Illicit Obsession

A Whitmore Elite Standalone

J.A. Owenby

Download Your FREE BOOK

Trigger Warnings

Please see my website for trigger warnings at https://authorjaowenby.com/about/illicit-obsession-trigger-warnings/

Dedication

For all the smut sluts who dream of being tied up and thoroughly fucked by a sexy, unhinged stepbrother ...

Jagger says, "You'll look beautiful with my baby in your belly, so be a good girl and take it all."

Playlist

Take You Down by L'FREAQ
Do You Really Want To Hurt Me by Nessa Barrett
Wicked by Miki Ratsula
Ready For It by ? (No artist listed)
Babylon by Babychaos
Monster by Chandler Leighton
I Wanna Be Your Slave by Maneskin
Haunted by Isabel LaRosa

Prologue

Jagger

"What the hell is this?" I blinked rapidly, trying to clear the haze from my eyes. "Where am I?" Despite the struggle against my restraints, it took me a few seconds to realize that I wasn't going anywhere due to the tightness of the ropes. I frantically searched around the room in an attempt to figure out where I was.

A dark chuckle bounced off the cement floor and walls. "Don't worry, Jagger Whitlock, it's all a part of the plan," the disguised voice said. He peered at me through the holes in the skull mask as he paced a circle around my chair. I recognized him from the society invitation video. *Fuck, what the hell did I do?*

"What do you want?" Despite the chilly air against my bare chest, beads of sweat formed on my forehead. The bastards knocked me out, drug me out of the field house, and tied me to a chair. Apparently, it would have been too much for them to grab some sweatpants for me. Instead, I shivered in nothing more than my boxer briefs. I had no idea who I'd pissed off, but I mentally skipped down that long list.

"You're one of the chosen. Try to relax and enjoy the ride." The fucker laughed even more.

My blood boiled in my veins. The familiar feeling of fury and hatred reawakened the beast inside me.

The masked and cloaked person didn't speak, but I felt the power bubbling beneath his skin. He might be crazier than I was. I wasn't sure if it was a good or a bad thing.

I attempted to control my breathing, but I had no fucking clue who was behind the mask and had taken me prisoner. If I bargained for my freedom, it would tickle his ego, and I would leave wherever I was in one piece.

"A brotherhood will fight for each other, but only if they have something on the line. Something to lose. In your case, you want a pro football career. I can make that dream come true, but why should I if you have no skin in the game?"

I blanched at him. "You can get me a pro ball contract?" A sense of foreboding enveloped me. This wasn't good. Whoever was talking to me was fucking with my head, and I strongly suspected I knew who it was. *Shit. This is bad. Real bad.* Until I found his weak spot, I had to play his sick game.

"If you can get me a deal with the Eagles, I'll give you my damn soul." Even though I realized it wouldn't serve me well, I gave him a disbelieving snort. "What are you, the devil's right hand?" What he didn't know was that I was the devil's left hand. Maybe we could work together and solve a big problem I had that refused to leave me alone.

The figure stopped in front of me and bent over, the nose of his skull mask a mere inch from mine. "I can make it happen, Jagger Whitlock, but what will you give me in exchange? I have no use for a wasted, dark soul like yours." He straightened, staring a hole right through me.

"Name your price. Hell, I've done a lot of dark shit in my life. I'm pretty sure I can offer you something you'll find valuable."

I shivered, sweat drying against my skin and making me even colder. Minutes ticked by without another word from him.

"What should I call you? Skull? I mean, you know *my* name. That doesn't seem fair, does it?"

He folded his arms in front of his chest. "You can call me King Cobra. I am the leader of a secret society, and if you pass the test, you'll join us."

I barked out a laugh. "Sorry, man. You should have led with that. You're wasting your time. I pledge to no one. This shit show wasn't what I signed up for." If he wasn't lying, it wasn't who I thought it was, which meant this situation wasn't as bleak as I first assumed.

A spotlight blasted through the darkness and I shrank away, trying to shield my eyes until my vision adjusted.

"It's easy, really. I'll make sure you have everything you want in exchange for your deepest, darkest secret."

My heart skidded to a stop, and I reminded myself to breathe. "No fucking way," I said quietly.

"Are you sure? You're ready to walk away from all of your dreams?"

"I don't know you, asshole. How am I supposed to blindly trust you?" I tugged on my wrist restraints again, as if they had magically loosened.

The light dimmed and moved, illuminating the rest of the small area. Several people stood on the other side of glass walls, all of them wearing the same skull mask and robe as the King Cobra, arms crossed over their chests in what could only be called a power stance. They looked immovable.

A voice began to filter into the room.

"Jagger," a female said.

My throat constricted as she continued to talk. "I love you, baby. Promise me we'll never be apart."

"I'll never let that happen," I replied on the recording.

"What the fuck? How did you get that?" I yelled over the recorded conversation. Her voice sliced through me like hot knives carving out my heart and tossing it on the cold ground.

"If our parents find out, they'll separate us," she said.

As hard as I fought against it, tears pricked my eyes. It had been years since I'd heard her speak.

"Tell us your secret, Jagger, then all of this will disappear. You can finally move forward. I'm doing you a huge favor."

My body trembled as the recording continued, with the sounds of us kissing and moaning as we made out. I remembered every sound, every breath. Even though I'd promised her, it had been our last night together.

Agony twisted my stomach into a million knots as I was overcome with grief—the soft lilt of her tone wreaked havoc on me.

"What happened, Jagger? What did you do?" the King Cobra asked.

I sucked in a huge breath, trying to clear my head.

"If you tell us, then you'll have everything you've dreamed of: a family, a career, and more women than you could imagine at your fingertips. Most of all, I can grant you hope. All I ask is for your darkest secret in return. Pledge your loyalty to each man here and they will do the same."

Frowning, I looked around the room at each person staring at me. I could have sworn a few of them nodded. Had they already talked about their pasts?

"Who are they?" I gestured to the strangers on the other side of the glass.

"Members. Each have shared their secret and now have successful lives and careers. They will forever be a part of the brotherhood. You can have the same thing. Once you tell us yours, they will share with you as well."

I swallowed hard, wishing I had some water. Closing my eyes, I listened to the recording continue to play. She had sent me the video later that evening. It was still on my phone, but I couldn't bear to watch it. Now, I was listening to it and so were the people in this room.

"You're a perfect fit for the society, Jagger. Name your price. We need someone like you."

"I want the pro deal. Nothing else matters. I have nothing left except football."

Moans of her pleasure filtered through the speaker, and it took everything inside me not to break down and sob.

"Then you'll have it. Don't misunderstand my intentions. I've hand-picked every member. You have skills and value. Let the society give you the world. All I need is something that proves to us that you're all in. Betrayal of the members is punishable by death, so are you willing to pay the price to make all your dreams come true?"

The recording finally stopped, and a heavy silence hung in the room as the others patiently stood and waited for my answer. I had nothing to lose. Whoever the King Cobra was, he realized what I would say, or he wouldn't have the recording. He was one clever son of a bitch. I had to give him that. If he could deliver on the pro deal in exchange for dirt that he already knew, what the hell was I really losing? The others had to share too. We would all be on an equal footing. I was familiar with the pledge process since my uncle was the president of an MC, the Dirty Bastards. I understood how that loyalty worked—a secret for a secret.

Taking a deep breath, I realized that if this asshole knew, anyone could find out, and that knowledge left me vulnerable. Hell, I would need some friends to help me bury it. All this time, I thought I was protected. As soon as I was finished here, I would need to find a way to erase my past once and for all. Maybe the King Cobra had done me a favor and saved my ass.

I squared my shoulders, ready. "I . . ." My voice cracked. "My biggest secret is—"

Chapter One

Jagger ~ Four Years Ago

My heart raced as visions of handcuffs and jail cells flashed through my mind. If I got caught, my comfortable life would be stripped away from me in an instant.

Sweat slickened my palms as I envisioned the police rushing in, handcuffing me, and shoving me into the back of a cop car. A million scenarios ran through my head, but the one on replay was how bleak my future would be if I were caught. The thought of spending my days inside a prison cell stole my breath. But no matter how wrong my actions were, I couldn't stop obsessing about my stepsister.

"Jag?" Ari's soft voice rippled through the air. I focused on her silhouette as she emerged from the darkness, her beautiful blonde hair accentuated by the moonlight spilling through the parted curtains of my bedroom.

"Close the door," I whispered.

Ari poked her head into the hall, shut it before securing the lock, and tiptoed to my bed.

"Every night I sneak into your room, I'm terrified we'll get caught. As hard as I try to talk myself out of it, I can't. With Mom's friends staying the night, too, it makes it even more risky."

"I know, baby." I motioned for her to sit next to me.

"Happy birthday." Her smile lit up my heart.

"What are you going to give me?" I raised my brow and soaked up her innocence. Ari was gullible and naïve except when it came to me.

Her giggle reached my ears. "Something special."

A loud groan worked its way up my throat, and Ari slapped her hand over my mouth and shook her head. "Shh."

Our parents' bedroom was at the end of the hall, but the guest room was next to us and another was across the hallway. I was paranoid as hell that Ari and I would get caught.

"Shh. If you want me to stay with you, we have to be quiet." Her long hair swept over my face as she leaned over and pressed her lips to mine.

Ari pushed me against the mattress until my head landed on my pillow. She leaned forward and smothered me with her sweet kisses, taking my breath away.

Over the months, Ari had grown less shy as I took our alone time a little further each week, but tonight held a hint of something deeper between us.

I gripped her chin and traced my thumb across her cheek. My chest painfully tightened, and fear of losing Ari trampled my heart. "We have to keep our secret, Ari. I can't ever lose you. If our parents find out, they'll separate us."

Ari's beautiful face hovered above mine. "Nothing will ever tear us apart, Jag. Nothing."

I wrapped her in a hug and placed a kiss on the top of her head. "I love you, Ari."

She peered up at me. "To the moon and back." Ari sat up, reached to the back of her neck, and removed her necklace with the dainty butterfly charm dangling from the thin gold chain. "Here, I want you to have it. I didn't have any money to buy you a gift for your birthday so keep this."

I held out my palm, and she placed the jewelry in my hand and gently closed my fingers over it.

"I should go."

I pulled her down for another kiss, losing myself in the warmth of her body against mine one last time before she left me for the night.

"Jagger! Wake up!"

My mother's voice reached my ears as I started to cough.

"Theo is waking everyone else. The house is on fire. We have to get out now!"

She jerked me by the arm and grabbed my shoes next to my bed. Thank God I'd slept in my shorts. I gasped for air as she led me out of my room and down the hall. Curls of black, thick smoke licked the sides of the walls, and I covered my nose and mouth with my hand.

"Dammit! Turn around! The fire is coming up the stairs!" Mom ordered.

I searched around frantically, looking for a way out as the flames grew closer, the heat almost unbearable.

"Go back to your room. We'll have to jump out the window."

"It's too high!" I choked out my response.

"We don't have a choice, Jag. Go!" Mom hurried back down the hall, pulling me along with her.

Seconds later, she ran through my room and pushed open the window. I watched in shock at the situation as she mashed on the screen and popped it out of the frame.

"Come on." Mom motioned for me to hurry up. "You've got this."

The flames traveled down the hallway, and I realized it was either jump or die. I had to fucking hurry, or my mom wouldn't make it out after me.

I scurried to the window while she gave me instructions on how to land. I peeked through the darkness lit by the orange and red flames.

"Come on, Jagger!" Mom's brother yelled up at me, his hands cupped around his mouth, and fear etched into his face. Mom's friends and my Uncle Gunner from out of state were below, peering up at me. Gunner frantically waved at me to jump, but someone was missing.

"Ari! Where's Ari?" I asked, panic gripping my chest like a vice, taking over my common sense. As I attempted to crawl back into my room, Mom shoved me out of the window.

"I'll find her!" she yelled after me.

Landing with a thud, I tucked and rolled on the unforgiving ground as the pain shot through my legs and knees. I didn't care, though. I pulled myself into a standing position and my Uncle Gunner hurried over to me. "She'll find her." His hands shook, and I realized that he was trying to convince himself as well. I glanced over to Mom's friends, who appeared terror stricken. Their faces twisted in horror as they waited for news.

An eternity later, Mom jumped out of the window—alone. As soon as she landed on the ground, I rushed over to her.

"Where is she?!" My voice cracked as I screamed her name. Tears streamed down my face, begging the night sky to give me a hopeful answer.

"I couldn't get close enough! Once I got back down the hall, the flames were too high, Jagger. I told her to jump out of her window!" Grief twisted her features as she looked at me. Her eyes widened as she bolted around to the other side of the house.

My pulse raced faster than a thousand horses as I rushed after Mom, searching desperately for Ari. No matter how loud I shouted, there was no response. My throat grew scratchy, like sandpaper raking over my windpipe, as raw emotions pulsed through me. She couldn't be dead. We were together only a few hours ago. Ari wouldn't leave me.

Rounding the corner, I came to a sudden halt when I saw that

Ariana wasn't there, but her father, Theo was picking himself off the ground. My legs shook uncontrollably as my gaze shifted up to the second story window only to see the house engulfed in flames. The knot in my stomach twisted into a violent wave of pain so intense, my knees buckled and everything around me spun.

I yelled until my lungs ached as the fire trucks and ambulance sirens grew closer. But it was too late . . . too late for me to save the one person I loved more than anything else in this world. My hands balled into fists as I pounded on the ground, screaming Ariana's name.

Mom wrapped me in her arms, her tears landing on my arms as we cried together. In the distance, I heard voices, but I couldn't register what they were saying. My heart had just shattered into a million pieces and no number of condolences could ever make it better.

Mom smoothed my hair. "At least your secret died with her."

I jerked away from my mother, staring at her in disbelief. How could she say something so cold right now? "You knew?"

"It's okay, Jag. I'll never tell a soul. Not even Theo."

Chapter Two

Jagger ~ Present Day

"Please, Jag? I need to." Her words teetered on the edge of whiney, annoying the fuck out of me.

I stared at the nameless chick on her knees, watching as her hands made quick work with the button and zipper of my jeans. She would look a lot prettier with her mouth full of my cock even if she were a jersey chaser. I was ramping up for a possible NFL career and she was ramping up to fuck the players, which meant I had little respect for her. Even so, I never turned down an opportunity.

My gaze traveled the length of her body, taking in her petite frame and flawless curves. Her faded jeans hung low on her hips, revealing a soft strip of skin between her tank top and waistband. I focused on the chick as her tongue moistened her pink-painted, full lips. A coy smirk played across her face as she leaned forward, lowering her head to meet my throbbing cock with her mouth. The sensation sent jolts of pleasure through me, and I let out an involuntary groan.

I shoved my fingers through her hair, hoping that I could lose myself for just a few freeing moments.

She paused then grinned at me. "I could get lost in your blue eyes for days." Her tongue swirled around the tip of my dick, and she nipped the sensitive skin.

"Don't bother. We won't see each other again after tonight, so give me the best you've got and maybe I'll remember your name."

"Cami." Her lower lip pushed out for a second before she parted her mouth and sucked me like her life depended on it. Hell, maybe it did, but I couldn't care less.

I leaned my head back against the couch, trying to enjoy the fruits of Cami's labor.

Quinn had invited us all to his house for a night of fun. We were far enough away from campus that it was safe to get wild without repercussions. The basement was our private party room. It was Kane, Quinn, Hunter, Remington, Anderson, and me, the best football players at Whitmore Elite and my best friends, who were privileged enough to be granted use for whatever purposes we damn well pleased. We'd had some wild nights here already and tonight was sure to be no different, especially with Cami kneeling before me, or so I thought.

I blew out a sigh, bored already with her performance. Wrapping my hand around my dick, I shoved her shoulder, sending her tumbling backward on her ass. "You're boring me. Go find some other guy's cock."

She gaped at me as she picked herself up off the floor and searched the room for another football player. "Ball slut," I muttered while I tucked myself back in my jeans.

The door opened and Quinn and Kane sauntered in, smiling at the group of ladies waiting at their beck and call.

"Hey, man. Can't find any good pussy?" Quinn asked as he walked over to me, slapping me on the shoulder. "I'm happy to sample all of them for you."

I chuckled. "You do that, just wrap your dick up. An STD would throw your game off on the field for damn sure."

Kane barked out a laugh. "That shit's not funny, yet it is." He rubbed his hands together, grinning like the asshole he was. Hell, we were all assholes, but we were on top of our football game, and the girls took good care of us. But I wasn't into it that night.

"I'm heading out. I'll see you guys later." I gave them a wave before I left, the girl's giggles reaching my ears as I ascended the stairs.

Although Quinn had a small group of about ten at the house, they had still made a mess in his kitchen. I would be pissed if no one picked up after themselves, but I didn't have a housekeeper like Quinn did either. Hell, I didn't even have a fucking place to live at the moment, but no one knew that tidbit about my fucked-up life except one other person.

I collected my motorcycle helmet near the front door and removed my keys from my pocket.

The warm early-autumn air held a hint of a cooler night, but I didn't care. It would be a great evening for a ride. I desperately needed to clear my head. We had a big game on Saturday, and I had to focus. Going pro was my only option to get the hell out of Oregon and leave my past behind.

An hour and a half later, I rolled up to the football training facility and hid my motorcycle at the back of the building. Only one person knew I was living here, and that was the man who had given me a key—Coach. When I'd arrived at Whitmore, I was working full time to pay for housing on campus, but my playing and grades were suffering because of it. Coach called me into his office and coaxed the truth out of me. Even though living in the locker room wasn't the best situation in the world, it was a hell of a lot better than what I had left behind.

There was a full-sized refrigerator, a microwave, a coffee pot, a small television, and a twin-sized cot in the room connected to Coach's office. Since the locker and workout rooms were all in the same facility, I had the use of the showers and bathroom as well. Nights I couldn't sleep because I was plagued with nightmares, I worked out. All Coach asked of me in return was to keep my mouth shut about our agreement and kick ass on the field. It wasn't difficult to agree to a roof over my head. Being safe allowed me to not give up on my dream of going pro. I owed Coach my fucking life, and I wanted to make him proud.

Once I was inside, I locked the door behind me and turned on a few of the lights. All I wanted was a hot shower and to crash. My ass was tired after two practices earlier that day. I'd hoped to blow off some steam with what's her name, but the second I saw her long blonde hair, the gut-wrenching memories hit my chest like a fucking ton of cement blocks.

I dragged my feet to my locker to grab my dirty clothes, spun the combination to the correct numbers, then it popped open. My gaze narrowed on a black envelope with my name written in gold calligraphy. Frowning, I reached for it. The only people allowed in the workout area were Whitmore football players, but that didn't mean the cleaning crew couldn't have left the mysterious piece of mail in my locker. A small vent would allow someone to slip something into it without any issue.

I flipped it over on the back, then lifted the flap. Curiosity pumped through my veins as I removed the black card.

Jagger Whitlock,

You're officially invited to join The Viper Society. This is a secret brotherhood for only a select few. Tell no one or there will be dire consequences. To learn more and accept, visit the website listed below and follow the instructions.

"What the hell?" I turned over the card, but there was only a big king cobra snake stamped on it. My laugh filled the empty room, echoing off the walls and tile floor. I grinned as I closed the locker and walked through Coach's office and into my adjoining room where I could chill and log onto my laptop.

Before I sat down, I stared at the butterfly necklace that hung from a nail in the wall. My heart curled in on itself in a vain attempt to protect me from the onslaught of memories that plagued my head about my past. But no matter how much it hurt, I refused to get rid of the piece of jewelry. It was the only thing I had left of Ari.

I stripped down to my boxer briefs before I sank onto the cot, the springs groaning beneath my weight. Setting the invitation on the mattress, I grabbed my backpack nestled in the corner next to my bed. I removed my computer, opened the lid, and waited as the screen came to life. In a few seconds, the website was loaded, and I watched as an animated cobra slithered across the landing page.

A figure wearing a skull mask and black robe appeared, then began to speak in a disguised voice.

"Welcome, Jagger. I'm sure you're curious about what the society has to offer." He spread his arms wide, laughing. "If you join me, you'll have girls at your whim ready to indulge in your wildest fantasies with no strings attached. They won't even know who you are." He tapped the side of his skull mask. "More than that, Jagger, I can make your dreams of going pro a reality. However, if you betray us in any way, your chances of playing will be ruined. Think carefully before you commit. Pay close attention to the following agreement. When you sign, you pledge your allegiance to the brothers and the society."

My heart pounded against my chest. Was this dude for real? He could help me go pro? In order to make that happen, he had to have connections somewhere. The wheels turned in my head, weighing the pros and cons, but all I could think about was what it would look like signing with the Eagles, Patriots, or any team for that matter. It had been my dream for as long as I could remember. Now, it was at my fingertips if this guy wasn't messing around.

I read through the terms and thought about what it would be like to belong to a group where we put each other first and watched each other's backs. Family. Other than my uncle, I didn't have anyone else, and certainly no one my age. Years ago, it had been different. I had people in my life that believed in me, and I would do anything for them as well. We never questioned why. We were just there for each other. No matter how hard I tried not to depend on anyone, the craving to belong and find my people was overshadowing any concerns about the society. It had been a long ass time since I'd had that in my life. Maybe it was exactly what I needed.

With sleep evading me, I pondered the society's invitation for a few hours. When I'd finally made up my mind and grabbed my laptop, I opened it to the website. Inhaling deeply, I e-signed my name. The second the imaginary ink dried on the agreement, the image shattered and disappeared. Only moments after, several member names appeared. Quinn was the first name I recognized and I chuckled. The motherfucker was almost as crazy as I was, and the fact that he'd already joined provided some reassurance.

The same voice spoke through my speaker and requested that I continue to the next page.

I did as I was asked, gawked at the information, then broke into a fit of laughter as I learned exactly what the society was about. Hell. Fucking. Yeah.

A loud noise caught my attention, and I nearly dropped my computer on the floor as I flew out of bed. No one should be here. Not even the cleaning crew.

Slipping on my tennis shoes, I hurried through Coach's office and searched through the darkness as three figures dressed in black hoodies bolted toward me.

"What are you doing here?" I demanded, my fists clenching and ready to do some damage. Unfortunately, the assholes wore black ski masks that covered their faces so I couldn't identify the intruders, which pissed me off even more. I attempted to dodge them but they had me surrounded.

Feet shuffled behind me and I attempted to turn, but strong hands grabbed my arms and forced them to my sides. *This isn't good.* The stench of chloroform filled my nostrils as a blindfold was slipped over my eyes, and my thoughts drifted into the darkness.

Chapter Three

Phoebe

"Babe, you look magnificent, if I do say so myself." I blew a kiss to one of my best friends, Teagan Mercer, who was standing in the middle of my bedroom.

"Are you sure?" She smoothed her black hair before she flipped it over her shoulder.

"You know I'm not going to blow sunshine up your ass." I shot her a pointed look.

Teagan covered her mouth, her giggle erupting through the air. Teagan, Everlee, Leighton, Gabrielle, and I had landed a cute house to share off campus. The second I'd FaceTimed my girls to tell them I'd been accepted to Whitmore for my sophomore year, and I was coming back to their side of the country, their squeals nearly burst my eardrums. It was worth it to see the expressions on their beautiful faces. I'd met my Fab Four when I was a freshman at Wahlberg Academy in New York state. We'd been inseparable until we graduated. They moved back to the West Coast, but I'd been forced to stay on the East Coast. Now that I was nineteen, it was time to strike out on my own, even if my parents didn't want me to come home. Our relationship had been strained since . . .

My stomach churned at the brutal memories racing through my mind. Teagan crossed the room, grabbed my wrists, and gently pulled me off the bed.

"When are you going to put yourself out there and sample some of the hotties on campus?" She folded her arms across her chest, waiting for an answer.

I wrinkled my nose at her. "I don't want to date anyone right now. My schedule is full with classes and studying. Besides, if I add anything else, I won't have time to hang with my bestie."

She rolled her eyes and squeezed my hands. "Phoebe, I love you, but you have to get your head out of books and join the real world. You're hiding. From what is beyond me. You're stunning and have curves in all the right places. I wish I had the hips and ass that you do. Not to mention these." She squeezed my boobs through my shirt and our laughter filled the room. Teagan and the girls had always been body positive, which made me love them even more.

Sadness snaked through me, and I did my best to shake the grief that still haunted me.

"I dated at the academy. Give me some time to adjust."

"Pff. We've been at Whitmore for a few weeks. It doesn't take that long to adjust to college. It's not like it's your first year at a university." Teagan looked up as the ceiling and tapped a contemplative finger on her chin. "You're going to the party with me Saturday."

I began to stammer out my reply, but she placed her hand over my mouth.

"Don't make me kidnap you because you'll fit in the trunk of my car just fine." She cocked her head.

There was no arguing with her. When Teagan set her mind to something, that was the end of the conversation. If I really wanted to dodge the party, then I would have to disappear that day. That wasn't a bad idea, but maybe it would do me good to get out for a while, wiggle my ass with my besties, and have a few drinks.

"Fine. But if I go, don't push a guy on me."

Teagan raised her palms in front of her, surrendering to my request. "Promise, but stop being a social pariah. You can't live in the library all year when there are so many ways to meet people. Debate club, drama club, or even check out a few sororities for next year. Hell, with our new quarterback, Kane Cooper, we have a real shot at ranking top 4 and, with a little luck, making it to the national championship game. That means you'll be alone on a lot of weekends since I travel with the cheer team to help Coach out. I don't like that idea. You need other people in your life when we're not around. With that said, I really hope our guys kick ass and go all the way." She bounced on her toes, clearly excited about the idea of the football team doing well that year.

"I said I'd go." I sat at the small desk in my room and caught a glance of my reflection in the mirror. My blue eyes were blank, soulless. I attempted a smile and busied myself with my biology and chemistry books in order to hide from Teagan. She could spot my vulnerability a mile away, and I wasn't up for any questions.

"If I'm going to go out and play this weekend I need to study." I stood. "But I need a snack and to check the mail. Daddy is supposed to send me a care package."

"Is Theo getting over being upset with you for returning to the Northwest?"

I grabbed my black windbreaker and put it on. "I think he's trying. Unfortunately, he wouldn't be straight up with me about why he didn't want me to come back. He shipped me off to boarding school for four years and insisted I attend a university in New York too. Not once did he allow me to come home, even for the holidays." I slipped on my Nikes, ready to make my short trek to the mailbox. "But you know that already." My shoulders slumped with sadness.

"I remember. At least he always brought the holidays to you. Remember when I went to visit my parents and Mom and I fought the entire time, so I came back to school early? I hung out with you and Theo in the penthouse suite he'd rented. Hell, we ate and drank ourselves silly. It was so much better than being at my place."

My heart sank for Teagan. Her mom was complicated to say the least, but she was verbally abusive to Teagan for no reason. Hell, even if Teagan had been a total failure at life, no one deserved to be talked to like she was.

"It was one of the best holiday breaks I'd had." I pulled Teagan in for a quick hug.

"Just proves that family isn't always blood. It's who loves and supports us."

"Damn straight." I released her, then headed out of the bedroom and into the hall.

"By the way, don't let Everlee catch you grabbing the mail. You know she twitches like a drug fiend to check it." Teagan snickered behind me as we descended the stairs to the main floor.

"Is it bad that I like to check the mail just to make her twitch?" I reached the front door and cracked it open. "Dammit. It's pouring out there."

Teagan gave me the umbrella from the coat closet. "Here." The moment she held it out, the wind blew into the house and jerked the door out of my hands. I stared at Teagan and groaned. It was an unusual day for the end of September with temperatures in the mid-sixties, and the rain made it feel colder.

"Girl, shut the damn door!" Cackling like the bitch she was, Teagan shoved me onto the porch and closed it in my face.

"Fuck!" I screamed, darting through the downpour to the mailbox at the end of the driveway. It wasn't far at all, but when we had a storm with high winds, I was pretty sure it was a trek through the jungle with wildlife poised and ready to attack. "You just wait, Teagan Mercer," I muttered to myself. If Everlee said one word to me about checking the mail, I would remind her that I saved her from being blown away. She should thank me.

Hurrying, I collected the small package and letters, then ran as hard as I could against the pelting rain. Shaking from the bone-chilling cold, I burst through the entrance and secured the bolt behind me.

"You look like a drowned rat, just prettier." Teagan laughed as I wiped the water from my cheeks and forehead.

"I feel like one thanks to you." I glanced at the package in my hand before I shuffled through the mail. A black envelope with gold calligraphy caught my eye. My forehead creased in confusion as I realized it had my name on it but no address, not even a return one. I gave the remaining letters to Teagan. "I want to open my box and see what Theo sent."

I headed up the stairs to my bedroom for a bit of privacy.

"If there are cookies or alcohol, you have to share!" Teagan yelled after me.

"Nope. Not after you shoved me outside to swim while you sat in Noah's Ark all nice and dry." I giggled as I returned to my room and secured the door behind me. In a few seconds, I anticipated Teagan would join me, but I wanted a moment to myself. It was a rare commodity in college with four roomies. I wouldn't change it for the world, though. Those girls were my sisters.

I sank into the chair and placed the box on top of my schoolbooks. Opening the little drawer, I rifled through pens, scissors, paperclips, and Post-it Notes in search for the letter opener. Paper cuts were straight from the devil, and I refused to get any more than necessary. I'd already paid my dues with pain.

Slicing the top of the envelope open, I removed a white card.

Dear Phoebe,

You've been chosen to attend the Viper Secret Society meeting. Only a select few are invited, so don't throw away your opportunity. Log onto the website below for details and instructions.

"What the hell? How could I be important enough to be selected?" I flipped the card over and grimaced. A large king cobra snake covered the back of it.

I tossed the invitation on the desk and shed my wet jacket, hanging it on the back of my chair to dry. Wiping my damp hands on my black hoodie, I sat down and opened my MacBook. Once I typed out the website, I sat back and watched as a snake slithered across the screen. A bright red dot on its back said "enter" and I clicked it.

A man dressed in a black cloak and skull mask appeared. "Hello, Phoebe," a disguised voice said. "Thank you for joining me. I'm sure that you have a lot of questions, but I'll address the benefits of you joining the society first. Incentives include spa days, where you will be pampered, waxed, shaved, plucked, massaged, and taken care of, and a safe place to live out your darkest fantasies and kinkier side of your sexual appetite anonymously and safely. Girls only dream of such luxuries, but I'm going to make it all a reality for you."

I sunk my teeth into my lower lip and continued to listen. Damn, all of that sounded like heaven. Since I loved books more than people in general and didn't enjoy trying to find a random hookup, the offer was a sweet deal. I couldn't afford a spa day, either, so being pampered and fucked senseless sounded amazing.

"The address, date, and time will scroll across the bottom of your screen. Be sure to write it down because in twenty seconds, the information will disappear."

I grabbed a pen and grocery receipt, ready to jot the information down.

"One more thing. No panties are allowed."

Shocked, my pen slipped from my hand and clattered to the floor. I scooped it up in a hurry, still needing to write the rest of the address before it disappeared. After I was successful, the screen pixelated then faded away.

"What the hell, no panties?" I blew out a sigh and realized the invitation was for tonight. "Dammit!" I glanced at my watch and pressed my mouth into a thin line. I had five hours to decide. I could chew on it while I took a shower and pulled myself together. Something inside me told me if I did go, yoga pants and a hoodie wasn't the right attire.

A tingle of excitement skated over my skin, leaving goose bumps in its wake.

Another problem I needed to consider, I had to figure out how to get past Teagan and the girls. The information had mentioned a skirt or dress, which I didn't wear often and would pique their interest along with triggering a million questions. Of all nights, this was when the weather had to be crappy, too. The wind would have my skirt above my head if I weren't careful. Forget that my kitty cat would be cold. Maybe I would wear my thong then shove it in my purse before I left the car. If I accepted the invitation. My mind whirled back and forth with the what-ifs, but my curiosity was most likely going to win.

From the safety of my Audi R8, I peered through the ink-black night at a building located in the industrial area. The rain and wind had chilled the fuck out, thank God. The girls were in their rooms study-ing, so it was easy to sneak past them.

My tummy flip-flopped with fear and curiosity. It was a dangerous mix and had landed me in trouble more than once.

I collected my handbag and climbed out of the car. My thong was tucked into the zippered pocket of my purse and out of sight. While I drove to the address mentioned on the website, ideas wracked my brain about the no panties event. Was it wrong that I hoped to get fucked ten ways to heaven? I needed it, and I'd rather hook up with some dude in a skull mask than have to commit to anyone on campus. I couldn't afford to get attached to someone. Neither could they.

Before I climbed out of my car, I scribbled a note and shoved it in the glove box in case tonight went south and my body was found. At least people would know about the invitation and society.

Loose gravel crunched beneath my high-heeled shoes as I hurried to the entrance. Following the instructions I was given earlier, I pressed a white button on a black box near the glass door. A buzz sounded right before the lock clicked open. Thrilled to be feeling something other than numbness, my hand hesitated before I grabbed the handle and pulled open the door. A long, dark hallway waited for me. My instincts told me to get the hell out of there, but I ignored it and began to walk slowly. After all, I'd lived through so much worse than an eerie dude in a skull mask and a fucking snake invitation. So. Much. Worse.

The air shifted around me, and I attempted to spin around but was stopped in my tracks.

"Hello, Phoebe," the voice said from behind me before a rag was slipped over my nose and mouth, and my world turned black.

Chapter Four

Jagger

"You ready, man?" Quinn asked as he collected a cloak and his skull mask from the closet. Apparently, the masks were equipped with voice disguisers, which was badass. Since several of us were trying to play pro ball, we didn't need any blowback for the crap that went down behind closed doors.

When I first drove up, I thought it was an old-school building. Per the instructions, I parked in the back and entered through the grey steel door. The hall was dark and creepy as hell, and I was grateful I had an idea of what I was getting myself into.

I entered the designated room and spotted a few tables and chairs scattered around. An old desk was nudged into one of the corners next to a filing cabinet. A few guys had their backs to me, but I would know them in a fucking lineup with hoods on their heads.

I approached my friends, grinning. "Hell, yeah. I have no idea who is behind the society, but I'm ready to find out."

"Same," Anderson chimed in from beside me.

"Dude, you're here too?" I chuckled as I slapped him on the back.

"We're all here. I mean, our small group of players we hang with. Kane, Sterling, you guys . . . There's no way in hell I would have shown up blindly if I hadn't seen your and Q's names on the list already."

"You and me both." I adjusted my robe, ready to start the action. "But if we accepted our invite to the society before we saw other names, then who was the first motherfucker who joined blind?"

Quinn's chuckle filled the room. "That motherfucker would be me." A mischievous expression flashed across his face.

"That doesn't surprise me. I don't think you actually look before you jump. One of these days, you're going to plunge right off a fucking cliff." I punched him on the shoulder. "Lucky for you, your team will scrape your remains off the rocks at the bottom."

Q rolled his eyes. "Thanks, asshole."

The door opened, and a tall figure dressed in a cloak and skull mask entered. Every guy in the room turned to see who the leader of the society was, but unless he removed the face covering and voice disguiser, we wouldn't find out that night.

"Gentleman, welcome. I'm happy to see everyone accepted the invite and passed initiation." He crossed his hands in front of him.

"As each of you know from the invitation, this is much more than a society. It's a brotherhood. We will fight for each other, watch each other's backs, and anything else that's called for."

I was about to test this motherfucker. "What about murder for each other?"

Tension clouded the air as he walked over to me.

"Even murder."

In my gut, I knew he was serious. I tipped my chin and stared him in the eyes. "Good. Sounds like my kind of brotherhood, and I'm in the right place. I've seen and done some shit but apparently, so has everyone else." After the initiation, we all had dirt on each other that could ruin our futures.

I could have sworn he grinned before he responded, but there was no way to tell beneath the mask. "You definitely are, Jagger

Whitlock. Your reputation as a crazy fucker precedes you on and off the football field. You were my first pick for the society."

I rubbed my chin, trying to track his mannerisms, but I was scrambling to identify him. My friends and some of my teammates were standing in the same room, so it wasn't one of them. Plus, there were plenty of other football players that weren't invited. When I watched the video, the King Cobra said twelve invitations were sent out. He would make thirteen.

He stepped back, exuding power and calm.

"There are thirteen rooms in this building, and each is created for any fucking fantasy you might have."

"Any?" Sterling piped up. "What about kidnap and rape?"

"It's ready for you, including the girls that want to play in return. They understand that they bow and serve us, no one else. If we snap our fingers, these bitches suck our cocks before asking how high to jump."

I folded my arms across my chest. "Our own groupies so to speak?"

He chuckled. "Call it whatever you want. If we're here fucking instead of picking up random chicks at a party that might cry rape the next day, then your asses stay out of trouble. Stupidity won't screw up our chances of going pro. Rest assured that the girls you use are well taken care of. They receive perks of belonging to the society just like each of you do. And of course, what happens here, behind these walls, stays here. If anyone gives the society or members away . . . there will be severe consequences."

Q pointed at me. "Jag will bring the shovel."

The guys chuckled. If they only knew how dark and twisted I really was, they would've thought twice before laughing.

"There are three honorary members who will prepare the girls for you. If the ladies should be tied up, chained, spread eagle and naked, then indicate that when you book a time and room. Toys and condoms are available in the cabinets along with anything else that you might need."

"Nice," Anderson said. "The last damn thing we need is a kid before we go pro."

"No kidding," Sterling muttered.

"Shall we begin?"

"Just so I understand, you like to boss everyone around like we're your little bitches, right?" I asked and smirked.

He crossed the room with lightning speed and wrapped his fingers around my throat. "If you want to remain here, you won't challenge me. Each of you will pick a deadly insect or animal. It will be your identity at the society. Am I clear?" He released me and stepped back.

My face flamed red. I wasn't embarrassed to have been called onto the carpet, but I was fucking pissed someone had the audacity to put his hands on me. I would deal with this issue when no one else was around.

"We're not here to fight, but I won't be disrespected. Are we all clear?" the King Cobra asked.

Twelve yeses echoed off the bare walls.

"Excellent. Get the hell out of here and go find a room."

That was all I needed to hear. I almost wondered if the King Cobra was Coach and this was how he kept his top players out of trouble. He could also be an asshole like that.

"You good, man?" Q said from beside me, our shoes slapping the tile floors as we strolled down the hall.

"Yeah. I'll deal with him another time." I slowed as we approached the rooms on both sides. Each door was closed. "For now, I'm going to enjoy myself. God knows the jersey chasers at the parties are getting old. I need a change."

"Same. Catch you later." Q walked away then hesitated as he reached for the doorknob. His gaze cut to mine, and we nodded before we slipped on the skull masks and activated the voice disguisers. We both opened the doors and stepped into our surprise fantasy for the evening.

My eyes widened as I focused on the dimly lit space. A floor-to-ceiling cabinet covered the wall to my right. A cage took up half the room, and I approached it—a girl with full tits, curvy hips, and a nice round ass huddled in the corner. Someone knew how I liked my ladies—with some meat on their bones. A black blindfold hid the majority of her face, and a gag was shoved in her mouth. The collar around her neck sported a thick chain anchored to the cement floor. Her hands were tied together, and she attempted to cover her nakedness with her arms.

Even with the blindfold, she was beautiful. Mesmerizing.

"Are you afraid?" I asked, my cock so hard, I thought it might rip through my black slacks, part of the King Cobra's mandatory uniform. I hadn't ever been this turned on before. I was in control. She would serve me, and I liked that idea way too much.

Swallowing hard, she nodded. I nearly moaned out loud.

"You're gagged since I wasn't in the mood for small talk tonight." I smirked, enjoying the ability to completely dominate her.

"Do you know where you are?" I was curious if she'd been snatched off the street or if she had been invited like the King Cobra said. This chick didn't look like she was having fun.

Again, she nodded.

"Are you here willingly?" I almost regretted gagging her, but that was my last question.

She nodded enthusiastically. Excellent. It was time for the games to begin.

I opened the cage and closed it behind me. She could only go somewhere once I unlocked her collar, assuming I could find the key.

Her perky tits rose and fell with her heavy breathing. I wondered if she got off on being terrified as much as I did on terrorizing her. It was probably some sick shit, but my past had made me a twisted man.

I reached out and smoothed her long blonde hair. "You're stunning." Looking around, I spotted the chair in the far corner of the cage and sat down. "Spread your legs, my pretty little slut. I want to see if your cunt is wet and ready for me."

She leaned against the bars and parted her creamy white thighs, exposing her clean-shaven pussy to me. I reached inside the cloak and unbuttoned my jeans, the sound of the zipper following.

I freed my cock and stroked it as my attention swept over her stomach and toned legs.

I stood and, within a few steps, closed the gap between us. Grabbing her hair, I jerked her head back and she yelped.

"Choke on this, beautiful." I tossed the robe over my shoulder before I removed her gag and held it in my hand. I shoved my dick into her mouth so hard and fast that she didn't have time to catch some air before I did it. I groaned as her full lips wrapped around my shaft. "That's it. You look so gorgeous right now, taking it like a good girl." I didn't move an inch, cutting off her airflow. "Your cheeks are bright red. I recommend you start sucking my cock if you want to breathe again."

Her body trembled, and I released my hold on her hair. She attempted to pull away, but I cupped the back of her head and ensured she could only move enough to have a trickle of air.

The chick's tongue swirled around my sensitive skin and I groaned. This bitch was so much better than the girls at Q's parties. Hell, I hadn't even fucked this girl, but I was about to lose my shit.

I pulled out of her mouth, and she broke into a coughing fit. Before she could say a word, I replaced the gag in her mouth. Wondering how long the chain would reach, I picked it up off the cement floor and stretched it out. She couldn't reach the door. I scooped up the chair and moved it closer, then I jerked her to her feet and led her to it.

"Bend over."

While she was feeling around for the back of the furniture to place her bound hands on, I grabbed a condom from my wallet in the back pocket of my slacks. I didn't want to leave her and search for a rubber in the cabinet.

Finally, she bent over, and I kicked her feet apart. Shocked, I frowned as my gaze landed on some dude's name carved into her lower back. Apparently, this chick liked pain. Who was I to judge?

I spread her ass cheeks, my attention gliding up and down her sweet slit. Even though she was here to serve me, tasting her pussy was a must. I knelt and massaged her clit with my thumb, coaxing a gasp out of her.

When I lifted the mask halfway, her scent filled my nostrils, and I rubbed the tip of my nose along her entrance. I bit and sucked her swollen bud between my teeth before I soothed it with a kiss. With each bite, a cry of pain escaped her, and my cock throbbed even more. Burying my tongue inside her, I stroked myself as I feasted on her sweet flesh.

My good little slut squirmed, grinding against my face as muffled moans of pleasure filled the room. Her legs trembled, and I backed away and stood. I moved her out of the way and tugged my pants down before I sat on the chair.

"Sit."

I guided her as she straddled me and eased down on my dick, her back angled toward my chest. She slid up and down, and I dug my fingers into her hips.

"Do you want to cum, little girl?"

She nodded enthusiastically.

I stroked her clit as I filled her wet pussy. Her juices slickened my thighs as I thrust into her harder, a feeling of déjà vu briefly clouding my thoughts. I reached for the chain that dangled to my left and pulled it, forcing her back where I could reach her better. My fingers found her throat above the collar and I squeezed.

"If you stop fucking me because you can't breathe, I'll snap your pretty little neck."

She froze for a second before she continued. I would love to think I wouldn't hurt her, but I would be lying to myself. Over the years, I had blood, plenty of it, on my hands. What was one more person?

The stormy reminders clouded my mind, and I shoved them into the dark recesses of my heart and concentrated on getting off.

To my surprise, she jerked and shuddered, her slick walls spasming around my cock with her orgasm. I let go of her throat, pleased that she'd liked the pain.

I gripped the sides of the chair, gaining more leverage as I thrust inside her over and over. Heat licked up and down my back, and my balls tightened with the familiar blissful feeling.

"Fuck!" I stilled, giving in to the intense waves of pleasure as I came. My body sank into the seat as I inhaled, and my mind calmed for a few seconds.

I kissed a trail up her back, then wrapped her long blonde hair around my hand. "I think I'll keep you. You're my good little pet."

Quickly, I picked her up off my lap and pushed her to the ground. Playtime was over. I had other crap I had to take care of.

Chapter Five

Phoebe

My black soul was clearly twisted. Burrowing beneath the blankets, I scooted down in my bed and groaned as I realized the beginning of a cold was settling in. Whether I only had a few sniffles or was full blown sick, I usually lost my voice. At least I didn't have to talk in classes that day.

The events of the previous evening had kept me awake for the majority of the night. I dreaded dragging myself from beneath the warmth of the covers, but eventually, I needed to get to class. But not yet.

As the memories washed over me, my thighs clenched. The last thing I'd expected was to be chained and blindfolded. At first, terror consumed me and ripped my heart from my chest. When I woke, the only thing I remembered was a funky smell, then nothing. My limbs tingled as I regained consciousness to find myself in a cage. Not sure who thought I wouldn't lift the blindfold and peek around, but they weren't very bright.

I sighed, my body aching for whoever I'd been with. The way

he'd touched me—fucked me. No one had treated me that way, and I hated myself for admitting that I liked it. Even though his words dripped in darkness, I could sense something different about him.

My phone buzzed with an incoming message, and I reached my hand out from the warmth of the blankets, patting the top of my nightstand until I located it.

My pulse skipped a beat as the name popped up on my screen. "Dammit." I grimaced and willed the text to disappear. Unfortunately, I'd lived through enough bad shit in my life to know that problems didn't go away on their own, and this was a big one.

A second message came through, and I surrendered, opening them.

The Devil:

Do you honestly think you can run from me?

Nausea swirled around in the pit of my stomach.

You'll regret this.

Panic blossomed in my chest as I threw my phone across the room. It bounced off the wall and clattered to the hardwood floor.

"Good. I hope you're broken." Unwillingly, I sat up and stared at the iPhone as if it were poison. I knew leaving New York would be risky, but I had to while I still could.

I squared my shoulders and marched over to the other side of the room where my cell had landed and scooped it off the floor. The screen had shattered, and I breathed a sigh of relief. If I couldn't see it. I couldn't read texts or see who was calling.

"Take that, motherfucker." I placed the broken piece of junk on my windowsill and walked to my adjoining bathroom. Maybe it would be nice not to have a phone for a while. If I wanted to, I could access social media on my MacBook, but I stayed far away from it. Plus, I could FaceTime Dad or anyone else from there as well. The fact that my entire life was trapped in a five-by-three piece of tech was daunting. Sometimes, a girl had to check out for a while to heal . . . or try to.

I caught my reflection in the bathroom mirror out of the corner of my eye and grimaced.

"Shit! Shit! Shit!" I touched the bruise on my neck from the collar I was forced to wear last night. If those assholes wanted to keep their society secret, they shouldn't have left marks where everyone could see them. There wasn't enough foundation in the world to cover it. "Asshole." My lips pursed together. Honestly, I loved rough sex. I was used to it, so returning to vanilla sounded boring. I doubted I would ever orgasm again if I tried a simpler sex life.

I used to not be this way—dead inside. After I lost the only guy I'd ever loved, I fell right into the hands of a . . .

I clenched and unclenched my fists, willing myself to snap out of it. I didn't have time to rehash the past. Turning on the shower, I realized I would need a damn turtleneck for classes, but I didn't own one. Teagan did, though. As far as I was concerned, wearing a turtleneck was illegal, but I did have a few scarves. With the weather having turned cooler the past few days, a scarf wouldn't look too out of place, and it would hide the marks and keep me warm.

Seconds before the professor closed the door to his class, I hurried in.

"Welcome, Ms. Jenkins. Nice of you to join us." Mr. Bowman's dark brow rose to his hairline as he shot me a disapproving look.

"Sorry." I flashed him the best smile I could muster up without appearing to flirt. Hell, he was too damn old anyway.

I settled into a seat near the aisle and slid my backpack from my shoulders. Teagan and I were supposed to meet up after biology. At the rate my day was going, I would need a stiff drink by noon. Although I'd tried to brush off the texts from earlier, dread twisted me into a fucking pretzel. The only time I was okay with being a pretzel was if a guy was balls deep inside me. Goose bumps peppered my skin, thoughts of the skull-masked stranger dancing through my mind again. Focus or flunk, girl.

Forcing myself to concentrate, I pulled out my iPad and took notes.

I caught a glance of a pencil from the corner of my eye before it tapped me on the shoulder from behind, and I took a tentative look.

A gorgeous blonde-haired guy flashed me a big smile. "I missed some notes, could you hang for a minute after class and share yours with me?"

Pink crawled up my neck and cheeks. I wasn't sure where the Whitmore University guys came from, but there were a lot that were panty-dropping gorgeous.

"Sure."

"Ms. Jenkins. Is there something that you'd like to tell the rest of us?"

Fuck.

"Sorry, Mr. Bowman. It was my fault. I was asking if we could share notes."

Mr. Bowman eyed the guy behind me. "I'm glad you're taking an interest in your grades, Anderson. After all, your team depends on you. If you need something, see me after we're finished for today. Otherwise, I think Ms. Jenkins needs to pay attention."

I bowed my head, my long blonde hair cloaking my embarrassed face. At one time, no one could humiliate me, but that was all before . . .

Clearing my throat, I returned to Mr. Bowman's lecture. Maybe Anderson would hang around regardless of what Mr. Bowman had said.

Half an hour later, I shoved my iPad and bio book into my backpack.

"Sorry about that," Anderson's deep voice said from behind me.

I stood and hoisted my bag on my shoulder and turned to him.

"It's fine. Mr. Bowman has it out for me. I was late twice and, apparently, that put me on his shit list." I shrugged.

Anderson flashed me a big smile, and I nearly melted on the spot. I tried not to be obvious about checking him out, but he was a cherry-flavored popsicle on a hot summer day—broad shoulders, nice jawline, and white teeth. I bit my lip, my gaze taking a slow hike down his chest to his jeans that hung low on his hips but clung to every yummy muscle in his legs.

"Do you play sports?"

Anderson tilted his head, studying me. "I get that you're new at Whitmore, but didn't you see the jocks all over the website and on social media?"

"You realize that sounds pretty egotistical, right?" I folded my arms across my chest.

Surprise flickered in his expression. "I didn't mean to be an asshole about it. It's just that Whitmore is known for its football program. I figured everyone knew who the top players were. Guess that does sound self-involved, huh?"

I pursed my lips, briefly deciding if I was going to forgive him for being a pompous ass. "I completely ignored the sports portion of the Whitmore website. My time is spent in the library with my nose in books or studying. Plus, I deleted all of my social media accounts years ago. Even my best friends stopped trying to show me Instagram reels and TikTok videos. It's not for me."

His shoulders briefly slouched, then a kind smile slipped into place. "I gotta respect you on the social media. It can be a crappy place sometimes. To answer your question, football. I would be down to try hockey, but Coach would kick my ass if I got hurt and couldn't play ball."

My eyes narrowed. There was something about Anderson that seemed genuine and I liked it. "I could see that not working out too well. Your coach being pissed at you, I mean."

"You can say that again." He rubbed the back of his neck. "So, are you still mad at me about the jock comment?"

"Nah, I rarely hold a grudge. I did like messing with you though." I grinned, showing him that I was a good sport.

"Then can I ask how your grade is in this class?"

"At the moment, I have an A in all of my classes. I'm happy to give you my notes."

"That would be so great. Maybe we can sit by each other and share?"

"Or." I pointed at him. "You should take the seat in front of me, so I can hide behind you. Maybe Mr. Bowman will finally leave me alone." I laughed as I left my seat and slowly walked toward the exit.

To my surprise, Anderson draped his arm around my shoulders. "Stick with me. I'll take care of you." Anderson's chuckle sent ripples of pleasure through me, and I wondered if he might have been the guy from last night. "What's your name anyway?"

Before I could open the door, Anderson beat me to it.

"Oh. A gentleman. Don't see that often anymore." I grinned as I stepped into the hall.

"I'm Anderson Nichols." He folded his arm across his waist and bowed. "At your service, beautiful."

My giggle echoed through the hallway. "My name is Phoebe Jenkins. It's nice to meet you, Anderson the football player."

"Likewise, Phoebe the book nerd. No disrespect, I think it's hot that you're smart and have good grades."

"Thanks." I beamed at him. That was new, but I was good with it. If Anderson noticed me because I was intelligent and didn't mind my curves, so be it. Before I headed off to meet Teagan, I got Anderson's email and shared my notes with him.

"Thanks. I'll share anything you missed. I gotta run. Practice calls."

"Later." I gave him a little wave before he left, my attention glued to his magnificent ass.

My chest tightened with anxiety. Hopefully, the universe was watching out for me. I wasn't sure yet. One thing I was clear about, it would be nice to have a friend in biology class. If I could surround myself with strong guys, I might be safe. Maybe.

Chapter Six

Jagger

"Are you excited to be back on the field after your injury last year?" Kane asked as he pulled on his shoulder pads.

"Yeah, the knee is as good as new, no thanks to the fucker that clipped me last season."

I flexed my fingers, adrenaline pumping through my veins at the thought of taking down the opposing team. Hearing the protective gear crack as I tackled a player made me happy. If he couldn't get up and stand afterwards, that made my dark heart sing a victory cry like a Viking left on the battlefield. My reputation on and off the field was that I was cold and calculating. It was true, and I owed it all to the shit show I called my past. Shaking the dark thoughts from my head, I reminded myself that I was about to walk out on that field and my future depended on me being sharp and attentive. Failure wasn't an option.

"Listen up, men!" Coach yelled over the chatter of the team and the clacking of the football pads.

We turned our attention to him, ready for our orders.

"Stay focused out there. This is our fourth game of the season, and the scouts are in the stands. Don't get cocky because we have a strong group of players this year. Keep your eyes on the ball. I believe that this team has what it takes to win the championship. Don't prove me wrong."

"Yes, sir!"

Anderson elbowed me in the side. "Ready to take these assholes down?"

I fist-bumped Anderson before Kane, Hunter, Quinn, and Sterling joined us. Without a doubt, these guys were the best offense I'd ever played with. I was honored to be brothers with them on and off the field.

Minutes later, we jogged from the locker room, through the tunnel, and onto the field. The referee tossed a coin. We had the ball.

Kane led us into position, the cheers of the fans almost deafening. Everyone was pumped.

"As we prepare for another game at Whitmore, the crowd mirroring the excitement of the players is really electrified," the announcer said.

I blocked out the chatter and noise as Kane threw the first play. The football spiraled into the air and down the field, right into my waiting hands. The second I caught it, a huge motherfucker ran into me. I landed on my back, the wind whooshing out of my lungs, but I kept the ball tucked under my arm.

"Get off me, asshole." I pushed him off enough to suck in a lungful of air.

The guy smirked at me then said, "Psycho says to tell you he's watching."

The blood drained from my face, and my world tilted on its side before it turned hazy. Rattled, I shook my head, wondering if I'd been hit it too hard and was imagining things. There was no way in hell Psycho would be at my game, or was there? Unease mixed with dread reached inside my chest and squeezed my heart.

"You alright? Way to get tackled on the first play," Anderson said, interrupting my thoughts and holding his hand out to help me off the ground.

"Yeah. I'm good." I tried to appear nonchalant as I searched the stands for Psycho, a sick feeling knotting in the pit of my stomach. If he was there, I wouldn't be able to find him. The stadium was packed.

To the best of my ability, I focused on playing and winning the game. Football was the only thing in my life that hadn't failed me. When I needed it most, it saved me more than once. I had an eerie feeling it was about to happen again.

After scoring two touchdowns, I was pumped and ready for more. The Hornets were a tight match for us, and as hard our team was playing, they were holding their own. We needed to catch the sons of bitches off guard.

The half-time buzzer sounded, and we jogged off the field and filed into the locker room.

"How's your knee, son?" Coach said from beside me.

"Sore but good."

"Let's ice you up. I need you healthy and on that field." He slapped me on the back before walking over to Kane and addressing the team.

As hard as I tried to pay attention to Coach, I felt like Charlie Brown, only hearing a muffled voice in the background. I wasn't sure what the hell had happened out there. I must have been hit harder than I thought because I didn't have a fucking clue who told me about Psycho. Just because he delivered the message didn't mean he knew Psycho. Hell, Psycho could have given him a crisp one-hundred-dollar bill and told him what to say before the other team traveled here from Washington state.

Even though I was hot and sweaty, a chill slithered down my back. Rage intermingled with guilt fueled my fucked-up soul as I vividly recalled the night that changed my life. To this day, I had no proof of who started the fire, but I had my suspicions. At this point, I was waiting for the right moment to exact revenge. When I did, it would feel damn good, even if I would serve eternity in hell for what I planned to do.

"Hell of a game, Jag," Kane said as I climbed into his silver Jaguar. My ass sank into the plush leather seat and I grinned. At one time, I'd been a rich bastard, but I walked away from every fucking penny. The money had cost me my goddamn soul, and I was determined to find my own path. I wasn't sure redemption was possible, but I toyed with the idea anyway. Some actions and choices weren't redeemable, and I was pretty sure I'd crossed that line.

"You too, dude. You were super tight in your throws out there. I wasn't sure we would walk away with another win, but we did." Our cheers echoed through the car as Kane pulled out of the university's parking lot and headed to the society. We were ready to blow off steam, and each of us had received a text that girls would be waiting at the society by eight that evening. I could definitely go for getting my cock sucked.

I leaned back in the seat and stretched my legs out, every part of my body battered and bruised from the Hornet's defensive line. The message the football player had delivered continued to fuck with me. As soon as the game had ended, I searched for him by the visitors' locker room, but I never found him.

I glanced at my friend. "Any idea who is behind the society?"

"Nope." Kane ran his hand over his short hair and drove onto the main road. "I'm thinking it's gotta be Coach, right?"

I shrugged. "I wondered the same thing, but I don't think it is. The last girl I fucked, I don't even know what she looked like. She wore a blindfold that covered her face. One thing I do know is she looked hella good naked." I rubbed the back of my neck; the thought of being inside her again had my dick begging to be set free.

"Did you get her name?" Kane asked.

"Nope. At the time, it didn't even cross my mind. Now I'm

wondering how to fuck her again." I frowned before I looked at Kane. "What about you? Did you like the chick you were with?"

A flicker of something I couldn't detect flashed across his stoic expression. "Yeah. She was fine. Not sure she's my type, though. It was probably the room I was in. Whoever designed it should have named it vanilla—a few toys but nothing big. Guess it's for those that want a tame time. That shit's not for me."

I barked out a laugh. "Same, man. In mine, the chick was blindfolded and had a chain around her neck. She was stark naked with her hands bound in front of her."

Bewildered, Kane shook his head. "Damn. I needed to swap with you, dude."

"Maybe you'll find that room tonight. Just point me away from the vanilla room, though."

"Sure thing." Grinning, Kane flipped on Spotify and "Take You Down" by L'FREAQ thumped through the speakers. It was an appropriate song as my thoughts shifted back to Psycho. Somehow, I had to find out where he was. I couldn't get blindsided—again.

Twenty minutes later, Kane and I were cloaked and masked. We walked down the hall in the opposite direction, both of us avoiding the vanilla room, as Kane called it.

Opening the door, I wondered if the gods above had heard my conversation with Kane on the way over to the society. Sprawled out and tied to a table was the same girl I'd been with the last time. Even with her face covered, I recognized her blonde hair and toned thighs.

"We meet again." My voice sounded odd beneath the skull mask and disguiser, but I liked that no one knew who I was aside from the other King Cobra Society members.

Although I couldn't see her expression, her body tensed.

"Who are you?" she asked, her voice hoarse beyond recognition. I wondered if she'd yelled her head off at the football game earlier. That was assuming she liked the sport.

I waited to respond, recalling that the leader had mentioned we should pick a deadly insect or animal. It would be stupid to call myself Jaguar. The second she heard someone call me Jag outside this room, she would put two and two together. I strolled around the room, my black dress shoes scuffing the tile floor. For whatever reason, the King Cobra had called for a uniform of a black shirt, black slacks, and black dress shoes. I assumed it was so that, if any of the chicks saw us, they couldn't identify us by our shoes or pants.

If any of the girls saw me shirtless, they would see the black mamba tattoo that covered my chest and wrapped under my arm and around my back. Choosing a snake might not be wise, either. But for that matter, I could keep my damn clothes on, then my tats couldn't be an issue.

My attention landed on her again. She was braless, and I drank in the curve of her breasts through her thin white shirt. Her long legs stretched out beneath her short denim mini skirt. "You can call me Black Mamba."

The corner of her lip kicked up in a slight smile. "Is that because you're deadly?" Her voice cracked with her question.

You have no idea. I cleared my throat so I wouldn't say something I would regret later. "I know how to adapt to my surroundings. I can survive anywhere."

She swallowed. "And through anything?"

Her question caught me off guard, and I wondered if she might also understand how to survive. Suddenly, I found myself intrigued by not only this girl's beauty, but her mind. *Who is she?*

"Yes."

Her tongue darted over her lower lip, and my straining cock nearly jumped out of my slacks.

My fingertips glided from her shin and over her knee. Goose bumps dotted her skin as I continued to trail upward. Although her arms were stretched out and bound to the table, her legs weren't. I pulled up her skirt enough to see her bare pussy. No panties again. My dick hopped into the driver's seat, and I crawled onto the table, parted her legs, and bit the inside of her thigh. Her scream filled the room and I chuckled. I hadn't broken the skin. Yet.

A red-hot, crazed-driven desire to claim her coursed through every cell of my being. I'd only been with her once, but the mere thought of another guy, in or out of the society, touching her drove me nearly insane.

"Who do you serve, my little cum whore?"

She bristled with my words, but she knew exactly what to say.

"You. But before you go any further, you should know . . ."

I ran my tongue up the length of her slit then around her clit. Sucking the hard bud between my teeth, I smiled. My pet had lost her thoughts. Moans of pleasure slipped from her pretty lips that would soon be wrapped around my thick cock as my cum shot into her mouth and down her throat. That was if I could stop fucking her with my mouth long enough.

"What were you going to say, my good little pet?" I spread her pussy apart, devouring her as she attempted to talk.

Her hips bucked off the table, grinding against my face as she whimpered and begged for a release. I wouldn't give it to her. Not yet. She had to earn it.

I moved away and fumbled beneath the damn cloak to free my dick from my slacks. I had to fuck her. Once I positioned myself at her entrance, I shoved into her fast and hard, her body rocking from the force.

"I hope you're on birth control because I'm going to cum inside you, and when I do, make no mistake that I'm claiming you as mine. No other man can ever touch you again unless I give them permission."

"Oh god. Fuck me good."

Her back arched off the table, her hard nipples poking through the fabric of her shirt. I leaned down and bit one, her scream of pain nearly making me lose my load inside her tight cunt.

"I requested you tonight," she grunted as I slammed into her.

Hesitating for a moment, I realized what she'd said. She'd wanted me too. I nearly laughed because I was pretty sure my pet would regret the day that she'd asked for me.

Pleasure zipped through me and I shuddered, filling her pussy with my hot cum, marking her as mine.

Her body tensed and shook beneath me as she released.

I pulled out of her, scowling under my mask. "Did I give you permission to cum, pet?"

Her chin trembled. "No."

"Then you'll be punished." I jumped down, tucked myself back into my pants, and zipped and buttoned them. Making my way to the top of the table, I stared down at her.

"Punished how?" she asked.

Her pitch rose with her question, but if I weren't mistaken, there was a hint of excitement in her words.

"First things first." I lifted the blindfold and she quickly turned her head in the opposite direction.

I assumed she needed a moment to adjust to the light.

Slowly, she faced me. Her big blue eyes widened as they landed on my skull mask.

Staggering backward, I struggled to clear my vision as my world skidded to a fucking halt.

Chapter Seven

Phoebe

The only thing that stopped me from screaming when I spotted the skull mask, was the second the Black Mamba saw my face, he swore a blue streak while practically running out of the room.

My ego had bitch-slapped me then kicked me to the curb. A few minutes later, another masked guy came in and untied me then told me to go home. With my tail between my legs and confusion buzzing in my brain, I hurried to my Audi as if the devil himself were chasing me.

As soon as I started the engine, "Do You Really Want To Hurt Me" by Nessa Barrett blared through the stereo speakers, startling the living daylights out of me. Tears welled in my eyes, and I leaned my head back against the headrest. I shouldn't have gone to the society tonight, even though I was wound tighter than a coiled spring in my grandpa's antique clock. I realized I'd been on edge since earlier that day.

I blinked several times, forcing myself not to cry, then shifted into drive and peeled out of the parking lot.

What was so wrong with me that the Black Mamba ran out of the room without any explanation? His reaction sat in my gut like sour milk. Inhaling a shaky breath, I refused to allow an asshole to undermine everything I'd worked so hard to accomplish. So what if I weren't pencil thin and a cheerleader like my friends. I refused to allow the world to dictate my definition of pretty, including that jack ass.

Shaking the humiliating thoughts from my overwhelmed mind, I sang along to the music as I shifted my focus back to the society.

"Shit!" I yelled and slapped the palm of my hand against the center console. The bass of "Wicked" by Miki Ratsula thumped through my body and calmed me. It had been a hell of a messed-up day, from the earlier texts to Black Mamba humiliating me.

I pressed a steering wheel button before saying, "Hey, Siri, text Teagan." Silence was my only response. A scream shot through me as I remembered that I'd thrown my phone and it was broken, sitting on my windowsill at home. An eerie feeling tiptoed down my spine, and I shivered in my seat. My foot pressed the accelerator, and my car picked up speed. All I wanted was to get to the house and shake off the bad day with a good yoga video. It was too dark outside to take a long run, so I would have to sweat out my frustrations another way.

After a good workout, I took an extra hot shower in hopes it would help my cold. Before I headed downstairs, I put on a pair of grey running pants and a P!nk concert T-shirt. I grabbed the white-and-blue checkered blanket from the back of the black leather recliner before I crawled onto the couch and turned on a romantic comedy. When my mood was bad, I tried to pull myself out of it by watching something funny. Since the roomies weren't around, I had the television to myself.

Settling in, I found "Sweet Home Alabama," and Reese Witherspoon lit up the screen in seconds. It was only eleven, but my eyelids fluttered closed only a few minutes into the movie.

"I'm sorry," I whimpered, a string of snot hanging from my nose as I pleaded.

"Silence! You know the consequences of your actions. On your knees."

"No."

I never saw his hand as it connected with my cheek, sending me to the floor. Tears streamed down my face as I scrambled backward. If I could reach the door, maybe I . . .

Strong fingers wrapped around my arm and jerked me forward. "I fucking said on your knees."

Without a choice, I did as he commanded. He cupped my chin and forced me to look up at him, his eyes as dark as his heart. I had to get away before he hurt me again.

"Do you honestly think you can escape me? I know your secret, little girl. I know what you did."

I shook my head. "No, you don't. There's no way."

Just as I hoped, he knelt in front of me. My adrenaline kicked in, but I was waiting.

"I will end you. Not even your daddy's money can save you now." He leaned in, hesitating for a split second.

My hand flew up, and my nails scraped across his cheek and chin.

"You little bitch!" He grabbed his face, blood seeping between his fingers.

I watched the red crimson drip to the carpeted floor. Reality sunk in, so I jumped to my feet and bolted to the door.

"Run! I fucking dare you," he snarled.

My arm shook as I fiddled with the lock then flung open the door and ran for my goddamn life.

A hoarse scream reached my ears and jolted me awake. Frantically, I searched around to see my roomies staring wide-eyed at me. Everlee trembled as she tucked her hair behind her ear.

"Babe, it's okay. You fell asleep during a movie," Teagan gently said before she touched my shoulder.

I flinched, my brain still struggling to comprehend where I was— a black couch with a matching recliner and tan accent wall.

"Look at me." I tracked the voice then turned to see my best friend sitting next to me. "It was a bad dream. You're safe and sound at home in Oregon. Leighton, Gabby, and Everlee are here too. See?" She pointed at the group of girls whose faces were drained of color.

"I'm okay." With a trembling hand, I wiped the sweat from my forehead.

"I'll get you some water," Leighton said before hurrying to the kitchen, her tennis shoes against the wood floor the only noise for a moment.

"Girl, you scared the living shit out of us. Are you okay? That must have been one hell of a boogeyman after you." Gabby's expression grew serious as she sank into the recliner while Leighton returned with a bottled water for me.

I twisted off the cap and guzzled the cool liquid, welcoming it on my sore throat.

"Do you want to talk about it?" Teagan asked, curling up next to me. She flipped her long black hair behind her and shoved a hand into her burgundy hoodie pocket. Teagan reached around and pulled me to her.

I rested my head on her shoulder. "No. I don't remember anything except a horrible feeling." I'd just lied, but I couldn't have them asking any questions. Some secrets couldn't even be shared with your best friends.

"I'm so sorry that I scared you guys." I tossed the blanket off me and sat up. "I'm exhausted, so I'm going to head upstairs."

"I'll go with you," Teagan said.

"Night." I hugged Gabby, Everlee, and Leighton before I made my way upstairs and to my room. Teagan was hot on my heels.

Dread twisted my insides. I'd known Teagan for a long time and suspected she hadn't bought my lie that I didn't remember my nightmare.

She closed the door behind us.

"What the hell?" Teagan hurried to the windowsill and grabbed my broken phone. "How did this happen?" She flashed the cracked screen at me as if I had no clue it was shattered.

"I dropped it." Lie number two, but I wasn't offering her any more information.

Teagan sighed and plopped down on the edge of my mattress. "What's going on, Phoebe? Don't bother lying to me like you did a few minutes ago. You're white as a sheet, so spill."

"Teagan." I sat next to her, tucked my leg beneath me, and tugged on the hem of my T-shirt. "I'm tired. The change in time zones, schools, and a full course load are stressful and . . ."

Teagan scooted up on my bed. "And?" Her big brown eyes flickered with worry.

I sunk my teeth into my lower lip, struggling with what to say. "The nightmare was about the house fire." It was the best I could come up with to tell her without having to traipse through memory hell when she demanded answers.

"Oh, hon. I'm so sorry. You've never talked about it other than your home burning down before you attended the academy. Would it help to tell me more? I can't imagine how horrible it must have been."

My shoulders slumped from the agony pulsing through my veins, and I stared at the wood floor. "No," I choked out. "But maybe you can sleep in here with me tonight?"

Teagan's smile lit up her face. "Just like we're still sharing a room. Hell, I miss those days."

"Me too."

Lie number three.

Chapter Eight

Jagger

I jerked off the skull mask, then shoved my hands through my short hair as I paced the society's office. No fucking way was it her. Apparently, that tackle had messed me the hell up and left me delusional. There had to be an answer to what just happened.

Stomping over to the desk, I spotted a folder with "Applicants" written across it in bold black Sharpie. I opened it and began flipping through the forms. I needed a name to go with the face I'd seen. *The pussy I'd fucked.*

Desperation and rage danced at the edge of my mind, daring one or the other to take over. I reached out with my foot and rolled the office chair to me, sinking into it. My pulse kicked into overdrive as I scanned the hundred-plus pages.

The creak of the door opening pulled my attention away from my task at hand. I glanced up to see one of the guys remove his mask. Anderson strolled in with a massive smile in place. "That was the best stress relief I've had in a long ass time!"

I rubbed my jaw, the stubble scraping against my palm. "Yeah. I'm enjoying the perks as well."

"You sure? If I'm reading the room right, you're pissed."

I blew out a sigh. "It's that obvious?"

"Yup." Anderson removed his cloak and went to the closet where he hung it up. "It's easier to fuck a chick when you remove the cloak. Plus, you don't have to deal with cum stains." He chuckled. "Mask intact, clothes intact. It's all good, man." He approached me and sat in a chair on my other side. "What's tickling your asshole, man?"

I shook my head at Anderson's question. The dude had a way with words.

"Do you know if these are the only applications for the society?"

"I do. There were one hundred-fifty invitations sent out. "Those" —he pointed—"are the ones that applied but are on hold. The forms for the girls that accepted are locked up in the bottom drawer of the desk. There's another office, too. It belongs to the King Cobra. The members meet in here where we have the masks and robes at our disposal."

I peered down and spotted two drawers, giving each of them a tug. I swore under my breath.

"I did mention they're locked, Jagger."

My eyes narrowed at him, then the corner of my lips kicked up when I realized Anderson was dangling the key from his fingers.

"Why didn't you tell me you had a key, motherfucker?" I reached over and swiped it away from him as he chuckled.

"You didn't ask."

I unlocked the drawers and pulled the largest one open. Another manila file folder lay on the bottom. I scooped it up then laid it on the desk. There were only about twenty forms.

"I assume you're looking for the girl you were with?" Anderson placed his elbows on his knees, his gaze attentive.

"Yup." I thumbed through the pages. "Gina, Louise . . ." I looked up at Anderson. "Louise? Who the fuck names their kid Louise?"

"Yeah, keep going." He nodded at the file.

"Jamie, Gertrude?" My shoulders dropped, my chuckle bellowing through my chest. "Can you imagine? Oh, you fuck me so good, Gertie."

Anderson threw his head back and laughed his ass off. "No! Dammit, you're going to ruin my fun. Every time I hook up, I'm going to wonder if it's Gertie now."

I returned to the applicants. "Phoebe, Maxine, Lauri . . ." I continued until I reached the last one. Puzzled, I stared at the stack of papers. "I don't get it."

"What's that?"

"I thought . . . No, I know what I saw. It was someone I grew up with from years ago, but . . ." Grief constricted my throat and clawed at my dark soul.

"Maybe the chick you used to know has a doppelganger. I hear that crap happens. Somewhere out there, we all have a twin."

"I never believed in that crap, but maybe you're right." Defeated, I sank back into the chair.

"You can always talk to her, man. If it's fucking with your head, then ask and be done with it."

"The problem is, I have no clue how to find out who she is. I mean, I never got her name. I was looking for the girl I hung out with when we were kids."

Anderson stood. "I can help you with that. Follow me."

Curiosity nudged me as I followed him down the hall. Anderson produced another key from his pocket before he opened a door. I strolled into the room behind him.

"The King Cobra's office." He waved at the tiny space.

"You have access?" I arched a brow at him. "Does that mean you know who he is?"

"Nope. He's only talked to me over the phone using his voice disguiser. Other than that, I find notes in my mailbox, like the keys and instructions of what he needs to have done. There's actually a spreadsheet that gives the girls' addresses and other details. You name it; we've got the info. It's on my laptop."

I folded my arms across my chest, watching as Anderson unlocked a big filing cabinet then produced his computer. He set it on the old, scratched desk then flipped it open. It whirled to life, and Anderson pulled up the Excel program.

"What room were you in?"

I frowned before I replied, "The third from the end on the right side of the hall."

"I need to get these numbered so we can track them better." Anderson grew quiet as he stared at the screen. "There we go. Phoebe. That's the girl you were with." Anderson rubbed the back of his neck. "She's a nice girl. We have a class together. Here's her number, so you can text her directly and set up the next meeting."

"No shit? Her number?" I grabbed my phone, ready for the digits.

"Not with that. You'll bring down the entire society, asshole." Anderson opened another filing drawer and tossed me a burner. "Use that for any and all society business. It's untraceable. The second Phoebe finds out who you are, she could go running to the press about the brotherhood and ruin all of our chances to go pro, so watch your step."

I turned the phone over in my palm. "Thanks, man. I'll make sure to use it." I hesitated, a thought occurring to me. "Who pays for all this anyway? I mean, the building, toys, and burner phones, that all adds up. It's not cheap."

Anderson shrugged. "I assume the King Cobra, but I don't ask questions."

I nodded, wondering what illegal activities were funding our sexcapades. "I'm not sure I want to know either." I poised my fingers over the screen, waiting. He rattled off the number as I plugged it into the burner.

"Thanks. I owe you."

A mischievous smile eased across his face. "Yes, you do. I'll collect later." He slapped me on the shoulder. "Have fun, and now that you know her name, I assume it's not the girl you thought she was?"

"Nah. Wrong one. Guess my head was fucking with me." I laughed. "This one." I pointed to my skull. "I'll catch ya later." I gave him a little wave before I left him alone in King Cobra's office. I had some business I wanted to deal with.

Thirty minutes later, I let myself into the locker room and strolled through Coach's office to my corner of the building. After tossing my keys on the makeshift shelf I'd created from a few old, sturdy plastic milk crates, I eased onto the cot and pulled out my iPhone. Regardless of what I'd learned from Anderson, I had questions and knew just the person to help me.

I brought up the number on my screen, then hit the green call button. Tapping the speaker icon, I stretched out on the bed and waited.

"Hey, Jag."

"Hey, Gunner. How's it going?" I asked, placing my arm beneath my head and propping myself up a bit.

"Same ol'. About to have church, but what's up?"

"It can wait. Tell everyone hey and let me know when you guys are taking another ride. It would be good to join for a weekend after ball season is over."

"I will but tell me what's going on. I've got time for my favorite nephew."

I chuckled. "I'm your only nephew." Tension slithered through my neck and shoulders as I prepared to tell him who I saw. Sitting up, I inhaled deeply and tried to clear my mind of the onslaught of emotions that slammed into my chest.

His silence told me he was listening.

"I think I need your help. You and the MC can find out anything. I mean, hell, you found me."

"It took too damned long, Jag. The situation shouldn't have gone down like that."

I swallowed over the lump in my throat, unwilling to dive deep into my dark past. "It was better than never."

My uncle blew out a heavy sigh, the weight of the conversation thick with pain and anger. He had no idea how grateful I was for him. I owed him my life.

"It pays when you have your hands in a lot of activities." Gunner's dark chuckle filled the line, and I appreciated him making light of it. We had to. He was a big part of my life, but even he wasn't aware of all my secrets.

Together with his MC, they had their share of illegal dealings, but we never discussed it over the phone. Half the crap they did, I didn't know anything about since I hadn't ever pledged. My focus was on football. Plus, even though I wasn't close to my mom, I didn't want to give her a heart attack if I joined.

"The fire . . ."

He released a low whistle. "We're going there?"

"Yeah. I fucked a chick tonight . . . she was wearing a blindfold so I couldn't see her face, but when we were finished, I lifted it." I scrubbed my cheeks with my hands, her image flickering through my mind. "Her name is Phoebe, but she's the fucking spitting image of . . ." Tears pricked my eyes. It had only been four years since I lost her. "Ariana."

I could hear rustling in the background, and I imagined Gunner was moving items around on his desk.

"Just like her? I mean, how well did you see her face, Jag? The past can wreak hell on us."

"I know. At first, I thought that's all it was and that the chick looks a lot like her, so I dug around and learned her name is Phoebe Jenkins. But it's not settling well in my gut. I've got a weird feeling."

"Jag, grief is a powerful bitch. You watched your home burn to the fucking ground."

"I know, but there wasn't a body." My nostrils flared as I struggled to sift through the pain of that night. It had fucking gutted me, ripped me to shreds, then kicked my ass straight to hell.

"That's because the house burned and everything in it turned to ash."

"I fucking know! I was there, goddammit." I choked on my words, my hands balling into fists.

"What information do you have on her?" Gunner's voice was even and calm. He knew how to handle me when I was about to blow my fucking mind.

"Her name and the fact that she attends Whitmore. I haven't seen her on campus, but it's a big school."

"I'll have Cupcake hack into the school's system and see what we can find. But first, Jag, you need to see her again and look her dead in the eye. If you have any doubt it's not Ari, then I need to know before I go snooping. You're already fucked up in the head, and this ghost could ruin you. Can't have that. No pussy is worth torturing yourself over."

"Ari was worth it, Gunner. Ari was."

A heavy silence filled the line.

"I've got you, man. Call me when you see her again. Any other info would help, too. I gotta go, kid."

"Wait. Do you have an update on the other situation?"

"I wish I did but we're all working on it. We've got your back, Jag."

A dangerous cocktail of disappointment, anxiety, and fear needled my skin. "Thanks. I'll talk to you soon." I disconnected the call, my chest heaving with the agony of revisiting that night. It had been the best day of my life, then it had all ended in a blink of an eye. I threw my head back and roared, cursing the heavens while my body trembled with raw energy and buried emotion.

There was no way I could sleep. I had to find out who Phoebe really was, which meant I had to get my crap together and strategize what to do.

Chapter Nine

Phoebe

"I've had it." Teagan slipped her arm through mine as we walked toward the gym's locker room after her P.E. class and my weightlifting class.

"Oh?" I flashed her an innocent look just in case she was pissed at me.

"Today, I was going to text you at least a million times, then I remembered that your phone was broken. We're getting you a new one. *Now.*"

I cringed. "Bossy much?" I scrunched my nose at her. "I have to study. Tonight won't work."

Teagan's gaze narrowed on me. "Listen, I completely understand taking a break, but Theo messaged me this morning worried sick about you. I told him you were fine, but your cell was broken and we were getting a new one after classes were over."

"What? Why didn't you tell me?"

Exasperated, Teagan rolled her eyes at me. "Bitch, please. This is the first time I've seen you today, and you have no fucking phone for me to call or text. You see my dilemma, right?"

An unexpected snort escaped me. "Now that you put it that way, I do."

My heart fluttered in my chest when I thought about the texts that caused me to throw my cell in the first place. I didn't want another one. I couldn't change my number or my friends and Dad would ask me a million questions. Other than not owning a phone, I had no other way to stop that monster. *He will show up in person if you don't reply soon.*

I attempted to shrug off my inner voice, but a cloud of unease rolled in the pit of my stomach. Stupidly, I thought he would give up if I lived across the country. I was sadly mistaken.

Teagan snapped her fingers in front of my face as we paused near the locker room entrance. "Babe? Where'd ya go?"

"Sorry. I was spacing out."

Teagan pushed on the door and released me. "Let's leave your car here. We'll get you a new phone then grab dinner. I'll bring you back."

"But—"

Teagan held up her hand, halting me midsentence. "Nope. We're getting it done. Be ready in twenty." Teagan spun around and hurried to go change.

I walked in the opposite direction until I reached my PE locker. There was no getting around it. I couldn't get away with not having a phone.

"You win again, motherfucker," I muttered under my breath as I turned the dial to the combination then grabbed what I needed for a quick shower. The coach had worked us hard in weightlifting class, and I was sweaty as hell. Too bad my past wasn't as easy to wash down the damn drain.

"See, that wasn't so bad, was it?" Teagan popped a french fry into her mouth, grinning at me as if she'd won the lottery. "Don't forget to add me to your Find My Phone feature. Not that I would expect to find you anywhere other than home and the library, but you never know." Teagan winked at me. "One of these days I'll talk you into attending a football game. Lots of tight ends to see."

"You'll have to bribe me, Teagan." I smirked before I added her to my new iPhone. "To answer your question, no, it wasn't that bad. Dad was my first message." I took a sip of my soda, chewing on the end of the straw for a second.

"I'm sure he appreciated that."

"He got onto me for not getting a replacement right away and scaring him. I'm sure Samantha got an earful when he couldn't reach me." I bit into my burger, staring at my food.

"Why are you so sad lately? You weren't like this at the academy. What changed?" Teagan leaned back in her seat, eyeing me.

"I'm good. It's an adjustment moving to the west side of the country." I flashed her a smile.

"You need to get laid. I know you were on the regular at the academy. My girl just needs a tune-up." She winked at me. "There's a party this weekend, remember?"

I pursed my lips into a thin line.

"You forgot about the party? Your mind is like a steel trap, and you don't ever forget shit." She leaned across the table and placed her hand on my forehead. "Hm. I thought for sure you had a fever."

I couldn't help but laugh. "Teagan, Whitmore classes are a lot harder than at the university I attended my freshman year. Did you know that moving is one of the top five stressors?"

"No, but it makes sense." She folded her arms. "So that's all this is? You're adjusting and stressed about starting a new college even though you're with your best friends again?"

"You know I love you all, and it's the reason I came. Dad was not having it but I told him I had a scholarship and a job to pay my bills. He had no say in my decision."

"I'm so proud of you. I think Theo would have caved and paid for everything at Whitmore, but it probably felt damn good to break away from Daddy's money."

I moaned. "You have no idea. He had zero input and control. It was amazing."

"Okay, so we'll celebrate the fact that you're standing on your own two feet. Let's do a little therapy shopping for Saturday night. If we win the football game, it will be hella rowdy. Drink up and fuck hard." Teagan laughed before she rummaged through her Louis Vuitton purse, then produced her credit card. "I've got dinner."

"Thanks. I'll pay next time." I grinned at her. "I really am glad to be here, Teagan. It's a relief to be with you and the girls again. Last year was super hard being apart from my besties." She didn't have a hint of how bad it had been.

She reached over and grabbed my hand. "We don't ever have to be apart again."

I wished her words meant more to me, but instead, they bounced around the empty chambers of my heart. I'd promised someone a long time ago that we would never be apart, too. Only hours after those words fell from my lips, my entire world turned upside down.

Chapter Ten

Phoebe

I applied my lip gloss, then smacked my lips before sliding the panel closed on the car's visor mirror.

"Where are we again?" I asked Teagan, who had offered to be the designated driver for the party. Everlee, Leighton, and Gabby were snug in the backseat because I called shotgun before we left the house. On the way home, I wouldn't care where I sat because I would be too fucking plastered to give a rat's ass.

"Some new football player's place. I forget his name. His parents are out of town, though," Everlee explained.

"Easy to forget. I suck at names," I muttered. Most of them anyway.

"At least the boys will be in a good mood and ready to play after the big win today," Gabby said, wiggling her brows at me.

I smoothed my lilac see-through top. Everlee, Gabby, and Teagan had sworn the color was perfect for my blonde hair and blue eyes. Leighton had chosen a black bandeau bra beneath the sheer purple, then they paired it with my dark-wash skinny jeans.

The girls grinned at me.

"You look fabulous, darling," Gabby said, clapping her hands together.

We broke into laughter. I had no clue what I would do without my girls, but I didn't want to find out a second time.

Since I hadn't been called to the society all week, I hoped to get fucked at the party. In fact, I wouldn't even mind giving Anderson from my bio class a ride. I mentally gave the Black Mamba a big fuck you for looking at me then running away like a chicken shit. If I ever saw him again, I would bite his dick for treating me that way.

We exited the car and slowly walked up the paved driveway. With parties this large, it was difficult to park near the house. If you did, it was hell to get out when everyone blocked your car. Teagan had hopefully found a good spot.

I glanced up, taking in my surroundings.

"Holy crap. I thought my home in Washington was big, but this . . ." Slowing, I gave the girls a bewildered look. The freshly manicured lawn with trimmed shrubs lining the walkway to the mahogany front door was a work of art. Daddy needed to hire whoever the landscaper was. The red-brick mansion hosted two white columns that guarded the entrance. A large balcony overlooked the property from the second story, and I guessed it was the master suite. Planter boxes with pink, blue, and purple flowers lined the edge of the porch as we approached the steps.

"I think you could fit two of my houses in this one," Leighton responded in awe.

I squared my shoulders, prepared to meet new guys and maybe some of the football team. "Are we ready to dance our asses off?"

We all linked arms and walked to the entrance as though we were going to take the party over. Hell, we had before, so why not this time.

Gabby opened the door, and we filed in as "Ready For It" resonated through the speaker system and a group of students danced in the middle of what I guessed was the living room.

"I say let's get lit first!" Everlee yelled at us over the music.

"I'm in!" My foot tapped against the black-and-white marble floors as the song pulsed through me. It had been a long ass time since I'd danced.

My dark thoughts wandered, dragging my mind back to the past. At one time, I had been a super social person, but after the fire, I hid from the world as much as possible. Now, I only spent time with my girls. I'd missed them horribly last year. When they left, shit got bad and fast. They protected me more than they would ever know.

The mansion was more amazing inside, with black marble floors and white pillars on each side of the hall that led to an open-floor plan. The living and informal dining area was packed with college kids laughing and drinking. I was ready to join them and let loose.

Fifteen minutes later, we'd worked our way through the crowd and reached the kitchen, where every kind of alcohol was waiting. Leighton located the whiskey and poured us all shots. We cheered over the music and downed them before filling our cups with our booze of choice. It would have to last a while since the lines were so damn long. Teagan joined us in the first drink, then she planned to chill for the rest of the night.

Gabby led us back through the crowd to the middle of the makeshift dance floor, where we swayed to the music. I sipped my coke and Jack in my red Solo cup, ready to lose myself for an evening.

"Phoebe! So glad you could make it!" I turned in the direction of my name.

"Anderson! Congrats on a kick ass game today." I winked at him, the alcohol helping me loosen up. He ran his hand over his short blonde hair. Sweeping my gaze over him, I settled on his focused eyes that hadn't left mine.

Anderson slipped his arm around my waist. "Thanks. I wish you would have been there at the game today. It would have been nice to see you in the stands cheering."

His smile weakened my knees. Maybe it was the fact that I was horny as hell, but damn, he looked even better than he usually did.

"Sports aren't my thing. I've never been to a game before, but maybe I'll reconsider for you." I flashed him a flirty smile.

Anderson beamed at me as we danced. The buzz of my phone broke through my thoughts, and I fished it out of my back pocket.

The color drained from my face as I read the text.

Satan:

You look gorgeous tonight.

Fear and adrenaline ripped through me, and my hand trembled as I attempted to shove my cell in my pocket again. I took a long gulp of my drink before I addressed Anderson. Is he here? I glanced around, but there were so many people, the messenger could have easily hidden behind the crowd.

"Sorry about that. What were you saying?"

Anderson's expression flickered with curiosity. "Are you okay? I'm guessing that text message wasn't anything good from your reaction."

I gently grabbed his shoulder and squeezed, his muscle rippling beneath my touch.

"What reaction is that?" Dammit! I have to work on my poker face.

Anderson tipped his chin. "It's like that, huh?"

"I have no idea what you're talking about, Mr. Nichols." I winked then danced a circle around him.

"Phoebe. If something is wrong, you can talk to me."

I moved my hips and raised my hands in the air. "I appreciate it."

He swept his gaze down my body, watching my movements.

"Damn, you look good enough to eat."

"Promises, promises." I rolled my eyes, giggling.

Anderson slid his arm around my waist and pulled me against him. He leaned down, his minty breath grazing my ear as he spoke. "I can make you forget all about that message that upset you. You should let me." He nipped my earlobe, and I arched my back, my breasts pressing against his muscular chest.

"Hang on." Anderson released me then produced his cell and

looked at the screen. "Dammit." He stared at me with disappointment flashing across his expression. "I gotta go. I'm sorry."

I couldn't stop my frown. "Are you sure? We were just starting to have fun."

He reached up and brushed my cheek with his fingertips. "Maybe another time." His hand dropped, and he winked at me before he walked away. My eyes latched onto the muscles flexing in his long legs and ass. Yum. I really would have enjoyed that ride.

Gabby quickly took Anderson's place, dancing with me. "You look bummed! If you haven't noticed, there are a million hotties here. The football team is loaded with sexy bad boys."

I laughed, trying to shrug off Anderson's sudden departure. At least it wasn't as awful as the Black Mamba's exit. Maybe Anderson's quick mood change didn't have anything to do with me, but it sure seemed like it. He was fun and sweet in class, and I had no problem hanging out. My brows knitted together. As soon as Anderson had checked his text message, he dipped. I was making a big deal out of nothing. The last thing I wanted to do was jeopardize my growing friendship. When I was with him, I knew I was safe, and that's exactly what I needed.

For the next couple of hours, I drank and danced with my girls as well as several guys. Each time the text message from Satan popped into my head again, I drank some more and blurred it out.

The tipsier I got, though, my two times at the Viper Society shadowed the idea of fucking someone else. Then, my cruel brain reminded me that the Black Mamba had left even more abruptly than Anderson had. I was beginning to wonder about the Whitmore guys.

A few hours later, "Babylon" by Babychaos pulled my attention to my friends, and I allowed the beat to consume me. My last drink was long gone, and I was on my way to sobering up. Too bad. Oblivion felt pretty damn good.

My cell buzzed against my ass cheek again, and I removed it from my back pocket. I squinted at the screen, attempting to read the blurry letters. Apparently, I wasn't that close to sober.

Unknown:

I thought I told you no one was allowed to touch you, my pet.

Looking up slowly, I scanned the crowd. The Black Mamba had told Anderson to leave me alone?

My fingers tightened around my cell as I considered my reply. I stared at the message again, then typed my response.

Me:

A girl has needs, and you've been MIA all week. That shit's on you.

I waited for his response, goose bumps dotting my sweaty flesh. I was well aware that my message would most likely push his buttons. That was my goal anyway. Maybe he would tie me up and spank me for flirting with Anderson. I would totally be down for that.

Unknown:

You tell yourself whatever you need to in order to feel better. Reality? I'm a busy man, but that doesn't excuse your behavior. You will be punished.

What the hell did that mean? I didn't do anything wrong.

Chapter Eleven

Jagger

Every nerve in my body stood on end as I caught sight of Phoebe across the room and watched Anderson walk away from her. I would have to deal with him later.

She looked stunning in her sheer top, with her jeans clinging to her curvy hips and luscious ass. My stomach flip-flopped as a harsh truth crashed into me. I had set my beer down the second I spotted her at the party. I needed a clear head to study her and make sure my mind wasn't playing tricks on me. As the hours ticked by, I was sure of one thing: Phoebe wasn't who she said she was. The moment I convinced myself of that, I questioned how in hell it was even possible.

My feet were frozen to the ground as I observed her, the tiniest details setting my heart on fire—the familiar waves of her long blonde hair, the glint in her blue eyes, and that perfect smile—the one she used to flash me when she snuck into my bedroom when we were teenagers and our lives were still uncomplicated. A sharp pain tore through my chest, and I slammed my eyes closed, barely able to breathe as a thousand questions raced through my brain—why would she do this? Why would she want to deceive me about something so damned serious? The voice in my head reminded me that it wasn't plausible for Phoebe to be who I so desperately needed her to be.

Doubt seeped inside me like a deadly poison, and once again, I questioned my sanity. Maybe Gunner was right. Grief could bend you over and fuck you in the ass without lube.

Clutching my burner phone I used for society business, I text Anderson.

Me:

Phoebe is off-limits. Stay away from her.

Anderson:

Dude, she's not even your type. She's a total book nerd and doesn't know a damn thing about sports. She didn't have a clue I even played football until I told her.

I quirked a brow at his assumption before I replied.

Me:

She's my girl at the society. End of discussion.

I tucked the burner phone away, still seething over Anderson's attempt to make a move on Ariana.

I stepped back into the upstairs hallway and grabbed my personal cell. Typing a quick message to Gunner, I kept my eye on Ariana.

Me:

I'm 95% sure it's her. I need to know the truth.

If I was correct, she had fucking betrayed me. My nostrils flared as the grief was suddenly replaced with hate. It was cold, deep, and consumed me to the depths of my dark heart. Quick as a tornado ripping through a city, I hated her more than I had ever hated anyone. The memories flickered through my thoughts, and I refused to give them any more space in my head.

Confusion shook and rattled me to my bones with unanswered questions. My guess? Ariana was a cold, heartless bitch under that gorgeous body of hers.

My shoulders sagged, the weight of the potential betrayal almost too much to carry. Son of a bitch, I'd fucked her at the society. In a moment of clarity, I knew why screwing her felt so right—even while she was blindfolded. Somewhere inside myself, I had suspected it was her all along. Only time would tell, though, and I was an impatient son of a bitch.

My emotions were firing off faster than a jet breaking the sound barrier. That girl was fucking me, and I wasn't even getting my dick wet. Turmoil squeezed my chest as my feelings bounced from love to hate, and now a burning rage surged through my veins as I thought about Ariana and Anderson. Hopefully, he was smart enough to heed my warning.

A possessive growl rumbled through my throat. The two of them could not happen. If I couldn't have Ariana, then no one else could either. She was mine to destroy, the same way she had destroyed me. And in the process of ruining her, I would demand answers. She owed me that much.

I cracked my knuckles, itching to touch her and force her to serve me. Grinding my molars, I ached to make her pay for all she had put me through. An electric thrill sparked inside of me as I imagined exacting my revenge. My dick sprang to life, enjoying the idea of punishing her. My thoughts spun in a million different directions as I struggled to grasp the possibility that the girl I'd lost was under my nose and had taken another name. My phone buzzed and I grabbed it, my eyes landing on the message from Gunner:

That's fucked, man. Are you going to confront her?

I smirked as I replied.

Me:

Hell yeah. Bitch owes me some answers.

Grey dots bounced on the screen as I waited for his response.

Gunner:

Keep me posted. I've been digging, and now that we know, I won't hack the records. Not at Whitmore, anyway. It looks like she spent her school years at Wahlberg Academy in New York as Phoebe.

Confused, my forehead creased.

Me:

When did she move there?

I glanced up, keeping an eye on her as my mind replayed Anderson slipping his arm around her waist a few minutes ago, and another growl escaped me. It was fucked up that I had a problem with him touching the girl I hated with every fiber of my being, but I was a complicated man.

Gunner:

Right after the fire, which means some shit was going on behind the scenes. Theo never makes a move without a reason.

Even in the years I'd spent with Theo as my stepfather, I knew what Gunner said was true.

Me:

But why? Do you think Theo knew the truth?

"Monster" by Chandler Leighton played, slowing the party's pace. I threw my head back and laughed. The song was fucking poetic. I was definitely a monster, and I was about to devour Ariana.

My cell buzzed with a response.

Gunner:

Hard to say. But, Jag, before you lose your fucking shit on her, I'd find out what happened.

I barked out a spiteful laugh.

Me:

Too late.

I replaced my phone in my back pocket, calculating my next move.

Ariana's cheeks were pink from dancing with her friends, and she lifted her hair, exposing the curve of her neck. I leaned against the banister, still hidden in the shadows. She said something to her friends as she walked away and headed for the front door.

Perfect. I hurried down the stairs, trying to remain undetected, which was nearly impossible. Elbowing my way through the crowd, I ducked through the kitchen and out the back door before Anderson caught up with me. The cool air greeted me, and I took a deep breath.

"Not now," I said irritation thick in my tone.

"Dude, your text message wasn't okay. You've not said anything about claiming Phoebe. You can't cockblock me like that."

I did *not* have time for his annoying small talk.

I made my way around the far side of the mansion, then I spotted Ariana in the driveway. My gaze narrowed as an older guy approached her and she backed away.

Unbridled fear coasted through Ariana's expression. I moved closer in order to hear what was happening, with Anderson right on my heels. If he was insisting on being on my ass, he had to stay quiet. I placed my finger over my mouth and he nodded. Hopefully, I could catch more than bits and pieces of Ariana's conversation.

Hidden behind a tree, I muffled my laugh. I felt like a cold-hearted stalker, but it didn't bother me.

"Why are you here, Peter?" Ariana asked, her voice trembling. "I left New York to get away from you. Don't you get that?"

He closed the gap between them and grabbed her wrists, shaking her hard. Anderson nudged me in the side, anger coasting over his face.

"You will *never* be free of me. I own you. Enough of your childish nonsense. It's time to come home." He sneered, the corner of his lip twitching.

What the hell? This ugly bastard thought he could get rough with her. No way was he taking her anywhere. She was mine. Always had been.

Peter slapped a hand over her mouth as a few stumbling, drunk girls giggled while they passed them. The group never even glanced their way.

The fucker quickly spun her around and pulled her against his chest. It was then that the moonlight glinted off the barrel of a gun. He and Ariana began to walk down the side of the driveway, where it was darker.

From Anderson's expression, I could tell he was about to blow a gasket. He might come in handy since I clearly had to deal with this asshole, so I motioned for him to come with me.

I followed them quietly, piecing together exactly how to deal with Peter. No one fucked with Ariana except me, and that disgusting son of a bitch was about to find that out. Not to mention, he had a gun trained on her, which made me nearly lose my mind. Fuck no.

Ariana dragged her feet, making it more difficult for Peter to navigate her. She elbowed him in the gut and attempted to run, but he tightened his grip on her and jammed the weapon into her side.

My molars clenched, images of my past flashing through my mind as I followed them. Peter took a right into the tree line of the property, trying to stay hidden. Quietly, Anderson and I darted across the driveway and ducked behind a large oak.

"We can do this the easy way or the hard way, Phoebe. It's up to you."

Without any concern for her safety, she spun around and head-butted him. Peter staggered backward, holding his forehead in his free hand. Ariana attempted to run, but he snatched her arm before she even made it a few feet away.

Anderson shot forward and I grabbed him before he blew our cover.

"Wait," I mouthed to him.

He nodded, ready to deal with the situation.

"You'll pay for that, you little bitch." Peter raised the gun and smacked her on the back of the head. Ariana dropped to the ground with a soft thud.

I bolted out from my hiding place and snuck up behind Peter, kicking his knee out from under him. He collapsed to the ground beside Phoebe, and I wrestled the pistol out of his grip. I placed it against his skull, grinning like the crazy fucker I was.

"Check on Phoebe," I ordered Anderson.

The moment he knelt beside her and checked her pulse, I returned my attention to Peter.

"Hello, Peter. Allow me to introduce myself. I'm Jagger Whitlock."

The color drained from his cheeks as he raised his arms in the air to protect himself.

"Don't hurt me. Please."

The only way I could deal with this bastard was to knock him out. I raised the gun.

"Nighty nighty, you son of a bitch." I whacked him against the side of the skull and watched as he collapsed.

Tucking the gun in the back of my pants, I flexed my fingers. I had my work cut out for me and would need both hands free.

Chapter Twelve

Jagger

I paced the small room, my tennis shoes slapping against the cement floor. Glancing at my watch, I wondered if enough time had passed before I called the hospital. Anderson had taken Ariana to the emergency room then got the hell out of there. Before he left, I made him swear on his fucking life that he wouldn't say a word to anyone about what had happened. I didn't need the cops breathing down my neck when Peter suddenly went missing. Anderson had reminded me of the society brotherhood. I was about to test the hell out of that promise.

Peter had struck Ariana, and I suspected she had a concussion, which put my idea for her on the back burner until she felt better. Maybe old habits died hard, but something inside me needed to know she was okay. *What if I'm wrong and it's not Ari?* After the hell I'd lived through, my instincts were spot-on mostly, but my emotions might cloud my judgment about who this Phoebe chick really was.

Anger flared to life as I mentally replayed Peter hurting her. Even though she was possibly a traitorous bitch, I had claimed her at the society, and it pissed me the fuck off the way he touched her—like he was familiar with her body. *Son of a bitch. It's his name on her body!*

Hair rose on the back of my neck, and I bristled as the voice inside my head told me I had tiptoed on the edge of insanity for too long and Ariana wasn't the love of my life.

Although that made sense to a part of my brain, I could spot Ari in a crowd of a thousand girls with blonde hair. I knew her. I knew the way she moved, the curve of her hips, and the way she threw her head back when she belly laughed.

"Fuck!" I scrubbed my face with my hands, searching for clarity and a shred of peace in my frantic thoughts. The memory of her soft kisses and innocence captured my heart all over again. If it was her, then . . . Goddammit.

A groan pulled my attention away from one of my problems.

"Where am I?"

I watched as Peter processed his surroundings. His expressions were almost comical. His brown eyes widened as his body shook against the table that I'd tied him to.

"Who are you?" he croaked.

Walking, I checked his ankle and wrist restraints. In a few minutes, he would tug on them as he screamed, and I needed to make sure he couldn't break free. Imagining the pain I was about to inflict, I inwardly grinned . . . I couldn't fucking wait. The son of a bitch had roughed Ariana up, and it was time for him to pay.

"Do you know who I am to Phoebe?" I wondered what she'd told him.

He nodded. "Jagger. Phoebe talked about you and showed me pictures of when you were younger. It's hard to mistake the ice-blue eyes and black hair."

Sweat covered his forehead, and I imagined he had one hell of a headache. Not my problem. A little voice in the back of my head nudged me. Even though I was positive it was Ari, I suspected Peter could shed some light on the situation. Regardless, before she was dealt with, I needed to confirm for a fact that she was indeed Theo's daughter. My hands fisted. If Mom and Theo had lied to me, then there would be hell to pay. Granted, I'd only been in their lives briefly since the fire, but the truth should have come out at some point.

"What's her father's name?" There was no use beating around the bush.

"I don't know. She just refers to him as Dad or Daddy." His gaze darted across the room, panic settling over his expression. "Why am I here? I haven't done anything to you." Spittle flew from his mouth, and I wiped my arm, disgusted.

To me, the reason was simple. "You touched what was mine."

His brows furrowed. "Yours?"

The stupid bastard had the audacity to laugh.

"You do realize you're tied down on a table in the back of an abandon butcher shop, right?" I sneered at him. "There are a total of four drains in the floor of this room. You should take a guess why." I loomed over him, enjoying the stages of denial then realization registering in his eyes. Maybe I had hit him harder than I thought if it took him that long to piece what I'd said together.

"You can't do this!" He tugged against the restraints.

"But I can. And I will. Again, why are you here?"

"I don't know, man!"

I made a buzzer sound. "Wrong! You dared to touch what is mine." I tapped my chin, pondering. "Plus, you were rough with Phoebe. In fact, you practically dragged her to your car while she was kicking and screaming. When you knocked her out, that was just too far for me. That's no way to treat a lady." I smirked. Phoebe certainly wasn't a "lady" at the society, but I had no problem with that.

"I'm sorry. I'll never lay another hand on her again." His chin trembled.

Anticipation could be a messed-up bitch. I chuckled at his fear. He wasn't that tough now that he wasn't hurting a girl. "I can spot a liar any day, so don't bother feeding me a line of bull."

His rumpled dark hair was plastered to his head as he profusely sweated. I'd turned the heat up to over a hundred degrees. My body was used to it since football camps and practices started in the hottest months of the year, but Peter struggled.

"I might be willing to negotiate your life for something, though."

"My life? You're going to kill me?" he squeaked.

"I haven't decided yet." I paced the room, my head hanging down as I pretended to contemplate. I wanted this motherfucker so scared, he pissed himself, but I also needed him to think he could work out a deal with me. "I'm not unreasonable, so let's give it a shot."

Hope sprang to life in his eyes, and he nodded enthusiastically. "Anything."

"Just tell me the truth. It's that simple." I snapped my fingers for added effect.

He licked his lips. "Then ask me whatever you need and let me go."

I strolled across the room and put some space between us, afraid of what I would do as he answered my questions.

"What's Phoebe's real name?" Leaning against the wall, I leveled him with an icy cold gaze and waited for him to answer.

Chapter Thirteen

Phoebe

I groaned against the bright lights, blinking rapidly in a vain attempt to clear my vision. My head throbbed like a son of a bitch as I glanced around at the stark white walls, the few chairs on the back wall, and the equipment next to the bed in the room.

"You're awake." Teagan stared at me with her doe eyes, fear etched into her pretty features.

"Where am I?" I whispered, my throat still raw and voice hoarse.

"You're in the hospital. Do you remember anything?" She moved from her chair near my bed to beside me on the mattress.

"A little." I rubbed the back of my head, wincing from the throbbing ache.

"You were attacked outside of the party, babe."

Moaning, I scooted over so Teagan could crawl into the bed with me. Dark circles had formed beneath her eyes, and I was pretty sure she was wearing the black lace crop top and boyfriend jeans she had worn last night. My head was too foggy from the pain, so I had no idea what day it was.

She settled in and rolled onto her side, propping her head on her hand. "Do you know your attacker?"

Her intense gaze told me she loved me but wouldn't buy the lies anymore and not to waste her time.

"Yeah. He's been . . . We were—" My pulse skipped a beat, and I shuddered. "He's terrifying. Was he arrested?"

Guilt graced Teagan's face, and she chewed on her lower lip, clearly stressed. "I don't know where he is."

The room tilted, spinning. *Peter is still out there.*

"Babe, why didn't you tell me you were in trouble? We're best friends. I could have helped."

She hadn't heard the half of it, but it was time I told her what I'd been hiding. Peter was in Oregon, and I might need help.

"You can't. It's why I tried to protect you and the girls. If you'd learned the truth . . . He threatened to hurt all of you if I ever said a word."

Teagan's expression twisted. "Tell me, now. From the lump on your head, he hit you hard. It knocked you out clean. This nutjob could have killed you. He's dangerous, Phoebs."

Cries shook my shoulders, and I hid my face behind my hands. "Please promise me that when I tell you, you won't hate me forever."

Teagan rolled her eyes. "Bitch, I could never hate you forever. Maybe a little while, but not forever." She flashed me a grin.

"It was Peter Jacobson."

Shocked, Teagan's mouth hit the floor. "Our high school history teacher?"

"We always talked about how hot he was," I said sheepishly.

She held up a finger as the realization smacked her. "Wait, are you sleeping with him?"

Bracing myself for Teagan to yell at me, I sucked in a breath and cringed. "I was until I moved to Oregon."

She shot out of the bed and paced the room. "You . . . I . . ." Bewildered, she tossed her hands in the air. "How long?"

"Three years." My voice was soft as the humiliation consumed me.

"Three years?" Her screech pierced my eardrums.

"You can't tell the girls. Please. It will only hurt them." I could only hope that by the time I was finished, Teagan would agree to keep her mouth shut.

Teagan snorted. "Now you want me to keep your secret?"

"If you'll let me finish, you'll understand why."

"Fine. But I'll remain standing for this." She folded her arms over her chest.

"At first, I figured it was innocent flirting. Peter asked me to stay after class one day after a test. I swear I thought he was going to accuse me of cheating, but he offered to work with me on a project."

Teagan tilted her head. "The essay contest for the achievement scholarship?"

"Yeah. Even then I knew I wanted to break away from Daddy's money and stand on my own two feet."

"I get it. You know my parents think they can dictate my choices as long as they are paying for everything." Her expression briefly softened.

"I realize Dad is trying to help, but I want to make my own decisions for a change. Sometimes he's too much . . ." I retreated into my head and tried to block out the bad memories.

Staring out the large hospital window at the cloudless, star-filled sky, I reined in the emotions that threatened to suck me into a dark hole. I had lost my entire world after the fire, but I couldn't talk about it with Teagan.

I cleared my throat and continued.

"It was as if Peter could sense that I was broken. At first, the attention was flattering. He made me feel special, wanted. It was our secret, and I felt alive again."

Teagan sank into the chair next to my bed. "We all want that, Phoebs."

"He took it slow, but after a few months of touching and kissing, he wanted more. So did I, or so I thought." I closed my eyes in a vain attempt to shut out the horrible memories, but I had to keep going.

"The sex was amazing at first, then he started to punish me if I didn't do what he wanted. Eventually, he coaxed my secrets out of me, then it turned into blackmail. If I handed in a paper and it wasn't to his satisfaction, he would strip me of my clothes, tie me up in his closet, and leave me for hours."

Teagan blinked at me as if she hadn't heard me correctly. "What? That's abuse."

"That wasn't the worst of it."

Her forehead creased. "The early mornings you crept into our room . . . it makes sense now."

"And the reason I wouldn't walk around the dorm in my bra and panties or wear a bikini . . ." I sat up slowly, my head giving me a big fuck you, but I ignored it. "My lower back," I whispered, pulling the gown to the side.

Teagan's gasp filled the room.

"Jesus. What the fuck?"

I remained silent and allowed Teagan to absorb what she saw before I spoke again. "I was in his office with him that evening and tried to run away. This was my punishment . . . and my nightmare the other night." I peeked over my shoulder at my best friend. Tears streamed down her cheeks as she stared at my exposed skin. "He carved his name into me. It took hours and he dragged out the pain until I passed out, then he would wake me again. Blood was every-where. Remember when I had mono? I didn't. It was a fake doctor's note so I wouldn't have to dress out for phys ed or sit in a chair all day while my back was healing. I was terrified someone would find out."

"Phoebe." Teagan's sobs echoed through the otherwise quiet room. "Why would anyone do something so horrible?" She walked to the side of the bed and wrapped her arms around me. "I've got you, girl. That monster won't ever hurt you again. I don't know how, but he will pay for what he's done to you, babe."

Relief flooded me as I hugged my best friend's waist and cried with her. Keeping that secret, plus the years of abuse, had nearly destroyed me. When it became too painful, I would close my eyes and think about the only guy that had ever mattered to me. Those memories had kept me sane—barely.

Teagan kissed my forehead. "You need security or a bodyguard or something. Tell Theo the truth, Phoebs. He loves you and wants to keep you safe."

I adamantly shook my head. "He won't let me stay at Whitmore and I'm not leaving. I love it here. I'm finally settling into a schedule, and I feel like I'm home."

Teagan's mouth formed a big O. "Your phone. Has Peter been calling and messaging?"

"Yeah. I threw the fucking thing after his last text. A lot of good that did; he showed up at the party."

"Fucking bastard. But how did he know where you were?"

My shoulders sagged. "I got scared and told him I was at Whitmore. After the big football win today, it wouldn't take much to listen to students talking or follow the line of cars to the party. I partied all the time at the academy, so it was probably the first place he looked for me."

Teagan's hands balled into tight fists. "Why would you do that?"

"He threatened to share my secrets. If he did, I would most likely go to prison."

Teagan's mouth dropped open, then she slammed it closed. "He has some serious shit on you?"

I nodded. "It's what he's blackmailing me with."

"I swear to you, no matter how crazy it is, I will never, ever turn you in. Babe, you need to talk to me, though. We can't figure out how to get rid of Peter unless I know everything."

Anxiety infiltrated my veins and slithered into every part of my body. It was too much of a risk to tell her.

"I can't. It will put you in danger."

"I don't care. I'll have my father hire a bodyguard for both of us. Plus, I'll take your secret to my grave. You have my word." She crossed her heart like kids used to in grade school.

Sweat beads formed on the nape of my neck, and my pulse wildly throbbed. I had always been able to trust Teagan, but this was huge. If anything happened to her, I would never forgive myself. From where I sat, I wasn't sure there was another choice. Maybe her dad could help without Theo learning about Peter. However, Mr. Mercer and my dad were golf buddies, so I couldn't take the risk.

"You can't tell your dad, but we have to figure out a way to stop Peter. You swear on your life no one will ever find out what I'm about to tell you?"

"Phoebs, you're my best friend. I don't want to lose you again. The year I was at Whitmore without you sucked."

Every cell in my being burned with guilt. My throat clogged up, and I heaved a sigh. "You say that now, but we'll see how much our friendship changes when you learn the truth."

Chapter Fourteen

Jagger

It had been almost twenty-four hours since I'd checked on Peter. By now, his head would be messing with him, and he's been wondering if he would die alone, tied to a table, or if I would show up again and offer him a grain of redemption. I wouldn't kill him today, but he didn't know that.

I hopped off my bike and removed my helmet before I scooped up the bag on the back of my motorcycle. Before leaving for the half-hour drive, I had packed food and water for the asshole.

The door to the abandoned building creaked as I let myself in then secured the lock behind me. Gunner and some of the MC guys had brought me here a few years ago. My uncle had told me we would return one day and use the butcher shop after finding what we were searching for. I was still waiting. Until then, it served a purpose for Peter.

My black combat boots scuffed against the cement floor as I approached. He was still tied where I'd left him. His limbs were probably so numb, he couldn't feel anything anymore.

"You smell like piss." I shot him a disgusted look. "Lucky for you, I'll hose you down while I'm here."

Peter looked at me as if I'd lost my mind. He would be correct in his assumption. "You're going to untie me?" His voice scratched over my skin like sandpaper.

"Yup. I even have food and water." I should make the mother-fucker earn it, but I wanted him to talk, which meant he needed energy and something to drink.

I set the bag on the floor, reached into the back of my jeans, and produced the gun I'd taken from him after he knocked Phoebe out.

"One wrong move and I'll shoot you in the kneecap."

Horror etched across Peter's face. "My knee? Why not just kill me?"

"Who knows. I might do that too," I said nonchalantly.

"We should get started. Since you passed out on me last time I was here, I'll ask you again. What's Phoebe's real name?"

I unfastened both of his ankles. "Move so you don't eat the floor when you stand up."

He groaned as he attempted to bend his legs.

"Her name, motherfucker." I waved the gun in front of him, reminding him of my promise to take a knee.

"Phoebe Jenkins."

I shook my head. "Wrong." At least, I thought so.

"I swear on my mother's grave it's Phoebe Jenkins." The corner of his mouth twitched. The bastard was lying. I untied his wrists, allowing him a trickle of hope. He flexed his fingers and moved his arms. It took him a few minutes, but he slowly sat up while I waited for his answer, my patience thinning.

"Stand up." Apparently, I needed to scare the asshole, just not enough for him to pass out again.

Peter slid off the table and tried to get his feet to work. His limbs were limp noodles from lying down for hours.

I pointed the gun in the direction I wanted him to walk. "Head to that corner." Backing away while I watched him stumble across the room, I turned on the water faucet and picked up the black hose. "You might need the wall for support." Laughing, I flipped the nozzle so the sprayer would blow full blast and soak the motherfucker. Hopefully, he would smell better.

"That hurts!" he yelled as I continued.

"And your point is?" I walked around Peter, washing the piss out of his jeans. A yellow puddle covered the floor as I sprayed the rest of him. Once I finished, I turned off the faucet and tossed the hose in the corner where I'd found it.

"You can walk for a few minutes." I collected the water and sandwich from the bag and approached him. "Eat slow or you'll be lying in your puke."

He snatched the food and bottle from my hand, his gaze cutting to the pistol. Peter might think differently, but I knew he was too weak to wrestle the gun from me. It would be fun if he tried though.

"Does Phoebe know what you're doing to me?" Peter glowered at me as he twisted the cap off his water and took a drink. He unwrapped the turkey sandwich and took a bite, chewing slowly.

"Not yet. You put her in the hospital. They're monitoring her concussion."

Something flickered in his brown eyes. Regret?

"Who is she to you?" I folded my arms, flexing and causing my biceps to bulge through my T-shirt.

"My girlfriend."

I flinched. His words might as well have punched me in the fucking balls. "For how long?"

His face turned ghostly white.

"How long?" I stomped toward him, barely containing my temper. Maybe it was time for some target practice.

"Since she was in high school." His voice cracked and hovered above a whisper as he cowered away from me.

I shoved my hands in my jean pockets. "She was a minor." I frowned. "Son of a bitch. Were you her teacher?" It was an educated guess, but I had hit the nail on the head with the sheer terror that twisted his face. I was going to make this bastard pay for taking advantage of a girl that needed to feel safe after she'd walked away from everything. Thirteen years ago, she'd lost her home and her mom, Maxine, who had died unexpectedly. Ariana had lived through enough.

"Did Phoebe consent?"

He smirked. "Oh yeah. She begged me for it. When she ran, I chased her and punished her." Peter's eyes widened as he realized he'd slipped up.

"How did you punish her?"

Rage blinded and gripped me, igniting an inferno inside me as he confessed how he terrorized and abused her. The son of a bitch had hurt Ari for three years. He was a fucking monster. My reflexes kicked in, and I grabbed the bastard by the throat and squeezed.

"My dick gets hard when I torture someone. I come from a long line of fucked-up men. You, Peter, picked the wrong motherfucker to mess with."

His cheeks burned bright red as he gasped for the air that I refused to give him. Peter's eyes began to glaze over, and I finally released him. I wanted to play with my prey for a while longer.

"I had hoped not to have to go this route because it's just . . ." I shrugged while he sucked in a lungful of air. "How do I say this? I'm getting bored with your bullshit. I've had to learn to read people for years. That skill meant I got to live another day, and you, Peter, are fucking lying to me.

"Recreational time is over." I gripped his bicep and pointed my weapon to the bed.

"You're going to tie me down already?" His voice was whiny and stomped on my last nerve.

"Seems you don't want to cooperate, so down you go."

He hesitated, and I released the safety on the gun. "Right or left knee?"

Terror twisted his expression, and he hobbled back to the table and lay down while still holding his water.

After I strapped him down, I asked him again. "Who is Phoebe?"

"I told you already! She's my girlfriend."

"Was. Not only am I in her life now, but she clearly said to your face that she'd moved across the country to get away from you. That's a drastic move, which tells me that you were hurting her."

"She's mine to do anything I want to with." He snorted, and I shook my head at his stupidity.

I reached for the tray above the table and picked up a pair of rusty pliers. Holding his index finger, I grinned at him. He was too weak to fight me. "This will hurt, Peter."

He started to scream even before I ripped the fingernail from its tender skin. "Who knew a fingernail could cause so much pain." I chuckled as tears streamed down his face.

"That's for touching Phoebe. You got a little rough with her against her will when you showed up uninvited to the party." I leaned closer, our noses only a few inches away from each other's. "I'm the only one on this fucking planet that can get rough with her. I claimed her tight cunt when we were teenagers. She has always been mine, and now I'm back to take her from you." I grabbed his middle finger, ready to pull the next nail.

"Stop! No! I'll tell you what you want to know!"

Chapter Fifteen

Phoebe

"I'm so happy to be home." I fluffed the pillows on my bed before I crawled under the blankets.

"Me too, and now that we have privacy without the nurses and doctors fussing over you, we need to have that talk."

Teagan and I had changed into our pajamas early. Even though my head was fine, I was still mentally and emotionally exhausted from the fight with Peter. The fact that he was in town terrified me, not only for my safety but for Teagan and the other girls as well. I lived with them. I was so relieved to be with them again; it never occurred to me that Peter would follow me across the country.

"I'm so sorry." My words came out breathy while I struggled to put a damper on my anxiety.

Teagan sat cross-legged on my bed and turned to me. "Let's get this over with and figure out what to do, Phoebe. I gave you my word that I would take your secret to the grave with me."

She says that now, but . . . Bracing myself to lose my best friends and serve time in prison, I reached deep inside myself for the necessary courage.

"I don't want to talk about it." I chewed on my thumbnail. "I killed someone," I blurted.

Teagan stared at me like I had six boobs and a green head.

"It was an accident . . . kind of."

She blinked at me, her disbelief and shock processing on her face. "Kind of?" The pitch of her voice spiked, and I cringed.

"The fire." Tears pricked my eyes, and I had to look away from her. It was too much to bear. "I set it."

Teagan's mouth hit the ground. "You're an arsonist? Is that how someone died?"

I swallowed over the grief and self-hatred, but it threatened to choke me. Maybe I could have escaped Peter a long time ago, but somewhere deep inside me, I needed to be punished for what I'd done. "Yeah."

"Son of a fucking bitch, Phoebe. That's a huge secret!" She hopped off the bed, planted her hands on her slender hips, turned her back to me, and walked away.

"I told you I could go to prison. I tried to warn you."

Teagan spun around on her heel. "Murder and arson, Phoebe, is a big fucking deal!" she hissed.

"It was an accident," I said in a weak attempt to defend myself.

My best friend's nostrils flared, and a flush traveled across her cheeks. She was pissed. I didn't blame her.

"It happened right before I met you at the academy." A tear slipped down my face, and I angrily swiped it away. "It was a hot summer night, and I couldn't sleep. Not wanting to wake anyone, I snuck out of the house and sat on the front porch. It was so peaceful, and the flurry of my thoughts calmed down. I'm not sure how long I was out there, maybe half an hour. When I was ready to go in, I literally had my hand on the doorknob and someone grabbed me from behind."

Teagan's brows shot up, but she remained quiet.

"She dragged me off into the trees and pressed a gun to my head. The girl introduced herself as Crimson." A shudder worked its way through me.

Teagan paced the room, chewing on her manicured thumbnail while I continued to talk.

"The second she told me her name, I knew it was bad. At first, I attempted to fight her, but she was too strong. Then, it dawned on me that if I wanted to live, I had to do everything Crimson told me to do. Honestly, I didn't think she would let me walk away. She was crazy and dangerous."

"Phoebs." Teagan's tone softened.

"Crimson walked me into the house with her gun trained on me. She said she would kill my stepbrother if I didn't set the fire." Swallowing hard against the agony, I tried to hold myself together.

"Holy crap." Teagan eased down on the side of the bed, her expression filled with worry.

"I struck the match, then we ran away. Crimson forced me to hide in the trees again and watch it burn. My . . . my stepbrother never made it out." I was unable to control myself any longer. A sob welled in my throat and before I could swallow it down, it escaped.

"You never told me that you had a stepbrother. Oh my God." Teagan pulled me against her. She smoothed my hair as my cries shook my body. "I'm so sorry you lived through that."

I gripped her forearm, clinging to my best friend. "I thought I would lose you if you knew the truth."

"Well, we were heading in that direction at first, but no fucking way, bitch. You're stuck with me."

Eventually, the crying slowed and I sat up. A nervous giggle escaped me.

"You always giggle at the weirdest times." Teagan wiped her damp cheeks and blew out a heavy breath. "I have a lot of questions, then we have to figure out how to deal with Peter and make sure you're safe."

I nodded, scooted back against my headboard, and grabbed a pillow to hug. "I'm listening."

"Okay, so I'm trying to get the timeline straight." Teagan cracked her neck, and her gaze narrowed. "Did anyone else die in the fire?"

More tears slipped down my cheeks. "No." As much as I wanted to tell Teagan more about my stepbrother, I wasn't sure I had the strength to do it. Maybe later. Our conversation was heavy enough.

"My dad, stepmom, and her relatives that were visiting all made it out."

"I bet they were so relieved to see you!" She flopped back on my bed and stared at the ceiling.

"They thought I died in the fire. Crimson held me hostage for three days."

Teagan bolted upright. She was making me dizzy, bouncing up and down, but I understood the need to move. I squeezed the pillow to my stomach in an attempt to comfort myself.

"Phoebs, did she . . . hurt you?" She took my hand in hers and gave it a gentle squeeze.

"No. I mean, she tied me to a chair and stuck a gag in my mouth. Other than that, she fed me, gave me water, let me walk around. It could have been worse."

"That's sooo wrong that you said that, but I was thinking the same thing. What happened? Did you escape?"

"No. Crimson let me go." I pulled at a loose thread on the blue pillowcase.

Teagan folded her arms across her chest, her eyes narrowing to slits. "That's kind of weird."

"It was, but I wasn't going to ask questions, ya know."

"You never got an answer about why she let you walk away?" Teagan asked.

"No. I have no idea why she decided to let me go. All I can think of is that Crimson needed me to get to something or someone else." I shrugged. Over the years, I've played the scenario in my head a million times, trying to make sense of Crimson's actions, but I only ran into a brick wall.

"Is this the first time you've really talked about it?" Teagan crawled up the bed and sat beside me, stretching her legs in front of her.

"I had to tell Dad and the cops some of it, just not that I started the fire. I blamed it on Crimson."

"Good! Goddammit, she held you hostage, Phoebs. The fire wasn't your fault, and neither was . . . your stepbrother."

"I wish I could believe you. I lit the match." My chest heaved with my tears, and I buried my face in my hands until my cries subsided.

"Dammit. With everything you've told me, I forgot about Peter. He knows what you shared with me?"

"Yup." I popped my p as I wiped the moisture from my cheeks. "I was desperate to talk to someone. There were so many times I wanted to tell you, but I was scared that you would hate me. I couldn't handle losing someone else. Peter was so sweet to me once I told him, then a few weeks later, he changed and started hurting me. I think he was just playing with my emotions, and when I realized it, I was in too deep and couldn't break things off with him. He had full control."

"Fucking bastard. Both of them!" Teagan slammed her fists into the mattress. "Geez, you went from Crimson to Peter. One abuser after the other."

"It's why I don't want to date anyone." I looked at her through swollen eyelids. "I don't trust myself to pick a decent guy."

"I'm sorry. I didn't understand the situation, or I wouldn't have been a brat about the parties and meeting someone."

"Don't be. It's good for me to get out. Hell, I don't mind a hookup, but other than that, no thanks." *It's why I like the society!* Black Mamba could be as rough as he wanted, but it never triggered me. Peter never hurt me during sex.

The love of my life had been rough, but he cherished and

respected me in his bed. I nearly barked out a laugh. We were teenagers, but the sex was mind-blowingly good.

My heart folded in on itself, and my stomach twisted into a million knots. I had killed the only guy I had ever loved. I clenched my jaw and forced myself to bury the pain once again. It was over. I'd shared the worst with Teagan, and now we could decide what to do about Peter.

"There's something else." Hopefully, she would understand what I was about to share.

"Crap. I'm not sure if I can handle anything else."

"It's not as bad, I promise, but you have to swear that none of this leaves this room."

"Girl, I ain't sayin' a word. I don't want Peter to come after me or anyone I love." She raised her hand to her chest. "I'm ready."

"My real name isn't Phoebe."

"Ohhhhh. Okay."

"My real name is Ariana Ellison."

Teagan's eyes nearly bulged out of their sockets. "Holy. Fucking. Shitballs. Theo is your dad, which means his last name isn't Jenkins like you both told me it was. He's *the* Theodore Ellison and you're his daughter?" Teagan shot me a look of disbelief. "I know you're his daughter, but holy crap. You really come from money, girl. Theo is famous. I've read an article about his tech inventions and company, TechG8, but I hadn't seen a picture of him." She smacked her forehead with the palm of her hand. A few seconds later, she peeked over at me. "Why the name change?"

"Dad wanted to protect me. Crimson was never arrested, and we were afraid she might take me again. It's also why dad shipped me off to the academy on the East Coast."

"Girl, you can't make this stuff up. I feel like I'm watching true crime or something." She slumped against the headboard.

"You have to keep calling me Phoebe when we're around everyone, okay? I can't jeopardize anyone else's safety."

A mischievous glint sparked to life in her brown-eyed gaze. "How about Phoriana."

For the first time in days, I laughed. Hard. "No! That's awful."

"AriPhoe?" She snickered. "Porana. Get it? Parana?"

Our laughter filled the room and I held my sides as Teagan continued to fire off possible portmanteau nicknames for me. "I love you. Thanks for making me laugh."

"Bitch, I love you too. Don't ever forget that I've got your back. Ever." She laughed. "Porana."

I smacked her with the pillow I held, laughing. Too bad the fun couldn't last forever.

Teagan blew out a heavy sigh before she focused on me. "Okay. Until we figure something else out, you're not to be alone. If you're in classes then find a big, strong guy to become friends with. Otherwise, I'll be around. I have pepper spray on my keychain, and we need to get you one as well. Tell Theo you need an Apple Watch. The new ones call 9-1-1 if they detect that you fall. If we're keeping this secret, that's the best I've got for us."

"I need to upgrade my watch anyway. If I'd been thinking about it, I would have told him I needed a new one when we got my phone. I'll call Dad and let him know I tripped down the stairs at the library and broke mine." I smirked. "It will sound more plausible."

Teagan laughed. "That will work. He won't question anything if you mention the word library."

Chapter Sixteen

Jagger

I lowered the pliers closer to his balls, itching to put Peter and me out of our misery.

"Tell me what I want to know and you walk away a free man."

Peter blinked at me before he licked his lips and began.

"Her name is Ariana Ellison. She changed her name before she enrolled at the academy."

Son of a bitch. Nausea rolled in my stomach. The truth barreled into me like a linebacker that weighed three-hundred pounds, stealing the air from my lungs. I was right. She was alive and well, not to mention attending Whitmore University. It was one thing to contemplate the possibility, an entirely different ball game to hear the information from someone else's mouth. Peter's words punctured my skin like a thousand jellyfish stings. What the actual fuck? All these years, I thought she was dead. Why didn't she tell me? My jaw clenched, then I gritted out, "Why?"

"Her father, Theo Ellison, never gave her an answer other than to keep her safe."

"From?"

"It took her a while to confide in me, but I could tell she was troubled. She was full of life with everyone except me. When I asked her if she was adjusting to the academy, Ari broke down sobbing. She said she couldn't tell me what had happened, but it was bad." Sweat dripped into Peter's eyes, and he blinked repeatedly.

"Keep going if you want to keep your fingernails intact. I've got time and you have nine more left." I quirked a brow at him.

"Eventually, I was able to coax it out of her. One thing about Ari, she was a wounded little bird. Stroke her just right and she'd do anything I wanted her to."

Without any warning, I grabbed his finger and ripped off another nail. His screams echoed through the room, bouncing off the cement walls. I should have thought ahead and brought my earplugs.

His shrieks finally died down into a whimper.

"What did she tell you?" I demanded, my tone sharp.

A crazy laugh escaped Peter. The pain was getting to him. Good.

"You mean the confession that slipped from her beautiful lips as she rode my cock?"

It took every ounce of restraint not to knock this stupid asshole out. He was clearly delirious, which meant I had to hold off on the torture until I had what I needed.

"Yup. What did she say?"

To my surprise, Peter's shoulders shook as he sobbed. "If I tell you, you'll kill me. I rather be tortured than die."

"Peter, Peter, Peter." I tapped the pliers against the side of the table he was lying on. "One way or the other, I will get the truth out of you. I certainly didn't waste my time knocking you out and throwing you in the back of your trunk. It took me a minute, but I found your keys and drove us where no one would ever look for you. You see, my uncle is the prez of an MC. One that won't even blink twice when I ask them to dispose of your body. Nothing really fazes them. For that matter, me either. You won't be the first person I've killed." I shrugged as though taking a life meant nothing to me. In his case, it didn't.

"Talk!" I raised the pliers a few inches above his balls.

This son of a bitch sobbed so hard, snot ran down his mouth and chin. As horrible as he was to Ari, he certainly couldn't take it in return.

"Okay, but promise me you'll let me go."

I paused, pretending to think about it. "If you're straight with me, and I know the words coming out of your mouth are the truth, then I'll give you the keys to your car and you can drive away. But if I ever see you or hear your name again, I will bury you fucking alive. Are we clear?"

"Y-yeah. I'll leave Ari alone. You can have her."

I stared a hole into him. "What is Ari hiding? Start from the beginning."

Peter licked his lips, the string of snot sticking to his tongue.

"She was in love with you, man. Like hard to the core obsessed with you. Ari never talked about you to her friends, though, just me. She was afraid they would hate her if they knew the truth." Peter swallowed. "One day after class, I found Ari curled into a corner of my office, crying. She was a mess. I tried to calm her down but it was no use. Then, I grabbed her face and ordered her too. She responded. The moment I was mean to her, a switch flipped inside of her. It didn't take me long to realize I could order her to do anything I wanted."

"Call her by her full name! She's Ariana to you," I snapped. The realization that she was alive threatened to override my senses again, and I had to stay in control.

Peter paused and flexed his fingers and nodded.

"At first, it was bending her over my lap and spanking her or telling her if she didn't get on my desk, spread her legs, and show me her pussy, I would flunk her. She craved it. Soon, I was obsessed with her. Ariana consumed me. One night in my office, I commanded her to tell me what she was running from. What was so bad that had ripped her to pieces." He swallowed and paused.

I lowered the pliers closer to his nuts and stared at him.

"Don't! I'm talking, goddammit!"

His sniveling disgusted me, and I was ready to get on with my night. I sighed. "You're wasting my time. If you want to leave, I suggest you finish the story now." The sorry son of a bitch was a blubbering mess, and I was growing restless.

"Ariana said that after she left your bed one night, she couldn't sleep so she went outside to sit on the back porch. She wasn't out there long when a lady came out of the shadows and grabbed her. She held a gun to her temple, then told her to set the house on fire. If she didn't, she would kill you."

I blanched at his words, struggling to piece together what he was saying. Ari set the fire?

"Who was she?" I fisted my hands, waiting to hear who had terrorized her and ripped her from my life.

"She went by the name of Crimson. It was some crazy ass stuff."

A cold sweat covered every inch of my body and my fists curled as white-hot fury swirled beneath my skin. Some sick fuck was behind the fire.

"Crimson forced Ariana back inside the house and to the basement. She made her pour gasoline on the floor. Apparently, she'd been in there before because there were several cans of gas waiting to be used."

"That would explain why the place burned so damn fast." As hard as I tried, the images of the red and orange flames licking up the walls and staircase, along with the overwhelming heat and smoke, tortured my senses all over again.

"Crimson took Ariana out of the basement, then she made her strike a match and drop it. They ran before the fire got started. Then, Crimson hid Ariana at the edge of the property line in the trees. She covered Ariana's mouth as she watched the only home she'd ever known burn with everyone she loved in it. Ariana said it was the most horrible thing she'd ever done, and if anyone found out the truth, she would go to prison for arson. It was too late to stop the inferno when she realized Crimson had lied to her about killing you. When the blaze kicked in, Crimson forced Ariana to leave the scene and held Ariana hostage just like you're doing to me," he snarled.

It took a minute for his words to really register in my gut, then they blew my goddamn mind. Some chick named Crimson made Ari set the fire. *Ari set the fire!* Memories of the night I left my heart on the lawn as the house burned to the ground ripped me to fucking shreds all over again. Why didn't she tell me she was alive? Why didn't Theo and Mom tell me the truth?

My world tilted, spinning as I struggled to keep my composure. I backed away and snagged several deep breaths as I processed Peter's words. Maybe he was lying, feeding me crap so I would let him live. Hell, my own mother and stepfather had lied to me and I knew them way better than Peter. The only way to learn the truth was to talk to Ariana.

"I want to make sure I'm clear about everything." Pressing my lips into a thin line, I tried to form the words. "You took advantage of a traumatized minor after she was held against her will and forced to set her own home on fire?"

"Man, I told you earlier. Ariana became my obsession. Everything I did was because I needed her. She's my sickness."

My pulse pounded in my ears and black dots danced in front of me. "And I'm your worst nightmare." I darted toward him before I plunged the pilers into his dick. His screams filled the room as I stabbed him over and over until I was soaked in my sweat and his blood. Panting from the exertion, I dropped the tool to the blood-splattered floor and looked at him. "As I said, Ari is mine."

"There's more, you fucking prick," Peter choked out before his head rolled to the side and his lifeless eyes stared at me.

"Goddammit!"

Chapter Seventeen

Jagger

"What's twisting your balls up, man?" Kane gripped me by my shoulder pad.

"Just a hell of a night. I'm fine." I shrugged his hand off, irritated that my playing was absolute crap today. At least it was only practice, but that didn't mean Coach wouldn't be riding my ass.

"Do you want to grab a beer after we're finished?" Kane removed his helmet and wiped the sweat from his forehead.

"Nah. I'm going to go to the society. Maybe it will help clear my head." I had no doubt it would when I took out my anger on Ariana. For the last four days, I had gone round and round hating her for not telling me she hadn't died but wanting to protect her from men like Peter. Hell, I'd at least taken care of one problem of hers. If I wanted to do the right thing, I would tell her Peter wasn't an issue anymore, but a sick part of me wanted to see her suffer and think he was still around. After all, she had put me through hell thinking I'd lost her when our house burned to the ground. As hard as I'd tried, I couldn't get over her. I compared every girl I fucked to Ari. I had given her my goddamn heart when we were in high school. She just hadn't known it until I kissed her on her birthday. That was all it took. I fell head over heels for my stepsister. It was twisted but felt so right.

At the mere thought of being inside her again, my cock sprang to life.

"Hell, I might go to the society myself." Kane tipped his chin at me. "Later." He pulled his helmet back on as we jogged to meet the other players and the coaches in the middle of the field before we were dismissed.

Coach clapped once, then peered over the top of his fingers at us. "Not sure what's going on with all of you today, but get your head out of your asses. This is a team. You're not a bunch of brainless individuals running over each other with no purpose. Keep your eyes on the ball and your teammates. I hope like hell I see a big change tomorrow because at this rate, you can kiss the next win goodbye and in the same breath our chances at post season anything."

"Yes, sir!" we all yelled in unison.

I already felt like shit. I didn't need to suck ass on the field as well.

"You're dismissed." Coach planted his hands on his hips as we broke from the group. "Jagger. A word."

Dammit.

I jogged to him. "Sir?" Guilt twisted my stomach. The coach had been more of a father to me than my own. He'd taken me under his wing and helped develop my skills on the field. He'd also taught me how to manage what little self-control I had. I had a reputation for being a hell of a player with a quick-ass temper.

"What's the problem? You're focus is out the window. Some girl got you by the balls?"

I removed my helmet and tucked it under my arm. "No. I didn't sleep well last night. The cot is old and uncomfortable," I said in a hushed tone. I wasn't lying, the bed sucked, but most days, I was too exhausted after practice to give a crap. I sure as hell wasn't going to tell Coach about what a fucking liar Ariana was. It was only a matter of time before I took care of her once and for all, then she would no longer be a problem.

"I'll get you a better one. You should have said something sooner." Concern filled his gaze.

"And sound ungrateful for a safe place to sleep? The only reason I brought it up is because it's affecting me on the field."

Coach slapped me on the back. "I'll have a new one for you before nine tonight."

"Thanks, Coach."

"Thank me by showing up as your best self tomorrow."

"You got it."

Coach's brow snapped up as he stared at me. "Go shower. You stink."

"Later." I turned and walked away, thoughts of Ari swirling in my head. Not only did I intend on fucking her senseless, but it was also time to have a little chat. I wanted some damn answers.

Wanting to observe Ari for a few minutes without her knowledge, I let myself into the playroom before she arrived. I was tucked into the corner and had pulled the cloak hood over my head. It allowed me to blend in as she entered.

Her shoulders were rigid with tension, and a part of me looked forward to helping her relieve her stress. There was nothing better for her than a good ride on my cock.

Maybe it was cruel, but I wanted Ariana to walk into the society room with a false sense of security—no blindfold, chains, or bindings on her wrists and ankles.

I leaned against the wall, my eyes glued to her as my throat constricted. Ari was beautiful, and it took everything inside me not to walk over to her and remove my mask. I wanted answers before I did, then I would reveal my identity. Maybe then she wouldn't be able to lie.

She gripped her clutch and flipped her blonde hair over her shoulder. Her short skirt barely covered her ass cheeks, and although I loved the view, I wasn't okay with her walking around in public that way. Regardless of my twisted love and hate for her, she was mine.

Ari cleared her throat, standing in the middle of the room. I had chosen the vanilla room for this visit. With its simplicity, it might be less distracting when I asked her questions.

"Hello, Phoebe." I stepped out of the darkness.

She practically jumped out of her skin. "Oh, hell. I didn't realize you were here." Ari pinned me with an intense stare, and I wondered if she was trying to figure out who the man was behind the mask.

I strolled over to her and reached out, my fingertips skimming along her soft cheek. "You're stunning."

Her tongue darted over her lower lip. "Then why did you hightail it out of the room when you saw my face the last time?"

A bark of laughter tore from my mouth. It never occurred to me that she thought I bolted because she was ugly.

"I had an unexpected call." I doubted she would buy my lie, but I wasn't going to tell her the truth . . . yet.

Her full lips pursed into a thin line. "I see. Well, I'm here again, so I guess I'll have to believe you."

I wrapped strands of her hair around my fingers as my brain skipped through the stupid tulips and betrayed me with the memories Ari and I had together.

"Kneel, pet."

Ari sank to her knees, the corner of her mouth lifting slightly. She liked it rough when we were teenagers; apparently, that hadn't changed. I was okay with it.

"Do you want me to fuck you, Phoebe?"

Hunger flashed in her blue eyes. "Yeah."

"Is your cunt wet for me already?" I grabbed a handful of her hair and forced her head back.

"Why don't you find out?"

Even though she couldn't see my face, I smiled. There was the feisty girl I'd fallen in love with.

"I have other plans for you tonight."

"Okay." Her sweet and obedient voice coasted over my skin, and I wanted to bury myself inside her.

"Tell me, Phoebe Jenkins. Do you know what it feels like to be so deeply betrayed that it carves your heart out of your chest?"

She blinked several times before she spoke. "No. I . . ."

I gripped her chin and forced her to look at me. "Tell me."

"I was the betrayer."

Thank God she couldn't see my shock beneath the mask. "What do you mean?" This was about to get good.

"I betrayed someone I loved and it . . ." She jerked out of my grip and stood. "I can't do this."

Ari darted for the door, and before I realized it, she disappeared.

"Son of a bitch!" I fisted my hands, frustrated that the evening hadn't gone as I'd hoped. It was time to step it up a notch.

An hour later, I looked at the new piece of furniture Coach had promised. My chest tightened with gratitude when I saw the twin bed with new blankets, pillows, and pillowcases. The navy blue was a nice splash of color against the white walls. I wondered if Coach's wife helped pick the bedding out. The idea that she cared enough to keep my secret softened my hardened heart. Maybe my mom would have done the same, but I never gave her a chance after Gunner found me.

I sank onto the mattress and stared at the ceiling. Ari had thrown me for a fucking loop earlier. Hopefully, the guilt of deceiving me for years was eating her alive from the inside out.

"Dammit." I scrubbed my face with my hands and groaned. I still had to deal with Peter, or rather what was left of him. I grabbed my burner phone for the society and placed a call to Anderson.

He answered on the first ring. "What's up, man?"

"I've got a sitch."

I rubbed my forehead, grimacing and questioning if I really wanted to do this. It seemed like the best choice, though, since my uncle was busy with other important matters out of the state.

"Can you reach out to Quinn and Kane and have everyone meet me at the society? I'll need a ride from there with someone, and we'll need some gloves and shovels."

Anderson blew out a breath. "No kidding?"

"No kidding. If the society is serious about protecting each other . . . Well, guess I'm about to find out if that's true or not."

"I can't speak for Kane and Q, but I've got your back no matter what," Anderson said, his tone full of sincerity.

"Thanks. I'll owe you a few." I rubbed my temple, hoping this would go well.

"A few?"

"Yeah. This favor is a big one. See you in a bit." I disconnected the call before I grabbed my motorcycle keys and helmet. It was going to be a long night.

The door to the abandon butcher's building creaked open as I led the way, Quinn, Kane, and Anderson right behind me.

I flipped on the light switch, and the room filled with the dingy light, exposing the blood splattered floor and Peter's body. His lifeless eyes stared at the wall to the left.

"Holy hell. You weren't kidding when you asked about

supporting each other even if it was a murder, huh?" Quinn folded his arms over his chest and assessed the area.

"Why did you kill him?" Kane asked.

"Because he's a sick bastard that liked to torture and hurt girls. Can't have scum walking around with free rein." I placed my hands on my hips.

"If any of you want to leave, now is your chance. Otherwise, I have to scrub this place clean and bury the bastard."

Anderson shot me a look. Since he'd helped me toss Peter in the back of my trunk before he rushed Ari to the hospital, he already knew who was on the table.

"Fuck that. I'm in. We pledged to the brotherhood, so let's see if we pass the test," Quinn said.

"An accomplice to murder will certainly give us dirt on each other. I've been through worse, though," Kane added, walking around the room. "Your secret is safe with me, Jag."

I nodded, appreciating the verbal commitment as I wondered what Kane had lived through that was more terrible than burying someone.

"Same," Anderson said, tipping his chin at me. "This son of a bitch had to be stopped. He was poison."

I rubbed my hands together. "Let's clean up. The bleach and other cleaning supplies are in the corner. Then we'll put the bastard six feet under."

Walking over to Peter's body, I stared at him, not regretting that I'd ended his life but still curious what else he would have told me. It would have probably been more lies.

Hours later, I strolled into Coach's office, then my room. I collapsed on the bed, exhausted. At least with three other guys, it hadn't taken us all night.

Rolling over on my side, I removed my cell from my back pocket and called Gunner. It was almost two in the morning, but Gunner stayed up late and needed little sleep to function.

He answered on the second ring. "Hey, man. How are things?"

"My ass is lying on a new twin-sized mattress, so I would say pretty damn good."

Gunner's laugh filled the line. "No more old cot, huh?"

"Nope."

"Nice."

"It's the little things, Gun." I grinned as if he could see me. "Had a hell of a night. I had to clean up my mess at the old butcher building, but it's done and ready for when you need it."

"What happened, or I should ask who since someone will eventually come looking for them and I'll need to make sure the cops stay off your ass."

"Peter Jacobson. Before I killed him for stalking and hurting Ariana, I made the time useful and he confessed it's her. She changed her name when she enrolled at the academy."

"For real?"

"Yup. It's got me twisted up in the head. Why would she lie to me? Why wouldn't Mom and Theo tell me?"

"Whoa. Back up, kid. Peter was stalking and hurting Ariana Ellison?"

"That's what I said." My tone was sharp and condescending. "It's been a hell of a few days. I didn't mean to be an asshole." I had no problem admitting when I'd screwed up, and I'd disrespected one of the few men that mattered to me.

"You need to chill, man. You've always been hotheaded, but when it comes to Ari, your decisions are driven by your obsession with your stepsister. Take a minute to shake it off and get your head right. I'll have my men take care of Peter. At least you rid the world of one more abusive fuck."

"Yeah, he pistol-whipped Ari in front of me. Knocked her smooth out. That crap doesn't fly with me. When I gave it back to him, he cried like a fucking baby. He won't ever mess with her or any other chick again."

"Does she know he's dead?"

"No. Not sure how to tell her. Eventually, I will. Maybe keeping her on her toes for a bit won't hurt."

"Jag."

Uncle Gunner's tone was no-nonsense, and I realized a lecture was about to happen. "You need to tell her, and she needs to know you're at Whitmore."

"Eventually. I might have some fun with her first. It's clear that she's not the same girl that I was with four years ago. Hell, she doesn't even realize I'm at Whitmore. According to one of my teammates, Ariana is a total book nerd and pays zero attention to sports or the players."

"This should be interesting, watching you try to convince your-self you're not still head over heels in love with her. Good luck."

I disguised my growl with a fake cough. Then, Peter's last words broke through my thoughts again.

"Unfortunately, I killed the bastard too soon. As the life drained out of him, he said there was more to tell me. That was it. He was gone."

"That's a bitch. Do you have any idea what?"

"No . . . but he told me that she was the one that set the fire."

"Seriously? Are you sure this motherfucker is capable of telling the truth? I don't trust a man that lays a hand on a chick. It ain't cool."

"I'm wondering the same, but Ari is the only one that can confirm his story. I'm just not sure I'm ready to hear what she has to say."

Silence filled the line.

Over the next few minutes, I told my uncle everything that had happened with Peter.

"Kid, I swear on my goddamn life, we will find the bastard behind this shit storm. I realize you're probably in shock. For now, I'll see if I can dig up anything new on her. My guess is that Theo tried to cover her tracks though. We might come up empty-handed on this end. You need to talk to Ari, Jag. Put all the anger and betrayal aside until you two sit down and you hear what happened after the fire. You've loved this girl since you were a kid, followed her around like a sick puppy. When you're in that deep, no one can turn those feelings off. You thought she was dead for four years. Haven't you lost enough time with her?"

I stilled as Gunner's words punched me in the gut. A part of me knew he was right, but I wasn't sure if I could forgive her. Ever.

Chapter Eighteen

Ariana

The September temps were perfect, and the morning sun warmed my skin against the cool autumn breeze as I sat on the back patio, studying. Dry leaves scraped along the pavement, giving me a foreboding feeling. Since I'd confided in Teagan, we had constantly looked over our shoulders for Peter. It terrified me that he'd slipped into the shadows. When he disappeared while I was at the academy, he was bidding his time until he could brutalize me again. He fed off terrorizing me.

The scars with his name on my lower back burned with the memories. Unless someone had suffered at his hand, they would never believe me if I tried to explain what a monster he was. Sick. Depraved.

"Babe, are you okay?" Teagan touched my arm, and I broke away from my thoughts.

"Yeah. Why?" I gave her an innocent look.

She scrunched her nose at me. "I worry is all. Why don't you come to the game and get out of the house? Anderson is playing, and you can root for him." Teagan tilted her head, her doe eyes pleading with me.

"No thanks. I have to keep my grade-point average up so I don't lose my scholarship." I sipped on the steaming mug of coffee in my hand. Truthfully, I loved having the place to myself on a Saturday or the entire weekend while the girls were at a game.

"This is going to be a tight game," Leighton said as she approached us on the patio from the kitchen.

"Yeah, the other team is undefeated too," Teagan agreed.

"Do you know why we love to be cheerleaders, Phoebe?" Leighton pulled up a patio chair and sat next to me.

"Why?"

"Because it's all balls and tight ends." She sunk her teeth into her lower lip and giggled.

"You can see it all from where we stand." Teagan shifted in her seat and crossed her legs. "Come to the game today. When it's over, meet us on the sidelines and we'll point out some of the guys to you. Most of them will be at the after-party as well, but use the guys for your study time instead of a book."

"That's a great idea! Then you can be selective about who you want to talk to tonight and have an opening line about seeing them on the field." Leighton's eyes brightened.

"I love you all for thinking about me, but you can point them out and tell me who is who at the party. I don't need to sit in the stands for hours," I pointed out to them.

Teagan released a defeated sigh. "Fine. Then we will see you at the party." Teagan stood. "If you change your mind, shoot me a text so that when the game is over, you can meet me on the sidelines. We can all get ready for the party together."

"I won't change my mind. I'll meet you here to get ready." Sometimes, I was stubborn, but I couldn't sit in the stands alone. Regardless of what the girls said, I couldn't force myself to go. It was a reminder of my stepbrother when he played in junior high, and it broke my heart every time I caught a glimpse of a game.

Leighton perched her hand on her hip. "Kane Cooper is the quarterback. He's new this year and the cheerleaders and fans are watching his every move." She grinned. "And when I say every move, I mean exactly that. He's at most of the after-parties, so check him out in jeans and a T-shirt next time. Just make sure you catch the drool before it lands on your top. Try explaining that to everyone."

"I'll remember that."

"Oh, and Quinn Astor is a running back. He has some dance moves that will make a kitty wet. I would happily take Quinn and Kane for a ride . . . at the same time." Teagan fanned herself.

"You do realize that just because you're telling me about them doesn't mean I'll know who they are at the party, right?"

The girls giggled. "We get a little excited about helping you hook up." Teagan squeezed my shoulder. "We gotta go."

"I hope they win," I added as they opened the slider and returned to the house, leaving me alone with my own thoughts.

The day dragged its feet, and as hard as I tried to focus on the assignments in women's studies, I couldn't. It was unusual that I couldn't escape in a book, even a schoolbook, but my brain bounced from the Black Mamba and the society to Anderson to Peter. Unable to calm my anxiety, I collected my books and headed into the house. Maybe a shower would clear my head.

Stomping up the stairs just to break the overbearing silence, I reached my room. My iPhone sat on the middle of my bed, and I scooped it up, not expecting to see any messages.

Unknown:

This is Anderson. Teagan gave me your number. She mentioned you might meet her on the sidelines after the game. You should.

I squinted at the screen. Why would Teagan hand out my number without my permission? She was starting to get pushy. Fine, if she was going to be like that, I would meet her there but chew her out for not asking me first.

Me:

For you, I'll be there.

When I arrived, the players walked off the field quietly. From the score on the scoreboard, they should have been celebrating the win, but they were somber. I found myself walking down the track, watching for Anderson. Teagan could wait. I tugged my Whitmore jacket tighter around me. I should have worn a sweater instead of a blue long-sleeved shirt. I was freezing.

Anderson strolled in my direction and removed his helmet. A group of players caught up to talk to him, but I couldn't make out what they were saying. Someone grabbed Anderson's arm and spun him around, but I couldn't see who it was since Anderson was blocking the view. Regardless of whether Anderson and the team barely won or won by a hundred points, I wanted to congratulate him. Even if I weren't a cheerleader, I could help keep his spirts up. I nibbled on my lower lip. I might want to keep something else up, too.

"Got it." His voice floated through the air, then he faced me again.

I flashed him a huge smile. "Congrats on the win!" Inwardly, I cringed. I'd overdone the excitement a little.

"Thanks. I'm surprised you showed up after the game." He grimaced.

White-and-black cleats caught my attention. My heart stopped beating as I glanced up and into the most piercing blue eyes I'd ever seen.

"Phoebe, this is Jagger. He wanted to meet you."

The color drained from my cheeks as I stared into my stepbrother's gaze, full of hate.

"Jag?" I croaked out. "You're alive?"

Anderson bowed out. "Catch you at the party, guys."

"You're alive?" My vision blurred as the world spun, and everything faded to black seconds later.

Reality flickered in and out as Teagan and her cheer coach leaned over me. The red letters on the side of the ambulance registered in my addled brain and I groaned.

"Are you okay?" Fear laced Teagan's words.

A gorgeous EMT knelt next to me. Gently, he took my wrist in his hand and checked my pulse.

"What's wrong with her?" Teagan's coach asked, hovering over me.

"Maybe it was simply a side effect of the concussion," I muttered.

Teagan cringed. No one knew about the hospital visit other than her. We'd told the roomies that I'd visited my dad while he was in town for a few days. No one questioned us.

"Your vitals are normal, but the side effects make sense," the EMT explained. "How long ago did you hit your head?"

I shot a nervous glance at my group of friends. "Monday."

"You can have dizziness and hallucinations for up to a year after a concussion. I'm guessing that's what happened. However, if you pass out again, you need to go to the emergency room. They might want to run some tests."

"Crap. Okay," I said as I slowly sat up, making sure the world wasn't still spinning.

"What do you mean, concussion, Phoebe?" Everlee barked out. She touched my back as she and Teagan helped me off the ground. Heat traveled up my neck and cheeks as I realized I was the main attraction. Football players and cheerleaders surrounded us with concern written in their expressions.

"I'm fine. I was checked out and released from the hospital Monday." *And clearly hallucinating!*

"Take it easy this weekend. If you become dizzy again, then get to the emergency room," the EMT instructed.

"Okay. Sorry to trouble you."

He flashed me a panty-dropping smile. "No problem. Just feel better." With that, he walked toward the ambulance along with his partner.

The cheer coach shook her head, her blonde ponytail swinging from side to side. "Get some rest and feel better." Worry flickered to life in her brown eyes before she turned to my best friend. "You need to watch her. If she starts acting strange, call 9-1-1 immediately, then call me if you need to."

"Yes, ma'am," Teagan muttered.

The coach shot me one last look of concern before she walked away.

"Girl, what the hell happened?" Teagan wrapped her arm around my shoulders.

"I thought I saw someone I used to know, but apparently, my head is screwing with me."

"Peter? Is he here?" Her attention darted around as she searched for the bastard.

I couldn't tell Teagan what had happened because I didn't know. I was pretty sure I'd hallucinated right before I blacked out and Jagger only existed in my imagination.

"Let's get ready for the party. I need to blow off some steam."

"Oh, hell no. You're not going. In fact, I'll stay home with you." Teagan's tone was firm, as if she were scolding a five-year-old.

"I'm going. End of discussion." Once I talked to Anderson, I could clear up my brain fart. There was no way Jagger Whitlock was alive.

Chapter Nineteen

Ariana

"I Wanna Be Your Slave" by Maneskin reverberated through the speakers, and college students danced throughout the house. The corners were filled with couples making out, and a game of beer pong was in full swing near the kitchen entrance. Since I had passed out earlier, I wanted to arrive fashionably late, hoping I wouldn't attract a lot of attention. Fielding questions wasn't on my to-do list. The only reason I showed up at all was to find Anderson.

Gabby, Leighton, and Everlee approached Teagan and me near the staircase.

"How are you feeling?" Everlee asked, slipping her arm through mine. "You scared the bejesus out of us. We had no clue you had even gotten a concussion!"

"I smacked my head really hard and I never said anything because it was a stupid accident. You have my word that I'm fine. I promise." I gave her a reassuring smile.

"Please take care of yourself. I would be devastated if you died." Everlee threw her arms around me.

"Everlee, don't make it worse," Gabby gently chided. "Phoebe, you do need to chill for the weekend though."

Teagan gave me a disapproving frown. "She shouldn't even be here."

Everlee released me, still looking worried.

"What are you doing here?" Gabby asked, wiping her palms on her black jeans. She looked as gorgeous as always, her teal crop top flattered her flawless complexion.

"I need to talk to Anderson, then I'm dipping. Netflix is calling my name."

"Good. And I can help speed things up," Leighton said. "He's in the kitchen playing quarters. The last time I talked to him, he was drunk, so keep that in mind."

My new silver Apple Watch caught the lights, reminding me it was there. Teagan's idea had worked well, and I liked the features and the bit of security the updated device offered.

"Thanks. I will. I'll catch you all at home." I gave each of the girls a brief hug and thanked them.

I nudged my way through the crowd with Teagan on my arm. It was a little more challenging to navigate, but before we left our house, she explained if I passed out again, she would be able to cushion the fall if we were connected. Since this mansion had marble floors, I was good with it. Cracking my skull a second time didn't sound like a good time. Anger flared up inside me, then was quickly replaced by fear. This situation was all Peter's fault. My gut churned with the mere thought of him. He'd been eerily quiet, which messed with my head way worse than if I knew where he was. Before I addressed that problem, I needed to talk to Anderson.

"Phoebe!" Anderson yelled as soon as I entered the kitchen. "You look fucking hot for passing out a few hours ago." He frowned as if he just remembered what had happened. It was as if his brain were trying to catch up with his mouth. "Are you okay?" he slightly slurred.

Anderson walked away from his game then affectionately squeezed my shoulders. "Concussions are serious, really serious. Football players die every year. Don't die, Phoebe. I like you . . . a lot."

Teagan elbowed me in the side, grinning.

I hugged Anderson and whispered, "I need to talk to you outside."

He wrapped me in a warm embrace and pulled me against his muscled and toned body. "I'll give you anything you want. Just ask." He gave me a loud kiss on the cheek. "I know where we can talk in private." He took my hand and led me through the people in the kitchen, swaying slightly every few steps.

I glanced over my shoulder at Teagan. "I'll wait here!"

Nodding at her, I returned my attention to Anderson, who had opened a back door for us. The crisp air was a breath of sunshine compared to the smell of sweat and booze in the house.

Anderson led me down the sidewalk, then through the pool gate. "There are a few chairs here." He pointed before he proceeded toward them.

"Sit."

"You don't have to be so bossy, ya know." I sat down, my anxiety kicking up a notch, a slight dizzy feeling creeping up on me.

Anderson sat next to me and took my hand. "You scared me today. Like really scared me."

"I'm sorry. Please don't worry." I squeezed his fingers, and the warmth of his touch traveled up my arm. "I do want to talk to you, though."

Before I realized it, Anderson leaned over and pressed his mouth to mine. He broke the kiss almost as fast as it happened. "Dammit. I shouldn't have done that."

"Fuck that. You should have." I grabbed the back of his neck and brought him in for another kiss, heat pooling low in my belly. *Jesus, he's a phenomenal kisser.*

His lips parted, his tongue caressing mine. I arched into him, moaning from how easily my body turned to Jell-O beneath his skilled mouth.

"I've wanted to kiss you from the moment we first met."

"Why didn't you?"

"Because I can't have you."

Surprised, I pulled away. "Says who?"

Guilt twisted Anderson's face, and the color drained from his cheeks. "You can't tell anyone I kissed you, Phoebs. I wish I could take you out and spend time with you, but . . . "

"But what?" I asked, my words dripping with irritation. "I'm my own person."

"I know." Anderson stood. "There's no way that I can explain it."

"Then who can?" I rose and stood toe to toe with him, anger lighting my short fuse.

"Let me see if I can help you get some answers." Anderson pulled out his phone.

Frowning, I pointed at the cell. "That's not your phone. I've seen yours in class."

Anderson turned stark white. "Don't ask any more questions. I'm drunk off my ass so ignore everything I'm saying and doing."

I folded my arms over my chest. "If you get me answers of why I'm off limits to you, then you have a deal."

Anderson fisted his hand and bit on a knuckle before he spoke. "You're feisty and sexy as hell. It sucks that you've been marked." His eyes nearly popped out of their sockets. "Fuck. I have to shut up. Do *not* talk to me anymore tonight." He focused on the phone, typing away. His shoulders sagged as he looked up at me.

"The Black Mamba wants to meet you at the society."

It took me a moment to realize what he said. "You're in the society?" I whisper-yelled.

Anderson's shoulders sagged. "Phoebe, if you care about me at all, even if it's only as friends, it's critical that you keep that secret."

My heart melted into a puddle at my feet. "Anderson, I would date you in a hot minute and I'm pissed that someone has decided *for* me that I'm off limits. One thing you don't know about me is that I'm a bit of a rule breaker." I grabbed the belt loops on his jeans and pulled him into me. "I would ride you all night long." I nipped on his bottom lip, my core throbbing for him to touch me.

"Oh God, why are you torturing me?"

I kissed him again to prove to both of us I could. His erection pressed against my hip bone and I sighed. "Before I leave, I need to ask you something."

Anderson reached up and gently brushed a knuckle across my cheek. "Anything."

"When I passed out today, I think I had a hallucination." Dread wrapped its fingers around my chest and pulled tight.

"What did you see?" Worry flickered in his hazel eyes.

"Please don't laugh. I just need to make sure I'm not crazy and it was only a side effect of the concussion."

"I won't. I swear."

"I thought there was a player standing next to you named Jagger Whitlock. I'm crazy, right? That didn't happen?"

A long, thick pause hung over us. "I can't say anything. Go to the society, Phoebe."

Chapter Twenty

Jagger

I grabbed my cloak from the closet and prepared for Ariana's arrival. This time, she would be secured so she couldn't run off. I wasn't in the mood for her to pull that with me again. My cock had been hard all day for her. She'd gotten into my damn head during the game, and I thought I would return the favor and have Anderson introduce me. What I hadn't expected was for her to pass out. When she hit the ground, Teagan, her best friend, ran over to her. It was my chance to go unnoticed before she woke up. According to Anderson, it was a side effect of the concussion, but she was fine and as spunky as ever. Ari had always been tough. It was nice to see that hadn't changed.

Jerking on the skull mask, I adjusted it before I proceeded to the room where Ari was waiting.

As soon as I opened the door, I grinned. There she was, naked and bent over the BDSM barrel. I approached from the side, her perky little ass tipped in the air, and her ankles and wrists were secured to the barrel.

"Phoebe. Welcome back. As you can see, you pissed me off last time when you ran. Good luck with that now."

Phoebe snorted. "You've got some nerve—"

Before she could finish, I raised my hand and smacked her butt cheek. "Silence. I didn't give you permission to speak."

She cried out, swearing a blue streak and something about trying to control her life. I laughed.

"It seems as though you need a reminder of who you serve. Don't you remember I'm the only one that gets to touch you?"

"If it pleases the king, I would like to date someone. Maybe he'll be down with a threesome," she spat.

My girl was feisty, and I understood why. She wanted Anderson, and no way in hell would that ever happen.

"I can arrange that." I strolled over to the cabinet with the sex toys and rummaged through the items until I located the anal beads. Grabbing the lube, I slicked them up.

"A threesome? I'm down as long as Anderson is one of the two."

I returned to her and dragged my finger down her sweet slit. My breath caught in my throat, and I stilled. Her scarred flesh was still slightly pink. Anger blazed inside me as I witnessed Peter's name carved into her skin right above her ass. Not just because it was his name, but the pain he had inflicted on her when I . . . I should have been there to protect her!! My legs trembled as I struggled to contain the fury and agony that had simmered beneath the surface, threatening to boil over and destroy me from the inside out. It was a good thing I had already ended Peter.

My hand shook as I massaged her clit, forcing myself not to look at Peter's name. Making myself breathe, I reminded myself that he could no longer touch her. He could no longer use Ari against her will. Pain rippled through me and caused me to forget why I hated Ari. Nothing mattered except that she was safe from the outside world. I just didn't know if she was safe from me.

The sounds of her approval filled the room. I knelt, the scent of her pussy driving me nearly mad. Since she couldn't see me from this angle, I lifted the lower portion of my mask until I could easily lick her cunt. Once I spread her sensitive lips, I nipped at her bundle of nerves. Jesus, she tasted good.

I plunged my tongue into her as I pinched the inside of her thigh. Her moans of pleasure overshadowed her cries of pain. I spread her ass cheeks apart and pressed the first anal bead against her puckered hole. Standing, I chuckled as she whimpered.

"Have you been fucked in the ass before, Phoebe?"

"N-no."

I eased the beads in one at a time until they filled her up. My cock jerked in my pants, begging to be inside of her. Quickly, I unzipped and unbuttoned my slacks. I was ready to fuck her so hard, she wouldn't be able to sit down tomorrow. Digging my fingers into her hips, I slammed into her without notice. She would have launched off the barrel if she hadn't been tied down.

"Oh God!"

I slapped her butt, and it stung my hand, but I fed off the pain. Her pussy clenched my shaft, showing me she also enjoyed it.

A primal urge consumed my body as I thrust into her, hungry and desperate. Her breathy moans intensified with each stroke, driving me further and further into a wild frenzy. We rocked together with an explosive intensity, and the air filled with the sounds of our bodies slapping.

Ari tensed beneath me, on the brink of an orgasm, but I wasn't finished with her yet. She whimpered as I pulled out. I moved to the side of her so I could see her expression while I asked my next question.

"Tell me, Phoebe. Have you ever been in love before?"

She blanched, her blue eyes wide with emotions I couldn't pinpoint. "Will you hurt me if I answer incorrectly?"

It was my turn to be surprised. "No. I want your honesty." All I wanted was the truth from her. It was a slow, agonizing burn inside me, and her words were the only way to extinguish it.

Her head lowered, then she looked me square in the face. "Yes.

One guy, and I've never loved anyone since him. So, if that's what you want from me, you need to look elsewhere. I'm not that girl for you. Fuck and hurt me all night long, but you'll never have my heart."

It took everything inside of me not to stagger backward. Thank God for the mask to disguise my face. "Who was he?"

She squeezed her eyes closed, tears sneaking out and trailing down her cheeks. "My stepbrother."

The room spun, nearly throwing me off balance. I didn't understand. If Ari loved me, then why had she disappeared? Why had she let me think she was dead?

As much as I wanted answers, I needed to be inside her more. Her last words had changed everything, and I was afraid if we talked about our pasts, I would lose her again.

My ongoing anger with Ari simmered down. *She still loves me.* Easing into her again, her pussy clenched my cock as her words sunk into my gut. There hadn't been anyone else. I was the only guy she'd ever loved. My heart truly beat again for the first time in years. Ari was alive, and I was inside her. Maybe fate had brought her back to me. I wasn't sure.

The protective walls I'd built around me crumbled with each thrust. There was so much to say, but I wanted to show her first. The conversation might break me all over again, and in these few minutes, I tried to pretend that I hadn't ever lost her. That she hadn't ever betrayed me, and that I had never died inside.

Reaching between her legs, I pinched her clit. Her tight cunt pulsed around my cock in response.

"Are you ready to cum for me, my pet?"

"Please let me."

"Good girl—asking permission first."

Sensing she was on the brink of her release, I reached up for the anal beads and slowly began to pull them out.

"Oh my god, that feels—" Her screams echoed off the walls as her pussy clenched and her body convulsed as she orgasmed.

I removed the toy then pounded into her deep and fast, chasing my release. A hard realization gripped my chest. If I was about to reveal myself, this might be our last time together. One part of me hated her; the other had never stopped loving her. I wasn't sure if I could walk away from her again.

Before I could try to prolong my time with her, my dick betrayed me. My body tensed and trembled, leaving me breathless as I finished.

Silence filled the room as I remained inside her, soaking up the feeling. Ari had been the only girl I'd ever loved, and she had confessed the same. Now I had to find out what happened to her after the fire.

Chapter Twenty-One

Jagger

I pulled out of her, then held my fingertip over Peter's name, etched in her skin. The motherfucker had placed it low enough that if she wore panties, I didn't think it would be visible, but I wasn't sure.

Slowly tracing the letters, she froze. "Peter," I growled.

"Please don't." Her cry lodged in her throat. "I'm begging you."

I ignored her, gently touching each letter. "Any man that hurts people like what he's done to you deserves to die." I knelt and untied her legs from the barrel, then her wrists. "Stand up and get dressed."

She straightened and rubbed her arms. Indents from the ties graced her pale skin, but they would fade in a few minutes.

Ari shot me a sideways glance as she slipped into her denim mini skirt and pink top. Her nipples poked through the thin fabric, and I longed to suck on them.

I strolled past her and removed a key from the pocket of my black slacks. Grinning, I slid it into the keyhole and locked us in the room. Ari couldn't run. She had to talk to me whether she liked it or not.

"In case you wanted to leave."

She frowned. "You locked me in?"

"Yes."

"Why?" She fisted her trembling hands but squared her shoulders.

My pet pretended not to be scared, and I wondered if she was having flashbacks of what Peter had done to her. My chest ached with the thought.

I walked a slow circle around her, my heart pounding so loud, I couldn't hear the sound of the noisy furnace in the old building.

"Was Peter your boyfriend?"

Ari shook her head. "I hate him. He's evil."

Good girl. "He must have been important for his name to be on your back."

Ariana stared at the floor, unmoving. "I wasn't the one that wanted his name on my skin." She looked at me, anger and fear dancing across her gaze.

"He did this to you without your permission?" I already had my answers but needed to hear them from her. If she didn't lie to me, I might believe her when she explained why she'd disappeared for four years, then showed up at Whitmore. It couldn't have been a coincidence.

"He does a lot without my permission. I've tried to get away from him, including moving across the country, but he followed me."

I stood in front of her, looking down at her upturned face. Her chest rose and fell with her heavy breathing. She was scared I would hurt her. I reached out and grabbed a handful of her hair.

"He can't harm you anymore, my pet."

"Wh-what? You know Peter?"

"You could say that. We became recent acquaintances." I leaned closer to her, the mask's nose grazing her cheek. "No one is allowed to hurt you. Ever. Peter had to learn that lesson the hard way after he tried to kidnap you and knock you out."

Her gasp filled the room. "*You* saved me?"

I released her hair and smoothed it. When we were teenagers, I loved to play with her long strands. They were soft and beautiful.

"Yes."

Baffled, she stared at me with her lips slightly parted. "Thank you. Thank you for saving me," she whispered, her voice choked with emotion.

My mouth went dry, and after several seconds, I replied, "You never have to thank me for that."

"He really won't bother me again?" Uncertainty laced her words.

"Never again." I debated telling her I'd killed the bastard, but I needed to see how the rest of the conversation would unfold first.

"I have no reason to believe you, but you saved my life. I'll have to work with that."

Ari was right, and I understood her reasoning.

My palms slickened with sweat, and my head pounded. A part of me wanted to show her who I was beneath the mask. The other wanted to continue with our charade at the society, but I had to put an end to her haunting my dreams.

"Why would you do that for me? We've fucked all of three times. Why are you telling Anderson I'm off limits, then dealing with Peter? I don't understand."

"What's your real name, Phoebe?"

Ari's forehead scrunched together, then her legs visibly shook. "Who are you? What do you want from me?" She backed away, placing her arms before her as if preparing to ward off an attacker.

"I won't hurt you. I'm on your side. Haven't I proved that already by dealing with Peter?"

"What does that mean?" She shook her head, her pulse throbbing in her neck.

"What's your real name?" I snarled, feeding off her fear.

"Phoebe Jenkins." Her chin trembled.

"You're lying!"

I backed her against the wall and pressed my body against hers.

My cock was hard and ready again. Stepping back, I forced her to her knees and quickly undid my pants.

"Suck my dick like your life depends on it."

Ari fumbled with my boxer briefs, freed my cock, and slipped it into her mouth.

"That's it. As long as you bow to me, I will always protect you."

She stroked my cock as she licked and sucked. I watched as my shaft slid back and forth between her pretty lips. Something about Ari on her knees sent me out of my mind. Briefly, I closed my eyes as she worked her magic.

I thrust faster, pausing in the back of her throat until her cheeks turned crimson from the lack of air. Jerking out of her wet hole, I pumped my cock a few times. "Open your mouth, my sweet pet."

She tilted her head back then opened it for me.

My moan filled the room as I jerked off, my cum landing all over her face and hair. Ari licked off the drops of creamy substance from her lips.

"Be a good girl and lick my dick clean. Every last bit."

She obeyed, her tongue making quick work along my semi-hard cock. Ari slipped the tip of me inside her mouth and sucked.

Once I was satisfied, I took a deep breath. This was how I wanted to remember her—on her knees before me, willing and compliant to my every whim.

I made my way to the cabinet and removed a towlette from the package. Returning to her, my emotions churned in my gut like sour milk as I gently cleaned off her face.

It was time, though, to call her on her shit. I tucked myself back in my slacks and fastened them before I spoke. "Do you prefer to be called Phoebe or Ariana?"

Ari scrambled backward and bumped into the wall. She hurried to stand, her cheeks draining of color. "No one knows my real name." Confusion clouded her gaze. "Except one. Teagan told you?"

"Why would Teagan tell me?"

"Because maybe she knows you outside of the society. She knows your real identity. There's no other explanation!"

"There is, Ariana." I slipped my fingers beneath my mask and slowly pulled it off.

Chapter Twenty-Two

Ariana

My head threatened to explode, and I slammed my eyes closed against the blinding pain. The side effects of the concussion still lingered and had left me reeling. I collapsed onto the floor, gripping my forehead as I was overcome with waves of nausea that surged through me like a wild storm.

"Ari, look at me."

The Black Mamba's voice cut through the air, and his firm grip on my chin forced me to meet his gaze.

"Jagger?"

"You're not imagining things, Ariana. It really is me."

My brow knitted as denial washed over me like an icy wave. "It can't be. You . . ." Cries choked my words off as fresh tears ran down my cheeks. "You died in the fire."

Too many emotions flitted across his handsome face as he watched me grieve his death in front of him.

Slowly, I reached out a shaky hand and brushed my fingertips over his sculpted jawline. I needed tangible proof that this man standing before me was real, not another figment of my imagination.

He grabbed my wrist. His deep blue eyes were cold and demanding when he finally spoke. "That's what you thought all this time? That I was dead?"

"I don't blame you for haunting me. I betrayed you. I'm so sorry. I'm so sorry."

The Black Mamba rose from his crouched position and withdrew his phone from his pocket before turning away from me without another word.

I gawked as a familiar figure entered the room dressed in jeans and a black T-shirt. "Anderson?" I knew he was a part of the society, but why was he here?

"Hey, Phoebs. I wanted to see if you're okay."

I sprinted toward him, throwing my arms around his neck. "I'm not. I'm hallucinating. I don't even think you're here. I wish like hell you were."

Anderson glanced over his shoulder at the Black Mamba and nodded. He returned his attention to me and gently cradled my face with both palms, engulfing me with warmth and a sense of security, like a shield protecting me from harm's way.

"Phoebe, it's okay," Anderson said.

"You don't understand." I sniffled through my tears. "The Black Mamba looks exactly like my stepbrother, but . . . my brother is dead."

As soon as those words left my lips, confusion and then anger contorted Anderson's expression. He dropped his hands and then whirled around to confront the Black Mamba.

"Really, asshole? You have some fucking nerve."

"Mind your own business, Anderson."

Anderson's legs ate up the space between him and the Black Mamba.

"She is my business!" Anderson pointed at me, his entire face red with anger.

I had no clue what was happening; I just wanted someone to take me home.

Black Mamba grabbed Anderson by the throat. "She's been my business since we were teenagers. She's mine. Get that through your head and help her before she spirals out, goddammit."

Anderson's nostrils flared. "I'll do this for her, but this isn't over between us, man."

I rubbed my arms, warding off the eerie chill. What if I wasn't hallucinating? How would I know the difference?

"Phoebe." Anderson took my hand in his. "What are you seeing?"

"My stepbrother." I licked my lips. "He died in a house fire four years ago, so I know he's not standing in front of me."

"What was his name?"

"Jagger . . . Whitlock." I looked at Anderson, terrified of what he would say next. Either the grief and blow from Peter had officially sent me over the edge, or . . . I couldn't even fathom the thought of anything else.

Anderson pulled me against him, holding me tight. "Phoebe, I don't know who told you that, but Jagger is alive. He's in this room. He never died."

A bubble of nausea worked its way up my throat and I repeatedly swallowed, willing myself not to puke all over Anderson.

I had to get myself together. Anderson wouldn't lie to me, but what had happened? How was Jagger standing in the room with me? My head spun with questions, then reality slammed into me, knocking the air out of my lungs. Jagger was alive. Why hadn't he told me he'd survived the fire? I'd punished myself for his death every day for four excruciating years. I allowed Peter to do horrible things to me because I thought I deserved it.

A seething rage burned through my veins and I pushed away from Anderson. I bolted to Jagger, and as I came into arm's reach of him, I clenched my fist and punched him in the nose.

"Phoebe!" Anderson cried out as he rushed toward me, but it was too late—I'd already hit Jagger a second time in his mouth, knocking his head back with a sickening yet gratifying thud.

In an instant, Jagger's iron grip wrapped around my neck and I gasped for breath, taken aback by the darkness in his eyes when they met mine. His upper lip curled into a cruel smirk as he drawled, "Hello, Ariana. So nice of you to join me."

He released me and I stumbled backward in shock. Blood trickled down his chin as he wiped it away. Jagger grabbed his nose and snapped it into place without flinching, the sound echoing off the room's walls. The air crackled with tension as fear tied my stomach in painful knots.

"How are you alive?" I asked through gritted teeth, my anger still boiling inside me. My brain could hardly comprehend how he stood before me unscathed after everything he had put me through. My mind raced and whirled like a fucking wind-up toy as I struggled to understand what was happening.

He slid off his cloak and then slowly opened each button on his long-sleeved black dress shirt until it hung open—there it was. The black mamba was ready to strike as it coiled around him like a living shadow. I remembered he had the outline done with his uncle's consent. If our parents had known about it, they would have come unhinged.

"If you still think you're hallucinating, then . . ." Jagger released his shirt and held his arms out for me to see. "It's really me, Ari." His voice sent goose bumps over my skin. "I'm alive." His lips shifted into an infuriating smirk as he added, "But tell me, how are you alive?"

Anderson remained quiet in the corner, watching the catastrophic show unfold.

I took a deep, cleansing breath to clear my addled brain. Surely, I hadn't heard him right. "What do you mean, alive?"

"What I said," Jagger roared. "Tell me what happened after the fire."

My heart raced and my hands shook as I considered how this could be real. Pinching the bridge of my nose, I steadied myself.

"Someone held a gun to my head and forced me to set the fire," I stammered, my throat tightening with every word. "As soon as I dropped the match, she dragged me out of the house and into the trees. She promised if I didn't cooperate, she would kill you."

My defenses crumbled as hot tears ran down my cheeks. "Her name was Crimson. She kept me hostage for three days, telling me that you'd died." A sob escaped from my throat as memories of that time flooded back. "Theo and Samantha flew me to New York and stayed for a week before dropping me off at the academy. But even when I begged them to tell me that you weren't dead, they never did. They just cried and grieved with me. Samantha prepared your funeral with flowers and pictures . . . and people showed up from everywhere. Since you died in the fire, it was a closed casket."

Jagger's expression contorted with shock and disbelief. He laced his fingers behind his neck, stared at the ceiling, and spat out a profanity-filled response. "What the actual hell?"

Forcing himself to look at me again, he said, "Ari, I think we were both lied to."

Chapter Twenty-Three

Ariana

I crumpled to the floor, the crazy reality of the situation finally soaking into my head and heart.

"You need to leave," Jagger said to Anderson, his tone bordering on harsh.

"I'm out," Anderson said, his tone heavy with concern.

The tip of Jagger's black dress shoes caught my eye as he sat beside me on the floor. I wrung my hands together, refusing to look at him.

"Ariana." His voice was void of anger this time, but I wasn't sure who I was dealing with: the Jagger that used to love me or the hardened man I'd witnessed as the Black Mamba. "I don't understand why we were lied to. But at least we know that neither of us left by choice. I didn't abandon you."

My gaze slowly lifted to his, and my forehead scrunched in confusion. "What do you mean?" Still in shock, it hadn't occurred to me to ask what had happened to him after the fire.

Jagger's jaw clenched and for a fleeting moment, I saw a glimpse of the monster that now lived inside him. He cleared his throat, the dark expression quickly shifting. *Who is he?*

"You don't need to know."

"Why? You know what I lived through."

Jagger glanced away. "It was a different time, Ari."

By the rigidity of his shoulders, it was clear that it was difficult for him to talk about the past.

"How did you end up with Peter?" His ice-blue eyes landed on me again.

"He was there for me after the fire. I thought he was a good person. Turns out I was wrong." *So damn wrong!*

I gulped, not sure I wanted the answer to the question I was about to ask Jagger. He's not just Jagger. He's my stepbrother. The love of my life. "What happened with Peter? You say I'm safe from him, but what exactly did you do?" My gaze widened as his lip curled into a sinister smile, chilling me to the bone.

"I couldn't allow him to hurt you anymore, Ariana. As far as I'm concerned, I did what I had to do."

I narrowed my gaze on him. "Which was?"

Jagger cracked his neck and rolled his shoulders. "When I ripped his fingernails out with pliers, he sang like a spoiled little bitch."

I gasped and scrambled backward. "Wh-what?"

Jagger rose and loomed over me. "I needed information." He gave me a half-shrug as if he'd done so much worse. Something told me he had.

"What was so goddamn important that you ripped out someone's fingernails?"

Jagger pressed forward until he backed me into the wall. He placed his palms on each side of my head, caging me in.

"You." His tongue darted across his lower lip, and it took everything inside me not to kiss him. "I saw you at the party that night. When you left the house in a hurry, I followed. Peter was waiting for you. The moment he got rough with you, I realized he had to be dealt with. As I told him, you're mine. No one has a right to touch you."

Confusion and rage clouded my mind. I wasn't an object that could be owned, but he'd saved my life. What the hell was I supposed to do with that mixed bag?

"I'm sure that made his day," I muttered.

"He also told me you started the fire." Jagger dragged his knuckles down my cheek, and shivers danced up and down my spine.

I slammed my defenses into place, unsure how Jagger felt about me burning down our home. "I had no choice."

"Peter told me that as well."

I looked away, relishing in the relief that Peter had told Jagger at least part of the truth. Tears pricked my eyes as I focused on him again. "I thought I killed you. All these years, it's consumed me." My voice cracked with the grief that had nearly destroyed me.

"Now you can sleep at night knowing that I'm alive and well." His words said one thing, but his expression another.

"What else did Peter say?" I took a deep breath and tried to calm my racing pulse.

"Not enough."

I waited for him to continue. Our conversation was like pulling teeth, slow and painful.

"If you still have questions for him, I have no doubt in my mind that you can coax . . . I mean torture the truth out of him." My brow quirked at him.

"Who is Crimson? He ran out of time before he could tell me about her," Jagger said.

I stilled as if deadly spiders surrounded me. "I don't know her real name. She was the one that forced me to set the fire, but it sounds like Peter told you that. After months and months of grief and depression, I confessed to him what happened. He used it against me."

"To control and hurt you."

"Yeah." My entire being ached from Jagger's proximity. I wanted to reach out to him, kiss him as though we hadn't lost four years. The man standing before me might be my stepbrother, but he wasn't the guy I fell in love with. I desperately needed to know if he still existed somewhere inside of Jagger.

"He said you were his obsession." Jagger shifted from one foot to the other, growing restless.

I nodded, unsure of how to respond. "What did you say?"

A cruel laugh rumbled through Jagger's chest. "I told him an obsession got people killed."

My eyes popped open. "Jagger. Please tell me you didn't."

He pressed his body into mine, and I placed a hand over his heart. The beat was steady and calm. Jagger wasn't tripping that he'd hurt Peter and tore out his fingernails. I wasn't sure I cared either. Peter deserved what he got after what he'd done to me. Flashes of him chasing me through the woods at night sent my pulse into overdrive. He hid my shoes, but I ran my ass off anyway. I concealed myself behind the trees and brush. Somehow, I'd managed to outsmart him, but my feet were cut and bloody, leaving a trail straight to me. My feet weren't the worst of it that night. He began his cutting rituals, but none were deep until he carved up my back.

I gritted my teeth, suddenly needing to hear that Jagger had hurt Peter—maimed him beyond recognition or fed his balls to him. The mere thought of that level of payback made my thighs clench with longing for Jagger. I was screwed up in the head if that turned me on.

Jagger leaned in, his nose brushing against my ear.

I grabbed his waist, heat pooling low in my belly as his dick pressed against his slacks and into my waist.

"What do you want me to tell you, my pet?"

Without my permission, a moan slipped from my throat.

"The truth. Tell me the truth."

He nipped my earlobe. "Here's the truth, baby. I thought about you every day for four goddamn years as I lived my own hell. You died in that fire and took my heart and humanity with you. What I had to do to survive would make a grown man beg for death." His hand trailed up my side then cupped my breast through my shirt and teased my nipple. "You haunted my dreams as I did unspeakable things. Horrible things. You can't handle the fucking truth."

"Yes, I can. I've seen darkness, Jagger. Don't underestimate me."

His fingertips danced a trail down my leg, then beneath my skirt.

"Spread your legs," he demanded.

My breath caught in my throat as he eased me apart and massaged my clit.

"As for Peter, I walked around with a hard-on for a goddamn week as I tortured him for what he did to you."

He pinched my bundle of nerves and I gasped, grinding my hips against his hand.

"He was tied to a table for days and pissed himself. Darkness and loneliness can kill a man, but the stupid bastard hung in there." Jagger nipped at my lower lip. "Are you going to cum for me, pet? Are you going to cum all over my fingers as I tell you how I killed him? Maybe your soul is as black as mine."

Shit! Shit! Shit! How was I getting so turned on by this? It was twisted as hell.

Jagger shoved a finger inside me, thrusting while he continued.

"Jagger." His name on my tongue sounded foreign to my ears. I dug my fingernails into my palms, trying not to give him the satisfaction of my orgasm while he confessed to a crime. A fucking crime. *Peter deserved it for what he did to me.*

"Peter told me how you explained about the fire, then how he manipulated and hurt you. He fed off your fear. If I had let him go, he would have gone after you again, and I couldn't have that." Jagger removed his hand then scooped me into his powerful arms and set me on the table in the corner. "Lean back and spread your legs."

What was happening was wrong, and I tried to will myself to leave, but not only was the door locked, I didn't want to. I craved my stepbrother, and I needed to fuck him without that damn mask over his head. Just us. Just like it used to be.

Jagger fully removed his black shirt and tossed it to the floor. "When Peter said he owned you." He clucked his tongue. The button on his slacks popped open, followed by the low hum of his zipper coming undone. He crawled onto the table and settled between my legs. "In case you forgot, I'm going to remind you that you're mine." Jagger shoved his thick cock inside me, stealing my breath. How a murder confession had turned into hot sex, I wasn't sure, but my body wasn't complaining.

"Do you remember the time our parents weren't home?" he asked.

"Which time?" I slid my fingers into his dark hair, my nails scratching his scalp as I bucked my hips against him.

"I tied you to my bed and licked your pussy until my sheets were soaked with your juices. When you were pleading for me to let you cum. If you did that now, I would discipline you for begging."

His blue eyes held mine. "And?"

"Oh, my dirty girl likes that?" He reached between my legs and massaged my clit while he continued talking.

I responded with a soft moan.

"Dirty girls get spanked when they don't behave." He thrust his hips and moved inside me. "I already left my handprint on your ass cheek, but it won't be the only time I mark you."

My brow rose, and a mischievous look flickered in his gaze. "What if I don't want you anymore, Jagger? What if I met someone else last night at the library and I'm super interested in him?" Burning jealousy zipped through every cell in my entire being at the thought of Jagger being with another girl, but I would never tell him that.

He roughly gripped my chin. "Make no mistake, Ariana. You will *always* be mine." He released me and ran his thumb up and down the sensitive swell of my neck. Jagger's fingertips danced down and between my breasts.

"Does that make you want to cum all over my cock? Thinking about how I own your body? You serve me."

"Jagger. Oh God!" I moaned as my inner walls spasmed around his dick.

"That's it, pet," he grunted as I began moving again. "Milk my cock dry with your tight pussy."

He leaned down. "If anyone touches you . . ." A guttural growl worked through his chest, his frenzied pace nearly rocking me off the table. "I'll kill them just like I did Peter." A crazed look twisted his expression as his body tensed, and he filled me with his cum.

Wrapping my legs around his waist, I rubbed my clit against him. Ragged breaths sounded through the room as my pussy clenched his shaft, draining the final drops from his cock as I released again.

Spent from the intense ride, I sighed, my limbs turning limp as noodles. Jagger pulled out of me without a word then hopped off the table.

His dark gaze raked over me from head to toe. "You look so beautiful with my cum seeping out of your cunt."

The rush of our sexcapade crashed, leaving me confused about my feelings for Jagger and what he'd done to Peter. Jagger had manipulated my body as he confessed, just like Peter had manipulated me.

His stare locked on me. The groove in his forehead deepened, and he averted his attention.

I mentally prepared myself to have my heart annihilated once more.

"Get dressed and go home."

My pulse thumped as his low, raspy voice filled the room, enveloping me in a thick fog and sending my emotions into a downward spiral.

I hopped off the table and tugged my skirt down. Jagger's cum leaked down my thighs, and I ground my teeth together. "You came inside me and now you're telling me to leave? Next time you want me, you can fuck your hand, asshole."

"Ari, I'll call you to the society when I'm ready to see you again." He tucked himself into his pants and zipped and buttoned them. Jagger reached for his shirt on the floor then shoved his muscled arms in the sleeves. His washboard abs rippled with each move, and I resisted the urge to lick every dip and valley. I snapped out of my hormonal haze, remembering what he'd said. Questions spun around in my head like a raging tornado.

"That's it? We lost four years with each other and you're kicking me out without a second thought? Like we don't have history?"

"Something like that." He turned away, clearly dismissing me.

My anger crackled through the room like a dry thunderstorm—dangerous and leaving destruction in its wake. "I never forgot you, Jagger. I never stopped loving you." The strain in my voice betrayed my grief.

I forced myself to breathe through the pain, willing the tears to wait until I was alone. I refused to give him the satisfaction of breaking me.

He kept his back to me, ignoring my confession. The cold, hard truth crushed my lungs and I struggled to catch my breath. I shoved the nearly debilitating ache to the side as I slowly walked to the door, heavy with grief all over again. I glanced over my shoulder at Jagger. "Let me out." I squared my shoulders. "What happened to the guy I loved? He held my heart in his hands . . . protected me at all costs."

Jagger slowly faced me, and his blue eyes pierced my soul. "He's gone, Ariana, and he's never coming back."

Chapter Twenty-Four

Jagger

I leaned into the curve of the road, feeling my motorcycle's powerful engine rumble beneath me. The need to feel the air on my skin fueled my decision to ditch classes. I had to clear my head, and as long as I was on the same campus as Ari, she consumed my every thought.

The last few days had left a hole inside me. I thought I was incapable of normal feelings again, but as I confessed to killing Peter to Ari, a little piece of me flickered to life. It was quickly extinguished when Ari wanted to try to pick up where we left off after the fire. That couldn't happen. I couldn't give her what she thought she wanted. I was too screwed up, and without even a second thought, I manipulated her not to leave the society room as I told her how I'd tortured him. I played her body like the strings on a guitar, bending her to my will. I should be ashamed of myself, but I felt nothing. *Liar! You still love her.* I gave the inner voice a big fuck you. I hadn't ever stopped loving Ariana, but I had no idea what to do with those feelings after thinking she was dead. The crazy thing? She was told I was dead too. It didn't make sense. I'd spoken to Mom a handful of times on the phone over the last few years, and she had never mentioned Ari's name. Neither had Theo.

The world blurred and my stomach churned. Why? Everyone had kept the secret from me, and I needed goddamn answers.

An hour later, I slowed my bike and pulled onto a paved road that wound through a state park. It had been a hot minute since I'd driven back there, but I had to make sure no one else saw me. Taking the next left, I carefully maneuvered the machine down a dirt path with jagged rocks jutting up from the ground. Thank God it wasn't far. I couldn't afford for my motorcycle to get trashed. Finally, I spotted the dilapidated ranger's station, mostly hidden by a grove of pine and aspen trees, but I still parked behind it.

"Took ya long enough," Gunner said, approaching me from the west side of the building.

"Good to see you too, man." I removed my helmet and sat it on the seat before I hugged him. "I see you brought a few men with ya." I grinned as I greeted Cupcake, Rigs, and Tiny.

"Safety in numbers." Gunner chewed on a toothpick, grinning. "Football serves you well. Seems like you've grown another inch and filled out since I saw you last." He slapped me on the shoulder.

"It's been twelve months." I shrugged. "The team is really good, so I'm hoping we have a hell of a year. So far, we've had a great season, and I'm eager to get in front of the scouts."

Tiny laced his fingers behind his head. "You'll go pro. We watch every game we can on TV, and you're too good for them to pass up."

I chuckled, appreciating the support. "We'll see." A heavy silence hung in the air.

Gunner folded his arms across his chest and rocked back on his heels. "You gonna fill us in, or we gonna stand here staring at each other like lovesick bitches?"

I kicked at the ground with the toe of my boot, searching for the right words. "You were the one that said you had something important to tell me, but I can start. I confirmed that Ariana was forced to set the fire. She was also held hostage for three days afterward."

Gunner shot me a "what the hell" look. "Who took her?" His jaw twitched, but his expression revealed zero emotion.

The familiar feeling of fury and hatred bloomed deep inside me. Gunner didn't speak, but I could feel the power rolling off him in waves.

"Some bitch named Crimson. You guys heard of her?"

The silence between us continued to thicken. "Gunner, what aren't you telling me?"

"She's crazy, Jagger. Stay away from her. I've never seen or met her, but the rumors are dark."

I laughed. "Not a problem if I don't know who the fuck she is. You all clearly do, so please, fill me in so I can deal with her like I did Peter for hurting Ariana."

Gunner crossed the room and grabbed me by the shoulder. "Don't even think about it, Jag. Crimson is out of your league. It's not only her, man. She's connected to . . ." He dug his fingers into my skin. "Psycho. We just found out. That's why I wanted to meet with you."

I swallowed excessively, attempting to clear the lump in my throat. Sweat dotted my forehead and upper lip as the dark clouds rolled through my head, bringing the horror back and dragging me to the pits of hell. The demons clawed at my soul and surrounded me in darkness.

"Jag. Jag? We've fucking got this, but you stay as far away from both of them as possible."

Every memory from those years snapped through my mind like a steel-tipped whip.

"Jag!" Gunner shook me and I stared at him, finally seeing him.

"Do you understand me?"

"Yeah," I finally managed.

He gave me a clipped nod, but a storm brewed in his eyes. It was then that I remembered Psycho's message on the football field. "He knows where I am." How had I forgotten that important detail? *Because I'm obsessed with Ari.*

"I'm sorry, what?" Gunner tilted his head and chewed on his toothpick.

"Too much happened with Peter and Ari after that. I totally forgot. But when we played the Hornets, one of their defense players tackled me hard then said that Psycho wanted him to deliver a message." I focused on the ground, scrambling to understand what was happening.

"Come on, kid. Spit it out," Rigs urged.

"He said that Psycho was watching me. I don't know if Psycho was at the game, or saw me on TV, or maybe he had someone else keep an eye on me." I looked at the men staring at me as if I'd lost my marbles. I had.

"How long ago was that?" Gunner asked.

"I think a few weeks. There hasn't been any indication that someone is following me, though. None."

"If he got that message to you, he knows exactly where you are." Gunner scrubbed his face with his hands.

"It's not like I was hiding. I'm playing ball for the best college team in the country." Frustrated, I blew out a heavy sigh. "I can't leave. Not now. Ariana is at Whitmore, and if Crimson and Psycho are working together, that mea—"

"That means they've most likely been partners in crime before the house fire. Not only was Ari used to set it, but for Psycho to draw you out and grab you."

The realization dawned on me, a sickening feeling coiling inside my stomach. "If Ari . . . that means . . ." I couldn't say the rest.

"If they know where you are, they know where she is, which means they know exactly how to get to both of you *again*. Ari should have never left the East Coast to come back here."

Chapter Twenty-Five

Ariana

I paced the length of my room, "Haunted" by Isabel LaRosa playing quietly from my Alexa speaker. Jagger had worked his way through my dreams, robbing me of any real sleep or peace. He hadn't contacted me in five days, and the darkness I'd been battling was too heavy to fight alone. It was clear that I meant nothing more to him than a piece of ass.

Throwing myself onto my bed, I screamed into my pillow. Questions that only he could answer ransacked my brain. Even worse, I was still trying to process the fact that he'd murdered someone . . . for me.

I groaned as I flopped onto my back and stared at the ceiling. Dad was right. I should have stayed on the East Coast, then I would never have learned Jagger was alive. Betrayal seeped inside me, stirring the pain and anger I'd tried to bury over the years. Dad and Samantha must have known Jagger hadn't died in the fire.

Pissed again at the lies that had torn apart my family, I stomped over to my desk and snatched up my brush and a hair tie. I had to talk to Dad about what happened and give him a chance to explain before I jumped to conclusions. But first, I'd had enough of someone else's crap too. Once I pulled my hair in a ponytail, I checked myself in the mirror. What I was wearing wouldn't work.

I hurried to my closet and grabbed my favorite jeans and an emerald-green top. In record time, I had fresh makeup on and was ready to leave.

Half an hour later, I parked behind the Viper Society's building, stashed my purse under the back seat, then tossed my blue windbreaker on top of it. From the looks of it, only a few people were there, and as long as I set my car alarm, I felt my belongings would be safe.

I ensured my phone was in my pocket and slid my keyring on my index finger before I locked the car and jogged to the entrance. I hadn't ever shown up unannounced before and wasn't sure if anyone would let me into the building. There was only one way to find out. Spotting the black box, I pushed the white button on it. To my surprise, the door popped open, and I slipped inside. Before I took two steps down the hall, a hooded and masked figure stepped in front of me, blocking my path.

"Who are you here to see?"

I jutted my chin up and squared my shoulders. "The Black Mamba. Is he here?"

"You don't have a meeting with him?" He folded his hands behind him.

"No. But I have to talk to him."

"I'm sorry. That can't happen unless he's summoned you." He grabbed my arm, and I jerked it away from him.

"It's urgent."

A disguised laugh echoed through the hall. "That's what they all say."

My eyes narrowed into little slits, and I mentally shot daggers into the asshole's heart. "What do you mean others? How many girls is he with?"

"You need to leave."

"Jagger! Jagger!"

The guy whipped me around so fast that I nearly tripped over my feet and fell. "Jagger!"

Seconds before he tossed me out of the building, he jerked me backward and grabbed a handful of my hair. "I highly recommend that you shut that pretty little mouth of yours, or I'll shut it for you. There's no one here by that name."

"Let her go!"

Before I could identify who gave the order, the asshole shoved me, and my knees hit the tile floor. Strong arms scooped me up and carried me down the hall. I wasn't sure who intervened, but they had great timing. After all the drama that had played out that week, I had a short damn fuse and was looking for someone to take it out on.

The cloaked savior ripped his mask off once the door was secured and locked.

"What the hell are you doing here? And what the hell are you doing using my real name?" Jagger fumed.

"What do you think I'm doing here? I haven't heard a word from you in five days and I have questions." I folded my arms across my chest, pissed all over again.

He blinked at me and shook his head. "I can't help you. You need to leave."

"No." I was sick and tired of fucked-up men dictating my life. "If you want me to go then answer my questions."

Jagger walked away and hung up his cloak in the closet. It was then that I glanced around. I must be in the office or somewhere similar.

"Ari. We're over. We had some fun at the society, but if you want to pick up where we left off, it's impossible."

"I never asked for that. I don't understand what happened after the fire. Why did everyone tell each of us we had died? It doesn't add up. Something is wrong, and you're the only person I know that has answers . . . and that I trust." I wasn't a thousand percent sure about the trust part, but I had to believe that there was a shred of good somewhere inside of him. He'd killed to protect me. As messed-up as it sounded, I felt safe with him, so I would take that for now. "But seriously, if you don't want me, then let me date Anderson."

Jagger shot across the room and backed me against the wall, breathing heavily. "No."

I shoved at his shoulders, but he didn't budge. "Sorry, Jag, you can't have it both ways. I'm not a sex toy that you put away in the cabinet after playing around. I'm a real girl, Geppetto." I tilted my head, wondering if he would get the joke we used to have when we were kids.

"Nice try, Ari. But I said no." He stepped back, his heated gaze never leaving mine.

A storm raged inside me. "I don't know what happened to you, but you can go to hell. Dad has tried to control me, then Peter, and now you." I fisted my hands and charged at him, punching him square in the chest.

He staggered backward, his eyes blazing with anger. His guttural growl filled the room as he rushed toward me. Jagger reached for me, and I ducked then stomped on his foot.

"Goddammit! What the hell? I have a game Saturday!"

"And this is my problem, why?" I landed a swift kick to his shin, feeling braver by the second.

"Because I'm trying to go pro and I can't play if I'm injured!"

"Whine to someone who gives a shit. And I'll tell you something else." I leaned down then rammed my shoulder into his side. His ribs were an easy target since he was a lot taller than I was.

Jagger landed on his ass with a thud, surprise coasting over his face. I straddled him then pinned his arms down with my knees. "This is how this is going to play out. I can date and fuck anyone I want to. You have no, and I mean no say in my life at all. When I walk out of this room, it's the last time you'll have to put up with me, but I'm not leaving without answers."

As the seconds ticked by, Jagger's expression softened. "What do you want to know?" he finally asked.

"Why did Crimson make me start the fire?"

Sadness ghosted over Jag's face. "Because she wanted to get to me."

That wasn't the answer I'd expected. Frowning, I said, "I don't understand."

"I just learned that Crimson's boss is named Psycho."

I gave a little shrug. "And? We all have a boss."

Jagger blew out a breath and briefly looked away. "You'll just have to hate me, Ari. I can't tell you, or it will put you in danger."

My anger deflated, and my shoulders slumped. "If you hate me, why are you still protecting me?" Every cell in my body wanted to reach out and touch him.

"I never said I hated you."

I rolled my eyes, irritation replacing the fleeting moment of compassion I felt for my stepbrother. "You have ten seconds to start talking, or I'm on my way out of here to find Anderson. I bet he's a better fuck than you are." Acid laced my words, and I hoped they cut deep. Jagger was being an asshole, and I wouldn't let him get away with treating me like I was insignificant.

A scream escaped me as Jagger easily rolled us over and pinned me beneath him. "Scream all you want. These rooms are soundproof and no one can hear you."

I glared at Jagger, willing him to disappear into a puff of smoke— no such luck.

"Ten, nine, eight—"

"If you want another dead body on your conscience, go ahead and date Anderson."

I sucked in a breath, not wanting to believe he would hurt someone he cared about.

"He's your friend and teammate. You won't do anything to him."

Jagger's dark chuckle filled the room. "Oh, I will. Make no mistake about it."

I groaned and shoved his shoulders. The sound of our breathing reached my ears, and I settled into the feeling of him on top of me. Even though he was driving me crazy, he meant more to me than my life. I reached up and brushed his bangs from his forehead like I used to when we were teenagers. His eyes darkened, and I felt his dick harden through his pants. Then, a thought occurred to me.

"If I can't be with anyone else then you can't either." My heart beat frantically behind my rib cage. I was taking a huge risk but had to see if it worked.

"I never seriously dated or loved anyone after you, Jagger." I licked my lips and hoped what I was about to say would penetrate his thick skull. "I've always loved you. I never stopped. No one has ever come close to what we had. What we might have again."

Slowly, Jagger's expression morphed from agony to relief to terror.

I wrapped my fingers around his bulging bicep. "Tell me you love me and I won't walk away. I won't date anyone else, and I'll save myself for you at the society too. Honestly, I'll do anything to keep from losing you again." Admitting that nearly gutted me, but I had to take a chance that I could break through the walls Jagger had so carefully built around himself.

Jag's head hung down, his hair brushing my forehead. His gaze finally met mine, and moisture welled in his eyes. "I'm terrified I'll lose you again, Ari. If we're together, you'll get hurt."

My forehead creased. "That won't happen. We're older, stronger." Even as the words left my mouth, Peter's abuse clouded my mind. "We're stronger together. Please don't let people keep us apart any longer." I reached for the tear that traveled down Jag's cheek. "I would give anything to kiss away your pain."

Jagger dipped his head and brushed his lips across mine in a gentle kiss. He brought his mouth to my ear. "I'm not strong enough, Ari. I've loved you since I was a kid. I understood we had to keep us a secret when we were younger, but they knew. Mom and Theo knew we were together. I think they were behind separating us."

I gasped. The thought hadn't occurred to me. Yes, they lied to us, but orchestrating the fire and separating us were entirely different scenarios. One that I wasn't sure I could digest.

"Are you sure?" I held my breath, waiting to see if he was guessing or if he had proof of their betrayal.

"No, but something's off. I couldn't protect you last time, but I'll be goddamned if you get hurt again."

"Then say it. Keep me safe by your side. Tell me that you still love and want me."

Chapter Twenty-Six

Jagger

It was wrong. I couldn't keep her tucked away at the society then insist she couldn't have a life outside of mine. Worse, I loved her with every fiber of my being. Once I realized we'd both been lied to, Ari started working her way back into my heart and fast. I wasn't kidding when I said she was mine, but I had to let her go or admit that there was no life without her. Not even football meant as much without Ari next to me. I wasn't sure how to protect her since we weren't together twenty-four seven. Telling Ari that I loved her might be a death sentence.

I stared into her blue eyes, all of her pain boiling to the surface. Weighing my choices, I knew in my gut that she wouldn't leave Whitmore just because I told her I didn't love her anymore. There had to be a way to be with her and keep us both safe. Giving up had never been my style, and I refused to do so now. I placed a kiss on her forehead before I looked at her.

"I love you, Ari. I never stopped."

Ari's body crumpled beneath mine, and tears streamed down her face. "What does that mean?"

"It means we're going to try. If you love me the way you say you do, then we'll figure us out. I can't lose you."

A cry escaped her, and she leaned up and pressed her mouth to mine. "Tell me again, Jag."

"I love you, Ari."

She wrapped her arms around my neck as we kissed, and for the first time in years, nothing else existed except for her. Beautiful, smart, and wonderful Ari.

"There are some things you need to know about me before you commit. It wouldn't be fair otherwise."

Ari smirked. "Because you've been so fair about the society and Anderson."

"You have a point." I pulled away and smiled at her. "We need to keep us a secret. At least until I figure out how to handle the situation around Theo and Mom." I climbed off her, then helped her up from the floor.

"We're not going to confront Theo and Samantha?"

"Not yet. On campus, if people ask, tell them that Anderson introduced us and we're hanging out." I wrapped a few strands of her long blonde hair around my finger. "You have to trust me on this."

She nodded. "I do. Somehow, you seem to know what happened after the fire, but I'm hoping you'll tell me more. If I'm in danger, then knowing the truth won't make a difference. It will help me be aware."

"I wish it were that easy, but I'll try." I pulled her body against mine, losing myself in the feel of her against Jagger Whitlock, not The Black Mamba.

Ari's stomach growled and broke up the moment. I kissed the tip of her nose. "I have to get to practice, and you should find some food to eat." If we were going to get to know each other again, I had to start somewhere with the truth. "Then meet me at the field house at eight. Don't let anyone see you."

Curiosity flashed in her gaze. "That's a strange request but I'll play along." She pushed up on her tiptoes and kissed me goodbye. I watched as she gave me a little wave before she left the room. How in the hell I would be able to focus on practice was beyond me, but if anything happened to Ari, I had nothing left.

The sun quietly slipped behind the mountain, painting the sky in brilliant blue and pink hues. My face warmed with the dying embers of the evening light, and I listened to the soft chirps of the crickets in the cool breeze. The rainy season would begin soon, and I promised myself I would soak up these moments as often as possible.

The sound of an approaching car distracted me from my peaceful moment. I pointed to the empty space beside me and indicated for Ari to park there.

She climbed out of her Audi, all smiles. Her long hair flowed down her back, the soft curls begging to be pulled, but I had to show her more of who I was before I believed she could still love me. I'd meant every word I'd said to her earlier that day, but Ari knew a different guy then. I came from almost as much money as she did, but that had all changed.

My gaze swept over Ari. Her black top clung to her curves, and her jeans hung low on her hips. My heart nearly leaped out of my chest. How could I have denied how much I loved her? "You look beautiful." I reached for her hand, then pulled open the door with my other.

"We're going inside?"

"It's a big building so you won't smell the jockstrap aroma." I grinned at her.

Her soft giggle made my cock jerk to life, and I had to remind him we were thinking with the big head tonight.

"I've never been in a guy's locker room before."

"You're not missing anything." I rubbed my thumb across the

back of her hand. It was surreal that she was next to me. There was no way we could get back what we lost, but maybe . . . just maybe. My stomach tightened with the thought of telling her about my past. It would make us or break us. If she couldn't handle it, I would ask her to leave Whitmore. I couldn't see her all the time and not be a part of her life.

"This is Coach's office." I opened the door and turned on the light.

"Why am I here? I mean, I want to support your football career, but I'm a bit confused." She tucked a loose strand of hair behind her ear.

"This." We walked to the other side of Coach's office, and I opened another door that led to my room.

Ari stepped in after me, looking puzzled.

"Ari, I live here. This is my room."

"What?" She shook her head and pointed to Coach's office. "Why aren't you in a house or even the dorm?"

I sat on the edge of my new bed and pulled her into my lap. "When I started my freshman year, I was working full-time to pay for my housing. I had a football scholarship for a full ride, so at least that helped. My grades and performance on the field were suffering though. When Coach found out, he set me up here so I wouldn't have to worry about a roof over my head. In exchange, he has my full dedication."

"But Theo and Samantha would have taken care of it." Her words trailed off. "You really do think they had something to do with the fire, don't you?"

"I believe they're involved somehow. I don't think it's Mom as much as Theo." Guilt weighed down my shoulders. "I've not had much to do with them since . . . . I started college. Before that actually."

"My dad?" Her voice hitched with her question. She stared at the wall and chewed on her lower lip. "When I was at the academy, Dad never allowed me to come home even over summer break. During the holidays, he would visit and bring Samantha sometimes. Other times, it was just him. I tried to ask him why I couldn't come back at least a million times, but he said it wasn't up for discussion. Do you think he was hiding something? I mean, that was a stupid question. Of course he is, but what and why?"

Rubbing her back, I took a slow and steady breath. "From what I gather, Mom and Theo didn't want us to know each other were alive. They needed us out of the way."

"Or Dad was protecting me. If Crimson . . ." Ari scrunched her nose in distaste. "What kind of name is that?"

I couldn't help but smile. "It's not her real name any more than Psycho is her boss's real name." I hoped like hell Ari wouldn't ask if I had that information. "Anyway, you were saying?" I asked, directing the conversation.

"If Crimson wanted you, maybe Dad didn't know that and he shipped me off to keep me safe." She shifted on my lap, and my cock throbbed. It took everything inside me not to throw her on the bed and ravish her.

"It's a likely possibility, but the fact that he didn't want you in Washington or Oregon are still red flags."

Ari leaned her head against my shoulder, and I pulled her close.

"I'm glad Coach believes in you. I do too, Jag." She glanced up at me and pressed a kiss to my mouth. "What happened to you after the fire? Where did you go?"

Time froze with her question. I knew it would come up sooner rather than later, but I wasn't sure what I could tell her.

I ran my hand up her back and massaged her neck. "Horrible things, baby."

Ari stood then faced and straddled me. "You admitted that you killed someone to protect me. Hell, even tortured him. That probably should have messed with my head but it didn't. It made me trust you more. I have no doubt that you will burn the world down for me." She touched her forehead to mine. "You know what happened to me with Peter. Secrets between us won't help us heal, Jag. You have my word that I won't judge you. Shit, you could turn me in for arson if you wanted."

"No way in hell would I do that. Besides, you were held hostage and forced to burn our house down."

"And the horrible things that happened to you . . . were you forced to do things against your will or was it your choice?"

My pulse spiked as the room spun. Flashes of my past assaulted my mind, and I struggled to pull myself out of the horror.

"Jag. It's okay. We're together again. That's all that matters."

I glanced into her beautiful blue eyes. "If you learn the truth, you'll walk out that door and never look back."

"You don't know that."

Maybe she was right, but most likely not. One thing I knew for sure was that I had to tell her that night and give her the choice to leave before I couldn't let her go.

"After the fire, I couldn't handle losing you, Ari, so I took off."

"You ran away?"

"Yeah. Packed some clothes and hopped on my motorcycle. I was going to visit Uncle Gunner, but I never made it."

"Why?" Ari's soft voice gave me the courage I needed.

"Because someone was tailing me. When they had the right opportunity, they grabbed me."

Ari's gasp filled the small room.

"I was in the bathroom of a gas station. It was one of those older ones, so the access was on the side of the building outside. The last thing I remembered was getting hit in the head and blacking out."

"Jag." She cupped my face with her hands and kissed me. "How many days after the house burned down?"

"Three," I whispered.

"The same day Crimson let me go without any explanation."

"Exactly. I suspect the reason she let you go was because I was snatched in broad daylight. I'm who they were waiting for. They used you to get me."

Even though I had mentioned it before to Ari, this time, it registered. Her body crumpled in on itself, and she collapsed against my chest. "I'm so sorry, Jagger. I should have done something to protect you. If I'd known . . ." Her shoulders shook with her sobs.

"Baby, it wasn't your fault. Please don't think you could have stopped it. Psycho was after me. He would have gotten to me one way or the other."

Ari lifted her head, and her eyes were rimmed with red. "Psycho? The same Psycho you said is Crimson's boss?"

"That one." I brushed the hair from her forehead then kissed her. "There wasn't a damn thing you could have done. Let that shit go right now."

"Bossy much?" A sad giggle escaped her, and I smiled.

"You know I'm bossy. And it seems like you still laugh when you're stressed."

Ari released a heavy sigh. "Why couldn't I have a different stress tic? Laughing gets my ass in trouble if someone doesn't know me."

"I can see how it would be inconvenient." I chuckled.

"I didn't mean to interrupt. Sorry."

"You're fine." I hesitated, not wanting to drop the next giant bomb.

Chapter Twenty-Seven

Jagger

"You were a teenager. What in the world could Psycho have wanted with you?"

I briefly closed my eyes, my heart pounding in my ears. "For bait." Unable to sit still, I lifted her off my lap and placed her on the bed. I shot to my feet and bolted out of the room.

"Jagger, wait."

Ari's hurried footsteps slapped the concrete floors of the building. She grabbed my shoulder and spun me around. She peered up, worry in her gaze. "Talk to me. What happened?" She held my hands, waiting.

"You're free to walk away, Ari. I won't call you to the society, and you and Anderson can go out."

"Wait? What in the hell are you talking about? We agreed to give things another try, Jag. Why are you flipping shit on me?"

I stroked her cheek, imprinting her beautiful face to my mind's eye for the last time. "I saved you from Peter, but no one can save you from me. I'm more of a monster than he ever was." He had been an easy problem to fix. I was already going to hell, so what was one more crime?

"I refuse to believe that. You risked everything to protect me from that bastard Peter. I know there's still a part of the guy inside you that I fell in love with years ago."

"Just remember what I said." I lowered my mouth to hers, enjoying her sweet kiss. "I love you, Ari."

"I love you, too." Tears welled in her eyes, but I knew her pain was about to become so much worse. "Tell me what you meant that Psycho wanted you for bait."

I took a few steps back, needing some space to breathe.

"Psycho and Crimson are part of a criminal operation. I've never met Crimson, but I know she's crazy if she works with Psycho. It's why I was afraid to be around you again. They're dangerous. Lethal psychopaths."

"So was Peter. He just didn't have a team or posse or whatever the shit people call it. What do they do?"

"They befriended kids." My throat grew tight and dry. I wasn't sure if I could tell her the truth.

She stared at me, a million possibilities of what I meant flashing in her expression.

"They used me as bait, Ari. I made friends with the kids at the dog park or wherever then Psycho kidnapped them." Agony slashed my chest open and ripped out my heart, not only for what I'd done in my past but for how Ari glared a hole through me.

"The Jagger I know would never do anything so horrible. Start talking fast, or I'm out of here." Her nostrils flared, and her heated gaze flashed with anger.

"I never wanted to hurt anyone, Ari. You have to believe me."

"I don't understand how that happened. Help me understand, Jagger."

I raised my hands in surrender. "I don't expect you to get it. It's why I said I would let you go."

She protectively folded her arms over her chest.

"They had a trained shooter on the kid. I saw Psycho shoot someone before, and there was no doubt he would kill one of them if I didn't do my part."

Ariana dropped her arms. "He's killed a kid?"

I rubbed my face with my palms, forcing the memories into the background of my mind. "I was terrified. They had me wired so they heard every word that was said when I was talking to the target."

"How old?" Tears slid down her cheeks.

"I can't . . . Please, Ari."

"Old enough to be at a dog park alone?"

I shook my head.

"Then where were the parents?" She screamed. "Where were the goddamn parents?"

"With the kids. I befriended them as well." I sank onto one of the benches in the locker room, numb. "A troubled kid trying to do some good and help families goes a long way with people."

"Oh my God, Jagger. You're right. You're a fucking monster." Ari walked away, her cries bouncing off the walls as she hurried toward the workout rooms.

I placed my elbows on my knees. With my heart in my throat, tears ran down my face. Tears for those years I'd lost, and tears for the kids and families I'd destroyed. Ari needed to leave. Deep inside, I knew that, or I wouldn't have turned her against me and shared my past. It was the only way I knew to protect her. But holy hell, did it hurt. Dragging my feet to my locker, I opened it and removed Ari's butterfly necklace. She would want it back now that she knew the truth about me.

Five hours had passed before Ari's light footsteps alerted me that she'd returned. Her eyes widened as her attention landed on the delicate necklace dangling from my fingers. "You kept it?"

I stood, my ass scolding me for sitting on the bench so damn long.

Glancing at her, I wiped my eyes. "Of course I did. Even through all the darkness, those memories of us together kept me sane." I briefly stared at the floor. "You should have it back."

Tears welled in her eyes as I walked behind her, then gently moved her long hair, my fingertips grazing the back of her neck. "I love you, Ari. What you think about me now won't stop how I feel." I slipped the necklace on and fastened it, her scent of vanilla and raspberries making me dizzy. Closing my eyes, I imprinted this memory to my brain. Telling her goodbye a second time was about to fucking kill me. I placed a gentle kiss along the curve of her neck. I took a step back and waited for her to tell me why she'd come back.

She turned slowly, and I braced myself for the worst.

Her eyes softened as she touched the butterfly. "Tell me the rest." Her voice was raw with emotion.

My shoulders sagged with the weight of her words, but maybe her wanting me to continue was a good thing.

"I tried to run after the first time they forced me to talk to a kid. They made sure I never tried it again."

She remained quiet.

"Psycho tied me to a chair, got out a gun, and shoved it in my mouth. He proceeded to play Russian roulette, and every time he pulled the hammer back . . . I was so scared, I pissed myself. The only way I made it through mentally was to think about you and football, but I honestly didn't think I was walking away alive." I took a shaky breath. "They wired me and made sure they had a gun trained on the kid and eventually the parent. I didn't want a kid to see his parent's head blown off. At the same time, I knew I was going to help grab an innocent child so they could . . ." My body trembled with my unspoken words. I dared a look at Ari, then at the floor. When I said the rest, I didn't have enough guts to look her in the eye. I swallowed repeatedly. "Sell them."

"Oh God. Oh. My. Fucking. God." Her sobs rang through the room, and my attention landed on her seconds before she reached me.

To my surprise, Ari wrapped her arms around my neck.

"I'm so sorry, Jag. What I lived through is nothing compared to what happened to you."

"It wasn't your fault, baby. We got tangled up with some dangerous people. I'm just not sure why." I stared at the floor, willing myself not to cry. Once I'd escaped Psycho, I swore I would never allow myself to be vulnerable again in my life. Yet here I was, gutting myself in front of my stepsister.

"Thank you for telling me, Jag. It's a lot to process, but there's no way you would have ever hurt anyone unless you were forced too. I can't believe that you're a bad person."

Her words reached into my soul, providing it a trickle of light.

"How did you get away?" She straightened and wiped the moisture from my cheeks.

"Uncle Gunner had been searching for me for two years. He knows a lot of people, but Psycho moved us around all the time. The one thing I was allowed to do was go to school and play ball, but even then, he had someone watch my every step.

You'd think I would be able to say something to someone at school, a teacher, counselor, or somebody, but that wasn't the case. Psycho had deep pockets and even deeper connections.

I had finally worked up the nerve to tell my history teacher. After class ended and the students had left, I asked to speak to him in the hall. Since the classroom had windows, I knew I could get shot if Psycho suspected anything. The hall was safer, or so I thought." I paused then licked my dry lips. "When I approached my teacher's desk, he opened the top drawer and revealed a gun. How he got it inside the school, I have no idea, but he had the means to buy off most people. As soon as I spotted the weapon, I looked at Mr. Anthony. He smiled before he told me that Psycho said to tell me hello."

"Holy shit."

"Yeah. I wasn't sure who was working for him and who wasn't. I was terrified all the time. It didn't take me long to realize that all I could count on was being the best football player on the field.

Even then, I changed schools every few months since Psycho moved us around to keep the cops off our trail. As I said, it took Gunner two years to finally find me. I was at a dog park, playing with the new target and his puppy. In the meantime, one of Gunner's guys snuck up on the man that had a gun trained on me from his hiding spot a block away. Tiny, Gunner's guy, took him out, then Gunner grabbed me and we ran. Not only did he save me, but he saved a lot of kids and their families. I owe him everything."

Ari's eyes widened. "Your uncle that's in the MC? *That* Uncle Gunner?"

"The one and only. I stayed with him for almost six months before I landed a scholarship at Whitmore. We knew that I'd be out in the open if Psycho wanted to come after me, but he hasn't. Until recently. He sent me a message through another football player, but I've not seen any signs of him."

"What? He knows where you are?" Ari's face turned ghostly white.

"Yeah. I don't know if he was trying to fuck with my head, or if he thinks he can make me work for him. I won't. I'll die first. Never again."

"Jag, you have to tell someone. Like the cops."

"Tell them what? I have no idea where Psycho is. He's a damn pro at hiding in plain sight. As I said, he moved us every few months. If there was even a hint that we would be caught, he packed us up and we left whatever state in the middle of the night."

"There has to be a way to stop him. But I'm still confused about why us? How did you end up on his radar, and why did Dad and Samantha hide the truth?"

"Maybe I sound paranoid, but I don't trust your dad, Ari. As for the rest of your questions, I don't know. Uncle Gunner still has his ear to the ground to see if there's any news on Psycho. He swore to me that Psycho and his people would be a thing of the past once the MC found them."

"Then let's help where we can. I won't say anything to Dad about us for now."

"Us?"

"I can't lie. What you told me is a lot to process, but as I said earlier, you're not a bad person. You were forced against your will to do awful things. I've walked in those shoes, Jag. I thought I killed you."

"Are you sure, Ari? There's no walking away. Ever. If you stay with me tonight, that's it. I won't let you go."

Ariana leaned over, her breath fanning against my ear. "I wouldn't have it any other way."

I held her against me, never wanting to leave.

She placed a kiss on the tip of my nose. "We should go. Get whatever you need for classes and practice tomorrow. You're staying with me at my place."

I quirked my brow at her. "Bossy much?"

She gave me an innocent shrug. "You knew what you were getting into, yet here you are."

A heartfelt chuckle rumbled through my chest for the first time in years. A flicker of hope was hot on its heels, but even I realized only the foolish allowed themselves to hope.

Chapter Twenty-Eight

Ariana

I'd danced on the edge of sanity that night, so sneaking my stepbrother into my bedroom was no big deal. I would handle the roomies later. Besides, if I could sneak Jag in, I could sneak him out. At least, I hoped.

No way would I let him stew in the hellish memories alone in a tiny little room after confessing his sins. Jag wasn't with me just for him, though. Having him next to me was my shield of protection against my nightmares. We had both lived through hell, but his words had gutted me in a way I never expected when he told me he was used as bait. I was afraid to close my eyes if he wasn't with me.

Luckily, the girls were asleep when we snuck in.

"This is nice, Ari. I'm glad you have good friends to live with." Jagger glanced around the living room, his gaze landing on the smiling pictures of me with Teagan, Everlee, Leighton, and Gabby. "I met them at parties last year. If you had ever mentioned me, they probably would have told you my first name and that I was playing ball."

"I only told Teagan about the fire, but I never mentioned you by name, only that you were my stepbrother. There was no way she could have known it was you. She's asked me to attend some football games, but I preferred time alone when they were gone, so I always declined." I led him through the living room and to the kitchen, to the food and alcohol. "I need a drink. Do you want one?"

"Yeah. It's been a hell of a day." He massaged the back of his neck while I collected some chips and items from the fridge to make sandwiches. "Get us a few sodas if you want." I pointed to the pantry on the other side of the room.

Jag's duffle bag was slung over his shoulder, and he carried the drinks and his plate of food. I grabbed a bottle of vodka along with my sandwich and led the way upstairs. Balancing my plate, I opened the door with my free hand. Once we settled in, I closed and locked the door behind us.

"I have no idea when the girls will wake up, but you can hide in the bathroom if someone knocks." I pointed to the door that was ajar. "I pay a little more for this room, but it was worth it not to share a shower."

"Five chicks in one house is a lot of bathroom time." Jagger chuckled and placed a potato chip into his mouth.

His gaze traveled with me as I reached inside my closet and produced a few red Solo cups for our drinks. "Yes, I keep a stash of cups here, so I don't have to run downstairs. Don't judge." I gave him the bottle of vodka then popped the top on one of the sodas. "Not sure how strong you like your alcohol. I figured it would be easier if you made yours."

"I have practice and classes tomorrow, so I'll take it easy." He flashed me a grin, and my insides melted all over the floor.

"I'm starving." I sat on my bed and pointed to the chair at my desk for him to sit down and eat. "You can shower in the morning if you want."

Jagger dumped his black duffle bag in the corner. It stuck out like a sore thumb against my white walls and furniture, but I wouldn't have it any other way.

"It almost feels like the old days," Jagger said between bites of his sandwich. "I'm sneaking into *your* room, though."

I gave him a shy smile. "It was a lifetime ago, but also just like yesterday."

"Do you think your friends will have a problem since we're stepbrother and stepsister?"

I blanched at his question. "Why would they? I mean, I understand creeping around behind Dad and Samantha's back because we were younger, but I don't know why anyone would have an issue with it."

"Ari, we practically grew up together. It's not like our parents got married when we were in high school. We were seven and eight when we met the first time. A year later, we lived in the same house."

"I can't control other people, but I don't give a shit what anyone else thinks." I took a long drink of my vodka and soda.

"You're telling me that if Teagan never spoke to you again and the girls asked you to move out, that I would be worth losing them?"

My heart dropped to my toes. "Is that what you think will happen? That we'll lose everyone else we love but have each other?"

Jagger set his plate on my desk. "I've seen a lot of darkness, babe. Enough to know that people rarely behave like we think they will."

"Then I guess it's a chance I'm willing to take. If shit goes south with the girls, I'll figure it out. As my grandma used to say, 'Don't borrow trouble.'"

"I get that. On the flip side, I've learned to try to be prepared for anything. It's kept me alive."

I took another drink, wishing the alcohol would quickly chill me out. The more he talked, the more I worried about the repercussions of our decision to be together. How would I deny a second chance with the only person I've ever loved to keep my friends?

"Guess the girls will prove that there are good people in this world. You have some of your football friends. Anderson clearly had your back. I'm guessing you texted him at the party when he and I were dancing. He backed off without giving you up. I had no idea what had happened."

Jagger's gaze narrowed. "That motherfucker has it bad for you. It pissed me off."

"Well, you don't have to hurt him now, Jag. Let's move on. I had no clue you were alive. Anderson might have been a good second to you. I don't honestly know since you got jealous and all possessive on me."

Jagger growled and rose from his seat. "No one will ever touch you again without my permission." He crawled onto the mattress, and I set my plate on the bed.

"Oh, does that mean I get a threesome?" I giggled as he pinned my body beneath his.

"Keep dreamin', baby. Keep dreaming."

Chapter Twenty-Nine

Ariana

I stared at the man in my bed as he softly snored. As hard as I tried, I couldn't sleep. Jagger's words about the girls and Psycho had royally screwed me up. Maybe I should hate and despise Jagger for his actions, but we had a history. I'd also walked in his shoes when I was forced to set the fire. How could I judge him when he had a gun trained on him but also on an innocent kid and family? I couldn't, and I would gamble away my savings on the fact that Jag was still a good guy. My guy.

The morning light streamed through the white curtains, surrounding my stepbrother in an angelic glow. I stopped myself before I barked out a laugh. Jagger had never been an angel, but it had been the reason I loved him so much.

His dark eyelashes fluttered, and sleepy eyes peered at me. "What time is it?"

I glanced at my alarm clock on my nightstand. "It's seven. Do you have practice this morning?"

"No. My first class isn't until ten. What about you?"

"Nine."

A slow, lazy grin eased across his face, and my pulse stuttered against my wrist.

"I slept my ass off last night." He propped up on his elbow and gave me a quick peck on my cheek.

"I'm glad. It was weird to have you in my bed." I ran my fingers over the dark stubble on his chin. "I'm glad you're here though."

"Can I shower?" He looked at me expectantly.

"Yeah. Do you want company?" I bit my lip, realizing I hadn't ever had shower sex before. It would be a great start to the day.

"I would love for you to join me." Jag sat up, the covers dropping to his waist and exposing his six-pack abs.

His biceps flexed as he tossed the blankets off and stood. My gaze swept over his muscular back, ass, and legs. Jag's black boxer briefs did nothing to hide his erection. He definitely looked good enough to eat.

Suddenly not tired anymore, I hurried to the bathroom and pulled my pajama top off. I giggled as I threw it at him.

"You'll pay for that." His raspy, deep laugh filled the room and I tugged on his wrist. I felt a bit better once we were tucked inside and the shower was running.

"I love to hear you laugh, but we have to be quiet if you don't want to be discovered. Plus, I should talk to Teagan first and let her know. The other girls can wait."

"I'm still not on board with the girls knowing, but I'm not sure how quiet you'll be when I'm fucking you senseless."

"Sounds like a challenge to me." I slipped my arms around his neck. "We have a lot to figure out. Honestly, I want to hide from the world forever, but that idea isn't realistic. And I want you to stay some nights here. I need to tell the girls, Jag." I placed my forehead against his chest.

"First things first, babe." He pressed his erection into my stomach. "We can talk later."

I looked up at him and grinned.

With a huge smile on my face, I hurried out of my room and into the hall. Jagger was still in the bathroom, getting dressed. We'd agreed that I would see who was at home and occupy them in the kitchen while he snuck out the front door. I wasn't sure it would work with four roomies, but we could try. It would be nice to stay in our little bubble if it bought us a few days without everyone in our business.

Besides, the most important people to keep our relationship a secret from were Dad and Samantha. We had to figure out what to do about them and Psycho, if he was stalking Jagger again.

An eerie chill skated over me, my brain recalling Jag's confession last night. I strolled through the hall then made my way down the stairs. Caught up in my thoughts, it took me a second to realize that Teagan, Everlee, Leighton, and Gabby were staring at me in the living room. Shit!

"Good morning, Phoebe," Everlee said with a wide grin. "From the sounds of it, you've had a really good morning."

Teagan tapped her chin and pretended she was thinking. "But who could the nameless guy possibly be? There's been zero clue that you've been hanging out with anyone."

I sure as hell couldn't tell her about the society, so I gave my friends the most innocent look I could muster up. "It's a mystery."

"Oh, you're going to play it that way, huh?" Gabby teased. "That's fine. We'll find out."

"My first guess is that it's a football player." Leighton folded her arms in front of her, staring a hole right through me.

"Why would you think that?" I struggled to hide my grin.

"Oh, I'm right." Leighton laughed.

Everlee walked over to me then slowly circled. A creak in the floor above us made me cringe.

"Oh hell, he's still here!" Everlee squealed.

"Shhh! Don't terrify the poor guy. He's not used to a house full of girls. You can't just steamroll him," I pleaded with the best puppy-dog eyes I could manage.

"Tell you what. Give us the deets, then we will scatter like little mice running from the cats." Everlee's brows rose with her suggestion.

Leighton's nose scrunched up. "Mice? Eww, gross."

Teagan lifted her chin. "I don't know if I'm hurt or more curious about why you didn't tell us about the guy upstairs."

My heart dipped to my toes. "No one was around when we got home. I assumed you all were sleeping, then we made some food and fell asleep. We only decided to give a relationship a try last night. This is the first opportunity I've had to tell any of you."

Hurt flickered in Teagan's gaze. "I didn't even know you liked anyone. The last conversation we had was that you wanted to focus on classes." Her doe eyes widened. "Peter?" she croaked out.

She might as well have punched me in the face with her guess. "Hell no. Besides, he went back to the East Coast. He won't bother me anymore." I sure as hell couldn't tell the girls he was dead. Although it comforted me, it would freak them out and they'd turn Jagger in. Not that there was any proof, but I didn't want to put Jag in that position.

"Teagan, I did mention to you that there was someone. It's just . . . Well . . . the guy upstairs is my . . ." I pinched the bridge of my nose, steadying my overzealous nerves. If I was going to tell them, I needed to start with the worst part. Dropping my hand, I bit my lip as my attention bounced between the girls, and I silently begged them not to judge me.

"You've not talked about anyone, Ari." Teagan slapped her palm over her mouth. I wasn't sure why she didn't attempt to cover her mistake.

My lips pursed together with Teagan's slip.

"Ari? Who the hell is Ari?" Gabby asked, confused.

I shot daggers at my best friend. Was she intentionally outing me because I hadn't told her about Jagger? Furious that she didn't even attempt to cover up the name, I folded my arms in front of me.

"If you ladies have a few minutes, I can explain things. Teagan, try to keep your mouth shut, will ya?" With that, I turned around and ran back upstairs. I burst through the door, startling the shit out of Jagger, who was sitting on the edge of my bed.

"They know you're here. I'm going to talk to them. Are you okay joining me?"

Jagger stood, his shoulders tight with stress. "I'm sorry I laughed too loud."

"They figured it out last night, I think. All four were waiting for me when I went downstairs."

"Fuck." Jag stared at the floor and placed his hand on his hip.

"I'm pissed at Teagan, but we might as well get it over with. It's Samantha and Dad that don't need to know for a while." I reached out to him.

"Uncle Gunner knows you're alive, too. But he won't say anything. I trust him with my life and yours." Jag slipped his arm around my waist and pulled me against his body. "Remember that I love you. The people who love and care about us will be cool about the situation."

I gulped, hoping he was right. "Okay. Let's go. Just smile and look hot."

"I know the girls, Ari. It's going to be all right." He rubbed my back as he talked.

"Shit. I forgot about that. Maybe it will work in our favor."

"Can't say for sure, but I've never had a problem with them." Jag placed a sweet kiss on my forehead. "If we're going to do this, we need to get a move on it. Classes await."

I blew out a big breath. "Let's go then." Leading Jagger out of my room and downstairs, we stood before my friends. Four shocked faces stared at us.

"You all know my boyfriend as Jagger Whitlock. To me, he's the love of my life and . . . and my stepbrother."

Everlee slapped her hands over her eyes and peeked between her fingers. "Holy shit. Stepbrother?"

Teagan's mouth nearly hit the floor. "Ari, you said he was dead."

"Who the hell is Ari?" Leighton asked, frustrated.

I glanced at Jagger, who remained quiet.

"I am. Why don't we sit down, and I'll explain what's happened over the last few weeks."

"Oh, I gotta hear this, Phoebe, Ari, whoever you are. You've got some serious 'splaining to do." Everlee spun on her heel and plopped into the recliner.

"What she said," Gabby added before she and Leighton sat on the couch.

Teagan remained standing, her arms protectively folded over her chest.

Jagger and I walked around the furniture and stood near the fireplace.

"I didn't mean to keep any secrets. As I said, it was only last night that we talked."

Jagger squeezed my hand, encouraging me.

"I'm sure you all remember that my house burned down. What I didn't share was that my stepbrother didn't make it out alive. Or so we were told by our parents. For the last four years, we both thought each other had died in the fire."

"What the hell? Why?" Gabby asked.

"We don't know," Jagger replied, finally speaking up. "It's one reason we want to keep our relationship quiet for a while. Clearly, we weren't trying to hide anything from you or I wouldn't have stayed the night with Ari."

Nice save, Jag.

"I guess that's true." Teagan huffed then plunked down on the couch. "I'm sorry I blurted out your real name." She glanced at me, sincerity written all over her face.

"So, you're not Phoebe?" Gabby asked, her forehead creasing.

"My real name is Ariana Ellison. After the fire, my father

changed my name to protect me from scrutiny and reporters. My father is Theodore Ellison."

Shocked mutters filled the room.

"Theo is my stepdad. He married my mom when Ariana and I were nine and ten."

"Oh, that's juicy. So how long have you two been hooking up?" Everlee asked, sitting upright in her seat.

I looked at Jag, and he gave me a little nod. "Since we were teenagers. Then the fire ripped us apart. We have a lot of questions ourselves, and I'm sorry we can't answer much else."

"Ari only learned I was alive and at Whitmore a few days ago. Maybe a week. Then we talked last night and decided we would give us another chance."

"This is blowing my damn mind," Leighton said, staring at us as if we were ghosts.

We were.

"So, you two are a couple and keeping it from your parents. What about at school?"

I looked at Jag, giving him the lead on that. We hadn't talked about it yet.

"I highly doubt anyone will run and tell our parents we're together." Jagger's expression filled with adoration as he looked at me. "A part of me wants all the fuckers that want to date her to know she's mine, but I think it's best if we kept it between us for now. We need to figure out the reason we were separated from each other."

The girls nodded, and Everlee chewed on her thumbnail. "I feel like there's some shady shit going down with your parents. I won't say a word. Besides, it's not my place to announce to the world that you two are a thing. As far as I'm concerned, I think it's hot that you both couldn't keep your paws off each other since you were kids." She winked at me.

"Good thing Jagger and I never hooked up," Leighton said, slapping her palms on the furniture. "Talk about awkward."

The group laughed, and I was grateful Leighton broke up the tension.

"I'm sorry we took you by surprise. I love you all so much, and I'll admit I was scared shitless to tell you that Jagger is my stepbrother. Some people will have a problem with it."

"Fuck them," Gabby said. "It's not like you're blood related. I think it's sweet that you two knew you were right for each other even as youngins."

"Exactly," Teagan finally said. "It's no one's business. I do have a question though."

"Yeah?" I braced myself for her harsh words.

"Jagger, do you have a twin?"

Laughter filled the house, and I leaned against him. "If he did, I'd claim both of them. Can you imagine how much fun that would be?"

"I don't share," Jagger growled.

Once we settled down, Everlee looked at Teagan. "How long have you known her real name?"

Teagan's gaze flitted from Everlee to me. "A few weeks."

I mentally willed her not to bring up Peter again. To my relief, she didn't share that secret.

"I have to get to class, but are we all okay?" I shifted my weight from one leg to the other, still anxious about telling them about Jagger. Once they had time to think about what we'd said, I feared they might change their minds about accepting us.

"Nope. I'm good," Everlee said. "I'm glad you're getting laid." She snickered.

"I'm happy for both of you," Gabby said. "I couldn't care less if you're stepsiblings."

"Same," Leighton responded.

I looked at my best friend and waited for her to say something. "I won't lie, the parental units have me questioning everything they told me."

"I get that. As far as you two together, it's cool. I'm glad you found each other again. It was clear that Ari wasn't going to move on from you, Jagger," Teagan said.

Jagger slid his arm around my waist. "I was having the same problem." He kissed the side of my head.

"I gotta go. I'll see you all after football practice."

"Jagger, will you be here tonight?" Everlee asked. "If so, we can order some pizza, but we'll need extra."

"If it's cool with Ari, I'll be here."

"Awesome. Maybe we can chat about making an intro to some of your friends." Everlee wiggled her brows at him.

"I'll take that too, please," Gabby and Leighton chimed in.

My gaze drifted to Teagan, who remained unusually quiet about introductions to some more of the football players. *Hmm. I'm not the only one keeping secrets.*

Chapter Thirty

Jagger

I slept better than I had since I'd lost Ari. Sharing a bed with her had provided a sense of peace I'd been chasing for years. Hopefully, it would help my performance on the field, too.

Ari's beautiful smile swirled through my mind's eye as I slipped my shoulder pads on in the locker room.

"You ready to kick some ass?" Quinn asked while he suited up.

"Hell yeah. We're on a streak. I can't be the one that screws that up." I shot him a mischievous grin.

"I know that look, dude. You're itching for trouble." Quinn sighed. "Don't get caught if you're going to play dirty."

"Don't even think about it, Jagger," Kane said from behind me. "Scouts are in the stands. Don't risk going pro because you still have beef with Cowling from last year."

I smirked. "Me? Have a problem with some prick that cheated and took my knee out the last game of the season? Nah."

"I'm not kidding, Jagger. Keep your personal problems off the field. It's not just you out there. We're a team. You cheat and it affects all of us." His gaze darkened. "We're brothers on and off the field."

My anger simmered down. Kane was right whether I liked it or not. We were tied together with the team and the society, and I had more to think about than just myself. I had them, and now Ari. She gave me a reason to keep my nose clean and feed the beast inside another way. Besides, she didn't know it yet, but I planned to knock her up when we graduated and I got a pro deal. My cock twitched at the thought of cuming inside her.

"I get it, man. I'll keep my nose clean."

"Good. Cowling isn't worth your career." Kane tugged on his jersey over his pads.

"Hmm. That was different." Quinn's brow arched at me.

"What do you mean?"

"You normally don't chill out that damn fast. No offense, but you're a hothead, man. Maybe the extra activities are helping." Quinn quirked a brow at me.

Quinn didn't have to say the society. I knew exactly what he meant.

"Probably. Getting laid is good stress management." I chuckled then straightened my pads and grabbed my helmet as my mind drifted to Ari soaped up and soaking wet in her shower this morning. I couldn't wait to celebrate another win later and get balls deep in her tonight.

The sound of Coach's whistle shrilled over the chatter. "Listen up!"

We all gathered around him, ready for our orders. "There are scouts in the stands, so let's show them what each of you have to offer." Coach continued to discuss plays and the strengths and weaknesses of the opposing team, The Wolves. I listened intently, exhilaration pulsing through every fiber of my being. I was itching to get the game rolling.

Twenty minutes later, I took my position on the field, ready. I tuned out the announcer and the fact that Ari was cheering in the stands. Teagan had given Ari a hard time for immediately accepting my invitation to the football game, but the girls had been cool about it. Now, Ari had a reason to be there and learn the game. As smart as she was, I was sure she'd catch on fast. My bet was that she'd fall in love with it too. At least I hoped so. If I made it to the NFL, she would be right by my side.

I spotted Cowling on the defensive line. He shot me a nasty grin, and I ignored him. If he pulled anything with me, I was ready, but I wouldn't step out of line . . . at least not on the field.

Focusing, I waited for Kane to make the pre-snap call. "White eighty! White eighty! Hut, hut, hut!"

Keeping an eye on the defense, especially Cowling, I zigzagged my way down the field, attempting to stay open, but these guys were on me tighter than a fly on shit. Kane got sacked on the first play.

Irritated didn't even begin to explain my mood. Our teams lined back up, and Kane called the play. Instead of throwing it, he tucked it under his arm and ran the ball, gaining us a first down. Coach would be pissed as hell that Kane took that risk. We couldn't afford for him to get hurt.

The fans cheered and screamed as Kane outmaneuvered the defense and sailed the ball down the left side of the field. I managed to shake Cowling, who was hot on my heels, then jumped for the reception. It landed right in my greedy hands. The second my feet touched the turf, I booked ass another forty yards before I was tackled by two big motherfuckers.

Quinn and Anderson jogged toward me. "That was sick, man. You good?" Anderson reached out to help me up.

"Yeah. Thanks."

"Got your back on and off the field," Anderson said.

Even though I hadn't talked to him about Ari after I revealed myself to her, he'd been cool and left her alone. I appreciated his cooperation. It would have been ugly if he hadn't backed off.

"QB's going to change up the next play," Quinn said under his breath. He clued us in before we lined up.

My fingers and toes tingled with anticipation as I waited for Kane to make his throw. When Quinn caught the ball, I barreled down the middle and protected him against the fuckers closing in on him at high speed.

The cheers from the stands were nearly deafening as Quinn scored the game's first touchdown. Pumped, I hurried to him and slapped him on the back.

"Do that a few more times and we'll be in good shape."

He set the ball down as more of our guys congratulated him.

I took a quick peek at my girl front and center in the stands, her smile lighting up her beautiful face.

"Yo, Jag. Focus. What the hell are you staring at?" Quinn asked.

Anderson chuckled. "One of the girls in the stands, I'm sure."

I nearly groaned with relief that Anderson didn't mention which one. Ari and I wanted to go public when we thought it was safe.

"She been to the society?" Quinn asked.

"Yup," Anderson said.

"Can we talk about pussy another time? We have a game to win," I reminded both of them.

"That's what after-parties and the society are for," Quinn added.

The guys and I jogged off the field, and I glanced at Ari again. Her eyes were trained in my direction, watching me on the field. For some reason, it made me feel powerful.

From the sidelines, I groaned as our defense failed us hard. Coach whipped his clipboard on the ground, swearing up a storm as the Wolves scored a touchdown on their second down. This game would be a bitch, so I had to focus and force Ari out of my head.

The first half of the game was intense, as each team continued to play hard, keeping the score neck and neck. At this rate, the winner would only be a matter of who had last possession.

The halftime whistle blew, and we jogged off the field. My ass needed a break and some water, but my mind spun with multiple possible plays.

When we reached the locker room, Coach ripped us a new one.

"Who the fuck are you? I must have the wrong team today because you're making stupid mistakes and handing the win to the Wolves." He shook his head and placed his hands on his hips as he paced before us.

"Coach." It probably wasn't the best time, but it was my only chance. "Permission to speak?"

Coach knew I never opened my mouth during a game unless necessary.

"What is it Whitlock?"

"While on the sidelines, I noticed that their number eighty-three and sixty-four stick together like construction glue. If we separate them, we break up their power couple." I continued to share my observations with the team.

Coach's eyes narrowed, then he rubbed his chin. "I caught the same, Whitlock. Let's try a few different plays and see if we can get some momentum."

Coach reviewed some new plays with us before he set the packages of bottled waters on the floor for us. It was up to us to go get one.

The second half was hella better than the first, and we walked off the field with a fourteen-point win. Although I'd expected hell from Cowling, he didn't mess with me. He trash-talked, but I ignored it by reminding myself that the love of my life was cheering for me.

I headed to the locker room with the rest of the team.

"Whitlock!" Coach called.

"Yeah?" I asked, approaching him.

"Damn good observations today. You played a great game." He slapped me on the back. "Seems like the new bed is improving your form too."

Before I could stop, my lips curled up into a big grin. "Yeah. Her bed is great."

Coach caught what I said. "Stay out of trouble, Jagger. Don't risk your chance at getting a contract over some pussy."

"She's more than that, but thanks for the warning." Truthfully, I didn't appreciate his words. It wasn't his damn business where I was putting my dick, but I knew better than to tell him that.

The rest of the team had hit the showers, leaving only a few stragglers behind.

"I appreciate everything you've done for me. Don't think I'll fuck it up. I won't." I wanted to point out that he'd just said my playing was stronger this game: case and point.

"Go wash up. You can't see her smelling like ass." He gave me a lopsided smile.

Laughing, I walked away, then I realized that I had forgotten to tell him to thank his wife for the sheets and bedspread. I turned toward him, walking backward. "Hey, Coach! I wanted to—" My body jerked back. "What the fuck?" As blood spurted from my left shoulder, my life played before me in slow motion. Confused, I looked at Coach. The smile slipped off his face and his eyes widened.

"Whitlock!" Coach bolted in my direction, the other coaches right behind him.

I slapped a palm over my wound, staring at the blood trickling down my hand and arm. Reality flickered in and out as my world blurred, then it faded to black.

Chapter Thirty-One

Ariana

I paced the hospital hall, pleading with the universe to save Jagger. He couldn't die. I just found him again. My head throbbed, and my swollen eyes burned from crying. Blowing out a shaky breath, I tried to inhale past the crushing agony in the center of my chest but I couldn't.

I stared at the waiting room with shoulder to shoulder football players and several of the cheerleaders. Coach was making rounds and talking to his team. He glanced up and made his way into the hall, joining me.

He pushed up the sleeves of his burgundy sweatshirt, his expression filled with concern. "He's strong, Ariana."

Since Coach had never met me, I used my real name to introduce myself. A part of me wanted to announce to the world that I wasn't Phoebe Jenkins but thought better of it. My boyfriend had been shot in the shoulder in a wide-open space with people around. It was too risky.

"I hope so. I don't understand how it happened." I did, kind of, but I couldn't admit that to Coach.

"How long have you known Jagger?"

Which answer should I give him? "We reconnected recently." Maybe that response would appease him, but it was also vague enough. The last thing I needed was for him to say something to Samantha.

"I contacted his parents. They should be here soon."

Shit! I'd been so terrified that he would die that the thought of calling Dad never crossed my mind. I had the support of my friends. I didn't need his kind of support that was filled with lies and half-truths.

"Thanks."

"When he pulls through surgery, he'll need to understand that he's out for most of the season, if not all of it. We'll have to see what recovery looks like. A shot to the shoulder could have killed him. Thank God the ambulance was still on standby after the game."

"I think he would have bled out if the EMTs hadn't acted fast." I shuddered at the idea. It had freaked me the hell out when I saw Jagger unconscious and bleeding all over the side of the football field.

"Yeah. We would have lost him. But something gives me the feeling that you're what he'll be holding onto."

I could feel the flush creep up my neck and cheeks, betraying any lie on the tip of my tongue.

"Ah, you're the girl he mentioned." Coach rubbed his lightly stubbled jaw. "Support Jagger the best you can. He'll need you to help him stay positive."

"I will. I'll take care of him when he's released from the hospital, too." My stomach flip-flopped with the possibility that he wouldn't make it home. Instead, I would be attending his funeral for real. I wrangled the negative thoughts and reined them in. There was no use entertaining any ideas except that Jag would live.

"Do you think his shot at the NFL is over?" An ache spread through my chest.

"I sure as hell hope not, but I'm no doctor. I have no idea what the damage is in his shoulder."

I blanched as nausea bubbled up inside me. "That would destroy him. He loves football. It's his entire life."

"I know. It's also kept him out of trouble. I'm not sure what he's lived through, but it's clear that it haunts him. The field is a good place for him to work out his aggression."

At least I understood that Jagger had never confided in Coach about his past. "I have no idea what to expect with his recovery, but I'll support him any way I can."

"I'm sure he'll appreciate it." Coach stared through the window into the recovery room. "The cops are here. I should answer some questions for them. I'll be around if you need anything, though."

"Thanks." I followed Coach and spotted Teagan, Everlee, Leighton, and Gabby. The girls refused to leave me alone at the hospital, and I was grateful for them.

I sank into a chair beside Teagan and leaned my head on her shoulder.

"Are you hanging in there?" Teagan asked as she slipped her arm around me.

I nervously picked at a hangnail on my finger. "No. Not even close."

"Me either, but I'm not in love with Jagger. I can't imagine how awful it is for you. I'm glad you were able to catch a ride with Anderson."

I glanced in Anderson's direction, who was chatting with some of his teammates. "I'm not even sure the doctor will tell us anything."

"Babe. You're his sister. You can see him and talk to the doctor until his parents arrive."

I straightened, hope blooming inside my chest. "Shit. I hadn't even thought of that."

"Just leave the step part off." Teagan tilted her head.

Seconds later, a man in green scrubs strolled in. His light-brown hair was threaded with grey streaks, and dark circles shaded his deep brown eyes.

"I'm looking for the family of Jagger Whitlock."

Every nerve ending inside me stood on high alert as I waited for the news that would shatter my heart or stitch it back together.

Coach stepped forward. "I'm his football coach. His parents are on the way, but it will be a few hours. Are you able to at least tell us if he survived through surgery."

"I'm Dr. Hewitt. He did pull through surgery."

The entire waiting room cheered and hugged.

"But there's more, and I can't disclose it to anyone outside of the family."

An anxious fluttery feeling descended on me and my palms turned clammy. I wiped them on my jeaned thigh.

Teagan nudged me, and I shot out of my chair.

Forcing down the fear that clawed up my throat, I blurted. "I'm his sister."

Every football player and cheerleader stared at me with their mouths hanging open.

"Your name?"

I gulped. "Ariana."

The doctor motioned for me to join him. Whispers and sideways glances from the others stirred to life. I looked at Teagan.

"Go. I'll deal with the gossip." She squeezed my hand.

"We've got this. Between the four of us, we'll shut the rumors down fast," Gabby added.

Everlee and Leighton nodded in agreement.

"Thanks. Love you guys."

I hurried to the doctor, not missing the frown of confusion that marred Coach's features.

Pausing, I turned and approached Coach. I pushed up on my tiptoes and whispered, "I'm his stepsister, but the doctor doesn't need to know."

Understanding coasted over Coach's face. "Keep me posted,

please." He patted my back, then I maneuvered through the crowd and joined the doctor in the hall.

"It seems that a lot of people care about Jagger," Dr. Hewitt said, glancing over his shoulder before he led me to the elevator.

"Yeah. He's a hell of a football player, and a good guy." I pursed my lips together. "Can you tell me anything else now that we're not around the team?"

The elevator ping alerted us it had arrived, and the doctor held the door open as we both stepped in. He pushed the fourth-floor button as the doors whooshed closed.

"He's stable for now, but he's not out of the woods. Jagger has to make it another twenty-four hours. Once he does, he should be on a long road to recovery. The bullet went through his shoulder, so that was a positive. However, it clipped the bone, so we had to remove some of the splinters. There's a risk of infection and a possibility that when he wakes up, shock might set in. During the surgery, we pumped him full of pain meds, so he'll be loopy for a while."

I attempted to digest the information. "I still can't believe he got shot at a football game."

The doctor's expression softened. "Since he was the only person shot, I'm guessing it was personal instead of a mass shooter. There were still plenty of people around, but from what the cops said, only one bullet was fired. They found the casing."

I couldn't feel much beneath the panic, shock, and nerves that kept my adrenaline spiked.

The elevator doors opened, and the doctor walked me past the nurse's station and to room 412. "Here you go."

"Thank you for saving him." Tears welled in my eyes. "Jagger and I are close, and I'm not sure what I'd do if I lost him."

Dr. Hewitt squeezed my shoulder. "He'll need you, so it's good to know he has friends and family to support him." He strolled over to a nurse in the hall and gave me a small wave.

A messy lump of emotion clogged my throat. I had no idea what to expect. I hadn't ever stepped foot inside an ICU room before.

From what the doctor said, Jagger was still sleeping, so there was no need to knock. I squared my shoulders, then pushed the door open and entered. A wail escaped me, and I covered my mouth with my hand, muffling my cries.

Jagger's face was pale, and he was hooked up to a heart monitor and an IV with two bags. His left shoulder was bandaged. Closing my eyes against the fear that he wouldn't live, I tried to still the dark thoughts rolling into my mind and focused on his chest's gentle rise and fall. *I can do this.*

Shaking, I walked to the other side of his bed and sat in the ugly green chair. "Hi, baby. It's Ari. I'm here." I took his hand and rubbed the back of it with my thumb. I'd heard if you talked to a patient when they were unconscious, they could still hear you. I wasn't sure if the same principle applied to surgery patients, but I wanted him to know that he wasn't alone.

"Almost the entire football team and several cheerleaders are in the waiting area. They're terrified and talking about the shooting. The cops talked to your coach, but from the little I overheard, the police have zero leads on the shooter. I have a feeling I know who it is. You're safe in the hospital, though. If I have to, I'll ask security to guard your room. Maybe that's not a bad idea. I have no clue what Psycho looks like." I gulped, realizing I was rambling about being in danger. That shit wouldn't help Jagger get better.

"I love you, Jag. I always have. You're my first and last love. You have to make it through this. I can't lose you again. Not after we just found each other." As hard as I tried to hold back the tears, I couldn't. They flowed freely down my cheeks. I stood, brushed Jag's dark hair from his forehead, and placed a kiss against his cool skin. "By the way, the parents will be here soon. I wish you were awake to help me talk to them, but I've got this, right?"

Realizing that I needed to make up a story about why I was next to my stepbrother, I wondered if I had enough mental energy to do so. It might be easier to tell them the truth. Besides, they owed us answers. Until then, I no longer trusted either of them.

Anger and anxiety swirled in my chest. They had a hell of a lot to explain.

"Ari?" Jag's voice was deep and throaty. "Ice."

"Baby, you're awake." I frantically looked around and spotted a yellow pitcher on his nightstand. "Hang on. Don't try to talk yet." I rushed to the other side of his bed, and grabbed an ice chip. "Open up, baby."

His lips parted enough for me to slip the ice into his mouth. He swallowed, his eyes glassy and heavy from the pain medications.

"Love you too." He looked at me, a loopy smile easing into place. "Glad you're here."

"Where else would I be, Jag?"

The creak of the door reached my ears, and I turned around.

"Ariana?"

Chapter Thirty-Two

Ariana

Surprise threaded Samantha's tone as she strolled into the room, looking disheveled and exhausted. Her blue eyes were rimmed with red and bloodshot.

Dad was right behind her, wearing a grim expression.

"Sup, Mom? Theo?" Jagger asked, grinning. "Long time no see."

As his heart rate climbed, I set the pitcher of ice chips down and focused on Jagger's monitor.

"Maybe you shouldn't be here right now," I said, standing between Samantha and Jagger. "It's clear that you're upsetting him. He needs to stay calm. He's not out of the woods yet," I explained in a hushed tone. I glanced over my shoulder. Jagger had closed his eyes, and I wondered if he'd drifted off to sleep again.

"Maybe we should take this somewhere else and let him rest." My attention landed on my dad. He looked like hell too.

"I think Ari has a good idea. We should talk, and I'd rather not do it front of Jagger while he's recovering," Samantha said in a hushed tone. "I need my son to get better." Tears streamed down her cheeks, and she quickly wiped them away.

Quietly, we slipped into the hall, and I closed the door behind me. Since I wouldn't be there, I couldn't monitor who entered and left Jagger's room. That didn't settle well with me. Whoever the shooter was, I had a feeling he was still around. I walked to the nurse's station and flashed the nurse on duty a charming smile.

"Hi. Jagger Whitlock is in 412. I would like to ask that no visitors are allowed until I return. There's some business I need to attend to."

"He's fresh out of surgery and in the ICU, so other than family, he can't have any visitors for a few days."

My shoulders sagged with relief. "Thank you. I'll be back shortly."

I turned to see Dad and Samantha standing behind me.

"Miss, what's your name?"

Shooting a look at the parents, I smiled. "Ariana. I'm Jagger's sister."

"Excellent. Thank you."

My gaze narrowed as I turned to Samantha and Dad again. "Let's get this over with." My tone was steely but not near as cold as my heart felt toward them.

Leading the way, I found a small waiting room. To my surprise, it was empty, which worked for us. Dad and Samantha sank into a couple chairs, and I closed the door.

"What are you doing here, Ariana?" Samantha asked, her voice cracking with worry.

I folded my arms across my chest. "Attending Whitmore."

The color drained from Samantha's cheeks, and a sheepish expression ghosted Dad's face.

"You didn't tell her?" I asked, incredulous that he kept that information from his wife.

"I didn't see any need to upset her at the time." Dad reached for Samantha's hand. "I couldn't stop Ari from moving. She received a full scholarship and had saved money from her job back east."

Samantha tucked her blonde hair behind her ear, staring at me. "Impressive. I always knew you were a bright girl with a big future."

"Thanks. I was bound and determine to come home. Picture my shock when I realized that Jagger not only was still breathing but played football at the same college."

Dad scrubbed his face, exhausted. Lies would do that to you—suffocate and cut you off from those who loved you. I was living proof.

"Imagine Jagger's surprise when he learned that I was alive, too."

The tension in the room escalated at breakneck speeds. "No more lies. We can get all of this out in the open."

"I need to know about my son first." Samantha wrung her fingers in her lap.

"Well, you saw him, so you realize it's bad. He has to make it through the next twenty-four hours. Any added stress or bullshit isn't allowed anywhere near him. Got it?" I placed my hands on my hips. I wasn't playing with them. I might be Theo's daughter, but they'd disrespected me with their deceit. They had to play by my rules if they wanted to know about Jag.

"What happened?" Dad asked.

I rocked from one foot to the other, attempting to ease my fear concerning Jagger. "The game was over, and most people had cleared the stands and field. There were about twenty still standing on the sidelines. I was walking toward Jagger to congratulate him on their win." Sweat beaded on my forehead and slicked between my breasts, my pulse whizzing with agony as I relived the moment that nearly stole Jagger from me. "We never heard the gunfire. Jagger was laughing with Coach one second, then his body jerked backward and blood seeped out of his shoulder. He grabbed the wound right before he dropped to the ground. The EMTs were still there. If they hadn't been . . ." I gulped air and tried calming my tattered heartbeat. I could feel what I'd witnessed churn in my stomach.

"Shot?" A sob shredded Samantha's throat as she stared down at the floor.

Confused, I studied Dad. "Whoever called didn't tell you?"

"They wouldn't tell us what happened, Ari. All the doctors said was that he'd been hurt at a game and was in surgery." His eyes misted over. "And that we needed to get here quickly."

He slipped an arm around Samantha.

"Damn. I didn't realize. I figured you had the details before you drove down." Compassion welled inside my chest. "I'm sorry. I know there's a lot of unanswered questions, but we have to be strong for Jagger. He knows that you both lied to him when you told him I died in the fire."

Samantha straightened. "It was to protect you both." Her eyes widened. "Not to mention that you are brother and sister and can't have a romantic relationship. What would people say if they found out? Your father's company could have suffered. It was in everyone's best interest, Ariana."

"Step," I said firmly, popping my p. "No blood relation."

"I love you both with all my heart, but . . . you and Jagger grew up together. It's wrong." Her mouth pursed, and I suspected her asshole had too.

Taken off guard by Samantha's confession, I wondered if Dad felt the same. "Dad? Get it out. Say whatever you need to say."

"I hadn't known about you and Jagger for a long time. Jagger was missing for years, so I assumed it was over between you two. He thought you died, then three days later, he was gone."

My jaw clenched, recalling the horrible things Jagger had told me he was forced to do. "The same time Crimson let me go."

"It was devastating for us, too, Ariana." Dad shifted in the orange plastic chair and folded his arms in front of his chest. "I figured the academy and a name change would keep you safe. It did. If Crimson was looking for you, she never found you again."

My hands fisted. "You let me think that Jagger had died in the fire," I snapped, my tone laced with hatred as I ground out each word. "He thought he had lost me, too. It must have been convenient to stand behind that lie since our relationship was an abomination."

"I never said that," Dad said, raising his voice. "My job was to keep you safe and I failed. When you were taken, it devastated me. You're my only daughter, and all I could think was that somehow, I'd put you in danger. I racked my brain to see how I'd let you slip through my fingers. Once I searched through your social media and laptop . . . that's when I found the emails between you and Jagger. How you snuck into his room when we were asleep." His cheeks burned red.

"Those private messages were pretty steamy, Dad. Serves you right for snooping."

Dad stood at his full height, looming over me. At forty-nine, he was in excellent shape. His black polo stretched across his broad shoulders, and his biceps bulged as he rubbed his palms together. When Dad was stressed, he rubbed his hands together as if the friction soothed his nerves. "If you ever have kids of your own, whether it's with Jagger or another man, you'll understand how difficult it is to make the right decision. Samantha and I talked it over, and we agreed that keeping you apart was for your own safety."

"It wasn't a coincidence that Crimson released you and Jagger was taken," Samantha said. "We searched for him for two years. Not one day passed that we didn't scour heaven and earth. We even hired Westbrook Security and worked with Pierce and Sutton Westbrook. Each time there was a lead, Jagger would disappear again."

"Then your brother, Gunner, found him," I added.

"Yes, thank God. After Gunner said that Jag was with him safe and sound, I puked. The years had been hell, and with the good news, my body rid itself of the fear, I guess." She paused, and I wondered if she was reliving that phone call with her brother. "I was so naïve thinking that Jagger would welcome me with open arms." Her bitter laugh filled the room. "We spoke once, then he said that he would reach out when he was ready. A week went by, then another. I called him and left a voicemail every day for a month, but he never reached out to me. I thought Gunner had brought my son home, but he wasn't the same boy who had been taken. His eyes were haunted, tortured. Since the night of the fire, I lost my boy. You lost your boyfriend, but I lost so much more."

I snorted, and Dad shot me a disapproving glance. Pressing my lips together, I swallowed my harsh response.

Samantha's expression pleaded with me. "You don't have to forgive us, Ari. We made some hard choices. Theo and I still have no idea who took Jagger or why. The only reason we learned about Crimson was because she told you her name. I'm still shocked she let you go."

"Me too, but Jagger wasn't. I was a way to get to him. That's all I know." I rolled my head and popped my neck, then I blew out a breath. "The fact is that you lied to us. Maybe you had a say in our relationship when we were kids, but we're grown now. You can't keep us away from each other. A part of me understands that you were trying to keep me safe, Dad. The other part . . . I'm not sure I can ever forgive either of you for the lies you told Jagger and me. For four years, I thought I murdered him in the fire. Do you have any idea how heavy that grief is?"

"The fire wasn't your fault, Ari." Dad's tone was gentle.

"It doesn't matter. You and Samantha let me think that I could go to prison if anyone found out the truth. That's some twisted shit. Jagger agrees. What he chooses to do concerning his relationships with the both of you, I have no idea. I'll support him either way. For me, we're going to be there for Jagger and help him recover. I'll be respectful, but once he's better, I'm done with both of you. What you did was selfish and coldhearted. Neither of you are the people I thought you were."

Without another word, I spun on my heel, flung the door open, and marched my ass back to my boyfriend's room. Fuck Theo and Samantha. I sucked in a deep breath, managing the tumultuous whirlwind of anger before I joined Jagger again. Plastering a smile on my face, I walked in. His soft snore reached my ears, and I sighed with relief. That would be the only time I planned to leave him, and it had scared the shit out of me. If someone took a shot at him in broad daylight, they were smart enough to sneak in and visit him at the hospital.

My heart hammered against my ribs as I sat beside his bed and watched him sleep. I wasn't sure if God existed, but I silently prayed to keep Jag alive and safe. But even I knew that hope was a dangerous drug.

Chapter Thirty-Three

Ariana

"How's that?" I fluffed Jagger's pillows behind him, then rolled over the tray on wheels. "The girls made you lasagna." I smiled at him. "After you eat, take your meds." I grabbed the blanket from the end of my bed and covered him. "At least the bathroom is nearby."

Jagger's stomach growled. "This looks amazing. Tell them thanks."

"As long as you're not dizzy, we can go downstairs. You're not stuck up here. I just don't want you to tumble like a deflated basketball." I cringed. "That wouldn't be good."

"No shit. I'd probably rip open the stitches." He picked up his fork and cut a healthy bite of lasagna that he popped into his mouth, moaning. "So much better than hospital food."

"Hey! Didn't the doctor say no sex until he was healed?" Everlee called up the stairs and into my bedroom.

"He said no such thing. My shoulder is healing, there's nothing wrong with my dick!" Jag yelled.

Giggles filled the house, and my heart warmed. "Like we would get busy with the door open anyway." I rolled my eyes, grateful for the lightheartedness. The girls had been phenomenal the week I'd stayed at the hospital with Jagger. Once he had cleared the twenty-four hours, he demanded that the doctor reduce the pain meds. He said they made him loopy and he could barely form a complete sentence. Once he was on a lower dose, to my surprise, he confronted Samantha and Theo for lying to him about my death. He made it clear that they'd crossed a hard line and he wouldn't forgive them any time soon. Even though Samantha pleaded her case, it was disregarded. I had no idea how it would play out in the future, but Jagger and school were my focus.

"I need to get some homework done. If you doze off after your pain meds, then I'll go downstairs. Just text me when you wake up."

Jagger set his fork on the side of his plate. "Babe, I don't want you to fail this term. Please don't fall back in classes because of me."

I sat on the edge of my bed and placed my hand on his leg. "I'm not that far behind since Teagan brought me my books at the hospital. Some of the instructors record their lectures in case a student has an urgent need and can't attend classes. I worked on my assignments while you slept. Remember?"

He shook his head. "Not really. The pain meds seriously messed with my head."

"I'm glad you're almost off them and you're home. That's all that matters." I squeezed his thigh, refusing to talk about the elephant in the room. "Eat."

The faintest hint of his smile peeked out. "You know what happens when you're bossy, right?"

"No." I feigned total innocence, knowing full well where the conversation was headed.

He smirked. "You get spanked."

I carefully slipped off the bed, not wanting to jostle his shoulder. It was in a sling for at least a few weeks.

"Good luck with that." I stuck my tongue out at him, and he

reached out to grab me, but I easily dodged him. "Getting slow, old man."

He growled as he returned to his lasagna. "I have a place for that sassy mouth of yours. You wait until I can take your ass back to the society."

My core throbbed with longing for him to touch me. At least we could work around his shoulder, but it would be pretty vanilla until he healed. "Oh, I'm scared." I pretended to chew on my fingernails. "Tie me up, hurt me, fuck me senseless. Sounds good to me. Until then, Jagger Whitlock, I call the shots since I'll be the one riding you." I winked at him before I walked away and swished my hips a little extra for his enjoyment. "I need to shower." I closed the bedroom door, then disappeared into the bathroom.

"How's he doing?" Teagan asked, setting two plates full of lasagna on the table for us, then she sat in the chair across from me. It had been a week since I'd been able to spend any time with my bestie, and I missed her horribly.

"He's okay. It's Jagger, so he won't actually tell me how much pain he's in or if he's scared about his future in football. He starts physical therapy in a few weeks at least." I speared a bite of the hot square of deliciousness.

Over the next hour, I updated Teagan on Theo and Samantha. It didn't get past her that I referred to Dad as Theo.

"That's some heavy shit, Ari. It trumps the rumors at school for damn sure."

I sank back into my chair. "I don't even care what people are saying. Haters are gonna hate. But, I feel so betrayed. Not by the assholes at school, but by Samantha and Theo. I expected Theo to be the hard ass against mine and Jag's relationship, not Samantha. He still went along with the plan to lie to me about Jagger, though."

Teagan took a sip of her drink, the soda bubbles still fizzing.

"Just goes to show that people will continue to surprise the crap out of you even when you've known them for years." She poked at her food and eyed me.

"I'm so sorry, Teagan. The guilt of thinking that I'd murdered Jagger, then the shit show with Peter, it really messed me up. I never meant to hurt you. Ever."

"I know. It's why we're still talking. I am aware that you defend the people you love, and one of those people is me."

"I do love you. I'm an asshole for not telling you more often. After almost losing Jagger for a second time, I had a lot of time to reflect while sitting beside him in the hospital. I've taken our friendship for granted, and I never want to do that again. Teagan, you make my world a better place. I'm so, so fucking lucky to have you as my bestie."

Teagan's eyes welled with tears. "Same, bitch." She took my hand in her free one. "If you've ever doubted my loyalty, I hope my actions have proved how much you mean to me."

"They have. I have your back too. Always." I sniffled as tears streamed down my cheeks. "The last four years have been hell. I'm still trying to wrap my head around the fact that Jagger is alive and here."

"When you guys return to classes in person, are you ready to deal with the haters?" Worry flitted across my friend's face.

"What do I need to be prepared for?" I took a sip of my soda, wishing there were a couple of shots of vodka in it.

As if reading my mind, Teagan hopped up from the table and grabbed the bottle of Froggy B. She unscrewed the cap, and before I could block her, she poured an ample amount into my glass. "I'll help you with Jagger. You need to unwind. Besides, the girls will be back early tonight. They're skipping the after-party to hang out with you and Jagger."

"Really?" I slowly pivoted my attention to the clock on the wall over the sink. I snorted. "It's eleven in the morning and I'm drinking. What does that make me?"

Teagan laughed. "Tired, exhausted, scared, and in need of some serious chill time. We've got you and Jagger, babe. Drink up."

I wiped the moisture from my cheeks and blew out a big sigh. "Thank you, Teagan. I love you."

"Love you too." Teagan leaned back in her chair, studying me. "Ari?"

"Yeah?"

"Who shot Jagger? That shit wasn't an accident. Are you two in danger?"

And there it was. "I don't know how to answer that."

Chapter Thirty-Four

Jagger

"This is bullshit. What the fuck!" I yelled at the television, where we watched Whitmore and the Bulldogs play. I jumped off the couch and cradled my arm in my hand and started pacing the living room. "I should be out there."

"I know, baby. Soon. At least we have the house to ourselves this weekend since the game is in Arizona."

Bummed that Ari had to babysit me, I was still grateful she was here. The last three weeks would have sucked without her.

I ground my teeth, hating that my shoulder wasn't healing faster. "Hell, I can't even make love to you right. I have to lie there like a dead fish and let you do all the work."

Ari tried to hide her smile, but I caught it. "It doesn't bother me. Not being with you sucks harder than I do when your dick is in my mouth," she said, probably trying to lighten my foul mood.

It had been weeks since I'd set foot on campus or the football field, and I thought I would lose my ever-loving mind.

My phone buzzed against the living room table, and I snatched it up. I frowned at the screen. "Coach wants me to call him."

"Really?"

"Yeah. Hang on." I muted the television, still glued to the game as I called my mentor.

"What's wrong, Coach?" My entire body tensed and I smiled. "Of course, I'm watching. Ari is too." My face burned as I witnessed the Bulldogs run up the center of the field and score a touchdown, giving them a ten-point lead. I clenched and unclenched my fist, wishing it were around someone's fucking neck. "Why isn't our defense on them?" I asked Coach, then listened for a minute, my forehead creasing. "You're missing it. I know it's a different view on the field than the television, but I see this. If you can fix these two things, I think the guys can still pull off a win."

My soul lit up as Coach and I continued to talk. Earlier that week, he'd sent over tapes for me to study the Bulldogs and review plays. Even though I wasn't on the field, Coach did his best to keep me involved. At least I could help my team from Ari's living room.

The halftime whistle blew, and I wrapped up my conversation with Coach. I tossed my cell on the couch cushion and stared at the most beautiful girl on the planet. With her in my life, I knew I could power through anything.

"That was pretty awesome that Coach called." Ari beamed at me as I strolled over to her.

"He's a good guy. All that football talk got my cock all hard, though." I patted my crotch and gave her a wicked little grin. "It's halftime, so . . . get naked. I need to fuck that tight cunt of yours. Relieve some tension."

"Are you sure? If you get dizzy or lightheaded, you promise me you'll quit?"

I pressed my lips into a thin line. "Yeah." *Sure, because I would stop when I was balls deep inside her.*

I stepped back and watched as Ari gracefully rose to her feet and began to undo each piece of clothing. I couldn't help but admire how her delicate body moved as she slowly revealed more and more of her naked flesh. Her nipples hardened with anticipation as she looked at me through her long eyelashes, and my breath caught in my throat.

"So beautiful," I whispered, lightly caressing the soft waves of her hair before undoing the zipper of my jeans. "Be a good girl and get on your knees." My cock sprang free, and a wave of desire rushed through me as she eagerly parted her lips. I slowly slid into her warm depths until I was against the back of her throat, and pleasure flowed through me as I started thrusting in and out.

I sensed my body nearing the point of no return, so I immediately withdrew from her mouth and gazed eagerly into her eyes. "It's time to take you on a ride," I growled, gesturing for her to bend over the couch. As soon as she obeyed, I lightly bit into the soft flesh of her ass cheek and heard a shocked gasp escape her lips. Her arousal increased as my touch traveled down while I trailed hot kisses to the base of her back.

When I reached her soaking wet pussy, I ran my tongue over her folds. I moaned. It had been too long since I'd tasted and feasted on her pussy. I licked and sucked her until she was begging for more. I added my fingers to the mix, pushing them deeper and deeper into her. Ari writhed beneath me, her body shaking and her slick walls pulsing with pleasure.

Unable to take it any longer, I withdrew my hand and rubbed the tip of my cock against her entrance, coating it with her juices. I slid into her, sucking in a breath as her pussy clenched my shaft.

I grabbed her hip and pressed her against me. She shuddered and whimpered as I drove into her harder and harder.

Ari's moans reverberated through her throat and filled the air around us as I increased my tempo. Lost in the moment, I shifted my hand to her back. Her skin was hot under my fingertips as I slammed into her.

"Cum for me, Ari." I panted. "Cum all over my cock."

"Jagger, oh God, fuck me."

"You ready for me to cum inside you?" I braced myself against her to keep my balance. Then, I dipped my finger in her juices and pulled apart her ass cheek. Pushing against her entrance, I pumped a finger into her puckered hole and drove into her pussy with my cock.

"Fuck," Ari moaned. "That's it, baby." Her nails dug into the back of the couch while she screamed my name and shuddered beneath me.

Her pussy clenched my shaft, and I shuddered as I spilled my load deep inside her.

Catching my breath, I stepped back with a mischievous grin. "Turn around and sit."

Ari collapsed onto the couch cushion, her chest heaving and a big smile on her face.

"Spread those legs and let me see my cum on your pussy."

She obeyed, and her tongue darted over her bottom lip. "Do you know what good girls get?" I asked.

"No." She squirmed on the leather seat, innocently looking up at me.

"Touch yourself. Let me watch you get off."

"Are you sure?" she might have asked the question, but I could tell from her glossy eyes that she wanted more. If we were at the society, I would have given her a dual vibrator.

Ari's attention remained on me as she massaged her clit, my cum and her juices mixing as she continued. Her back arched off the couch, her full breasts calling my name. God, I wanted to cum all over them.

My dick twitched again, and I reached down and palmed it. "That's it, baby. Nice and slow."

Her gaze landed on me stroking myself and a small smile graced her face. "Come here." She motioned for me to straddle her, and I willingly did so.

Ari flicked her tongue across the head of my cock, then sucked me.

"Be my good girl and don't stop playing with yourself." She licked and worked my dick while she played with her pussy with her other hand. Jesus, I could get used to this.

Her breath hitched, and I knew she was close to another orgasm. I grabbed the back of the couch and fucked her mouth. "I don't know if I want to cum all over those glorious tits or in your cunt."

Ari's lips tightened around my shaft as she released again. Watching her cum for me sent me spiraling, and I pulled out and jacked off all over her tits.

I grinned at her. "How was that for a halftime show?" I chuckled as I backed away and hurried up the stairs to the bathroom. A minute later, I brought her a warm washcloth and gently wiped her pussy and tits clean. Nipping the inside of her thigh, I looked up at her. "I love you, Ari."

My heart lodged in my throat. I would move heaven and earth for her. That fact had tied me up in knots, but now I truly understood what it meant to put someone else first.

Chapter Thirty-Five

Jagger

Cheers and applause filled the field house as I walked in for the first visit after the shooting. I grinned as I made the rounds and hugged my friends. Anderson and Kane had dropped by Ari's place, but talking with all the guys hanging around was hard. I knew they had questions. So did I. As much as I loved being with Ari, I needed to see a few of my teammates to have some private conversations.

"Speech! Speech! Speech!" the team chanted.

It was one of the rare times in my life when I was a bit embarrassed. I raised my hand to quiet the room. "Thanks, guys. Man, I've missed being on the field with you more than you can imagine. I appreciate all the phone calls, texts, bad memes, and TikToks. It's kept me sane."

"Along with your sister!" a guy on the second string yelled. Shit, I didn't even know what his name was. He'd apparently lost his fucking mind, but I decided now was as good a time as any to quiet the bullshit rumors down.

"Stepsister. Ari said she was my sister in order to be able to talk to the doctor after . . . after I was shot." Sweat beaded on my forehead, and the room spun slightly. Thankfully, I had a wall to lean against. "Any of you fuckers even think about touching her, you'll regret it. I'm an asshole, and I'll always protect what's mine. Ariana Ellison is mine." My heated gaze swept the group then landed on Anderson. He tipped his chin up, then he cracked a smile at me. We were good. I would talk to him one-on-one later, but for now, we were both clear our friendship hadn't changed.

"What's it like fucking your stepsister?" the same guy asked.

Anderson cleared his throat and held up his finger, indicating for me to hang on before I lost my shit. Anderson walked to the back of the group, then a loud whack filled the area. The asshole guy's head bounced forward, and it took everything in me not to burst out laughing.

"Don't talk shit to an upperclassman or you'll be dealt with outside of the team." Anderson glared at him, and the team's chuckles echoed off the walls.

I rubbed my jaw, grinning. The poor asswipe had no idea what he was getting himself into. Hopefully, Anderson's warning sunk into his thick skull.

"Anyway. I won't be able to play until next season, but the doc says I'm healing nicely. I started physical therapy and it sucks almost as much as Coach making us run suicides." I laughed as Coach entered the locker room.

I'd already talked to him about returning, and he assured me we would work together over the summer. The important things were to stay focused and heal.

I intended to do precisely that.

"Thanks again for all the support." I tapped my fist against my heart.

Everyone clapped as I joined my friends.

"Dude, I hate to admit it, but it's sucked without you." Quinn patted my good shoulder. "We've got some society business to handle as well."

"I was able to talk Ari out of babysitting duty this afternoon. I was hoping to hang with you, Anderson, and Kane for a bit."

"You bet. We can fill you in on everything you've missed. Plus." Quinn leaned in. "Did they ever find the guy that took a shot at you?"

A trickle of fear crept down my chest. "No. It's another thing I wanted to talk to you guys about. I need help keeping an eye on Ari. I'm not sure she's safe."

Quinn staggered backward before he caught himself. "And everyone else around you?"

"It's about her and me. There's not a threat to anyone else as far as we can tell."

Quinn's eyes widened. "As far as you know. That's a gamble, dude."

"I get it, but think about it for a minute. One shot was fired. One bullet casing was found. No other shots. If it were about anyone else or a random shooting, I wouldn't have been the only one taken down." I slapped him on the back and hoped my reasoning calmed him. "Let's catch up at the society where we have some privacy."

"Yeah. Sounds good."

Memories of joining the brotherhood and fucking Ari returned front and center in my mind as I walked into the building and to the meeting room. That time, I wouldn't grab a mask and cloak. It was all about talking to my friends and asking them for help. I wasn't sure how much I needed to divulge, but the society had brought us all closer, and I trusted them. At least with most of my secrets.

The sound of my tennis shoes echoed off the walls, the only noise in the building. I reached the door, strolled into the room, and closed it behind me.

"About time, asshole." Anderson grinned at me and popped a potato chip in his mouth. "Hungry?" He held the bag out, but I declined.

Since Quinn and Kane weren't there yet, it was a perfect opportunity to chat with Anderson.

"Are we good? About Ari? I know you had a thing for her. I can't blame you." I flashed him a smile, then sat across the table from him and propped my feet on the corner.

"Yup. Gotta say that Ari seemed unimportant when you dropped, man. Nothing against Ari, I'm just saying the team and I were worried about you."

"I appreciate it. The whole thing has been difficult. It's why I wanted to talk to you guys. I trust you all with my life, and . . ." I rubbed the knots in the back of my neck, hoping to relieve some of the tension. "I'm concerned about Ari. I'm not sure she's safe either. We're both taking a chance still attending Whitmore."

Andersons' face fell. "You got in some deep shit, didn't you?"

I nodded. "Yeah. As much as I want to, I can't tell you guys everything. I can give some details, though. Enough for you all to keep an eye on Ari when I'm in classes or helping Coach with scouting our opponents."

"At least you're coming back. Honestly, I didn't think you would ever walk onto the field at all, so I'm glad he's keeping you busy. It probably helps you still feel involved and a part of the team," Anderson added.

The sound of the door opening broke up our conversation. I glanced over my shoulder at Kane and Quinn and the rest of the guys joining us.

"Good to see ya, Jag," Kane said, holding his fist out for me to bump.

"Good to be here. Is this place running okay without me?" I laughed as the others sat down.

"We're managing," Quinn smirked, grabbing his crotch. "I do love the variety the society has to offer. I'm not sure how I was selected, but there's no complaining here."

"Same," the guys said in unison.

"Me too. I just had no clue the first chick I would be with was Ari."

"I'm so damn confused. I thought her name was Phoebe." Quinn looked at the other two. "Didn't you?"

"That's part of the reason I'm here, to explain some shit."

"Then get started, we're listening," Kane said. He laced his fingers behind his head, his expectant gaze focused on me.

"Ari had to change her name for a while. Well, her dad changed it to protect her. She went by Phoebe Jenkins for several years, but I've always known her as Ariana Ellison. When I got shot, she revealed herself as Ariana and informed the hospital she was my sibling."

"Man, I wish you could have been a fly on the wall when she mentioned to the doc you two were related. Pretty sure everyone was shocked shitless. Especially those of us that knew you'd hooked up with her at the society," Quinn said.

I eyed Anderson. "Did you tell them?" Other than Anderson, I had no idea how they would have learned who I'd fucked.

"Chill. It's common knowledge who fucks who. It's all on the spreadsheet and was emailed out when you were in the hospital. The King Cobra had several guys wanting the same chick over and over, so this was the easiest way to handle it."

"I never got an email." My brow rose, and I questioned his honesty. In my gut, I knew that Anderson was loyal. I was just overly cautious after I took a bullet to my shoulder.

"You've only been with Phoebe." Anderson cleared his throat. "I mean Ari, so I didn't send it to you while your life was hanging on by a thread. Would have been rude."

I nodded. "I get it. Thanks for the update."

Quinn raised his hand like he would in class. "Why? Why did Ariana need to be protected?"

I pinched the bridge of my nose before I continued. "I fell in love with Ari when we were teenagers. Our parents got married when we were nine and ten. Some people find that gross, but we're not biological siblings, so I'm not sure why people think it's their business to object."

"I find it kind of hot." Kane shot me a lopsided grin.

"We had to sneak around a lot." My cock sprung to life at the memories of her running down the hall naked when our parents weren't there. When we had vacation days from school and Theo and Samantha worked, we fucked on every surface of the house. Those were the good days before shit got complicated.

"One night, our home burned to the ground. Ariana was told that I died, and our parents told me that she died. Imagine my shock when I saw her at Whitmore."

"Holy shit. That's fucked up," Quinn muttered, grief clinging to his tone.

I had no idea what Quinn had lived through, but at that moment, I realized he had serious ghosts in his closet. I understood what that was like. It could eat you alive from the inside out.

"Why, though. Unless they strongly disapproved of the two of you seeing each other, then what was the point?" Anderson asked.

"Ari and I thought we were doing a good job at keeping a secret, but the night of the fire, my mom told me she knew that we were together." I set my feet on the floor and straightened in the chair.

Kane blew out a low whistle. "So they lied to keep you two apart? Dude, that's twisted shit."

"I suspect there's more, but I don't have any proof."

"What do you mean?" Anderson leaned forward and propped his elbow on the table.

"It's just a gut feeling, but I think Ari's dad is hiding something. As soon as I found Ariana again, I got shot. Whatever is going on is personal as shit. I'm worried that being in Ari's life again also puts her in danger." I hoped I made enough sense without having to dive into any more detail, but from the looks on my friends' faces, they needed more to go on before I could ask them to keep an eye on Ari when I wasn't around.

"What are you not telling us?" Quinn asked, staring a hole right through me.

"I don't want to put you guys in danger by sharing too much, but the night of the fire, Ari was kidnapped for three days. Once they had access to me, they let her go. My parents and family searched for two years before they found me. I can't tell you anymore."

"What the actual fuck? You both were held hostage? Well, shit, that makes sense as to why you're itching to keep Ari safe, too. Hell, I thought getting shot just made you a paranoid motherfucker." Quinn rubbed his jawline, focused.

Anxiety pulled and tugged at my insides. "It has. I have a guess who might have been behind the trigger, and I need to deal with it. In order to do that, I have to take off for a while."

Silence descended over the room, and I watched as my friends processed what I'd said.

"How long will you be gone?" Anderson asked, sadness clinging to his expression.

"I don't know. Hopefully only a week or so. My uncle is in an MC, so I'll be working with them to track someone down that has answers. I've not talked to Ari about any of this yet, but I need to make sure she's safe before I leave."

"From the sound of it, she's safer away from you." Quinn gave me a pointed look.

"I know. It's why I've gotta jet for a bit. I love her, and I didn't protect her after the fire. I can now." I had dealt with Peter too, but I sure as hell couldn't share that with anyone other than Kane, Quinn, and Anderson.

"I'm in," Kane said first.

The others agreed, and we discussed how to ensure that Ari remained safe while at school. Asking the guys for help wasn't the hard part, though. It was making Ari understand my decision to leave.

My cell buzzed, and I stared at the screen and read Gunner's cryptic text.

The eagle has landed.

I blinked multiple times. Fuck! Fuck! Fuck! Ari and I had run out of time.

Chapter Thirty-Six

Ariana

I stared at Jagger as if he'd just told me he had a family that lived on Mars and he visited on weekends.

Jag paced my bedroom, his ice-blue eyes pinning me. "Ari, this isn't up for fucking discussion. Pack your bag, *now*."

"I can't skip classes, Jagger. I'll flunk out and lose my scholarship." I tapped my toe against the wood floor, hoping that he would understand he was overthinking the situation. "You leave if that's what you have to do. I'm staying."

Jagger's temper snapped like an overstretched rubber band. He stormed over to me and grabbed my shoulder with one hand. "You're not listening. I'm not giving you a choice. You can either pack a duffle bag with what you want to take or I'll throw you on my bike without it. We're leaving."

"You know, it might help if you told me why you're freaking out. I don't care how long we've known each other, threats to kidnap me won't work well. It wouldn't for any girl, Jagger." I attempted to pull away from him, pissed that he thought he could control my life. A lesson would do him some good, and I was about to teach him.

Jagger tightly gripped the back of my neck and placed his forehead against mine before he whispered, "I don't trust that your room or phone isn't bugged. Call me paranoid, but I was shot a few weeks ago. Shit is getting real, and I have to keep you safe. I was going to go out of town on my own until I got a text message that changed my mind. You're coming with me. It's not up for debate. This is life and death, baby."

His words slammed into my chest like a freight train, stealing the air from my lungs. I looked into his eyes. They were heavy with desperation and love.

I swallowed over the lump in my throat and willed my overactive pulse to slow before I spoke. "Crimson?"

Jag shook his head. "Worse. Tell the girls we're going to spend a few weeks at Theo and Mom's place You can still keep up with your schoolwork online, so grab whatever you need then pack a week's worth of clothes. You have to keep it to necessity only since we're on my bike.

"We could take my car, Jag."

"No. I want people to think you're here."

"Can you tell me where we're going?" I asked, my voice thin with anxiety.

"Not now. I will soon, though." He gently squeezed my arm.

My brain scrambled for the right words to say to the girls, but since Jagger was still recovering, it should be easy to give them a reason. I hated lying to them, but I wasn't sure what was worse than Crimson unless it was . . . Fear scraped its ugly nails down my spine and I shivered.

"You have to tell me what's happening when we're tucked away safe, Jagger. You promise?"

His eyes bored into mine. "I swear. Right now, we have to get the fuck out of here."

His words squeezed my chest, and I pushed up on my tiptoes, kissing him. "I need to talk to Teagan before we go."

"I understand." Jag smoothed my hair, and I leaned into his touch. "Give me fifteen and I'll be ready."

In record time, I had what I needed for school, including my computer, jammed in my backpack. Once I packed clothes, shoes, and toiletries, I rolled up my phone and laptop chargers. I stuffed them into my bag before zipping it closed. I had zero inkling how Jagger would balance everything on his bike, but I trusted him.

"I'll find Teagan. She's probably grabbing breakfast in the kitchen." I blew out a breath, my heart heavy. My stomach churned with reality. I hated being unable to talk to Teagan about what was really happening. When I'd told her about Peter and the fire, I thought my days of lying to her were over. The only thing that offered a tiny bit of consolation was that not telling her the truth would protect her and the girls. Hell, I didn't even have the whole story yet. I had a feeling Jagger had played it like that, so I couldn't tell Teagan anything until we were gone.

"I'll load up the bike. If I were you, I would go to the bathroom and put your hair in a ponytail. The helmet will help, but if it's flying everywhere, it will be a mess to comb out."

The corner of my lips curved upward. "You remember how I hated to have my hair brushed when we were little."

Jagger's chuckle warmed me. "I'll never forget those screeches when Mom had to work on your hair for an hour because you refused to brush it all week." He kissed me on the cheek. "I'm glad that's changed. Not sure I could deal with you having a rat's nest." He scooped up our duffle bags then headed to the front door.

I grabbed my backpack and put my purse into it. A nagging feeling twisted my stomach into knots.

Hurrying downstairs, I found Teagan at the table in the kitchen.

"Hey." I gave her a warm smile.

"Morning." Her spoon paused in midair, milk dripping from it as she stared at me. "Are you okay?" She shoved the Raisin Bran in her mouth then wiped the corner of her lips with the back of her hand. "So ladylike, huh?" She laughed. "I'm starving."

I wondered what had caused her to be so ravenous, but I didn't have time to ask. Nervously shifting my weight from one foot to the other, I urged myself to tell her we were leaving.

"The parental units called and they want us to come home for a while. They've lined up a physical therapist for Jagger, and I need to focus on school. I'll have to finish my classes online for now. It won't be for long. We'll be back before you know it."

Disappointment flashed in Teagan's gaze. "I'm guessing after Jagger was shot, it scared the shit out of them."

"It did." I hadn't shared with Teagan that I'd basically told Theo and Samantha to fuck off. It was a good thing since it made my cover more believable.

"I'll miss you. Hell, I might even miss Jagger." Teagan stood, then threw her arms around me.

"Love you," I whispered with more emotion in my voice than I'd meant to let slip out. I couldn't tell Teagan I had a bad feeling or she would worry.

"Love you, too, Ari. Be safe and let me know when you get there." She returned to her seat and offered me a supportive smile. "I'm glad your folks are being so awesome and helping you both, especially after the rift between you guys."

If she only knew the truth. "Me too. I'll call you later. Please tell the girls bye for me, and I'll hop on our group chat as soon as possible." I gave her a wave before I hurried to the bathroom before I met Jag outside.

"The weather is gorgeous." I soaked in the sun on my face and took a deep breath of the fresh autumn air.

"Perfect day for a ride." Jagger handed me my helmet.

"You're going to have to drive, Ari. I can't with my shoulder."

I stared at him in disbelief. "I haven't driven a motorcycle since we were teenagers," I stuttered.

"Yeah, but you've driven one before. It will all come back to you. I've got you, babe. You can do it."

I smirked at him as I pulled my helmet on. "Looks like you're the bitch this time." I winked at him as he groaned.

"I'm not a bitch, Ari. I'm just your backpack." Jagger chuckled.

I fastened the strap beneath my chin before I hopped on.

"Ready, baby?" Jag winked at me as I started the motorcycle and waited for him to climb on behind me. The engine rumbled between my thighs and I grinned. Maybe the ride might be fun. I mentally laughed that my brain would go there under the circumstances.

I rolled out of the driveway and took a left. He wrapped his arms around my waist, holding on for life. It had been a long time since I'd been on a bike.

Eight hours later, we had arrived in Montana and I turned down a dirt road and slowed. The crunch of the gravel beneath the tires alerted the homeowners that we were approaching.

I parked and cut the engine in front of a gorgeous, modern, rustic home. An abundance of trees surrounded the house, and I released a sigh. This place was peaceful and quiet with no expectations . . . yet.

My stepbrother climbed off the motorcycle, and we removed our helmets. He held his hand out, offering to assist me.

I placed my palm in his and looked around. "Where are we?" I asked.

"One of my uncle's places."

He grabbed our bags and led us to the entrance. Jag unlocked the front door and waltzed in. I gasped, soaking in the comfort and safety of the blonde redwood floors and open plan. A cozy stone fireplace begged to be used. The worn-in brown leather couch and chairs complimented the living room that opened to the dining and kitchen area. I noticed the staircase to the left and wondered if the bedrooms were upstairs. The minute I stepped into the fortress, I realized I never wanted to leave. Even though we were here under shitty circumstances, this house felt safe and inviting.

Jagger released my hand and dropped his keys on the brown and white granite counter. He ditched his jacket and tossed it onto the kitchen island. "Uncle Gunner will be here soon. He stocked the fridge for us. Are you hungry?"

"Why don't you let me make you something. If there's anything good to drink, I'll take some." I strolled over to the refrigerator and opened it, peeking inside. "How's your shoulder feeling? It was a long day. My legs are definitely sore."

Jagger's grin lit up his face as he reached into the cabinet to my left. "I can help you with your legs."

"Promises, promises." I laughed as I pulled out the turkey breast, cheese, mayonnaise, and tomatoes. "Sandwiches work?"

"Perfect. The shoulder hurts like a bitch after the ride, but I'll take some Advil and a few shots of whiskey." He retrieved a bottle of Jim Beam and sat it on the counter. "Is this okay?"

I set the ingredients next to the alcohol, then began to open the other cabinets in search of plates. "I'm not picky at this point. I just want to relax and get our bellies full. Afterward, you have some explaining to do. I love and trust you, it's why I'm here with you now, but you asked a lot of me to walk away from my friends and school. It's a good thing you're worth it." I winked at him.

He turned to me and closed the gap between us. Jag brushed his knuckles across my cheek, leaving goose bumps in their wake.

"I love you, Ari. I'll fucking move heaven and earth to keep you safe. I lost you once. That shit can't happen again." He pressed a kiss to my mouth and I sighed. He stepped away before he opened the cabinet to the right of the refrigerator. "Paper plates. Gunner doesn't do dishes."

"What? He has someone wash his dishes?"

"Really, Ari?" Jag laughed. "Have you washed a dish in your entire life? Theo is loaded, and from the first day Mom and I moved into the house, we had a housekeeper. We didn't even clean our rooms or do laundry."

"Yeah, well. Okay, we were spoiled, but we still figured it out." After searching for a knife, I focused on making sandwiches. Jagger picked up a bag of plain potato chips and tossed them on the counter.

"I had to learn to do everything after the fire." His voice was low, haunted.

Unsure of how to respond, I whipped up our late lunch and watched him make us some stiff drinks.

I replaced the food in the refrigerator, then climbed up on the barstool next to Jagger. He slid my glass to me, and I snatched it up and chugged half of it.

"Damn, girl." He topped the drink off with more whiskey and coke.

I giggled into my hand before I grabbed the bag of chips. "I'm stressed. I have no idea why we're here. I can guess, but not having a concrete answer is fucking with my head."

"I know. I'm sorry." Jagger picked up his glass, took a long drink, then replaced it.

"It will make more sense when Gunner and the guys arrive. They can help explain. My uncle sent me a message to meet him here and to bring you. That shit was going down."

"I assume that you know what he's referring to."

His lips pressed into a thin line, and an unsettling feeling curled into a tight ball in my stomach.

Jagger was about to respond when the front door opened. Startled, I nearly fell off my seat.

Chapter Thirty-Seven

Ariana

A tall, lean guy with sandy-blonde hair and a well-kept beard entered the house. His hazel eyes landed on me, then he grinned. "Ari, it's been a while. It's good to see you again."

"Hi. Thank you for opening your home to us."

"Anything for my nephew." Gunner chuckled as he embraced Jagger carefully.

"How's the shoulder, Jag?"

"Good. Making progress and hope to be on the field soon."

My eyes widened as my gaze swept over the guys filing into the house. There were at least five, all wearing jeans and black leather cuts with a flaming skull on the back.

"Ari, this is Slim, Cupcake, Rigs, Boomer, and Tiny."

Suddenly overwhelmed by their presence, I smiled and gave them a little wave. As discreetly as possible, I slid off the barstool and inched over to Jagger. He placed a kiss on my cheek.

The men went to the kitchen, where they grabbed food and beers. I snatched my drink up and drained it dry, the ice cubes clinking against the glass. Although I trusted Jagger, his uncle and the MC were intimidating as hell.

I poured myself another drink as the house was filled with chatter and laughter.

"Pace yourself, babe. We're about to have a serious conversation. You can have all the whiskey you want afterward."

"Shit. It's that bad?" I replaced the cap on the bottle of Jim Beam and waited for my stepbrother to answer.

Jagger slid his arm around me and led me to the couch, where we sat. The men remained standing, serious expressions settling in.

"Jagger told me some details about you and Crimson, but I'd like to hear it from you," Gunner started.

The hair on the back of my neck bristled, and I glanced at Jagger for confirmation that it was okay to share with the MC.

He took my hand in his. "Go ahead, Ari."

I forced away the dark memories and focused on what was in front of me—a room full of people who cared about Jagger and me. Over the next several minutes, I shared with Gunner and the others about Crimson forcing me to start the fire and how she held me hostage for three days. I wasn't sure if Jagger had told them about Theo shipping me off to the academy, then lying and telling me that my stepbrother died in the flames, so I gave them the quick and dirty version.

Gunner shot his men a pointed look, his expression filling with compassion as his gaze landed on me. "I'm sorry you had to deal with that shit."

I bit my lower lip before I responded, "It wasn't as bad as what Jagger went through with Psycho."

"That's why we're here. Jag, I couldn't risk telling you on the phone or in a text, but one of our guys spotted Psycho in Oregon near Whitmore. It's why I messaged for you two to get the fuck out of there."

Frowning, I placed my palm against my chest. "I don't understand. Psycho? He was the one that forced you to do those . . ." I stopped myself before I uttered the words.

Gunner cracked his knuckles as though he were headed into a fight.

"Fuck!" Jagger said, his knee bouncing.

A heavy hush fell over everyone, and I glanced at Jagger. For the first time since Jag and I had reconnected, I saw sincere fear flicker in his gaze.

"Was he the son of a bitch that shot me? Do we know?" He stood and walked around the back of the couch, pacing the room with a hand on his hip.

Tiny cleared his throat before he spoke. "We've heard shit through the other clubs we're in contact with. Psycho has laid low for a long time, but it seems he wanted to pay you a visit. From the chatter, he was the one that shot you."

A maniacal laugh escaped Jagger, and goose bumps peppered my arms.

"Jagger?" I asked softly. "What is it?" Impatience jetted through me as I waited for an answer.

Finally, Jagger spoke, but not to me. "I want that son of a bitch to die a slow, painful death for what he's done. Where is he?"

"Wait." I jumped off the couch. I wasn't sure I wanted to be a witness to a murder plot. Pushing my fear aside, I dug deep for the courage to ask the question that had burned a hole in my stomach. It was necessary, but I was terrified to hear the answer. "I know you talk about them by those names, but why did they pick Jagger? Or me? All I know is that they're crazy and psychopaths, but I don't understand the connections."

I stared at Jagger as the words left his lips. My brain took a moment to register what he'd said. Seconds later, it felt like a nuclear bomb detonated in my head as the truth crashed down on me.

Stunned, I staggered backward. "What?" My attention swept over the men, their grim expressions supporting what Jagger had finally revealed. I walked to him and cupped his face as tears welled in my eyes. "Psycho is your father?"

"Yeah."

My blood chilled in my veins. What kind of father kidnapped his son and forced him to be the bait to capture and sell kids? Nausea swam up my throat, my stomach churned, and I swallowed my fear.

"He's never going to stop looking for you, is he?"

Jagger licked his lips, and his icy blues flashed darkly. "No. And in some ways, Ari, I'm just as much a monster as he is. I should have walked away when I saw you alive and well. I'm too selfish of a bastard to let you go again, though. I'm risking your safety, yet I did it anyway."

"Why would you not tell me he's your father or that the danger isn't over?" My legs trembled, and I wished like hell we didn't have an audience.

"Because I stupidly thought I'd won and he'd moved on. I'm sorry, Ari."

I dropped my hands and focused on my feet, my heart in my throat. My mind reeled as I recalled our conversation in the locker room when Jagger told me what Psycho had put him through. His nickname fit him. My skin buzzed with anxiety as I muddled through the possibilities. I could wish Jagger good luck and walk out that door or stay. But there was only one choice to make. Deep in my gut, I knew I would never turn away from Jagger any more than he would me. I loved him with every cell in my body and would do everything possible to end his nightmare.

I took a long, calming breath and wiped my sweaty palms on my black skinny jeans. "How do we take the son of a bitch out? The sooner he and Crimson are dealt with, the sooner Jag and I can move on with our lives . . ." I looked at Jagger. "Together."

A relieved smile eased across his handsome face.

"Hell, yeah. Jag, you got you a fine bitch, man." Tiny held up his beer before he took a swig.

I ground my teeth. "Bitch?"

"Uh, shit. No disrespect, Ari. I meant it as a compliment." Tiny flashed me a grin.

I wasn't certain how to take it, but I had other things to do than get my feathers ruffled.

"I need to make sure I'm clear. If Psycho is Jagger's biological father, then who is Crimson?" My attention bounced from each man, then landed on my stepbrother.

"Psycho's partner," Gunner responded. "They work together."

The sudden realization disoriented me. "I'm in danger because I'm associated with Jagger, not because I'm Ariana Ellison, daughter of the tech god," I mumbled, thinking the situation through.

"Yup," Cupcake said, finally chiming in. "They're known across the world for being crazy ass fuckers. They won't hesitate to put a bullet in your head to get to Jag. Shit, I was shocked Psycho didn't end Jagger with that shot he took, but I don't think that's what he wants."

My vision blurred and my pulse pounded in my ears. Pain gripped my heart and injected me with its ugly poison.

"He wants Jagger to work for him again," I managed, my voice hovering above a whisper.

A low whistle filled the room, and I snapped my attention to Cupcake. "Dude, you haven't fucking told her yet?"

The color drained from Jagger's cheeks, and his shoulders visibly tensed.

"What. Is. It? Tell me now, Jagger." I fisted my hands, willing myself to remain standing upright.

Chapter Thirty-Eight

Jagger

This wasn't how I wanted shit to go down. Not even close. When I moved to Whitmore to play ball, Gunner and I figured out exactly how to handle the situation in case Psycho came after me. I hadn't ever disclosed it to anyone other than my uncle, but he had shared the information with a few of his men, including Tiny and Cupcake.

My gut twisted into knots as Ari glowered at me. "Ari, I had to prepare for any possibility. Now that he's back and so are you, this has to end."

Ari's baby blues glared hate fire in my direction. Hell, at this point, I fucking deserved it. Too bad it didn't change anything.

"You're going to put yourself out there and bait him, aren't you?" Her nostrils flared.

Guilt—my constant companion—reared its ugly head right along with the shame. "I know it sounds fucked up, and it is. But I'm the best chance to take the fucker out. Crimson too. I won't be alone."

"Hell no. We're not letting our guy go out there solo. We'll have his back from every direction. As soon as we have clear shots, we'll take him out. We've already tracked Crimson to a place a few hours from here. She'll be easy to deal with after she gets the news that Psycho is dead. Those two have no fucking feelings or conscience except for each other. Craziest shit I've ever seen," Tiny said.

Ari turned to me, and my pulse pounded in my ears. "Did you know? When you told me to pack my bag this morning, did you know that you were going to offer yourself as bait?" Tears pricked her eyes.

"If Psycho showed up again, it was always the plan. I had no idea you were alive, Ari. As for today, the idea is to keep you safe, but I'm going to deal with Psycho as soon as the opportunity shows up. It was simply a matter of time before Gunner tracked him. I didn't know my uncle and his men were close until a few minutes ago, when Gunner explained everything." It wouldn't work in my favor if I told her I'd met with the society guys to watch out for her. That before Gunner messaged me, I was going to try and draw Psycho out to end him once and for all. Plus, I couldn't reveal the identities of my brothers.

She pinched the bridge of her nose, remaining quiet while she stared at the floor. Unfortunately, our scheme was probably the only way to coax Psycho into the open so Gunner and his men could take the son of a bitch out.

"I want a gun," Ari said, her tone clipped and heated.

Shocked didn't even begin to explain what I felt. "You know how to shoot? Since when?"

"Peter. When he was pretending to be my friend, we went to a shooting range in the middle of nowhere and he taught me how to shoot along with firearm safety. If you're meeting Psycho, I'm fucking going too. So before all of you get your panties in a twist and object, get me a damn gun. There's no way this is happening without me."

Someone's snicker caught my attention, and Ari quirked a brow at Tiny. "Problem?"

"Not mine. You're all Jagger's." He turned to me. "Ma man, you've got a spitfire on your hands."

I grabbed Ari's wrist and pulled her against me. "I wouldn't have it any other way." Let's hope the plan worked and Ari and I could walk away and start our life together for real. *If it were only that simple.*

"I'm furious with you." Ari sunk on the edge of the king-sized bed with a navy comforter. I propped the pillows against the headboard.

"I get it. By the time I realized I was in too deep with you again, it was too late."

"You should have told me, Jagger."

Exasperated, I shook my head. "I didn't know that Psycho was around for sure until we got here, Ari. How was I supposed to tell you about it if I had no clue what was happening?" I blew out a breath, tamping down my temper. "Listen, be mad at me, but it's too late to walk away. You had your chance when I told you what Psycho forced me to do."

Her blue eyes blazed. It was clear my pep talk was anything but.

"Do you love me, Ari?" I knew the answer or she wouldn't still be here, but I needed her to say it.

"Since I was twelve." Her voice was soft. It had been a fucked-up day, and all I wanted was to be inside her, hold and touch her, keep her safe.

"If I said you could leave right now and I would never reach out to you again, would you go?"

A long silence filled the space between us and my pulse shot up. *Fuck! She would.*

After several more seconds, she replied, "No. I lost you once. I can't lose you again. Four years was bad enough." Her expression softened as she crawled up the mattress then straddled me. "There's a good possibility that I'm as twisted as you are. I'm convinced that we couldn't live through what we have and not come out warped in some ways."

I brushed the stray hairs from her ponytail off her cheek. "Maybe we're the right amount of fucked in the head to be a perfect fit for each other."

She briefly closed her eyes. "Why does that actually make sense?" Ari rocked her hips against me, and my cock grew painfully hard.

"No more attitude then. I made the best decisions for us that I could. We're alive and here together. That's what matters." I tapped my finger against the tip of her nose.

"For how long, Jagger?" Fear flickered across her beautiful face. "What if this goes wrong and we have to say goodbye to each other? I don't think I can live through losing you a second time."

I leaned up and kissed her. "Nothing and no one will ever come between us again."

"You say that, but you can't promise me. We don't know." She ran her fingertips down the front of my white T-shirt, her nails scraping over the material.

"Are you saying that I'm lying?" I gripped her hip hard.

"Maybe." A mischievous smile graced her mouth.

I licked my lips, remembering her scent and taste tingling against my tongue. "I think you need that attitude fucked out of you." She quivered against me.

I fisted her ponytail and tilted her head back. "You're not ever leaving. You're staying right here with me. If you try, I'll deal with you."

Ari's audible gasp filled the room, her nipples poking through her bra and the thin fabric of her purple top.

"Suck my dick, pet."

Silently, Ari slid down my legs and unbuttoned my jeans. The low hum of the zipper reached my ears, and she freed my throbbing cock.

"On your knees."

She climbed off the bed and knelt before me, looking up expectantly.

"That's my good girl. Open wide." I traced her mouth with the tip of my dick, aching to fuck her. "Take it in. All of me."

I nearly came as she eased my shaft between her full lips. Catching her by surprise, I hit the back of her throat, reveling in the feel of her hot, wet mouth. "You're so goddamn beautiful with my cock shoved into your mouth. Your cheeks are turning red as you wait for me to allow you to breathe. You're under my complete control, and I bet if I touched your sweet little pussy, you would be drenched." I pulled my hips back, allowing her a breath.

She continued to lick and suck me until I thought I would explode. It was too soon. I needed to fuck her.

"Take your clothes off and get on the bed."

Ari slowly removed her shirt and black lace bra before tossing them on the floor. She shimmied out of her jeans and, last, her matching thong. She climbed on the mattress, giving me a full view of her gorgeous ass. Ari turned and parted her thighs.

"Good girl." My attention focused on her spread legs, my cock growing harder each second. "Who do you belong to, Ari?" My voice was low and husky. I wished like hell we were at the society, but at least we had our room and a bathroom.

Her gaze stayed glued to mine. "You."

"Good girl." I stroked my dick, keeping focused on her perfect body. "Don't ever forget that I own every piece of you now: your cunt, your ass, and your mouth. Most of all, your heart. Are we clear?"

"Yeah. Only you." Her eyes darkened with need as her gaze followed me.

I opened the nightstand drawer and removed a pair of handcuffs. "My uncle and I share similar tastes." I motioned for her to move toward the headboard. "Spread your arms."

Her chest heaved as I secured her to the slats of the bed. "Do you want me to fuck you hard, my pet?"

"Yes." Her response was breathy.

I grinned like the devil I was before I ran a finger over her soaked pussy. "So wet, baby. If we were at the society, I would bend you over my knee and spank you. Then, I would find the perfect plug for that tight asshole, lube it up, and fuck you with it before I left it in your ass. I love that it makes your cunt even tighter."

"What are you waiting for? Fuck me, Jag. Please." Her begging made me only want to torture her more.

I balanced on my knees and positioned myself at her entrance, rubbing my cock up and down Ari's slick core. I slid in a little before easing out and repeating the motions.

Raw need surged to the surface as Ari moaned softly with the slow pull out and soft push back in.

"You're so tight." I grunted, pushing all the way into her and stilling. I growled before I slammed into her.

"Yes, baby. So good." Ari rocked against me.

My thrusts were rough and precise, with pushes directed to her sensitive bundle of nerves.

"Cum for me," I demanded, and she shivered beneath me.

Delicious desire licked every inch of my skin. I let out a harsh growl, grabbed the back of one of her thighs, and began plowing into her hard and fast.

Ari arched off the bed, and my name left her as her orgasm ripped her and she trembled beneath me.

Before she finished, my lips parted, then I jerked and released inside her. Ari's core pulsed around me. Eventually, our bodies calmed, then I leaned down and kissed her.

"No one fucks me as good as you do, Ari. No one."

From the expression on her face, she was about to respond with a sassy comment but thought better of it.

I moved down, admiring her cuffed to the bedframe and spread out for me. There was something about my cum all over her pussy that nearly sent me out of my fucking mind. Maybe I would make her stay that way for a while so that I could enjoy her surrender.

Ari tugged on the cuffs. "Are you forgetting this?"

I grinned like a kid in a candy store and stood next to the bed. "No." I cupped her chin, and my lips hovered over hers. "You're for my viewing pleasure. Don't ever forget it."

Chapter Thirty-Nine

Jagger

Ariana and I grew restless with Gunner's orders to stay inside and lay low. The house was in the middle of ten acres, surrounded by pine and aspen trees. It was well hidden, but that also meant if someone knew the property layout, they could sneak up on us. I didn't like it one bit, and my pissy mood let everyone else realize I wasn't happy about it either.

I shifted on the couch, staring at my laptop. It seemed I couldn't focus on my assignments while Ari and Teagan chatted on the phone in our bedroom. Ari promised not to blow our location. Since she finally understood what was at stake, I knew she wouldn't want to involve Teagan or her friends. She would never forgive herself if something happened to them.

The door opened, allowing a stream of bright golden sunlight into the semi-dark room. I closed my computer and set it on the coffee table.

"Hey, anything new?" I asked my uncle as he strolled over to the couch and plunked down.

"Fuck no. It's annoying as shit. Psycho left Oregon, but he seems to be trying to shake our tail. Makes me think someone wasn't as discreet as they should have been. Kid, he's probably on his way to Montana, taking all the back roads possible so he won't be spotted. At least he doesn't know where this house is. You and Ari should be fine."

I tapped my foot, irritated by how helpless I was with only one functional arm. What if I had to fight Psycho? I reminded myself that my gun and ammo were in the nightstand drawer in the room Ari and I were using. Gunner also let her choose a handgun from his vast collection. He'd even taken her out back to his shooting range that he'd built, and she fired off some rounds. She was a damn good shot, and although I hated to admit it, Peter had taught her well.

"Okay, but if he's on his way here, then who tipped him off that we're in Montana?" I asked.

"Jag, it could have been anyone. Our information is rolling down the hill through other MCs. I might use them for help, but I sure as fuck don't trust any of them. It's just like that."

"Are you saying one of your guys let it slip? I'm confused." My heart hammered in my chest. My uncle hadn't answered my question. "Gunner, I can't afford any fuckups. Did one of your men let it slip or not? And if so, why are we still here?" My nostrils flared, my temper kicking into high gear.

"Jag, chill the fuck out. Do you honestly think I wouldn't have already tracked that info down and handled it? None of my guys would rat you and Ari out. They're clear it would cost them their fucking lives. All I'm saying is that maybe you were followed and didn't know it. Psycho has a lot of men working for him across the country. If he wanted eyes on you, then that's how it plays out. The only way to change that is to take the motherfucker out."

"Sorry. You're right. Waiting makes me anxious." I shoved my hand into the front pocket of my jeans. "I should be playing ball and spending time with Ari. Instead, we're hiding from a sick son of a bitch. I feel like a sitting duck if he sneaks up on us. He had Crimson grab Ari and he took me. We might be older and have more life experience, but I'm one-handed."

"Jag, we have security cameras on the property and even in the woods surrounding the house. My men are on watch twenty-four seven. We're all packin'. You're as safe as you possibly could be. Just chill, man."

Surprised by the new information, my eyes narrowed on him. "Why didn't you tell me about the cameras before?"

"Because I know how you're wired. You'd be sittin' there staring at the camera feed instead of making sure you don't fall behind in classes, or studying the opponent's football plays Coach sent you." Gunner shot me a cocky look. "You're my favorite nephew. I've got your back. Always."

I sat on the edge of the couch, my head dropping between my shoulders. "It's different now that Ariana is with me. I failed her once. I can't do it again. I love her, Gunner. I would gladly give my life to save hers."

"You better not," Ari said from the hallway.

Caught off guard by her presence, I glanced up, spotting Ariana leaning against the wall with her arms folded. We were both on high alert, and every noise made us jump.

"Come here." I reached out and motioned for her to join me on the couch. When she got close enough, I pulled her into my lap and wrapped my good arm around her. Our gazes connected, and my heart dropped to my toes. I loved Ari so much that sometimes, it fucking hurt. "Would you not do the same for me? If you had the chance to save me, but it meant giving up your life—"

She placed her fingertips on my mouth. "Without a second thought. I killed you once; I'll never let it happen again."

"No, you didn't, but I understand what you mean. It's the same for me. I couldn't keep you safe from Crimson. I wouldn't hesitate to keep you safe now."

"Well, hopefully it won't even boil down to that. You two can stop talking death and nonsense." Gunner stood, then made his way to the kitchen. "Tiny is grilling tonight, so bring your appetite. The beef and booze will abound. We'll throw down some cards and cash too. We need to lighten up this drab ass party." He winked at us before grabbing a beer from the refrigerator.

Ari's brows knitted together. "It's ten in the morning," she mouthed to me.

"Hair of the dog." I grinned and ran my knuckles down her soft cheek.

She nodded, realizing that Gunner was hungover even though she couldn't tell.

"I'll let you kids study." Gunner chuckled. "I actually do mean study. Keep your fucking grades up. Both of you." Gunner gave us a two-finger salute before he disappeared out of the house.

"How's Teagan? Is our story still holding up?"

Ari carefully climbed off my lap and walked to the door. She flipped the locks in place before she returned.

"Yeah. She doesn't suspect anything especially since we talk every day. It's the most normal thing I can do with her, ya know? If I had cut off communication, she would call Theo and our cover would get blown."

"I agree. Plus, I never told Gunner you and Teagan were in touch, so I would keep that between us."

"I figured. Not to mention, he's dictating everything we do. I'll be damned if I can't talk to my bestie. It keeps me sane while we're hiding."

"Me too. I've messaged Anderson and Quinn a few times. Guys don't chat as much, so it's not suspicious to message them every few days."

Ari propped her feet on the coffee table. "Jag, how is this going to play out? I know you and Gunner are close, and I'm guessing you two have discussed the strategy at length."

I massaged the back of my neck, where a nagging pain began

throbbing. "You and I will let the MC deal with Psycho and Crimson. The guys will close in and take them out the second they step onto the property. It will be quick and over with."

Ari stared at me, burning a hole in my head. "Let me get this straight. We're just hanging out here? I feel I should be doing something for fuck's sake. Sitting here is driving me insane."

"No. I would much rather you stay safe right here next to me. Let them handle it. Our hands will be clean if it goes down the way we hope."

"Other than we're an accessory to murder, but lately that's not a big deal." A faint smile curved her lips. "You're rubbing off on me. I was shocked about Peter, but relieved. Now, I'm like, let's take Psycho and Crimson the fuck out." She slapped her palms over her face and groaned.

"If I hadn't dealt with Peter, he would have come after you again. The more those asshole men are pissed off, the more they take it out on the girl. Couldn't have that. Eventually, he would have broken you and maybe killed you."

She gulped. "I know. And I'm grateful to you for taking care of him. I really am."

"As for Psycho and Crimson, they're not human. They're fucking evil walking this earth hurting innocent people. We take care of them, and when we do, we save a ton of lives in the process."

Ari turned toward me and tucked her leg beneath her. She propped her elbow on the back of the couch, her blue eyes locking on mine. "I know. It's why I'm on board." She paused and reached for my hand. Averting her gaze, she worried her bottom lip with her teeth. "What if we could speed up the plan?"

A bark of laughter tore from my lips. "Are you saying what I think you are?"

She gave me a shrug. "Since your shoulder is healing, I'll volunteer as bait. We know Psycho is headed to Montana, right?"

I frowned. "How long were you listening to my conversation with Gunner?"

Ari twisted her mouth. "Most of it. In my defense, if you two wanted to speak in private, then you shouldn't have had an important conversation in the middle of the living room. Just sayin'."

"You're not going to be bait, Ari. Forget it."

A crease dented the smooth skin between her blonde eyebrows. "It's not your decision," she snapped.

I shot off the couch and stood, hovering over her. "You're cute when you're feisty, but I said no. You are not going to offer yourself up as a goddamn target to crazy fuckers. End. Of. Discussion. I will tie you naked to the bed for a week if you test me."

Her face glowed as she pinned me with a hot glare. I knew she was about to go behind my back, so I would have to take extra precautions and not let her out of my sight. Even if I objected, Gunner might go for her idea. That shit couldn't happen.

Ariana only spoke to me the rest of the day if she had to. I wouldn't admit it, but I enjoyed dancing on her nerves. Everywhere she went in the house, I was right behind her. When she tried to shut me out of the bathroom, I shoulder-checked the door and pushed my way in. She yelled at me that she couldn't pee in front of someone, so I turned my back to her and stood next to the window she could have climbed out of. Gunner had been in and out all afternoon, and we could smell the grill starting up. It would be easy for her to crawl out, find him, and pitch her plan. Not going to happen. My work was cut out for me during dinner and card games, though. Even then, I refused to let her outsmart me. I knew exactly how to handle her.

Ariana rubbed her stomach and grinned at the guys. "I ate too much, but it was so good. Thank you for cooking, Tiny."

Tiny beamed at her, stood, and bowed. "You're welcome."

Laughter erupted, and I relaxed for the first time since Ari had come up with her stupid idea. Maybe it was the food or the beers I'd had. I made sure to pace myself with the alcohol but continued to pour Ari's drinks. Once she was drunk, I could tuck her into bed and cuff one wrist to the bedframe. From how she slurred her words, I was close to achieving my goal. When she passed out, I would talk to Gunner and make sure he didn't agree to her putting herself up as bait.

Three poker games later, Ari's eyes were glassed over. Guilt elbowed me in the side but I ignored it. I intended to keep her safe and would do anything to make that happen.

"It's only eleven, but I'm so ready to go to sleep." She yawned then glanced at me. "I'm drunk." Her giggle made me laugh.

"That's all right. I'll walk you to our room. You needed to relax." I kissed her forehead, wishing I could carry her down the hall, but my shoulder was still healing.

We both stood, and I wrapped my arm around her before glancing behind me. "I'll be back in a bit. Get ready to have your asses kicked in the next game."

The guys continued to talk smack as I managed to get Ari situated. I suggested that she go to the bathroom, then get into bed. She crawled under the covers once she changed into sweatpants and a cute sleep tank.

"Thanks for taking care of me, Jag. I love you." She snuggled beneath the blankets and fluffed her pillows. In seconds, her soft snores filled the room. She wasn't going anywhere, and my conscience told me not to cuff her. I would check on her again shortly, but I wasn't worried about her taking off with the amount of alcohol in her.

"Love you too, baby." I pressed a kiss to the side of her head before I quietly slipped out of the room.

Relief flooded my system as I walked down the hall, ready to join the guys for another round of poker. I adjusted my sling, wanting to throw the damn thing away, but the doctor had said to wear it for one more week. At least I had physical therapy exercises, which were painful as hell, but my shoulder wasn't stiff and seizing up on me.

I glanced up, stopping in my tracks as my gaze swept over the empty room before me. "What the fuck? Where did everyone go?"

"Gunner said to tell you they had an emergency to handle. Get some sleep, kid." Cupcake drained his beer before he walked out the front door.

I locked it behind him, wondering what the hell had happened.

Chapter Forty

Ariana

"Baby?" I reached for Jagger, my hand landing on his bicep. I smiled as I squeezed it, watching the love of my life sleep. His jet-black hair was slightly rumpled, and I resisted running my fingers through it. He was exhausted and needed his rest.

Muffled voices and laughter floated in from the living room. I struggled to remember how I'd gotten in bed, but one of the guys must have carried me. I blinked, trying to clear the haze from my vision. The world spun, and I grabbed my stomach in a lame attempt to control the butterflies. My legs and toes tingled, and I tried to touch my mouth, but my arm fell to the side.

Jagger's eyes popped open, his steely gaze terrifying me.

"Jag? I . . . . .. can . . ." I attempted to swallow, but I was losing the use of my limbs. My lips grew numb, and my arms and legs were heavy.

"Move," I finally managed to say.

"No." He blinked a few times, staring at me.

Fear wrapped her cold fingers around my heart and squeezed as the bedroom door flung open. The hall light illuminated a tall, broad-shouldered man.

I tried to scream as he strolled into the room and I saw his face. One half was normal, the other severely burned, and thick scars twisted his expression.

"It's nice to finally meet you, Ari. I think you'll be a wonderful addition to the family."

Somehow, I managed a frown.

"I'm sorry, where are my manners? Let me introduce myself. My friends call me . . . Psycho. In your case, your angel straight from hell."

I jerked myself awake, my head throbbing like a son of a bitch as I attempted to lift it. Before my brain could register what was happening, my stomach rebelled, and I puked all over the floor. Heaving, I tried wiping my mouth with my hand but couldn't move my arm. My dream came rushing back, and I detected voices in the distance, and a whoosh of panic spiraled through me.

"Fuck! Fuck!" I looked around, scrambling to comprehend where I was. My attention landed on Jagger. His head lolled forward as he sat in an upright chair. His arms were tied behind him, and his ankles were bound to the front. At this angle, I couldn't tell if he was breathing. Warm, prickly fear clawed its way through my chest.

"Jagger! Jagger!" I whisper-yelled. "Wake up." I nearly cried with relief when he moaned.

"Baby, listen to me. It's Ari. I need you to wake up." No response. I stared at the cement floor, dread pooling in the pit of my belly as I saw two drains in the middle of it. *Shit. This is bad. So bad.* I tugged on the ropes that restrained my wrists, willing my frantic breathing to calm down so that I could think.

I focused, identifying a long table, a water hose, a tray of tools, and a gun. Jagger's gun? A lot of good it would do us over there.

"Fuck. My shoulder." Jag winced as he lifted his head. His confused gaze landed on me, then scanned the area. It only took seconds for the panic to register on his face.

"Jagger. I'm here with you. Stay calm." It was a stupid thing to say, but the only thing that came out of my mouth.

"Ari?" His dark brows knitted together. "What the hell? Why are you tied to a chair? Where are we?"

"I don't know. But it doesn't look like a place you'd bring friends to."

Jag shook his head. "It looks similar to where I held Peter, but it's smaller." A light went off in his eyes. "Motherfucker. I've been here before."

My insides twisted into a million knots as I waited for him to talk. The silence between us continued to thicken until the entire room pulsed with the words we were both terrified to speak.

A door opened, and my attention landed on black combat boots as they thudded against the floor. Every cell in my body trembled while I dared look up into the face I had thought I'd dreamed about.

Half of his mouth curved in an evil smile. "Excellent. You're both awake."

Jagger gritted his teeth, his chest heaving with fury. "Fuck you."

Psycho's maniacal laughter bounced off the concrete walls. "Good to see you too, son. I see your shoulder is healing nicely."

"How could you shoot your own son, you sick fuck," I blurted before I could stop myself.

Psycho slowly walked to me, his hands folded behind his back. He leaned down, his nose nearly brushing mine.

"Don't touch her, goddammit. I'll do whatever you want, but don't fucking touch her," Jagger growled.

"He always loved you the most. Even more than his pops." Psycho's tongue flicked out and he licked my lips. Without thinking, I opened my mouth then chomped down on it as hard as I could. Startled, he jerked back, blood streaming down his chin. "Fucking bitch."

I wished I'd been able to cut his tongue clean off, but he could still talk, which meant I'd failed.

I never saw his hand coming as he hit the side of my head with his fist.

A scream tore from my throat as the pain blinded me. Jagger's muffled voice broke through the fog, but I couldn't make out his words. For now, I decided to shut up and pretend to be unconscious.

"What the fuck do you want?" Jagger hissed.

"Can't a father have some quality time with his son?" Psycho asked.

"You call kidnapping me father and son time?"

I eyed Psycho's boots through my hair that was covering my face as they moved around the room.

"You walked right into it. I couldn't have arranged it better."

Jagger full-on snorted. "You planned for Ari and me to stay at Gunner's, or are you talking out of your ass and had one of your men follow us?"

"I didn't tail you. I also didn't shoot you." Psycho tsked. "Thought you had that part figured out. It's clear to me that I didn't teach you very well the first time. Maybe we'll get it right while you're here."

"If you didn't put a bullet in my shoulder, who did? I'd like to have a little chat with the fucker."

I held my breath, wondering if Psycho would reveal who had shot Jagger or if he was simply messing with his head.

A second set of heavy footsteps had me peeking in that direction.

"Meet your shooter, Jag." Psycho cackled, and the hair on the back of my neck stood on end.

My heart folded in on itself as Jagger muttered his name, shock lacing his words.

Chapter Forty-One

Jagger

It took everything inside me not to rip him to pieces, but even I knew I was completely helpless against Psycho and Tiny.

"Does my uncle know that you betrayed us?" I ground out, my shoulder throbbing like a son of a bitch. At least the stitches had healed already.

"Ah, come on, Jagger. Don't be a bad sport about it. I got paid well to not kill you." Tiny chuckled. "It wasn't personal, man. It was just a job."

"Not personal?" I was so pissed, my voice shook. "Nothing is certain. Who's gonna draft someone with a shot shoulder? You might have ruined my chance at going pro. Worse, you could have hurt someone else."

"It's all business, kid. I needed the money. Ma has cancer and someone's gotta pay the bills." He had the audacity to shrug. I glanced at Ari, but it seemed that she was still unconscious. If we lived long enough for me to explain how Tiny had betrayed us, she would be as shocked as I was.

I pressed my lips together, wishing I hadn't lied about where Ari and I were. Even if Teagan didn't hear from Ari for a day or two, she would have no idea where to tell the cops to look for her. Fuck!

"You know damn well my uncle is looking for Ari and me. He won't stop until he finds us, Psycho. He hates your fucking guts."

Psycho's expression turned grim. "That makes me so sad, Jag." He and Tiny burst into laughter.

He looked at his watch. "I gotta jet, but I wanted to make sure Tiny hadn't drugged your and Ariana's drinks enough that they killed you both. I'll have to give him a bonus for a job well done." Psycho slapped Tiny on the back as they walked out of the room and closed the door behind them.

As soon as the footsteps down the hall subsided, I looked at Ari. "Are you okay? Ari?"

She raised her head slowly, her blue eyes tormented. She spat on the floor, blood mixing with her saliva.

"You shouldn't have bit Psycho's tongue. He's probably soaked in disease." I winced when the words left my mouth. It was stupid to add one more fear to Ari's plate.

"It was disgusting, but I just reacted."

I was thirsty as hell, and I suspected that she was too. My heart slammed painfully against my rib cage. I'd led Ari straight into the devil's den when I thought I was protecting her. Tiny had watched us, waiting for the right moment. The son of a bitch had been working with Psycho the entire time. Hate simmered beneath my skin, threatening to drive me over the edge. If I got free, they would both regret ever touching us.

"Jag?"

Ari's voice pulled me from my murderous thoughts.

"Tiny shot you." Sadness flashed in her blue eyes and she swallowed. "I'm so sorry. From what I could tell, you considered him family."

My shoulders slumped, and I stared at the ceiling, the bitter, fiery aftertaste of betrayal burning my insides. "I never saw a sign, but I wasn't with him on a regular basis." A flicker of hope ignited in my chest. "If Uncle Gunner can find us, we have a chance to get out of here alive."

Ari didn't even blink when I said alive. Maybe she thought we were dead people walking. She might be right, but I couldn't afford to entertain the what-ifs.

"The hall is long. I think we must be at the end of the building. Usually, there's an exit door. I can't swear to it, but maybe." Ari offered me a wistful expression.

I frowned at her. "How did you come up with that?"

A haunted look flashed across her face. "When Peter locked me in closets, it wasn't always the same one. It took a while, but I was finally able to calm my heartbeat down enough to listen to my surroundings: footsteps, voices and how far away they might be. If they were closer to the room I was kept in and shit like that. I had three years of practice but eventually, I could close my eyes and kind of piece together the layout and halls. I wasn't great at it, but half the time I was right."

Stunned, I gawked at her. "It's crazy what you can learn when it means you live or die."

"Jag, you watched Tiny walk in. What was behind him?"

I racked my brain, attempting to think of any detail that might help us, but I came up empty.

"It's okay. When the door opens again, let's try to see what's out there. Once we know, we can figure out what to do next."

"Ari, unless we can get to my gun sitting on that tray over there, there's no use. Psycho won't get close to you again."

"Oh, stepbrother of mine." I flashed him a grin, using the exact phrase I had before he kissed me the first time. "Peter might have helped more than we gave the bastard credit for. I hope he's burning in hell, but I underestimated his usefulness."

I suspected disbelief was written all over my face.

"I need to think, so help me and keep an eye on the door."

I nodded, unsure of what was running through her head. "Hey, Ari?"

She looked at me.

"I'm sorry I got you caught up in this shit."

"Jag, it wasn't your fault. You had no idea Tiny was working with Psycho. You can't go there. Save your energy. We'll need it soon."

Her stoic expression did little to reassure me. "If we don't . . . I love you, baby. I'm so grateful to have found you again."

"I love you too, Jag, but we'll have more time together. I'll be damned if we don't walk out of here with our arms around each other."

Wasn't I supposed to keep her calm and protect her? I focused on the entrance, my brain running different escape scenarios.

I jerked myself awake when the door opened. Psycho was alone, which gave me a better view of him. A large red E on a sign over a door caught my attention. Psycho strolled over to us, holding bottled water in each hand.

"How did your face get messed up?" Ari asked.

"You sure are a polite one." Psycho twisted the top off the bottle and held it to her lips, allowing her a few sips at a time. "Only a little or Tiny will be cleaning puke up."

She took two drinks, then he replaced the lid.

"I figure we're either not walking out of here alive, or you're going to hold us hostage and put us to work like you did Jagger after the fire. In my opinion, no questions are off limits."

Psycho gave me a drink, his expression void of any emotion. It didn't surprise me. His nickname fit him well.

"I pissed the wrong people off. One of the kids Jag snagged for me got away after I had the money. They didn't like it when I explained that it wasn't my job to keep up with the kid after they were sold. Even though I had men guarding the temporary house we were in at the time, the son of bitch torched it with me inside." Psycho laughed. "He wasn't too happy to meet up with me a year later, but I was the last thing the fucker saw before I slit his throat."

I suspected Ari regretted asking the question. Right after Psycho got what he deserved, Gunner found me and I escaped. This was the first time that I'd seen Psycho's deformed face. It was fucked up for sure, but he was uglier on the inside.

Psycho set the bottles on the floor between our chairs. "We've got a long night ahead of us. The boss is coming in, then we'll have our orders of what to do with you two. My vote is to cut our losses and kill you, but even I have someone I gotta ask first."

Sweat glided down my temple. Gunner needed to hurry the fuck up. We were running out of time.

Chapter Forty-Two

Ariana

Fear pulsed through my veins, sending my heart rate into overdrive. Psycho had left several hours ago, and I'd been hard at work.

"Jagger, can you see my hands?"

Jagger leaned back on the legs of his chair, frowning. "Yeah. Ari, you're bleeding."

"Good. How much? I've lost the feeling in my arms so I can't tell. On the bright side, I can feel my shoulder and that's what I need to move." I groaned, moving my wrists against the ropes as best I could.

Jagger's gaze narrowed. "Ari, your wrist is covered in blood, but I think you could slide out of the rope." Excitement clung to his words.

"That's the plan, baby. That's the plan." I gritted my teeth so hard, I feared breaking a molar. My hand wriggled free of the ropes with a quick jerk of my numb arm.

"Jesus, you did it." Jagger's expression was full of pride.

"Don't get excited yet. Let's hope no one checks on us for a while." I winced from the sharp tingles in my limbs and wiggled my fingers. It took me some time, but I finally lifted my arms and set them on my lap. I grinned at Jagger. "I can move better now." I wiped the blood on my black jeans. My wrists looked worse than they actually were. "Over the years with Peter, I was able to slip out of the ropes several times. The rope burn is brutal, but it works."

"No one ever noticed your bruised and bandaged wrists? Not Teagan or the girls?"

"When you have a secret, you'll go to great lengths to hide it. Peter liked to tie me up for sport in the winter and fall. If someone saw the marks, there was a chance I would expose him for the sick monster he was. He bought my clothes to handle that problem, including long-sleeved shirts and several windbreakers with elastic sleeves so they wouldn't ride up. I was always cold, and no one thought twice about me wearing a jacket, even inside."

"What about a shower or bath?"

"Teagan and I shared a room and bathroom. She was the only person I needed to be careful around." My explanation was calm and collected, and I knew that a part of me had mentally checked out as I retold the horror that Peter had inflicted. Thank God the fucker was dead, but I had bigger problems to deal with.

Voices floated down the hall and I froze for a second. Realizing the rope had dropped to the floor, I leaned down and scooped it up. Quickly, I wrapped the bloodied rope around one of my wrists, then put my arms behind me. "Does it look like I'm still tied up?"

Jag leaned back, eyeing my shitty job. "I think it will work."

"Let's hope so."

Silence hung in the air between us as we waited to see if the door would open. My heart pounded so hard in my ears that I had trouble listening.

Several minutes later, the men's footsteps faded, and I blew out the breath I hadn't realized I was holding.

"Hang on." My ropes landed with a thud, then I leaned over and worked on the ones that bound my ankles to the chair. I glanced at Jagger, who was paying attention to my every move. "Pissing Peter off beat the hell out of being a Girl Scout. They don't teach you how to get out of certain knots. After the first time the bastard tied me up, I googled and watched YouTube videos on survival and how to get free." I left the ankle ropes near my seat in case I needed to secure myself again.

"Holy crap. My legs." I went to work, furiously rubbing my calves and encouraging the blood flow. "As soon as I can walk. I'll untie you."

"Do you have any clue what to do?" Jagger looked at me expectantly.

"What, you don't? My badass boyfriend is scrambling?"

He jerked back as if I'd slapped him. "I've got one, but you might not like it."

"Maybe it's the same idea." I placed my palms on the sides of the seat and slowly pushed myself up, managing to get my feet steady beneath me. I took a tentative step and, seconds later, another. Pins and needles pricked my skin, and I fisted my hands, forcing myself to walk to the back of Jagger's chair. Kneeling, I frowned. "It will take me a minute. The knots are tighter on yours."

"Probably because you have tiny wrists and I don't." Jagger glanced over his shoulder, trying to watch.

"Got it." I held one of his arms and placed it in his lap, massaging it awake.

"Fuck. They're so numb." He wiggled his fingers.

"I know. Wait until you stand. It doesn't feel very good. Fortunately, we've both had enough crappy experiences that it's made us strong." I looked at my boyfriend, adoration in his gaze. "You're incredible."

I hurried to the other side and worked on his right arm. "How's your shoulder?"

"No idea." A smart-ass grin slipped into place. "I can barely feel my arms and hands, but I bet it's going to be pissed at me when I have feeling in my body again."

"Probably." I knelt before him, working on the ropes that bound his ankles. "What's your idea?" I needed to hear what he had to say first. Rubbing his legs, I gave him my undivided attention.

He lifted his arm and pointed to the ceiling where several wood beams crisscrossed. "I'll get up there, and when the fuckers come in and see us gone, I'll shoot them."

"See if you can stand up." I reached out to him and rooted my feet to the floor, leaning back as I helped pull him from the chair. I placed his palms on my shoulders and walked backward several steps. "I know you're capable of walking, but if you eat it, then we're risking your shoulder and I need you intact."

"I know. It's why I didn't refuse the help." He winced. "Fuck. You're right. Walking doesn't feel too good."

Once Jagger could lift his feet like a normal human being, he walked over to the tray of tools. He handed me a pair of rusty wire cutters. "Hide these on you in case we need them."

Jagger grabbed his gun, slid back the slide-lock, and peered inside before he removed the clip and counted the bullets. "If we're smart about firing shots, we should have enough to get the fuck out of here."

I looked up at the beams on the ceiling. "One of us needs to be up there, the other down here."

Jagger shook his head. "No. We both go up. The second they spot the empty chairs, they're going to run out searching for us. We'll save our bullets, hurry across the hall, and out the exit door."

My eyes widened. "Why didn't you tell me you saw it? I couldn't see shit from my angle."

"Sorry. I thought you would have said something."

"It's fine." We didn't have time to argue anyway.

Muffled voices grew nearer and we scrambled to our chairs. I quickly tied his arms behind his back and his feet to the chair.

With my heart in my throat, I loosely secured my ankles, groaning when I realized we'd left the gun on the fucking tray.

"Hurry!" Jagger urged me.

The door opened as I barely finished wrapping the rope around my wrist, hoping it looked like I was still tied.

Psycho entered the room with a wicked grin on his face. "Boss is here to say hello. If you're lucky, you might even get out alive."

My attention bounced from him to the hallway, and I held my breath as the tip of a black shoe appeared.

I wasn't sure who gasped first, Jagger or me, but shit had just gone off the fucking rails.

Chapter Forty-Three

Jagger

My mask remained in place, refusing to crack from the anger swirling in the depths of my chest. I opened my mouth but nothing came out. My attention landed on Ari, her eyes wide with shock.

"Don't look so surprised, honey," my mom said.

"Samantha? What are you doing here?" Ariana asked.

"I have business to attend to." Her blue eyes flashed, then a wicked smile slipped into place.

"But Psycho called you the boss. I don't understand." *This is a mistake, right?*

"That's because I am. Everything you've seen and experienced, Jagger, is all me."

Psycho coughed and shot her a dirty look.

Samantha ignored him. "Behind every successful business is a woman. She might not be seen or heard, but she's the driving force." She looked at Psycho. "Oh, darling. Don't get your feelings hurt. Sulking isn't a good look on you."

"Does my father know that you're a crazy bitch?" Ari spit out.

Samantha laughed. "He's one of the stupidest men I've ever met. I could have auctioned off children in the middle of the living room and he wouldn't have noticed."

Ariana visibly bristled. "He's highly intelligent, Samantha. Don't talk shit about him. At least his business is legit and legal."

Mom strolled over to Ari and leaned down, getting in her face. "Are you certain about that?" She smoothed Ari's hair as if she were a little girl that needed consoling.

Ari's cheeks burned red. I wasn't sure if Samantha was serious or playing mind games. My bet was on the latter.

"Mom, if you let us go, we'll leave town. Theo never has to know." I tried to control the sound of the voice, but I was unable to hide the wobble. I thought Ari had betrayed me, but Mom working together with my dad was over the fucking top. Not once had I ever suspected her actions or intentions.

Psycho threw his head back and laughed so hard, his belly shook.

Mom stood tall, making a tsking sound. "I have much bigger plans for the both of you." She tucked her blonde hair behind her ear, studying us.

"Is this because Jagger and I are together? You made it clear in the hospital that you weren't okay with the idea. If that's the problem, it's easily solved," Ari offered.

My brows furrowed, but I remained quiet and let Ari finish.

Mom shook her head. "No. For the record, I couldn't care less if you're fucking your brother."

"Step," I interjected. "We're not blood related, so quit with that shit."

"Jagger, always so tough. It's a shame that you'll never make it to the big show. You're very talented." Samantha walked over to the tray, her face turning crimson. "Who the hell left a gun in the goddamn open? What if they got loose and shot you when you opened the door?"

Psycho hurried over, grabbed the weapon, and shoved it in the back of his pants. It took everything inside of me not to groan. "I'll talk to Tiny. He was the one that brought the kids in."

"It had better not happen again. These aren't your average college students. They've seen and lived through a lot. They're smart. Under no circumstances should anyone let their guard down around them. Understood?"

Psycho looked like a sad puppy that had been scolded. "Of course. It shouldn't have happened. I'll deal with him."

"I'll see you kids later. Try to stay out of trouble." Mom laughed as she and Psycho strolled through the door as if it were perfectly normal to kidnap her children.

As soon as the lock clicked into place, Ari and I breathed a sigh of relief.

"That was close. If one of them had walked behind us, they might have noticed the ties." Ari slipped out of the ropes, then untied her ankles.

"I'm glad they didn't, but Mom took the fucking gun." I ditched the restraints then unbound my ankles from the chair. Standing slowly, I tested my legs, but they felt almost normal.

"There's an exit door across the hall. I saw it for sure this time." Ari stared at me, hurried over, and threw her arms around my neck. "I'm sorry, baby. Both of your parents are crazy."

I pulled her against me, holding her tight and nuzzling my nose in her hair. "It explains why I do the crap I do."

Ari stepped away, her intense gaze connecting with mine. "You are *not* your parents. There's zero comparison."

"I wish that were true, but I killed Peter without blinking an eye. He wasn't the first. I just pick my targets carefully. There have been plenty of times in my life I've questioned my sanity. My saving grace is you and football. It keeps me centered the majority of the time."

I dipped my head and pressed a kiss to her mouth. "I love you. I'm sorry you got wrapped up in all this madness, but the other part of me is glad you're by my side. We're better together." I realized I spoke the truth. I just wasn't sure we would make it out alive.

"Yeah." She pressed up on her toes and kissed me. "We need to get out of here. We don't know where that door leads too. For all we know, we're on a remote island with water for days." Ari cringed as soon as the words left her mouth.

"I know. Similar thoughts have fucked with my head too. There's only one way to find out, though." I rubbed her back, imprinting this moment with her in my mind. It might be the last chance I had to tell her. "Ari, if we make it out of here in one piece—"

She placed her fingers against my mouth. "*When* we get out of here."

"When." I inhaled a long, deep breath. "I want to propose and get our own place to live. I have no doubt that you're the one for me. If you still love me after this is over, what do you think?"

Her smile lit up her face. "I can't answer until there's an actual proposal, but I would love to move in together. You're always at my house anyway."

"Now, victory over these sons of bitches will taste even sweeter." I kissed her on her forehead, bracing myself to run for my life again. This time, I would have my girl with me instead of leaving her behind like I had after the fire.

My nerves pulsed with anxiety as I took Ari's hand, and we crept to the door, listening for voices.

She tugged on my arm, reached into her back pocket, and produced the pliers. "This is what we have to work with. Are there any other tools we could use as weapons on the tray?"

"Shit. I almost forgot. There are some screwdrivers. They'll do the trick if you jam them into the side of someone's neck." I rushed over and grabbed the two I'd seen earlier. Shoving them in my jeans pocket, I nodded. I lifted my head, my heart thundering as Ari's gaze seared through me. "Ready?"

"As ready as I'll ever be." She squeezed my hand.

With my pulse racing, I flipped the bolt and pushed the door open enough to peek out. "It's empty," I whispered to Ari. The exit door was only a few feet away, so we should make it as long as we were quiet.

I stepped into the hall, my chest tightening with anxiety. If anyone had told me I would be kidnapped and held hostage by my parents, I would have laughed so hard, I'd have pissed myself.

Ari and I crawled across the hall, counting to three under our breath. We pushed against the metal bar on the door and it opened with a groan. Wide-eyed and terrified that we'd alerted Psycho, we bolted out. Seconds later, a piercing alarm rang through the building.

"Run!"

Ari took the lead, zigzagging through the pine trees as if her life depended on it. It did. I pumped my arms, my shoulder giving me a big fuck you as voices started to close in behind us.

"Go, baby. Go. If you get away, bring help!" I motioned for her to run the opposite direction.

Ari tripped over a branch but gripped a smaller tree and managed to stay upright. "I'm not leaving you behind, Jagger. I can't."

"You can, Ari. Go. I'll distract them."

Ari looked over her shoulder, and several men were closing in fast. Ignoring my pleas, she grabbed my arm, and we ran through the woods. Thank fuck we were both in good shape or the terrain would have kicked our asses. A slope suddenly appeared, and Ari lost her footing. She busted her ass then tumbled down the hill.

"Ari!" I hurried after her, digging my heels into the ground to stop myself from falling too. God, I hoped she was okay.

Ari sat up slowly and brushed the leaves and dirt off her face.

"There they are!" Psycho yelled from the top of the steep slope.

Three men shot out from between the trees directly across from us, their expressions morphing from alarm to anger in seconds. They scrambled for their guns, and we were surrounded before Ari had a chance to get up.

Shaking and gasping for air, I groaned as every drop of adrenaline in my body flooded my bloodstream. We weren't going to make it out alive.

Chapter Forty-Four

Jagger

I landed with a thud on the cement floor before the door closed. Ari had kicked and screamed, giving the men hell until they knocked her out. She was tossed in a different room this time, across the hall. My new problem was that the entrance only opened from the outside. From where I was, it looked like a wall—no doorknob, only a keyhole.

"Fuck!" I groaned, picking myself up off the floor. I stumbled to the table and sank into the chair. I scrubbed my face with my cut and bloody palms. How was I going to get to Ariana? If they touched her, I'd fucking come unglued on them.

Standing, I walked the room and kept my legs moving. When Ari and I started to run, I could tell we hadn't eaten in a while. The only water we'd had were the little bits Psycho had provided. We were weak and dehydrated, which slowed us way down.

My gut twisted into knots as I sank into the chair, sifting through different ways to get Mom and Psycho to set Ari free. But before I had time to piece together what to do, the door opened.

Fearing the worst, I rose to my feet. Anticipation halted my breath in my lungs. My vision blurred, and my pulse pounded in my ears as my mother stormed in.

"I hope you're proud of yourself. All you did was manage to piss me and your father off. Things will be much worse for both of you."

It crossed my mind to apologize, but I didn't owe this bitch anything.

"Why?" If I was stuck in this shitty room with her, I wanted answers.

"Why what?"

It took a moment before I realized she had a bottle of water and a sandwich. She placed them on the table, her eyes never leaving mine. "Eat. I can't have you looking like shit. Your handsome features are what make you so valuable."

I grabbed the water, untwisted the cap, and downed a few gulps. It took everything inside me not to guzzle all of it at once. Finally, I sat in the chair across from my mother.

"What did I ever do to make you hate me so much that you used me as bait to kidnap little kids?" I sniffed the sandwich, then picked at the roast beef hanging from the side.

"It's not poisoned, so eat." She pointed to the food in my hand. "I'll bring you another one if you behave." She arched a penciled-in brow at me.

"Is that why Psycho snatched me up? Because you thought my looks would be good for business?"

My mother crossed her legs and smoothed her black slacks. "It was his idea. As you and Ari began to hook up and other girls started calling you after school, I knew you would fit the job perfectly."

I barked out a laugh. "Job? I never got paid."

"You had a roof over your head, food to eat, and clothes on your back. You were provided for." She tapped her red, manicured nails against the table. "At first, Psycho and I thought you might want to join the family business, but Psycho realized you had a soft heart for the kids and their parents. Our hopes to train you to take over fizzled pretty damn fast."

Befuddled, I shook my head. A beat of silence hung in the air. Finally, I took a bite of the sandwich, and my stomach growled in agreement. I set it down, chewing slowly. My mouth was dry, but the mayonnaise and tomato slices helped. I would see how it settled and if I got drowsy before I had another bite. I didn't trust her not to drug my food no matter what she said.

"What about you and Theo? You clearly never broke things off with Joe." I held her stare as I used my father's real name.

"Theo is a smoke screen. He's good in bed, works hard, and loves his family so much that he can't see the shit show in front of him. It's sad really."

"Are you and Joe . . . Did you even get divorced?"

"We did. Joe and I were young and toxic when we were together. At the time, I wouldn't embrace his dark side. After I took you and left, I met Theo. Not long after, Joe reached out. I realized I missed him terribly, and when he told me how much cash he was making." Mom gave me a little shrug. "Being a housewife and waiting for my husband to come home wasn't for me. I mean really, do I look like a Stepford wife to you? I wanted to live on the edge. Also, I knew you could bring us in a lot more money. Joe and I planned the fire and Ari's part in it. It came together beautifully. Everyone won. Theo got a large sum for the damages, you joined your father, Ariana was out of the way, and I steered the business from behind the scenes."

I rubbed my chest, where my heart pounded. The palpitations were full of fear, anger, and shock. "I don't even know who you are. My own mother has lived two lives, pretending to be a caring parent and wife."

"I'm sure it will sink in over time. You deserve the truth." The corner of her pink-painted mouth twitched.

"Which means you're going to kill me or force me to work for you again." Not feeling sick to my stomach or drowsy, I took another bite of my sandwich and slowly chewed as I stared a thousand holes into her. Hatred rolled to a boil, consuming me.

"No one will die . . . today. I'm here to welcome you back into the fold. With those beautiful blue eyes, dark hair, and gorgeous body, you'll bring more girls for us to sell than we could possibly manage. We'll need to hire more help. When I gave birth to you, I had no clue that you would be the best investment I ever made."

I scoffed at her. "How do you live with yourself? You're selling children, Mother. Children!" Cold, hard fury brewed in the pit of my stomach, and I itched with the urge to hit her. Never in my life had I wanted to lay hands on a woman, but she wasn't a woman. She was a fucking monster. All bets were off. My fingernails dug into my palms and I stood slowly.

"Just in case you get any big ideas in your thick skull, Psycho is holding Ariana at gunpoint." She reached into her slacks pocket. "If I push this button, he pulls the trigger."

A burst of panic strangled my throat. I mentally kicked myself for ever involving Ari in my life. I was toxic, a monster just like my parents, and I hated myself for it. Whatever was left of my heart shattered as the realization hit me like fucking hurricane, stealing my breath.

"That's why you want Ari. To control me."

"She's the only person that you've ever loved. Not me. Not your father. You like your friends, but Ariana is your person." Mom stood and smoothed her blue blouse. "Now, Ariana is *my* person." With that, she walked out of the room and left me with my dark thoughts.

Chapter Forty-Five

Ariana

"Where is Jagger?" I asked, my chin shaking with anger and fear. Jagger and I had almost escaped until Psycho's goons appeared out of nowhere.

"Jagger is having quality time with his mother," Psycho said around the toothpick dangling from his mouth. He propped his feet on the table and folded his arms over his chest.

After we were caught, Psycho tossed me into the room like a sack of flour. I cried out as my knees connected with the cement floor. It took me a few minutes to pull myself up into the chair. The sharp pain was horrendous, but I could bend my legs, which told me I had no broken bones. Running at this point wasn't going to happen, so hopefully, in a few days, I would return to normal.

Psycho's gaze narrowed on me. "You really don't remember, do you? At first, I thought it was all an act, but now I ain't so sure."

I rubbed my forehead, confused. "I have no clue what you're talking about."

He snorted. "Just proves my point. You don't remember meeting me after the fire?"

"I've never seen you. Even if your face hadn't burned, you wouldn't look familiar." His comment unsettled me, something strange stirring in my chest, but I couldn't pinpoint what it was. "Did I meet you when Jag was young? Honestly, he never talked about you, and neither did Samantha. Now that I think about it, I never even saw a picture of you." I smirked. "Sounds like your kid thought you were the real father of the year." Samantha's words bounced around in my head as soon as I said that. I wasn't sure if she was fucking with me about Dad's job not being legit or if there was truth to her statement. At this point, nothing would surprise me. For all I knew, Theo was mentally unstable and Samantha's partner in crime.

"The first time I saw you was right after Crimson snatched you."

Shock waves rippled through me, and I licked my dry lips. "I don't remember. I'm sure the trauma messed with my head and I've blanked out parts of what happened."

Psycho scratched his chin, the stubble whispering beneath his fingertips. "I suppose so."

"I remember Crimson." My palms slickened with sweat, and I rubbed them on my jeans.

"She's hard to forget," he grumbled.

Even though Psycho's nickname definitely fit him, I'd just realized even *he* had a weak spot.

"Why do you let Samantha talk to you that way? It's demeaning. According to Jagger, you run the fucking business. What's the deal? I figured a tough guy like you wouldn't allow a bitch to order you around." I drummed my fingers against my leg, wondering if there was any way to turn him against Samantha.

He answered me with his silence. Then it hit me. I leaned forward and propped my elbow on the table. "Oh hell, you've got it bad for her. Does she know?"

"Shut the fuck up, you have no clue what you're talking about."

Grinning, I crossed my legs. "I think I do. You're in love with her and would rather she treat you like shit than not have her in your life." I was grasping at straws, but my intuition rarely led me down the wrong path. If I'd listened to it concerning Peter, I wouldn't have landed in hot water with him. But desperation breeds desperate choices, and I couldn't pull myself out of my depression and grief when I thought I'd killed Jagger. God, I hoped he was okay.

"It sucks when the other person doesn't love you back," I whispered, ensuring my tone was compassionate. "I felt like that about Jagger for a long time."

He snorted. "You're a kid. What do you know about relationships?"

I held my hand up in surrender. "Hey, I just want to help. I think if she knew how you felt, maybe she would look at you as an equal in the business. It's worth a shot, isn't it?"

"What do you care?" Psycho grumbled, pouting. "I do everything for her: run the show, manage the workers, arrange the sales . . . "

"I can give you some pointers if you want. It sounds like she doesn't look at you as the smart guy you really are. I've been there." I hoped he couldn't see through my thin façade that I actually gave a fuck. I'd read in psychology class that kidnappers and serial killers don't humanize their victims. This was my lame attempt to become Psycho's friend. There was no way I could tell if it would work or not, but I didn't have anything to lose.

"Yeah? Whatcha got. If it works then I'll make sure you're treated a little nicer."

Not what I'm looking for, but it's a start.

"Isn't that funny. We both want to be treated better." I faked a yawn and leaned back in my chair. My stomach growled, and I placed my hand on it. "Some food and water would be nice. Maybe we could eat lunch together."

He glanced at his watch. "It's six thirty-two in the morning."

I tried to hide the surprise on my face. "How long have Jagger and I been here?"

Psycho flashed me a devilish grin. "Two days."

I groaned. "No wonder I'm tired and hungry. Have you ever gone two days without eating?" I asked, my voice teetering on whiney.

"All the time. You'll live."

The sound of the door opening distracted me from the monster babysitting me to the well-put-together woman waltzing in. One hand held a bottled water and the other a sandwich. Please, God, let those be for me.

"Samantha." I gave her a salute. "I would say it's nice to see you so soon, but I would be lying."

Samantha frowned. "You always were a smart-ass." She turned to Psycho and tilted her head to the door. "Leave."

Glancing at him, I waited for his attention to dart to me. "Told you," I mouthed. If anything, maybe I was fucking with him. It gave me something to do while I bided my time to try to find Jagger and escape again. If they thought I would work with them without a fight, Samantha and Psycho were sadly mistaken.

Psycho scooted his chair back, the metal feet scraping across the cement floor. He walked past Samantha and grumbled under his breath.

"He certainly isn't the chatty type." Under different circumstances, I would never talk to my kidnapper so casually, but this woman had helped raise me from the age of nine. The evidence was right in front of me. She was a hundred percent monster, but I still couldn't wrap my head around it.

She placed the water and sandwich on the table before she settled into the seat beside me.

"Where's Jagger?" The deep longing to know he was alive and unharmed made me flash my vulnerability like a stripper on a bad day.

"He's fine. Safe and sound." She cleared her throat and pointed to my sandwich. "Eat. You'll need your energy."

"For?" I opened the water but only allowed myself a few small drinks.

"You'll see." Samantha folded her hands in her lap.

"Did you ever love my father or, for that matter, your own son?" I unwrapped the sandwich and sniffed it.

Samantha laughed. "Jagger did the same thing. It's not drugged. You have my word."

I snorted. "Because your word is worth so much." Pulling the slice of tomato from between the bread, I popped it into my mouth.

"I love Jagger. Theo . . ." Her lips pursed. "He's a necessity."

I nodded and nibbled at the roast beef hanging off the side. As much as I wanted to wolf the food down, I had to take it slow and make sure she wasn't drugging me. Plus, I didn't want the food to come back up in record time.

"You should tell Jagger you love him. From this angle, it looks like you're a monster without the ability to feel anything except greed."

"My goodness. You don't hold back, do you?" She tilted her head, studying me while I took a full bite of my food. "You'll learn to be polite and do what you're told. If you don't, I'll hurt Jagger. If you comply, he stays safe."

I lowered my sandwich to the table, staring at her. "Don't you fucking touch him," I seethed. "You've done enough harm."

"Then you better stop being a little bitch." She smiled as if she'd won the game. Samantha had no damn clue how wrong she was. I'd learned a lot over the years with Peter, and I was happy to use Samantha as my guinea pig to try some new tricks, including escape.

I sank into the hard plastic chair. "He's been hurt enough. I can't be the cause of that." My voice cracked with emotion. Slowly, I looked at Samantha. "If I promise to be good and do what you say, could you give Jagger a message for me?"

Her brow rose. "What is it?"

Tears welled in my eyes. "Please tell him that I love him and . . . I'm sorry his mother is such a cunt."

Samantha moved so fast that I never saw her open hand coming until her slap nearly knocked me backward.

"Little bitch!"

I rubbed my cheek, laughing. Apparently, I was losing my

fucking mind talking to her that way. Betrayal did nasty shit to people. Closing my eyes, I felt the room spin and opened them again. My chest heaved with my frantic breathing, images flashing in my head and an eerie feeling of déjà vu tiptoeing down my spine.

"I highly recommend that you settle down, Ari. You'll have a new life, and if you earn it, you and Jagger can spend some time together."

I sat up and stuffed my sandwich in my mouth to keep it fucking shut. Samantha stared at me and offered me a sweet smile. "It's fascinating. All these years and it's still working."

I brushed a few loose strands of hair from my face. "What are you talking about?" I reached for my bottle and took a sip, allowing the water to roll over my parched tongue.

"I'm shocked but so happy. This is a huge game changer in how we run the business."

I swallowed excessively, attempting to clear the lump in my throat. "What was the game changer?" My hand fluttered to my chest, where my heart pounded against my ribs.

"Your stepbrother."

Chapter Forty-Six

Ariana

I stopped midchew, waiting for her to explain how Jagger had changed her business for the better. Considering that she kidnapped and sold kids, I wasn't okay with her revelation.

The few bites of food I'd eaten rolled in my stomach, and I willed them to stay down. If I was going to try to escape again, I needed all the energy I could get.

"When Jagger and I moved in with you and Theo, Jagger figured it would be fun to skip school. He thought Theo and I were at work. When he snuck into the house, he checked all the rooms to make sure no one was there. When he opened our bedroom door, he caught Joe . . . well, Psycho and me in bed together. Later, I found out that Jagger overheard us talking about how to nab us a new kid to sell to the highest bidder. Like a stupid child, he threatened to turn us in."

"I'm guessing if Jagger did tell the cops, you and Psycho talked your way out of it." I sipped my water.

"He never told them because we slipped him a drug that blocks your memory. It's similar to what doctors give to their patients right before surgery. You remember what happened before and a few hours after, but not during those moments. It was new on the black market and had some glitches. A few years later, Jagger remembered and accused me of the same thing he'd overheard us talking about. It was clear that we had a problem on our hands."

I listened intently, my legs shaking with what I suspected would be shared next.

"Joe and I decided that Jagger needed to be removed, so we decided a fire was needed."

"I was there. I recall all those horrible details of setting the fire and being held hostage. Too bad you didn't use the drug on me."

"And why would I want you to not remember those good times?" A wicked grin curled Samantha's lips. "It kept you in line and away from Jagger. I had to make sure our tracks were covered."

The room swayed, and I clutched my stomach. "You're insane."

"Maybe, but it's so much fun." She gave an innocent half-shrug. "After your time with Crimson, you were so easy to manipulate and control. It was as if you'd died inside."

"That's because I thought I killed Jagger," I growled, mentally picturing myself strangling the bitch.

Her gaze thinned, and she leaned farther onto the table, pinning me with a steely glare. "Here's a fun trivia fact for you. I'm Crimson's boss, Ariana. I arranged for her to kidnap you, force you to set the fire, and hold you hostage for three days until Joe could grab Jagger."

I gripped my bottle so hard that water sloshed over the rim and the plastic crinkled. I stared at her, unseeing, as my heart rate spiked. My chin trembled, a rush of confusion and anger hitting me all at once. "*You* were behind it all?"

She threw her head back and laughed as if she'd told the best joke she had ever heard.

Just then, a knock on the door pulled our attention away from the conversation. The entrance cracked open, and I nearly tumbled backward and out of my stupid chair.

A familiar, beautiful woman entered the room, smiling warmly at us. Her blue eyes sparkled, and not a single blonde hair was out of place. "Hey, bestie." She hugged Samantha, then sat next to her. "It seems I've missed some fun." She gave me a little wave. "My, haven't you turned out to be a gorgeous girl since I saw you last. It was a shame our time together couldn't have been longer." Crimson joined us at the table.

An onslaught of memories of those three days with her bombarded me, making me feel sick.

The ladies laughed while I stared wide-eyed at them.

"Kelly, or as you call her, Crimson is my best friend." Samantha leaned her head against her friend's. "It was easy enough to fool you all. Whenever I needed to manage the business, I told everyone I had to take care of my elderly aunt for a few days. Theo never questioned me."

My stomach dipped hard and gave me a firm fuck you on its way down to my toes. My attention bounced back and forth between them. "Does Jagger know that you're behind Joe putting him through hell?"

"Before I gave him the memory blocker, yes. I met with Joe and Jagger saw me and started to ask questions. It was a touch and go situation at first. For whatever strange reason, the memory blocker worked on Jagger later, but not when he caught Joe and me in bed along with our conversation. Then, we found the right dosage and the drug finally worked on him. My son is our first success."

Kelly clapped her hands together and squealed. "This means that when we befriend a family, we can slip them the drug, spend time feeding them false memories, and not worry about them identifying us. We'll never serve time in prison."

My mouth gaped open. "What the actual fuck?" I muttered. "If you're the boss, Samantha, then who is the mastermind behind the entire crime ring?"

Samantha feigned innocence. "It wasn't Joe, that's for damn sure."

The ladies' laughter sliced through my chest as white-hot rage blazed to life inside me.

Samantha squared her shoulders, pride rolling off her. "Joe and I are partners, but I call most of the shots."

"So Jagger and I were pawns to move you along in your twisted game of chess?"

"You and Jagger weren't just pawns. You were the best choices we could have made." Samantha winked at me. "Look at you, Ari. You're all grown up, beautiful, and smart. You'll attract the girls and guys alike."

I slammed my fist on the table. "I will *not* help you!"

Samantha shot me a dirty look as she reached inside her pocket and removed something similar to a key fob. "Psycho is babysitting Jagger. If I punch this button, his orders are to kill him. I suggest that you rein in that nasty temper of yours right now or you will have Jagger's death on your conscience . . . for real this time."

"Looks like you might need this as well." Crimson removed her gun from the back of her pants and slid it across the table to Samantha.

Checkmate!

Chapter Forty-Seven

Jagger

I paced the small area, swearing at the top of my lungs. It had been hours since Ari and I had been recaptured and Samantha left my room. Every time I referred to her as my mom, it made me sick in every sense of the word.

After running multiple scenarios through my head of how to break the fuck out of here again, defeat won out. I'd searched the door, but there was no way to open it from the inside without a key.

I had no idea how long Ari and I'd been missing, but surely someone was looking for us by now: my teammates at the society, Teagan and Ari's friends. Maybe Theo couldn't get in touch with Ari and he'd called the cops and sent a search party. Unfortunately, we'd lied to everyone about where we were.

Exhausted, I sank into one of the chairs and laid my head on the table. Images of Ari's smiling face eased my anxiety a little bit. I promised her a proposal if we got out of here, and for just a few minutes, I allowed my thoughts to wander in that direction. Maybe my subconscious would work a plan while I thought about the only girl I'd ever loved.

A gunshot jerked me up straight and I ran to the wall. I banged my fists on it as another shot was fired. "Ari! Ari!" I choked on my tears as additional shots rang out, my mind playing dirty tricks on me that Ari was lying on the floor bleeding out. I had to fucking get out of here. "Ari!" I pounded and screamed at the top of my lungs for what seemed like an hour before I heard the lock click. Stepping back, I raised my hands to protect myself. I didn't have a clue of what was happening in the hall or who was about to walk in.

The door flung open, revealing Samantha and another lady. Ariana was right behind them with a gun trained on them.

"Move. Now!" she ordered.

"Jagger, check Kelly to see if she's armed."

As I was too astonished to move, Ari had to repeat herself. Yells and another shot fired off, pulling me out of my fog.

"Kelly?"

"Jagger, search her. She's your mother's best friend, also known as Crimson. I'll explain later."

It only took a moment for me to frisk Kelly and remove the firearm from her calf holster. In a few seconds, I checked to see if there was a bullet in the chamber. Apparently, Kelly came locked and loaded.

"Come on, Jag." Ari stepped back, keeping an eye on the women.

A loud crash rang through the building, and I hurried to my stepsister.

"Later, Mom." I trained my weapon on her as Ari began to back out of the room.

With a quick move, Samantha lunged in our direction. Before I had time to fire, Ari took out both of Samantha's knees. She screamed as she crumpled to the floor in agony, blood spilling on the floor.

"Are you having fun now, Samantha?" Ari asked, steel in her voice.

"You little bitch!" Kelly lost her fucking mind and charged at us just like her best friend had. How Crimson could do the same thing as Samantha but expect a different result was beyond me.

I stepped in front of Ari then fired off a shot. Kelly dropped to the floor, her unseeing eyes wide open.

Samantha screamed then burst into tears. "You shot my best friend in the head? You stupid son of a bitch!"

Ari nudged me in the ribs with her elbow. "Let's go."

We slipped out of the room and closed the door behind us. Ari and I were at the opposite end of the hall from the exit door, but from the sounds, shit was still going down somewhere in the building.

"Cover me," Ari said, hurrying to check the exit. She pushed on the bar and poked her head outside. "It's clear." She waved me forward.

I jogged to her, my heart pounding so hard, my chest ached. She slipped outside, and I was inches away when a loud voice boomed,

"Stop right there!"

Ari's eyes widened, then she peeked around me. "Gunner?"

"Jag? Ari?"

"Holy fuck. Thank God you're here." I lowered my gun and slumped against the wall. Ari tore past me and ran to Gunner at full speed, her weapon still in her hand.

She nearly tackled him with her embrace. "I'm so happy to see you."

"Man, you two gave us a scare and half. Are you okay?" Gunner held Ari close, then he released her and looked her over.

"Jagger? You hurt, man?" He walked down the hall toward me.

"Just my ego." I cracked a grin at him before I hugged him. "How the hell did you find us?"

Gunner rubbed the back of his neck, then he pointed at Ariana. "She and Teagan Mercer have each other added to the Find My iPhone feature. It's a smart thing to do these days. When Teagan couldn't get in touch with Ari, she drove right to our house. She banged on the door, demanding to know where you two were. I had barely walked in myself, so I had no idea you guys were gone yet.

Once we searched the premises and neither of you turned up, I knew something was wrong. Besides, both your phones were on the nightstands. Ari's backpack and your duffle bags were still there, too."

"Tiny. It was Tiny," Ari blurted. "He took us when we were asleep. I thought it was all a dream, but he drugged us at dinner."

I pulled Ari against me and kissed the top of her head. "Can we get the hell out of here?"

"Wait." Ari produced the key to the room that held Samantha and Kelly and pushed the door open. "You might want to see this."

Gunner's mouth pressed into a thin line, then he walked to the entrance and peered in. "Son of a bitch." Gunner's gaze bounced from his sister to us. "How the hell did all of this go down?"

"He killed her. Jagger killed Kelly!" Samantha pointed at me.

"Ari shot her in the kneecaps so she couldn't follow us. She needs medical attention." I stared at Samantha. "Or not."

Ari closed the door again and gave Gunner the key. "She's your sister, and now she's your problem. I never saw a fucking thing." She patted him on the arm then took my hand.

"The fight is over, so we're good to go. I'll have one of my men take care of Samantha."

An ache consumed me. I wasn't sure how I would feel if my mother suddenly showed up dead or if I had the opportunity to talk to her again. Maybe that made me as much of a monster as she was.

Ari and I snuggled up on Gunner's couch a few hours later, and Teagan sat at the other end. Gunner, Cupcake, Rigs, and a few other men from the MC occupied the living and dining area.

Ari explained about the memory blocker, that Kelly was Crimson, and Samantha was behind the entire criminal ring. Silence hung in the air once she finished providing all the details.

"You wouldn't have ever found us if Teagan and I didn't share the

Find My iPhone. Thank God," Ari whispered, choking on her emotions.

"Girl, it saved your life." Teagan's eyes welled with tears.

"No shit. From now on, I'm going to watch out for you too," Ari said, pointing at Teagan.

If I wasn't mistaken, guilt flashed in Teagan's gaze momentarily. I wondered if Ari caught it.

"When Teagan nearly busted the door down and we realized you both were missing, I called in a favor to another MC. One of the men has an infrared drone, so he flew it about twenty miles in each direction. That fucker was cool as shit and military grade, and it could cover long distances without any problem. There were two buildings out in the middle of nowhere, and one showed movement inside. We were able to get a count, then we took down the guys guarding the entrance of the abandoned warehouse."

"How many people were there?" Ari asked.

I tightened my hold around her waist as she leaned against me, her back to my chest.

"Ten or so." Gunner laughed.

I wondered what happened to them, but I trusted Gunner would tell us later. "And . . . Tiny?" I asked, searching each man's face as I waited for Gunner's response.

"No need to worry about him ever again. He broke the code and betrayed us all. You don't walk away from that kind of sin."

Teagan's eyes widened. "I won't ask."

"Good. Don't," Ari said.

Over the next hour, we continued to discuss everything we'd learned. Samantha's name never came up, and I didn't mention it either. I would pull Gunner aside later and find out how he'd decided to deal with her. After all, it was his sister and my mother. It would be hard to bury the past, but I was ready to make a fresh start with Ariana by my side.

"I guess I'll talk about the elephant in the room," Ari softly said. "What happened to Psycho?"

"I'll fill you in on that shit when we don't have additional ears around." Gunner tilted his head toward Teagan.

"Sorry. I wasn't thinking."

"Let's get some food in our bellies and some drinks in our glasses," Gunner said, standing from the barstool.

Chatter erupted throughout the room, and Ari looked up at me. "I love you." She kissed me, and I allowed myself to get lost in her touch.

"Love you too, baby." I winked at her then focused on Teagan. "Love you too, Teagan. You're my hero."

Teagan's cheeks flamed red before she burst into tears.

Ari slid across the couch and hugged her best friend as they finally cried together.

Chapter Forty-Eight

Ariana

I sat at the desk in my bedroom, grateful to be home with Jagger and the girls after the shit went down with Samantha. It was almost too bizarre to be real.

"I can't believe it's nearly Thanksgiving," I said to Jagger, who was stepping into his jeans. His muscles rippled in his legs, and my gaze skated up to his washboard abs. I could look at them all damn day.

"I'm ready to settle into a schedule again." Jagger grabbed his grey sweatshirt and pulled it over his head, blocking my view. "And get back on the field."

Once we returned to Whitmore and discussed it with the girls, Jag told Coach he was moving in with me. It was nice to have him next to me at night. I slept better, and the nightmares didn't plague me as often.

"I know. At least Coach is using you to help with plays and on the sidelines. If for some reason you aren't able to play again, I think you would make one hell of a coach."

Jagger smiled, but it didn't reach his eyes. "It's a backup for sure. But I'll do whatever I have to in order to return to normal. The physical therapist doesn't see why that can't happen. Tiny at least shot my left shoulder instead of my right. It still fucks me up, but . . ." He placed his hands on his hips. "I'm trying to find the ray of light in this dark, fucked-up mess."

I stood and smoothed my teal top before I closed the gap between us. "I know. Me too. Maybe Samantha and Psycho's business is over and we saved some kids. If that's the case, then I would do it over and over again."

Jag pressed his forehead to mine. "Same. I think about how many children and families I hurt already. Maybe this was the universe's way of giving me a sliver of redemption by ridding the planet of a few more sick bastards." Jagger pulled me against him and gently kissed me. "A part of me is still in shock that my mother was behind it all."

"And the memory blocker. I still can't swallow that she tested the drug on her son. She has zero conscience."

Jagger brushed my hair from my forehead. "It's twisted that she experimented on me, and it's still hard to process." He hesitated, sadness flickering across his face. "Ari, I stand with you on taking time away from Theo. I'm angry with him too. But he's the only family other than Gunner we have left. Now that we have all the pieces of the puzzle, maybe think about forgiving him. My mom tricked him too. He lost his wife and his daughter."

I frowned, not liking where the conversation was going. I wasn't ready to forgive Theo yet. He'd lied to both of us for years. Plus, they weren't a few white lies. If they were, then it would be a moot point. Theo willingly chose to let me believe that I'd killed my stepbrother. How would I pretend that never happened?

"Where's this coming from?" I placed my palm on his chest, the steady beat of his heart soothing my unruly emotions.

"I knew my dad was twisted, but I thought Mom was a good person. When her charade was shattered, it felt like a hot knife stabbed me in the chest. Both of my parents are straight-up evil, which makes me think I'll end up like them. But my point is that you never know how much time you might have with Theo."

I worried my bottom lip with my teeth. "Samantha . . . Do you believe she was playing mind games when she said that Theo's business isn't legit?"

Jag took a deep breath. "I'm not sure. We've never been around Theo at work. It's not like we've overheard phone calls or saw him sneaking out and meeting shady people. Honestly, I think she wanted to fuck with your head. It's her talent."

"If he is then I don't want anything to do with him, Jagger. It makes more sense to keep him at arm's length." I scrunched the soft material of his sweatshirt beneath my fingers.

"What if you're wrong? Then you've pushed him away when this might be a good time to make things right." He rubbed my back and placed his chin on the top of my head. "Do what feels best for you. Just promise me that you'll consider it. If he died tomorrow, would you be okay with how it ended?"

When I finally realized where Jagger was coming from, my heart hurt for him. "I'm sorry you didn't have that chance with your parents."

Jagger remained silent as we held each other.

The doorbell rang, and I stepped back. "You ready to have some fun and celebrate with our friends?"

"Hell yeah. It will be good to see everyone." He took my hand and led me down the hall and the stairs.

"Can someone get that?" Gabby called from the kitchen.

"I got it!" Excitement bubbled up in my chest. This was our first Friendsgiving, and I was so excited. Flinging the door open, I offered them a huge smile as my attention landed on Kane, Quinn, Anderson, and another guy.

"Hey, come on in," Jagger said.

I laughed as the teammates filed into our home, each holding a bottle of alcohol. We'd agreed the girls would cook and provide the food and the guys would bring the booze and mixers.

Kane slowed. "Ari, this is Sterling. I'm not sure if you've met him or not."

"Thanks for having me." His sandy-blonde hair flopped into his eyes and he brushed it aside. He looked at Jagger and raised a bottle of tequila. "Hey, man. Good to see you. How's the shoulder. Miss your ass on the field with us."

"Me too. Can't wait to get out there and crack some pads." Our friends laughed as I closed the door.

Quinn sniffed the air. "Something smells really good. I think I need to check out what's happening."

I remained in the living room as the guys headed to the kitchen. Laughter filled the house, and my heart twisted into knots. None of our friends knew the truth about Samantha and the kidnapping except for Teagan, and she'd sworn to keep our secret, taking it to her grave. I realized she was scared as well. We were still waiting to see how things unfolded but were afraid to ask Gunner about his sister. At least Gunner had let Jagger know that Psycho would never be a problem for us again, or anyone else for that matter. I understood what that meant. As for my wicked stepmother, I didn't want more blood on our hands than we already had, but a part of me wanted to know if Samantha was alive or not. Surely her arrest would have made the news, but we hadn't heard or seen a single thing. The criminal world dealt with people very differently than the cops and the legal system. In this case, I appreciated that fact.

Jagger returned to the living room with two blue Solo cups in his hands. He'd been able to ditch the sling and moved much more normally.

"Here. Your fave, vodka and cranberry juice." He gave the glass to me and kissed me.

I took a drink and choked. "Damn, baby, did you make this?"

Everlee popped her head out from the kitchen and waved at me. "Glad you like it!" She laughed as she disappeared.

"She's having fun with all the guys' attention. Maybe she'll find someone soon."

"You never know what's around the corner." Jag sat on the couch and pulled me into his lap.

Kane and Quinn joined us, and I listened to them talk about football and the upcoming game. I felt calm and at peace with my life for the first time in years. I'd fought my ass off and had to claw my way out of hell to get there, but even Peter had served a purpose. I'd learned a lot of skills with his sick games. At least I could be grateful for that.

The afternoon turned into an evening as our group ate, drank, and laughed. Not only was the house full of love, but so was my heart. Although I had the girls at the academy, I still had a huge hole inside myself after I lost Jagger. Not anymore.

Jagger and I returned to my bedroom around ten-thirty. The guys had left, and I suspected they were going to meet up at the society.

"How did your friends take the news about you leaving the society?" I sank onto my bed and stretched out.

"They weren't surprised. We can use the rooms if we want since you're one of the first girls to be invited that joined." Jagger climbed onto the mattress with me, smiling.

"Oh yay!" I laughed. "I won't lie, I would have been sad if we couldn't pop in on occasion."

Jagger cupped my chin and turned my face to his. "My girl likes to be dominated, huh?"

I rolled my eyes. "You already know that. If I didn't, I would have dipped out after the first time I was there." I traced my fingernail down his chest. "Who runs the society, Jagger?"

An ornery grin graced his gorgeous features. "I'm sworn to secrecy, so if I did know, I couldn't tell you. But we have no fucking clue."

I sat up and crossed my legs. "What? You don't know whose running it? I figured by now you would."

"No. We've talked to him, but he has his skull mask with the disguiser on as well as his cloak."

"Do you guys have an educated guess after spending time with him?"

Jag shook his head. "We thought it was someone on the football team, but he had the girls ready for us right after the games."

I cocked a brow at him. "Jag, he could have set it up earlier that week. He only needed a few people at the door to lead each girl to the rooms, right? The King Cobra didn't need to be there." My mind scrambled with the ideas of who it might be. "I still think he's a football player."

Jag laced his fingers behind his head, thinking. "Why?"

"I mean, I'm not with you guys, but I know Anderson and you are members. If I had my guess, so are Quinn, Kane, and Sterling."

Jagger clenched his jaw, the muscles twitching. *Bingo.*

"You're all football players, but more than that, I'm guessing the society is also a brotherhood. It makes sense; it's like the fraternities. Sure, it's about parties and getting laid, but it offers a lifetime friendship. That's why I think it's one of your teammates or he wouldn't have selected the guys that he did."

Jagger's eyes narrowed. "I am curious to find out. Since this is the first year, I suspect he's checking to see if he can trust everyone. Hell, I would remain anonymous, too, until I was sure the society was going to work and there were good people in place."

My phone buzzed in the back pocket of my jeans and I removed it. "Huh. Speak of the devil." I held up the screen to Jagger.

"Are you going to answer it?"

I stared at the name, wishing Theo wasn't calling. I'd had an amazing day and he would most likely ruin it. Against my better judgment, I answered.

"Hey." It was a big change from how I typically greeted him. That time, my voice wasn't full of love and eagerness to hear how he was doing.

"Thanks for taking my call, Ari. I know you made it clear where you stand, but I have some news."

"Jagger is with me. Can I put you on speaker?"

"Sure."

I tapped the screen and set the phone on the bed between us.

"Hi, Theo."

"Hey, Jag. How's the shoulder?"

"Better. I should be on the field again soon, thanks to my physical therapist."

"That's great." A pause filled the line. "I won't keep you long, but I wanted both of you to know that I was contacted earlier. Samantha was taken to a hospital by an anonymous person and she was treated in Montana. She couldn't remember how she'd gotten there, and the cops were just able to track me down. Apparently, she has Joe as her emergency contact, not me. They tried to find him for almost a week. When they couldn't locate him, they reached out to me."

My stomach dropped to my toes, and I forced myself not to puke. She isn't dead.

"Interestingly enough, Gunner also contacted me. He told me to divorce Samantha and get as far away from her as possible. He shared with me about what she was involved in, kids." Theo's voice trailed off, and I wondered if he felt guilty for putting us in harm's way.

"It wasn't your fault, Theo. No one realized what she was a part of," Jagger said.

My head snapped up, and I stared at him. The genuine expression on his face backed me down. Theo had been the only steady and decent parent Jagger had ever had. He still needed that, even if I didn't want to have Theo in my life.

"Thanks, Jagger. That means a lot. I'm not sure how to fix the rift between us . . . for lying and allowing Samantha to manipulate me into believing I was making a good decision keeping you two apart. Maybe you can forgive me, maybe not. To try to make up for it, I'll cover your tuition and expenses until you both graduate. You can attend anywhere you want. I also have no problem with your relationship. I hope that you've found something special. True, deep love is hard to come by."

Jagger rubbed his jawline. "Actually, you have a bank account with Mom, right?"

"Yeah. But she has a separate one too," Theo admitted. "We both do."

"Do you have access to hers? If the FBI hasn't gotten involved, you need to drain them, Theo. Move the money into yours and take her name off any financials, insurance policies, etc."

"I know. I already called my lawyer to get ahead of this before it blows wide open. If it does at all. She's convincing everyone she has amnesia."

"That's such bullshit. She remembers," I said.

"She's a great actress for sure. But, Jag, I'll drain her accounts then set you and Ari up with those funds. If it buys you a house or whatever you want . . . Well, after all the shit you two went through, she owes you big."

Jagger chuckled. "I like the way you think. I would be happy to take her earnings."

"It's dirty, blood money. I don't want it." I shot Jag a look, unhappy that we hadn't discussed it.

"Ari, how you feel makes sense, but we could do something good with the funds. Money isn't evil or good. What you do with it makes the difference. Go out there and change lives. Or, since you and Jagger saved future kids and families, consider it payment. However you need to process it."

I frowned. I hated that what Theo said made sense. "Maybe we can donate some of it to Ashton Kutcher's foundation. He helps bring home kids and people in sex trafficking."

"I would love to do that," Jagger agreed and took my hand in his.

"I'll let you two go, but if you want . . . if either of you want to call or visit, I would love to see both of you." Guilt and pain threaded Theo's words.

"I'll be in touch, Theo. I know Mom can be a con artist, and I think you got caught up in her shit." Jagger glanced at me. He wasn't asking me permission to have a relationship with my father, but I was okay with it. My stepbrother would be good for Theo and vice versa.

I cleared my throat. "I can't forgive you yet, Theo. You let me think I killed Jagger and it nearly destroyed me. Maybe someday I can, but not yet. I need some time."

"I understand, Ari. I'm truly so sorry. I love you so much." Theo choked on his words, and I realized he was crying. Good. I hoped he felt as shitty as I did.

"Jag, I'll reach out to you tomorrow. I'll tap into her accounts now. I know where she hid the passwords," Theo said.

"Thanks. Have a good evening."

"Night," I said before ending the call. Glancing at Jag, I rolled my shoulders, trying to break up some of the tension. "I support you in your choice with Theo, but I ask that you support mine, too."

Jagger rubbed the back of my hand with his thumb. "Of course. I wouldn't have it any other way."

Chapter Forty-Nine

Ariana

Jagger had left earlier to hang out with his friends.

Since the girls were all at their parents' places for the Thanksgiving holiday, I did some retail therapy by myself. Having alone time was rare, and I also treated myself to some sushi.

It was almost five in the afternoon when I returned. I called out to see if Jag was back, but the house only greeted me with silence. I set my bags near the door before going to the kitchen.

Spotting a blue piece of paper on the dark wood of the kitchen table, I picked it up.

I'll be back around five. Get naked and lie on the couch. No touching yourself.

Grinning like crazy, I peeked at the clock on the wall over the sink—ten more minutes. I hurried upstairs to our bathroom and freshened up. While brushing my teeth, I heard the front door open and froze. Fuck, his watch must be faster than ours. I quickly rinsed and dried my mouth.

"Ariana!" Jagger's voice boomed through the home.

I took my time strolling to the top of the stairs and looked down at him, butterflies running amok in my belly. "You're early."

"You need to set your clock correctly," he growled. His heated gaze swept up and down the length of me. "Why are you still dressed?" He rubbed his chin, and I guessed he was thinking about how he would punish me.

"Because you're early," I said sweetly, making my way down the stairs, my body tingling with anticipation. I stood transfixed by his every move and his gorgeous features.

He made his way to the couch and picked up a brown bag from the coffee table. Jagger glanced at me as he dumped the contents on the glass top. Curiosity reared its head as I joined him. Oh. Shit. I sank my teeth into my lower lip as my focus landed on the items: rope, lube, butt plugs, and a dual vibrator. Jagger's hand traveled up my back, then he wrapped my hair around his fingers and pulled until I landed on my knees. "Do you know what tonight is?"

My insides quivered with excitement. I was pretty sure I could guess from the toys in front of me.

"What?"

"I'm taking every part of you tonight. Not being naked when I got home." He tsked. "You've been a naughty girl, Ariana."

I gawked at him.

I did as he asked, peeking up at him.

He flipped open the button on his jeans and lowered his zipper with his free hand. He freed his thick erection and rubbed it against my mouth. "Naughty girls don't get to cum."

I grimaced. Dammit.

"Open."

I did as he commanded, and the smooth skin of his shaft glided over my tongue.

"That's it." His attention was trained on me as I sucked his dick, the otherwise quiet house filling with his grunts as he moved his hips.

Almost as quickly as he'd shoved himself into my mouth, he stepped away. "Take your clothes off."

He watched me as I discarded my shirt, bra, shorts, and G-string. Standing in front of him, I shivered as his gaze latched onto my bare pussy. Without a word, he shucked off his shirt, jeans, and boxer briefs then sat on the couch, his erection resting against his stomach. "Bend over." His voice was gruff and sexy as hell, sending shivers of anticipation through me as he patted his thigh.

I settled over his lap, my butt in the air. Jagger spread me apart then ran his finger up and down my slit, but this time, he smeared my juices up to my asshole. No one had fucked me in the ass, but I'd let Jagger know I was ready. Apparently, he was, too.

He smacked my ass cheek and I jumped. He leaned over my back, pinning me down as he slapped my butt repeatedly. Tears filled my eyes from the sting, but I refused to let him know.

He rubbed my tender skin, then slipped a finger inside me. "So wet."

I whimpered as he fucked me. "Does that feel good, baby?"

"Yes," I responded breathlessly.

He immediately stopped and swatted my ass one more time. "Sit." He moved me off his lap before he stood. Jagger ripped open the package of the dual vibrator before he disappeared into the kitchen. I heard the water running and realized he was washing the toy. I wasn't sure I was supposed to find that sexy as hell, but I did. He returned and sat on the edge of the coffee table, his eyes hooded with desire. "Fuck yourself."

I leaned over and accepted the vibrator. Spreading my legs, I positioned myself on the couch where he had a full view of my ass and pussy. "I need the lube."

Although Jagger sometimes pushed my limits in the bedroom, he also understood that my comfort was important. There were a few places he had wiggle room, but not with anal sex.

He gave me the cherry-flavored lube, and I used it to slicken up both tips, then turned the toy on. The soft buzzing filled the area, then I ran it over myself before I eased it in. A gasp escaped as pure pleasure pulsed through me. "Oh God." I pushed it all the way in, then out. Jagger's attention was glued to me as I writhed on the couch before him. His hand wrapped around his shaft and he stroked himself.

"That's it, baby. Take it all. Get ready for me."

I cupped my breast, tugging on my nipple. "Jagger." My eyes fluttered closed as the familiar feeling pooled low in my belly.

He knelt, taking over the vibrator. His tongue circled my clit, and I grabbed his hair as I bucked against him. Nipping and licking, he brought me to the edge then stopped. He gave me a mischievous smile as he crawled on the couch and hovered over me. Then, he startled me and forced his cock into my mouth again.

His hips thrust faster as he shoved the tip to the back of my throat. He growled as his hot liquid coated my lips. I swallowed it greedily, sucking every drop from him.

Jagger pulled out then stood on the floor. "You took that like a good girl." His dick began to soften, and my lip jutted out. "Don't worry, my pet. This time will be well spent. Stand up and bend over the couch."

At times like these, I didn't have to say much, and I relaxed and let him set the tone. I got up then eagerly bent over.

"Spread your legs."

I gave him the access he wanted and waited for his next move. "Goddammit. Just looking at you has my cock getting hard again." He knelt then ate my pussy like I'd never experienced before. He nipped the insides of my thighs as he shoved his finger into me long enough to get it slick, then he pressed it against my asshole and pushed as he sucked on my clit.

How in God's name I wasn't supposed to cum was beyond me. I clung to the soft leather, my moans filling the house.

Seconds before I was about to lose it, he rose from the floor, and my body yearned for his touch. I glanced over my shoulder, watching as he picked up the lube from the couch, squeezed some in his hand, then stroked his shaft. My eyes were glued to him as his dick fully hardened again. Grabbing the vibrator, he slid it into my core and turned it so the shorter end wouldn't penetrate my ass, but he didn't turn it on.

He pumped me a few times with the toy, then he moved his cock to my tight hole. He pressed against me and pushed the tip in.

"More," I pleaded.

"You're so tight, baby. That sweet little ass is all mine." He eased in some more, still fucking me with the vibrator at the same time with his other hand. Jagger removed the toy and tossed it on the couch. His fingers dug into my hips as he worked his long dick inside me. Currents of electricity surged through me as he picked up the pace.

My whimpers and moans escaped me as he reached between my legs and pinched my clit. Jolts of pleasure mixed with pain rippled over my flesh.

"Do you like me in your ass?" He smacked my bundle of nerves before he massaged it.

"Yeah," I answered breathlessly. "Fuck me, Jagger."

"Who do you belong to, Ari?"

"You."

"No one will ever touch you again. This is all mine. Say it." He reached for my throat and squeezed.

"No one ever again," I said.

His fingers tightened around my neck as he pumped into me. My senses heightened as he blocked my air, and I drowned in exquisite waves of pleasure. The rush of the blood to my head while he fucked me was beyond anything I'd experienced before, and I loved every second.

"Cum for me, Ari."

My body seized as black dots danced across my vision as an intense orgasm ripped through me, peaking his release as well. He jerked, his hold on my neck loosened, and I sucked in a much-needed breath as I returned to earth. Panting, I nearly collapsed on the couch, but he was still inside me.

Jagger dotted a few kisses on my back before he eased out, then he slapped me on the ass and disappeared down the hall of the main floor. I sat down, my core and butt throbbing from pain and the aftermath of our playtime. The water running in the bathroom let me know he was cleaning up. When it turned off, his feet padded along the wood floors and to the living room.

Jagger once again knelt and tenderly cleaned me with a warm washcloth. He kissed the inside of each thigh then rose, his expression full of adoration. "Are you hungry? I'll cook."

I grinned at him. "How could I refuse that offer?" I placed my hand in his, then he tugged me off the seat and into a standing position. I rested my palms against his chest and peered up at him.

Jagger smoothed my hair and kissed me. "I love you, Ariana Ellison."

"I love you, too, Jagger Whitlock."

He wrapped me in a warm embrace, and we stood there completely naked and vulnerable with each other—skin to skin, with no more fronts or façade, just our hearts beating in sync . . . for each other. At that moment, I realized that home wasn't a place. It was a person. And wherever Jagger was, I finally understood it was where I belonged. That I was home.

Chapter Fifty

Jagger

I stood by Coach on the sidelines, watching my friends play without me. It sucked big time, but at least I was with them in person. We had a six-point lead, and it was closing in on halftime.

Kane threw a beautiful pass up the middle of the field. Quinn ran his ass off to catch it, but number thirty-nine on the opposing team clipped Quinn and knocked him out of the way. The offense caught the ball and intercepted it.

"Dammit!" I fisted my hand and listened to Coach swear a blue streak. The game was way too close for that to be happening. I glanced into the stands, spotting Ari in a bright red jacket. I returned my focus to the game, chatting with Coach about strategies.

"When can you play again, Jagger? We need you out there," Coach said.

"I might make the last one if we're in playoffs." Regret that I ever trusted Tiny infiltrated my being. "Even if I do, I'm not in shape. So, next season."

Coach grimaced but nodded. "You have to heal correctly or you'll never be out there. I'd rather you wait."

"Why don't you bump Samson from second string into my place. I know you have Ty there now, but I believe Samson is stronger. Just my opinion."

Coach's eyes narrowed. "You think he has what it takes?"

"I do. I've watched him in practice. He's spot-on with his catches and can dodge the defense. He's light on his feet." I folded my arms over my chest. "Just don't give him my spot." I grinned at Coach.

"Don't even worry about that. Your position is safe. You're one of the best running backs I've seen in years." Coach walked over to Samson and chatted with him.

Samson's face lit up, and he jumped off the bench, ready for his chance. I hoped he wouldn't blow it. He had a lot of potential.

Whitmore had the ball again, and Coach sent Samson in. It was easy to tell when players were hungry for an opportunity because they worked their butts off on the field. By the third play, Samson caught the football and hauled ass down the field and into the end zone one second before the halftime whistle.

The crowd went wild, and my teammates were all over Samson, congratulating him. If he kept playing like that, he would be on the first string by the next game.

With a massive grin, Coach approached me again and slapped me on the back. "Great call, Jagger."

"Thanks. Let's hope he keeps it up and we can gain a better lead. Until then . . ." I tugged on my shirt. I hadn't suited up but wore my team jacket and jeans instead.

"Coach, aren't we heading up to the locker room?" Anderson asked.

"In a few. Grab some water and have a seat until I tell you."

Anderson frowned but didn't argue. He let the team know they were hanging tight for a few.

Coach patted me on the back. "Good luck, Jagger."

My stomach was in a million knots as I approached the referee, who gave me his microphone. He helped me clip it on before I jogged onto the middle of the field. Applause filled the stadium as the Whitmore fans stood. I waved, grateful for all of their support.

"Thanks. It's good to be on the turf again," I said into the mic. "As we all know, it's been a hard year, but one amazing thing has happened." Searching the sidelines for Ari, I spotted her surrounded by Everlee, Leighton, Gabby, and Teagan. The girls had talked her into joining them on the sidelines for the halftime show. The ladies were trying to hide their smiles but failing.

"Ariana, can you join me?"

The shock on Ari's face when I called her to the field was almost comical. Her friends nudged her forward, pointing in my direction. She broke into a run, her jacket flying behind her. Ari's cheeks and nose were pink from the cold.

"This is Ari." I held her hand, and she waved at everyone in the stands. "We were reunited this year, but I've been in love with her since I was twelve. Ari is my stepsister, but she walked away with my heart when we were teenagers. Unfortunately, we were separated after our house burned to the ground. Both of us thought the other was dead."

The crowd gasped, and I took that moment to look at the love of my life before I continued.

"It seems fate had other ideas because Ari started attending Whitmore this year. Not long after, we ran into each other."

Ari giggled, and I suspected she remembered how we fucked each other at the society.

"One thing I've learned is that life is short. In a blink of an eye, everything can change. After four years of thinking Ariana was dead, when I saw her, I knew I never wanted to be apart from her again." I turned to her and dug in my pocket for what I needed. Thanks to Theo transferring my mother's funds to my new bank account, I was able to make my dream into reality. Dropping to a knee, I flipped open the little blue box, the one-carat princess-cut engagement ring catching the lights on the field.

"I never want to live without you again, Ari. You're the love of my life, and I can think of nothing more I rather do than start our next chapter together. Would you do me the honor of marrying me?"

Silence filled the stadium, and I assumed everyone was holding their breath like I was. If Ari said no, it would destroy me, but I had to take that chance.

Ari reached out and placed her cold hand against my cheek, her eyes welling with tears.

"I love you with every fiber in my being, Jagger. Yes, I'll marry you."

My shoulders relaxed, and I slipped the ring on her finger before I stood. Once again, the stadium erupted with cheers and applause.

I wrapped Ari in my arms and kissed her hard. "Thank you, Ari. Thank you for saving me."

She embraced me and buried her face in my neck. "I love you. Thank you for making your way back to me."

I promised myself that I would always protect Ari and return to her no matter what our future looked like. She was my rock. My home. I'd lived with and without her. I would move heaven and earth never to lose her again. She was *mine*.

***

Want more of the secret society, football, and masked men? There are three more standalones! Click here to download Ruthless Obsession in Kindle Unlimited! *Turn the page for a sample of our morally gre hero watching his prey.*

Ruthless Obsession Sample

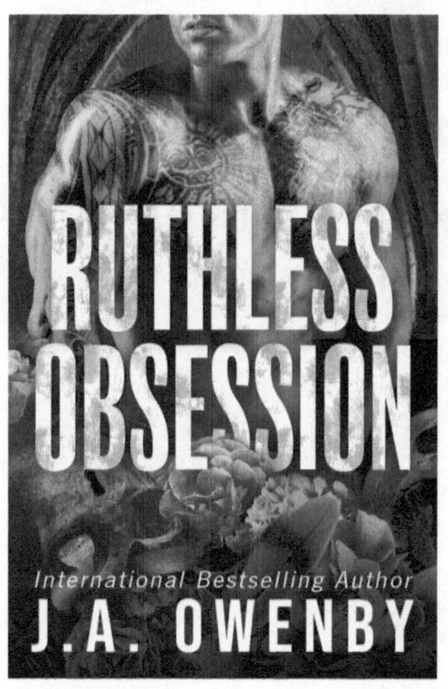

I ask for nothing. I bow to no one.
Then Teagan Mercer arrives on campus.

She's to blame for destroying my life,
but I refuse to let her ruin my shot at the NFL.
I will never forgive her for what she did,
and I have the power to make her pay.
When the memories come rushing back,
I'm falling into the darkness that nearly destroyed me.
But this time, I'm taking her down with me.

★★★★★ "Unlike Anything You've Read In A Dark Enemies-to-Lovers book!" ~ Kristin, Goodreads Review

This full-length novel is a **dark, secret society, sports, enemies-to-lovers standalone** *featuring a damaged hero, a strong, calculating heroine, and a lot of kinky times. No cheating, no cliffhanger, and a happily ever after guaranteed!*

Download Ruthless Obsession on Amazon or **FREE** in Kindle Unlimited! **Click Here!**

Turn the page for the Sample of Ruthless Obsession.

Prologue

My hard-on painfully strained against my jeans as I leaned against the tree. The rough bark rubbing the sleeve of my navy polo shirt as I watched her every move.

A ray of sunshine trickled through the red, orange, and yellow leaves, spotlighting the dark brown highlights in her otherwise black hair. Teagan Mercer was stunning. She was more than beautiful with her toned legs, curvy hips, and perky tits. But her eyes ... those doe-like eyes could melt the hardest of hearts. Except for mine. The only thing I wanted to see were tears in them while I made her beg for mercy.

I rubbed my clean-shaven jaw, then stuffed my hand in my pocket as I watched her frown at her phone screen. My dick twitching at the mere thought of bringing Teagan to her knees.

"Teagan!" A pretty blonde strolled across the lush green Oregon grass. The rain would begin soon, but the last remnants of autumn stubbornly clung to the air.

Teagan's head whipped up, then she stood and hugged her friend, Ariana Ellison, the daughter of Theo Ellison who owned TechG8. Theo wasn't who I was concerned about interfering with my plan, though. It was Jagger Whitlock, Ariana's stepbrother, and now boyfriend. Not to mention, Jagger's uncle was the prez of a one-percenter MC club, the Dirty Bastards. They were ruthless if you messed with them, and my goal was to stay off their radar.

From my research, Teagan's friends adored and protected her. Fine. Whatever. But taking down Teagan was a different game than messing with Jagger and the club. I wasn't stupid enough to fuck with them, which meant that I'd spent my summer researching everything about Teagan and her peers. Since this was my first semester at Whitmore University, it increased my chances of laying low, since not many people knew me.

Playing football, though, would put me in the spotlight. Under the leadership of Kane Cooper, we were going places. Fortunately,

Jagger was playing this year after a scare with a knee injury. Our team had the potential to be fucking unstoppable.

"Speak of the devil," I muttered as Jagger approached the girls, who were now sitting on a burgundy-colored blanket that Teagan had spread out on the ground. The corners of Jagger's mouth tilted up in a smile as he joined them, then kissed Ariana.

I liked his style. Possessive. Dominant. His reputation preceded him. He was loyal to his friends but a real motherfucker if he didn't like you.

A flicker of jealousy flashed across Teagan's expression. Then she turned away, I assumed to try to disguise her feelings. Her tongue slipped out and swiped over her cherry-red bottom lip. But I saw her vulnerability. Her longing.

I peeked at my phone, checking the clock. Our class wasn't for another hour, but I wanted to arrive after Teagan to strategically choose my seat, which meant that I had enough time to swing by my house and rub one out. My dick was pleading for a release as I thought about all of the ways that I was going to make Teagan pay for ruining my life. I planned to humiliate and torture her until she confessed her sins.

A shiver skated down my spine. I almost felt bad for her, but then I reminded myself what she'd cost me: everything. It was my mission to dismantle her piece by piece until she was completely destroyed. The mere thought nearly made me come in my jeans.

Chapter 1 ~ Teagan

"I really don't want to go." I groaned for added effect while I crawled onto my bed. "Are you sure you can't come with me and visit your parents?" I batted my eyelashes at my best friend, Ariana, while I tugged on my grey, oversized Whitmore University hoodie. As soon as classes were over for the day, I'd hurried home and thrown on some black yoga pants—comfort was everything.

Ari grinned at me before she delivered the soul-crushing no. "Jagger has a big exam on Monday, so being on the road, then spending time with Dad—Theo—isn't ideal. I don't have a problem with Samantha, except that before she married him, she was aware of the fact ..." Ari's expression twisted, hurt flickering in her blue eyes.

"It's okay, babe. Like, we don't even have to talk about it. I'm here when you need me." I rolled onto my back, stretching across the full-sized mattress in my room. Gabrielle, Leighton, Everlee, and I shared a place during the school year. As long as our grades were good, the parents covered the costs. The bedroom was smaller than at home, but I didn't have to share it with anyone, which was worth the boring white walls and drab, dark wood floors. I'd tossed up some artwork and bought a bright teal comforter and throw pillows to perk up the space. Oregon winters were grey and wet, which meant my mood tanked unless I took extra precautions to feel better.

Ari tucked a lock of her blonde hair behind her ear and gave me a sad smile while she extended her legs in front of her, crossing them at the ankles. "I'm sure I'll eventually get over the betrayal, but not yet." Ari wrapped her arms around her waist, her cranberry shirt bunching up slightly.

"If my dad did something like that, I would feel the same. Just give yourself some space." I gently squeezed her jean-clad knee. "I'm always here for you to talk if you need me."

Ari placed her hand over mine. "I know, and I love you for it. When are you leaving to go home?"

"Around eleven tomorrow morning, after my class." I pressed my lips into a thin line. "I'm going to surprise the folks, so if you change your mind, you can stay at my place and never see your parents." I grinned at her, realizing I was trying to win a losing battle. Before Ari and Jagger started dating, we always traveled together, and I would miss my sidekick something awful. I'd made a new playlist for the road to keep me company.

"Speaking of your parents, how are things with your mom?"

"Shit. It's why I'm surprising them this weekend. That way she can't plan ahead and give me a bunch of lame excuses why she can't be in the same room with me." I glanced away, the inescapable pain tugging at my heart. My mom had never been easy, but when I turned fourteen, she changed. At first, I kept my distance, but after witnessing what Ari and Theo had gone through, I wanted to make things right with mom. She was the only one I had.

"You're doing the right thing, Teagan." Ari offered me a supportive smile.

"Well, it won't be the same without you. Guess I'll just have to wait for our girls' weekend and shopping trip. We score in Oregon with no sales tax."

"Not to mention better stores than back home. Usually have to go to Seattle for a good selection." Ari pulled her knees to her chest and propped her chin up. "What about Gabby, Leighton, or Everlee? Could they go home with you?"

I placed the back of my hand against my forehead. "Cheer practice. You remember how it is during football season."

"Every minute of your life is dedicated to the team." Ari's expression softened. "Do you miss it?"

After three years of high school drama and being the youngest person in the history of the Wahlberg Academy team to make captain, I'd had enough shit to deal with for a lifetime. Granted, I did miss the sport and competitions. If I wanted to, I would try out next year. I was at the gym five days a week, staying in shape and continuing to perfect my flips and jumps.

"Part of it. I do *not* miss the bitches." I sat up and twirled a strand of hair around my finger, pondering what I wanted to do for the evening.

Ari stood and picked up her handbag. "I should pick up something for dinner on the way home. You're welcome to join us."

I waved her off. "Nah, I have a suspicion that you and Jagger fuck on every counter of your kitchen." I screwed up my nose in disgust, thinking about eating my food where they'd christened the surface.

Ari giggled and swatted my leg. "We clean and disinfect, thank you very much. At no time have you ever come over to eat and propped your elbows in my ass print."

A heavy sigh slipped through my lips. "I want someone to make ass prints with."

Ari tilted her head. "I have a feeling you're going to find your guy this year. Whoever or wherever he is, he's looking for you, too."

I rose, then hugged her. "If you're right, then I'll pay for a trip to Mexico for the four of us."

"Oh, I'd better get busy finding him then." Ari released me, giggling. "Text me later, bitch. Please be careful on your way to Washington tomorrow, too."

"Always."

I walked Ari downstairs and to the front door. Leaning against the frame, I watched as she climbed into her new blue Audi R8 parked next to my red Audi R8. Our cars were nearly identical except for the color, and mine was a convertible. Ari and I had been sharing and choosing similar clothes and vehicles for years. We weren't biological twins, but we were similar in so many other ways.

A chilly, wet wind whipped into the doorway, and I shivered before I waved and hurried back into the house. It would be nice to have dry weather in Spokane, even if it were only for a few days.

I strolled into the spacious kitchen I shared with the girls and spotted a small stack of envelopes on the table. Everlee was a mail hooch. For whatever reason, she loved to check the secured mailbox daily. Sifting through the pile, I spotted my name. It wasn't often that I received anything, but there it was—a beautiful black envelope with *Teagan Mercer* written in gold calligraphy. I frowned when I realized there wasn't a return address.

Carefully opening the sealed flap, I removed a white card, and my eyes widened as I read the message.

You've been chosen to attend The Viper Secret Society. Use this code to log in for additional information. Come alone and tell no one.

Holy. Fucking. Shit. I'd heard rumors about the King Cobra but had never known anyone that had been allowed to witness it first-hand. From what I understood, it was an honor to be selected, but that was all I knew. Whispers of kinky and group sex had traveled around the college campus, but only a few times. I had no problem with the rumors if they were true. God only knew it had been far too long since I'd been laid.

I sank into the dining table chair, my heart banging against my chest. I glanced at the note again, then shot out of my seat and up the stairs to my bedroom. Gathering my MacBook from the desk, I plopped down on the bed and typed in the website that had been provided on the note. A large King Cobra appeared on the screen with a red 'enter' button on its back.

The snake pixelated, then disappeared. The sound of footsteps thumped through my speakers as a hand reached out and pushed open a door. Riveted by the theatrics, I carefully input the code.

"Hello, Teagan," a disguised voice said. "Thank you for replying. Please join me Thursday evening, October twenty-first, for a night that you'll never forget. Pay attention to the rules."

A white skull mask with black eyes appeared, and strong hands steepled their fingers together. Unable to see the color of his intense gaze, I focused on the details that were scrolling on the screen next to him. I scooped up my phone off the bed and took notes of where and when. Once again, he impressed the importance of keeping the invitation and participation a secret. Honestly, it would be easy not to tell anyone. The girls would fucking freak if they knew, then Ari would tell Jagger, and he would never let me leave the house. He was almost as protective of Ari's friends as he was of her. Almost.

"See you then," the voice said, then the screen faded to black.

Scowling, I grabbed the notecard and typed in the web address again. Nothing. An empty white page with a 404-error message instead.

"Dammit," I whispered, staring into space and trying to decide if I would accept the invitation. At least I had a week to decide. Sex with a stranger might be a lot of fun. No strings, no talking, no accusing stares or awkward conversations.

The sound of the front door opening reached my ears, and my attention darted around my room. I jumped off the bed and shoved the notecard back into the black envelope, then tucked it between a few books on my desk.

"Anyone home?" Gabrielle called out.

"Hey, I'm here," I responded, then descended the stairs to talk to her. Hopefully, I could focus enough on what she said and not what I would most likely be doing next week.

J.A. OWENBY

Edited by: Anne-Genevieve Ducharme-Audran

First Edition ISBN: 978-1-949414-85-1

Download Your FREE Book

Also by J.A. Owenby

The Beautifully Damaged Series

Beautifully Damaged

Beautifully Broken

Beautifully Shattered

The Whitmore Elite Standalones

Forbidden, A Whitmore Elite Prequel

Illicit Obsession

Ruthless Obsession

Sinful Obsession

Toxic Obsession

The Love & Ruin Series

Love & Sins

Love & Ruin

Love & Deception

Love & Redemption

Love & Consequences, a standalone novel

Love & Corruption, a standalone novel

Love & Revelations, a novella

Love & Seduction, a standalone novel

Love & Vengeance

Love & Retaliation

Love & Betrayal, a standalone novel

About the Author

International bestselling author J.A. Owenby grew up in a small backwoods town in Arkansas where she learned how to swear like a sailor and spot water moccasins skimming across the lake.

She finally ditched the south and headed to Oregon. The first winter there, she was literally blown away a few times by ninety mile an hour winds and storms that rolled in off the ocean.

Eventually, she longed for quiet and headed up to snowier pastures. She now resides in Washington state with her hot nerdy husband and three purebred Siberian cats who insist on using her computer as their napping spot. She spends her days coming up with ways to torture characters in a way that either makes you want to throw your book down a flight of stairs or sob hysterically into a pillow.

J.A. Owenby writes new adult and romantic thriller novels. Her books ooze with emotion, angst, and twists that will leave you breathless. Having battled her own demons, she's not afraid to tackle the secrets women are forced to hide. After all, the road to love is paved in the dark.

Her friends describe her as delightfully twisted. She loves fan mail and wine. Please send her all the wine.

You can follow the progress of her upcoming novel on Facebook at Author J.A. Owenby and on Twitter @jaowenby.

Sign up for J.A. Owenby's Newsletter:

https://authorjaowenby.com/newsletter/
Like J.A. Owenby's Facebook page:
https://www.facebook.com/profile.php?id=100064095791999
J.A. Owenby's One Page At A Time reader group:
https://www.facebook.com/groups/JAOwenby